F

Lyn

DIRT CHEAP

a novel by

Lyn Miller-Lachmann

CURBSTONE PRESS

This is a work of fiction. Names, characters, places, and incidents are either the product of the author's imagination or used fictitiously. Any resemblance to actual persons, living or dead, educational institutions, business establishments, events, or locales is entirely coincidental. If you think this may be your town, start digging.

Printed in Canada
Cover design: Susan Shapiro
Cover photograph: Joe Raedle/Reportage/Getty Images

 This book was published with the support of the Connecticut Commission on Culture and Tourism, National Endowment for the Arts, and donations from many individuals. We are very grateful for this support.

Connecticut Commission on Culture & Tourism

NATIONAL ENDOWMENT FOR THE ARTS

Library of Congress Cataloging-in-Publication Data

Miller-Lachmann, Lyn, 1956-
  Dirt cheap : a novel / by Lyn Miller-Lachmann.—1st ed.
     p. cm.
  ISBN 1-931896-29-1 (pbk. : acid-free paper)
  I. Title.

PS3613.I5626D57 2006
813'.54—dc22

                              2005032340

published by
  CURBSTONE PRESS   321 Jackson Street   Willimantic, CT
                              06226
    phone: 860-423-5110   e-mail: info@curbstone.org
              http://www.curbstone.org

Acknowledgements

In the long journey between conception and publication, many people helped point the way. Marjorie Agosín and Christine McDonald challenged me to write the novel, which I had abandoned years earlier. Danilo Figueredo, Ann Frantti, Elizabeth Janicek, and Byron Park offered suggestions and encouragement as I worked on the initial draft. Samantha Dunn's tough love approach convinced me that I could do better; she motivated me to throw out much of what I had written and start over. During the long rewriting process, Courtney Walsh was always there. Through his explanation of the Kaddish, Rabbi Matthew Cutler at Congregation Gates of Heaven in Schenectady, New York, guided me to the finish.

From my critique group at the Barnes & Noble in Colonie, New York, I would like to thank Ann and Bill Goodwin, Nick Kling, Lee Kolesnikoff, Hugo Matson, Debbie McDaniel, Robyn Ringler, and B.J. Rosenfeld. From my critique group at Professor Java's, also in Colonie, I thank Ken Fitzpatrick, Eric Luper, Mary Nicotera, and Leonora Scotti.

Tim Hall, the editor of *Struggle*, and Charles Willett, of *Counterpoise*, provided opportunities for me to audition early chapters in print and before a live audience.

Without Marnie Mueller's support, this novel may never have seen the light of day. She brought the manuscript to the attention of Alexander Taylor and Judy Doyle at Curbstone Press. I am honored to be a *compañera curbstonista*, along with dozens of poets, novelists, and essayists part of a press that for more than three decades has embodied the literature of social engagement in the United States. I am grateful for Jane Blanshard's keen editorial eye and my publicists Jantje Tielken at Curbstone and Caitlin Hamilton for their enthusiasm and hard work in bringing the novel to the attention of readers.

I am forever indebted to my husband, Richard Lachmann, for his unwavering support during all these years of writing, rewriting, agonizing over every critique, and rewriting again. My two children, Derrick and Maddy Lachmann, grew up with the book and offered advice and encouragement on ever-more-sophisticated levels. I am so proud of them and believe that my experience has taught them something about persistence, pursuing a dream, and daring to speak in a strong voice that is their own.

At Congregation Gates of Heaven, where I teach seventh grade in the Sunday school, members take turns participating in Sabbath and High Holy Day services. Before we enter the sanctuary, we meet with the rabbi and recite the Shehecheyanu, a prayer that gives thanks to God, the Creator, who has supported us, protected us, and brought us to this important moment. It is the prayer that I recite as I reach this moment in my journey and my book goes forward into the world.

To Maddy and Derrick

Search Continues for Missing Boy

COLD SPRINGS, August 16 – The search continued along the Yellow River for Luis Espada, 5, who fell into the river on Sunday while fishing from the North Springs Bridge with his father and brothers. Rescue teams were called in early Monday morning from towns and cities within a 50-mile radius of the accident. The search began in the North Springs area but has now spread three miles downstream through Yellow Springs Heights to the northern edge of Yellow Springs. So far, searchers have found no trace of the boy.

Espada and his family had recently arrived in the United States from the Dominican Republic and had lived in Cold Springs for two months when the accident occurred. They resided at 102 Wallman Street in the Flatlands neighborhood.

According to authorities, this is the fourth serious accident to occur on the North Springs Bridge in two years. In May, Jason Breyer, 18, a senior at Yellow Springs High School, drowned when he fell from the bridge after a night of drinking with friends. After Breyer's death, North Springs mayor Albert Marinello had called for the construction of a ten-foot-high fence along the bridge, and he renewed those calls on Monday. "How many more kids have to die before we make a decision to do something?" Marinello said in a morning press conference.

One: This Much Was Known

At the bottom of the riverbank, a mile upstream from his family's home, Nicholas Baran shot a photo of the Hometown Chemical Company plant across the river. The plant had been abandoned fifteen years ago, four years before Holly bought what she called her dream house. A grove of trees and bushes along the northern edge of the bluff shielded the view from Yellow Springs Heights so that no one could see the carcass of the plant, only the river itself flowing toward Cold Springs Harbor and, eventually, to the Atlantic Ocean. For as long as he lived here, Nicholas loved to walk the footpath next to the river. He said the river eased the constant tightness in his throat and chest, the clenched fist that squeezed him often to the point of suffocation. The path was exactly two miles long, a good half-hour walk from the wooded bluff where the neighborhood began to where it flattened out into the small tract houses of Yellow Springs.

Nicholas snapped on the heavy-duty latex gloves and leaned out as far as he could over the river. He dipped a plastic lab-specimen cup into the water. The cool, murky liquid pushed over the top, and the ripples from his trespass lapped at the shoreline where he set the filled cup. He crouched and with a teaspoon scooped mud from the riverbank into another cup. He tightened the lids, dropped the two containers into a zippered plastic bag, wrote the date and location of the samples with a permanent marker, and shoved the plastic bag into his black canvas shoulder bag.

A quarter mile downstream he collected another set of samples. The morning haze had burned off, and beyond the shadow of the bluff the sun painted the still river in hues and textures of blue and gold. Even in the shade, Nicholas could feel the rising humidity. Careful not to touch his face with his hands, he lifted off his wire-rimmed sunglasses and wiped his forehead on the sleeve of his t-shirt.

Just before the next stop he spotted a search team dressed in shiny black and orange wetsuits with "Woodlawn Rescue Squad" printed on the back. He waved at the three standing at the edge of the river. Taking a break, he guessed, because none wore headgear, standard equipment for a search and recovery operation but in this instance an especially good idea.

"Any luck?" he asked as he approached.

One searcher shook his head. "What are you doing down here?" another asked.

Nicholas pointed up the riverbank. "I live in the Heights. When they built the neighborhood, they put in this path so people could go jogging or ride their bikes."

"Yeah—well, if you see anything let one of us know," another searcher said. "Don't try to handle the body yourself."

Their headgear back on, the men unfolded a net and waded into the murky water. As he waited for them to drift farther away, Nicholas ran his gloved finger along the rough edge of a specimen cup's lid. He had liberated the cups—two dozen of them—from his doctor's office over a period of several months. No big deal—go into the bathroom and stuff a handful of them into his shoulder bag. All for a worthy cause. Just for the hell of it, he took a photo of the Woodlawn Rescue Squad and continued collecting samples.

Small bunches of men in wetsuits dotted both sides of the river as he rounded a bend. He sighed heavily. It would be almost impossible to collect more samples without attracting attention. He wouldn't have picked this day if it hadn't been for the end of the summer session at his community college and the fact that his friend Rich would have the entire organic chemistry lab to himself until after Labor Day. He had already lost a couple of days because of the reporters and TV cameras, but when the searchers didn't find the boy by Tuesday, the news media had gotten bored and left.

What was the kid doing fishing in the river anyway, Nicholas thought. Eating those fish would have been like eating poison—that is, if there were any fish alive to catch. But then again, the family had arrived only a couple of months ago, and they had no way of knowing.

Some activity near an outcropping of rocks a hundred yards away sent Nicholas running. A pair of searchers was hauling in a net. By the time he got close enough to see, the net was almost all the way in, and he could make out a muddy bundle the size and shape of a large backpack like the ones his kids lugged to school. One of the searchers lifted the bundle from the net and carried it the rest of the way to the shore.

But when they unrolled it, it wasn't a backpack; it was the little boy. He had a name, Nicholas reminded himself. Luis Espada. And as they laid him face up on the riverbank, now slick from the water that had drained off, the men turned away and stripped off their headgear.

"Aw, jeez," one cried out. "Can we get something to cover him up?"

Their eyes averted, the two dragged the net ashore and threw it over the boy. One of the men reached for his two-way radio.

Nicholas stuffed his gloved hands into the pockets of his baggy shorts and jogged up to the searchers. He noted the writing on their wetsuits, "Yellow Springs Rescue Squad." The locals. One was a heavy, balding fellow, and the other was a muscular guy in his twenties, with a buzz cut except for a thatch of dark brown hair on top. Nicholas didn't recognize either of them.

"Is that the boy?" he asked, his voice suddenly shaky.

"Yeah," the older searcher responded. "You with the press?"

Nicholas nodded yes. "Can I have a look?"

The older one shook his head. "You don't want to. Trust me."

As if he knew his partner's warning wouldn't make a bit of difference, the younger man gave Nicholas a contemptuous glare. "Here's what, *paparazzo*. *You* keep an eye on the body. We have to call the authorities."

Nicholas waited until they were far enough away, then he knelt next to the boy's head. The chemical smell of the river mixed in his nostrils with the sour stench of death and decomposition, and he steeled himself against what he might see. Before his illness, he had prided himself on his strong stomach. But even though he had been in remission for almost three years, the chemo treatments had left him with a persistent queasiness, as though the fist compressing his throat and chest had migrated downward.

Knowing he didn't have much time until the searchers returned with the cops and everyone else, he exposed the body with a powerful yank of the waterlogged net. His stomach contracted, and he swallowed hard against his breakfast rising to his throat. He'd expected the body to appear bloated—from what he'd read, all drowning victims look bloated when they're recovered after a few days. But Luis's amber skin had begun to peel off, and his wide-open eyes, the softest of his tissues, were black holes consumed by acid. Nicholas swallowed again and in a single motion stripped off one of the boy's sodden, muddy socks. Handling it with his fingertips to avoid squeezing out any of the water, he dropped the sock into a plastic bag. Then he took out his camera and snapped pictures of the body until the roll was spent.

He replaced the net and knelt next to the boy one more time. "Hey, little buddy, I'm going to find out what did this to you," he whispered. He stood and backed away. Trees and water spun around him. His blood pounded in his ears.

I'm not going to be sick, he told himself. He didn't have time to be sick. Now that the body had been found, the cops and reporters would be all over the place within minutes. And three hundred yards downstream, he could collect all the samples he wanted with nobody asking questions.

* * *

His son, Tony, collided with him in the kitchen later that morning, causing Nicholas to knock over the glass of water he had poured.

"Sorry, I didn't know you were here," apologized the scrawny twelve-year-old, whose short dark-blond hair stuck out in every direction, as though he had just gotten out of bed. Tony reached for a paper towel to wipe the floor.

"It's okay." Nicholas opened the refrigerator and took out the plastic jug of distilled water. He gulped the cold liquid directly from its mouth, trying to wash away the smell of the little boy's decomposing body, avoiding his son's clear gray eyes as he drank. He drained the jug and tossed it into the recycling bin under the sink.

Tony stood there watching. Nicholas would have expected him to go back to his computer or his video game, but the boy shifted his weight from foot to foot. His slender fingers tugged at the unraveling sleeve of his rec basketball league t-shirt. "Dad, can you take me shopping this afternoon?" he finally asked. "I need stuff for my new school."

After what he had seen on the riverbank, Nicholas could not imagine spending an afternoon with Tony at the mall, pretending everything was all right. Besides, he had to drop off the samples and the film. The last thing he wanted was for Tony to find out what he had been doing all morning, what he suspected about the river. For whatever poison had settled in his bone marrow had probably seeped into the growing young bones of Tony and his big sister, Rosie, and into the bones of all the children of Yellow Springs Heights.

"So can we go?" Tony pressed.

"Is your mother working late tonight?"

"She didn't say. Why?"

Nicholas sighed. "Then she can take you. Don't you wear a uniform anyway?"

Tony frowned. "I still have to get it. And I need a binder and notebooks and—"

"Well, I can't do it today. I have to go to the office."

"Can I come with you?"

"No. Meetings." He knew he was leaving Tony alone in the house again, unless Rosie decided she was tired of hanging around her friends' houses all summer long. But the boy had neither drained the liquor cabinet nor burned the place down, so he was a lot safer at home than at the college chemistry lab where, with the river's secrets and his father's secrets, there was no end of trouble he could get himself into.

Two: The Pied Piper of Colbert Hall

Holly noticed the blinking light of the answering machine when she arrived home from work, her briefcase in one hand, the day's mail in the other, and her purse dangling from her shoulder. Tony must have missed the call, as loud as he blasted his stereo. He'd be deaf by thirty but kids never thought about the future, where they'd be twenty years from today and the consequences they'd have to live with because of their reckless choices. And the music he played. Melody-challenged, Nicky termed it. Nicky had taught her to appreciate jazz, though at the time of their marriage she'd immersed herself in a punk phase destined to cause her embarrassment for years thereafter.

In those days she longed to write poetry like Ginsberg, sing her poems like Patti Smith so that the words rose to the ceiling and drew the energy of everyone in the concert hall toward her. She longed for the energy to seize her, make her bold, give her a presence larger than herself—shy, earthbound Holly Meggett, straight-A student, good Catholic girl from stiff-upper-lip Minnesota. But whenever she tried to write poetry the words never soared but instead dropped with a thud onto the blank page.

Now she believed that hardcore punk was a taste for the young, unbecoming of anyone her age. Not like the classic rock her daughter preferred. So she tuned out the cacophony, the lyrics she couldn't understand because she was no longer accustomed to their cadence and logic.

Her manicured fingers leafed through the catalogues and bills. Two credit card statements on the same day. Another had arrived a day ago, and she hadn't yet brought herself to open it. Tomorrow was payday for both of them. Nicky would hand over his check. She would leave the grocery money inside the second volume of Marx's *Capital*, make the minimum credit card payments and deposit the rest to pay the mortgage. She wouldn't even think about the remaining balances, what they added up to. She turned up the volume on the answering machine and pressed the play button.

"This is Marc Martineau calling for Nicholas Baran at 3 p.m. on Thursday. I'm calling on behalf of the Yellow Springs Heights Community Association." For a moment Holly savored the Cajun accent, the sign that he, like her, had come to this place from somewhere else. But as the message continued, the sweetness turned to sour fear that clogged her throat as though the president of the Community Association had reached his huge hand through the machine to choke her. "Some of the fellows from the rescue squad thought they saw you down at the river this morning. I'd like to discuss this matter with you. Please call me at my office or at home when you get a chance."

"Nicky, what on earth have you been doing?" she said aloud. The call should not have surprised her. Nicky's collecting water samples from the river was more premeditated than most of the things he did. And ever since Barbara and Roger's death a year earlier, he had been obsessed with Hometown Chemical Company and the poisons they must have poured into the river. He'd demanded the entire family drink bottled water, though he wasn't one to spend money unnecessarily. Her grip tightened around the leather handle of her briefcase. *There are no coincidences in the world of Nicky Baran.*

After a while, she recovered her equilibrium and went upstairs to change clothes. The door to Tony's bedroom was open. She rapped several times before he turned the music down.

"Hi, Mom." He appeared grateful to see her. He didn't like being left at home alone all day. Nicky had promised to spend more time with him now that he had the month off from teaching.

"Where did your father go?"

"He said he had meetings at his office." Tony glanced at his feet, then back at her. "Can you take me to the mall tonight. I need my uniform and other things for school."

"Sure," she answered. He grinned, his fist clenched. It seemed so easy with these kids—buy them something, make them happy. "Did he say when he'd be done?"

"No." Tony waited a few seconds, then asked, "Can we eat at the mall too?"

"Why not?" She caught herself before adding, *God knows when he'll be home.* Nothing worse than dragging the kids into their battles. Her parents had taught her that. They had stayed together for their girls and by force of habit and fear of hell continued to do so even after all three had moved away, though it took one of the larger houses in Eden Prairie to keep the two of them under the same roof.

She had just shed her business suit for a cotton skirt and t-shirt when she heard the back door slam. She called for Nicky.

"Yeah, I'm home," he shouted back.

Downstairs again, she saw he had deposited his filthy black canvas shoulder bag on the new white sofa in the family room. She moved the bag to the laundry room. "Nicky, we need to talk."

He draped his arm around her and tried to kiss her, but she jerked her head away. His breath smelled of alcohol. He liked to hang out in the bars near the college with his friends, but he rarely drank enough that she could smell it on him.

"Marc Martineau from the Community Association left a message for you. He said some people saw you down at the river—"

"Fuck him." Nicky strode over to the machine and punched the erase button.

She followed him from the laundry room past the family room into the kitchen. "What were you doing there?"

"Collecting more samples." Nicky glanced up at the ceiling, as if to make sure Tony wasn't on his way downstairs.

"I saw them bring in the little boy who drowned." He pressed his thin lips together until the color drained from them. She noticed his throat tighten as he swallowed. "You're not going to read about this in the papers or see it on the news, so I might as well tell you. Some of the chemicals that company dumped in the river had eaten his eyes and the flesh from his body. It was the most sickening thing I've ever seen, and it took all I had not to pollute the river any further."

Holly shivered despite the heat that pushed central air conditioning to its limit. The chemicals in the river and what they might have done to the boy didn't shock her. The terror between her ribs was instinctive, her worry about his blood cells and the state of his digestion and nutrition a vestige burned into her memory of the months of chemo and the bone-marrow transplant—for her only secondhand. She wondered about his trauma, the scars he carried inside.

"You were supposed to spend the day with Tony."

"That's why I went out early. I didn't expect to find what I did." He pushed the hair from his forehead and leaned against the kitchen counter. "Can I ask you to cook tonight? I was planning to grill some burgers outside, but I really need to lie down in front of the baseball game for a while and forget about all this."

"I'll call for a pizza. Do you know if Rosie plans to be home for dinner?"

"She stopped by to pick up some clothes before I left for the office. She says she's sleeping over tonight and will get a ride to work tomorrow."

She's avoiding us again. I would too if I were sixteen, with all the lies and secrets to make me think the worst. But Holly missed her daughter, who seemed to attract attention and friends wherever she went, who had grown up so confident and self-assured in spite of her father's neglect and the aggregate of her mother's losses.

* * *

In my dreams I still see him as he was then: little Nicky Baran standing on a long folding table that served as a makeshift stage, five feet five inches of pure energy, a spring wound tight, small, and hard, exploding in a torrent of words. Perspiration beaded his flushed face and plastered his dark brown hair to his head and neck, and as he spoke into the microphone he paced the table in his shabby black canvas high-tops, so often coming close to the edge but never falling off.

Two thousand students, almost a third of the student body, had assembled in front of Colbert Hall, the administration building, to demonstrate against the university's investments in apartheid South Africa. Nicky was the final speaker before the march, the one who would fire up the crowd, and fire them up he did. Sometimes shouting with indignation, sometimes pleading and hoarse, sometimes speaking in a whisper the audience strained to hear, he matched his wide-ranging voice to the words of a speech that seemed to exist only in his head. He described the murder of Stephen Biko, relentlessly and graphically telling the story of the young man lying on a cold prison floor, his skull crushed by guards, drifting in and out of consciousness for days and then being driven seven hundred miles on a surreal journey from Port Elizabeth to Pretoria only hours before his death. Holly felt the tears forming under her eyelids and rolling down her cheeks, and when she glanced over at her roommates, Cindy and Gwen, she saw them crying too.

Nicky, his voice now almost gone, pointed to the audience and screamed, "What do we want?"

He held out the microphone, and the audience's chants echoed across the quadrangle. "Divestment!"

"When do we want it?"

"Now!"

Six times they repeated the chant. Nicky tossed the microphone to a fellow organizer and jumped from the table, doing a single flip on the way down. Those standing near the front gasped, then roared.

Even though no one had invited her to join the sit-in after the march, Holly wanted to rush the administration building and stay there until none of the university's money went to that—or any other—police state. She, the good Catholic girl who could only dream of words making her larger than herself, stood ready to follow Nicky Baran straight to hell if that was where he wanted to lead her.

* * *

Many other students must have felt the same way she did because by his senior year the five foot five, skinny as nothing Nicky Baran had become the most feared student on campus, at least by the administration. Veteran of demonstrations against J. P. Stevens' labor policies, nuclear power, defense spending, and the U.S.-backed dictatorship in Chile, he had come to be known in the campus newspaper and everywhere else as the Pied Piper of Colbert Hall. Rumors swirled around him. A girl in Holly's dorm said he had once been the state gymnastics champion of Massachusetts, thus the flip from the table at the end of his speech. Another said he grew up in a trailer park somewhere in central Massachusetts. A third said he came from Boston and his father was a professor at M.I.T. The only thing any of the stories had in common was the state of Massachusetts.

Later she would learn that he had grown up in a Jewish family in Worcester, where his father owned a scrap yard. When he was ten, his mother died suddenly of a cerebral hemorrhage. His brother, twelve years older than he, had already moved to California by the time of their mother's death. Afterward, Nicky and his grieving father had moved to a trailer park for older adults, where children were not even permitted. He'd never competed in gymnastics, though—his father had neither the time nor the energy to drive him anywhere. This skill, like many of his others, came from the recklessness and dumb luck of a motherless, unsupervised, and often lonely boy.

*　*　*

Now that she had reached middle age, the stage when teenage children considered their parents pathetic, it helped Holly to remember how she and Nicky had come together in the first place. She had joined the demonstration and march but had not been one of the two hundred "invited" to the sit-in because—she guessed, nobody told her—she had developed a reputation as a nerd who'd never do anything to get arrested or put a blemish on her record. Both her roommates had been invited, as had her boyfriend at the time, a long-haired activist named Gary Johansen. And as she watched Nicky standing with three of the other organizers, none of whom she knew well, she wondered which one had cut her from the list. Gary had explained that the list grew out of the need to enforce discipline, to make sure the people sitting in would stay in the building and not start a riot. Sacrificing some individuals for the greater good—which made sense except to the one sacrificed, she'd told him. He hadn't sympathized, and it made her wonder if they'd really had anything more in common than increasingly predictable sex and the fact that both had come to this Ivy League university from Minnesota.

After the march she returned to her empty dorm, took out her contact lenses, and stood in the hot shower for forty-five minutes, supposedly washing her waist-length light brown hair but mainly pampering herself after her disappointment. She was sitting in the living room of her suite in her bathrobe, reading a book for her senior American lit seminar, when she heard a knock at the door.

It was Gary. He already looked tired, even though the sit-in had begun only three hours ago.

"They sent me to get you," he said. "If you want to be part of the sit-in."

She closed the book. "Who's 'they'?"

"The organizing committee." He paused. "Well, actually, Nicky. Your roommates talked to him."

"Thank you, Cindy and Gwen," she murmured. She threw on some jeans and a t-shirt, grabbed her sleeping bag and toothbrush, and went out into the warm late-April night. The line of campus police outside Colbert Hall didn't stop her and Gary as they entered. Two "peacekeepers" from the student group waved them past.

Gary took her through halls littered with lounging students to the university president's office on the fourth floor. The size of the office astounded her, as did the presence of so many ragtag students in a place that should have contained only rich and powerful old men.

Nicky sat on the floor. He thumbed through a stack of papers, his back against the president's huge antique wooden desk. Cindy and Gwen were chatting with some guys in a nearby corner next to a row of ornately carved floor-to-ceiling bookcases. Holly gave each of her roomies a grateful hug. Gwen grabbed her arm and brought her to Nicky.

Nicky jumped to his feet. "Hi, Holly."

She nodded, holding her breath. After so many demonstrations, she stood face to face with the Pied Piper himself. He was about her height and had on the same tight blue jeans, faded black t-shirt, and high-top sneakers he had worn earlier that day. He had a narrow face, with delicate features and the shadow of a mustache and beard. She could make out reddish and light brown streaks in his unruly dark brown hair, which he kept pushing back from his face as he talked. But the thing she noticed most were his eyes—dark, piercing, and intelligent, they seemed to take in everything around him instantly.

He glanced at Cindy and Gwen. "You have some great roommates," he said, his voice almost a whisper.

"Th-thanks."

He hooked his thumbs on the belt loops of his jeans. She noticed he wore no belt. "It wouldn't have been right to invite two roommates and leave the third one out. Especially one as pretty as you." He grinned, and his thin lips parted to reveal slightly crooked teeth.

At that point, a young woman dashed into the room and whispered something into Nicky's ear. He nodded. "Okay. I'll take care of it."

"What's the problem?" Holly asked.

"Bathrooms. Not enough bathrooms for the women. Problem with the university just going co-ed." He turned and surveyed the president's desk. "Okay, what can we do here?" he mumbled to himself as he scrounged a bunch of paper clips.

Not knowing what Nicky wanted her to do, Holly followed him out, along with the other woman. He paused in front of the university president's private washroom, then twisted the largest paper clip and picked the lock. "All yours," he announced to the other woman. "Don't make a mess."

He asked Holly to walk with him as he continued down the darkened hall. Students were just beginning to bed down for the night. As she quickened her pace to keep up with him, he explained the rules. No property destruction. No stealing. No graffiti. No drugs. On the third floor, a student was smoking a joint; its orange tip glowed when he inhaled. Nicky snatched it from the student's hand and crushed it under the heel of his sneaker.

A male voice called out, "You're such a fucking Stalinist, Baran."

"Eat dogshit," Nicky fired back.

He laid his arm on her shoulder and pulled her closer to him. She shivered under his touch. His warm breath smelled of the cinnamon gum he was chewing. "We can't have dope in here," he whispered. "It hurts our credibility and exposes everyone here to a lot of other criminal issues that have nothing to do with the divestment."

"That's fine," she said. "I don't smoke."

"I didn't think you did." After about a minute of silence, he asked, "Holly, have you ever been tear-gassed?"

"No. Why?" This was beginning to sound scary.

"Because the university might use tear gas to get us out of here. I don't want you crying—" He paused. "Well, actually, you *will* cry if they use tear gas, but I don't want you cursing me and the ground I walk on if something happens."

"I won't."

"Promise?" He squeezed her shoulder.

"I promise."

* * *

The sit-in ended without the launch of a single tear-gas canister. The university promised to suspend new investments in South Africa and to look into selling old ones—at least until the current crop of organizers graduated—and the students, Holly included, received one year of disciplinary probation. Nicky, along with the other organizers, received two, though it didn't matter because they graduated six weeks later. For his faithful sentry work and his less-than-faithful advocacy of her, Holly dumped Gary as soon as the sit-in ended. Not that it mattered, for this was the free-love seventies and he'd started sleeping with someone else during the sit-in anyway.

That summer they moved to New York City. Nicky began graduate school in modern European history, studying Gramsci to figure out why the other four thousand students hadn't come to his demonstrations. Holly got a job as an editorial assistant in the juvenile trade division of a publishing house. They married in the Municipal Building with no one but two friends as witnesses. Nicky's father had died of a heart attack at the beginning of Nicky's junior year, and Holly didn't tell her parents about the wedding.

A boy from a central Massachusetts trailer park and a girl from a staid suburb of the Twin Cities—in New York, they were in paradise. And everybody liked them. Nicky received his doctorate the year Rosie was born. His department hired him as an assistant professor on tenure track. Holly moved up in the publishing company to become a senior editor. They traded their cramped student digs for a two-bedroom apartment on the Upper West Side near the university and started saving for the co-op they would buy when he got tenure. Her parents had reconciled themselves to her marrying a Jewish boy without their blessing, and her mother had discovered the joys of shopping in New York— this was in the pre-Mall of America days—so she flew out to help take care of the baby.

* * *

In all those years Holly never questioned her good fortune; she just kept taking advantage of it. In the eighties they detested Reagan, protested his military buildup and his war in Central America, enjoyed their work immensely, and loved each other, Rosie, and the City. Surrounded by so many important and famous people, Nicky only occasionally spoke at demonstrations, but he poured all his dramatic ability into his teaching. In his second year as an assistant professor, the students voted him Teacher of the Year. A year later his dissertation was published, and the following year she became pregnant with Tony. In her worst nightmares she could never have imagined what would happen next.

It amazed Holly how, for better or for worse, a single person could set off a chain of events that changed another's fate forever. It happened because when one reacted to that event, it had consequences. And in dealing with those consequences, one faced even more consequences. Soon, it became a spiral and hard to figure out where it started and who started it.

In her and Nicky's case it started with a senior professor of medieval history named Branscum. He taught at the university where they had received their undergraduate degrees, but neither had taken a class from him or met him face to face. She'd majored in English and had no interest in the history of the Middle Ages. Since Nicky had majored in European history, he knew Branscum was an outspoken right-winger and timed his enrollment in the required course to the professor's sabbatical.

Branscum, however, knew well the Pied Piper of Colbert Hall. He had denounced the radicals in the conservative campus newspaper, and most of the students had laughed at his Neanderthal ravings.

But in the eight years between graduation and the publication of Nicky's book on Gramsci, Branscum helped found an organization called the National Association of Restoration Scholars. In the Reagan era, NARS received funding from right-wing foundations, which allowed the group to go after untenured leftist professors. Nicky was Branscum's first victim. Holly once spotted a headline in the graduate student newspaper that said it all: "Nemesis Launches Crusade Against Young Professor's Attitude."

Though published by a prestigious university press, Nicky's book was missing several footnotes. Having worked in publishing, Holly knew this sort of thing happened from time to time and should have been caught by a good editor. Even so, things like this never became major issues unless somebody had a vendetta.

The scholarly journals erupted with articles about the missing footnotes and the allegedly falsified work. Even the *New York Times* picked up the story. A year after the first barrage, Nicky's department voted not to consider him for tenure. He applied to hundreds of universities for new jobs, and received only three offers. One was for a one-year position; another offered him two years. Springs Regional Community College hired him with tenure on the spot.

Nicky would say that in the scheme of things having one man ruin your career couldn't be compared to one man taking your life—or killing the rest of your family and leaving you to live with the guilt—which happened in so many places in the world throughout history. Political martyrs fascinated Nicky. He'd convinced Holly to name Rosie and Tony after two of them. Though at the community college he taught as many classes as a public-school teacher and had no time for research, he said they should be grateful he had a full-time academic position, one that allowed him to teach those very same working-class kids he had once been. While preparing for careers in offices and hospitals, hundreds of them made room in their schedules and crowded into his modern European history classes semester after semester. Eight times the students voted him Teacher of the Year. He missed only his first year, a sabbatical year, and the year he went to California for his bone-marrow transplant.

*   *   *

Maybe because Nicky had always been wrapped up in his work, it was easier for him. But Holly still remembered the slights, the people they had regularly socialized with who after the tenure vote avoided them as if they had a contagious disease. The parents of Rosie's friends who turned away, leaving the toddler to wonder what had happened to her playmates. The whispers behind Holly's back when she was drooping with Tony, "Poor thing, expecting another kid. How are they going to support themselves?" When she overheard one of Nicky's graduate students say to a friend, "If they'd known earlier, they could have had an abortion," she cried for an hour. Then she went down to J & R Music World and charged a thousand dollars on her credit card for a new stereo receiver and speakers.

Though Branscum set the downward spiral into motion, Holly blamed her tendency to soothe herself with physical and material comforts for accelerating it. When she knew for certain Nicky would be teaching in a community college in a boarded-up industrial town in Connecticut, just beyond the far fringes of the New York metropolitan area, she insisted on selecting their house. She wanted to settle into something clean and spacious and safe, like the community in which she'd grown up. Nicky offered to stay back with their infant and four-year-old and left instructions: "Something with a roof."

Holly's mother flew in from Minnesota, and together they went house hunting. After days of trooping through dingy resales, they found a model house in a neighborhood-under-construction in Yellow Springs Heights. All around the model stood bulldozers and mounds of dirt fill that shored up a thirty-foot-high bluff overlooking the Yellow River. The view was, in her mother's words, "exquisite." The realtor sold them on this *tabula rasa* out of which would rise huge, luxurious modern homes, expansive front lawns with fluffy green grass, and jacuzzis on the screened-in back porch (optional). And there were what he called the "amenities"—a hike and bike trail along the river, a clubhouse and playground and pool for the children and for neighborhood events, landscaped cul-de-sacs, the close friendships that would naturally grow out of this planned community.

That weekend she put a deposit on 15 Butternut Court, a four-bedroom colonial on a cul-de-sac. Despite the piles of dirt and construction materials scattered all around, the realtor guaranteed the house would be ready by the middle of August. It was four times the size of their apartment in New York and a stretch financially, even if she got a job nearby. Nonetheless, she returned to New York proud of herself for having made a decision, for putting an end to the uncertainty that had tormented her ever since Branscum had published the article about the missing footnotes. With the new house, she figured, she had bought them nothing less than a fresh start.

At that time she never even saw the abandoned chemical plant a mile upstream and on the other side of the river. She didn't think to question. Not then, and not later, after Nicky's injury on the ball field and the terrible diagnosis—not only a wrist broken in two places but also leukemia.

She saved all her questions for God. But Nicky, who had lost his faith when he'd lost his mother and who refused to accept as coincidence a circumstance that cruel, had to go looking for answers.

*   *   *

When I awaken from my dreams, I realize what we've lost. I see it in my rough, dry skin, in my sagging breasts and thighs, in the thickening around my middle, in my limp, unmanageable hair that I have to keep short and spiky to look halfway decent. I am no longer beautiful and strong, and no matter how much I try to keep the illusion going by shopping in the same stores where Rosie shops, I can never bring myself to wear the things I buy.

Even more, I see what we've lost in Nicky's gaunt, worn face, in his eyes burning bright with the fever of his crazy mission that he promises he will finish before he dies. And if he does finish, he'll leave me alone with two kids, a worthless house, and a bunch of hostile neighbors with worthless houses as well. So sometimes when I awaken and he's still asleep, I'll stroke his dark brown hair now streaked with gray and whisper, "I promised I would never curse you or the ground you walked on no matter what happened. But you've got to promise me two things, Nicky baby. You're never going to finish, and you're never going to die."

I am no longer strong.

Three: Flowers for a Drowned Child

Sandy Katz rehearsed the words: *Lo siento mucho. I'm very sorry*. Translated literally, the phrase meant, *I feel it very much*. What did she feel? Not their sorrow, for at the age of twenty-three she had never lost a child, a sibling, a parent. She didn't know what it was like to have someone standing beside her and the next instant gone forever.

She stroked the delicate yellow petals of one of the flowers she had bought to take to the Espadas. The small plastic vase sat on the coffee table in her living room, and from her second story window she could see much of her block of Wallman Street. She regarded the two- and three-story frame houses—some separated by narrow driveways, others only by footpaths. The houses' faded and dented aluminum siding, the decrepit cars parked in the street, the tiny vegetable gardens dried out by weeks of no rain, the cracked sidewalks with weeds poking through, and the overflowing garbage cans at the curb gave her neighborhood a hint of the sorrow she couldn't fully comprehend.

On the next block stood the building where Luis Espada's family lived—a partially burned-out four-story tenement with peeling yellow asbestos siding and a collapsing gray roof. The building bordered a vast weed-choked vacant lot, two blocks wide and more than a mile long, where the city had torn down houses forty years earlier to build a highway, but the highway had never been built. A day ago she had stood on her front steps and watched the funeral procession, a hearse and a single rusted brown station wagon with New York license plates that cruised alongside the vacant lot and slowly disappeared from view.

Now there were no cars parked in front of the Espadas' tenement, and she wondered if it was too late, if the rest of the family had also gone away and she'd bought the flowers for nothing. She took the vase and left her apartment.

Downstairs, Paulie Amato, her landlord's eight-year-old son, sat on the front steps, his elbows on his knees and his chin resting on his two small fists. He stared at the street, his face expressionless. His twelve-year-old brother, Ben, picked through her Sunday *Cold Springs Post-Examiner*. The paper must have been delivered after she'd returned from her early morning run and her stop at the florist across the street from Mercy Hospital. The comics lay spread out on the porch, and the upper half of Ben's body was hidden behind the sports section. Just beneath the paper's jagged bottom edge his belly hung over the waistband of his jeans.

"Yankees won," Ben said to his younger brother. He read the story aloud while Paulie glanced listlessly in the direction of the comics.

Sandy set the vase on the railing and collected the rest of the paper. Luis's drowning and the recovery of his body had fallen out of the news; the right-corner headline now read, "Company Reaffirms Commitment to Hometown, Cold Springs." She glanced at the subtitle: "500 Jobs at Stake." Not another threat of layoffs. Except for Burnham University, Cold Springs had so little industry, just two hospitals, a couple of insurance firms, the phone and the power companies, and the national headquarters for Hometown Chemical Company. She skimmed the article. The giant biotechnology firm that had bought the chemical company sometime the year before—she hadn't been paying attention then—promised the mayor the Hometown division offices would remain in Cold Springs, but the closed-down factories in the area would not reopen.

Ben lowered the sports section. "What's up, Sandy?"

"Nothing." He hadn't apologized for dismantling her paper, and she wasn't in the mood for a confrontation. On Tuesday, the day before her boyfriend, Mitch, left for Chicago, Ben had burst out of his family's first-floor apartment while Sandy was reading Paulie an article about the search. She still remembered the door slamming behind him and the sharpness of his voice.

"Is that the spic that drowned in the river?"

"The word is Hispanic, Ben," she said. "I was asking if Paulie had ever seen him." From his usual place on the steps, Paulie seemed to see everything else.

"He don't know no spics. Do you, Paulie?" Ben's voice cracked with the question.

Paulie shook his head. "I never seen him."

Then Mitch spoke up. "Ben, I don't like you using that word. That boy's family came here for a better life. Just like your family and Sandy's and mine."

Ben stared at his unlaced no-name sneakers.

"Do you understand what I'm saying?" Mitch's voice dropped.

Without looking up, Ben mumbled, "Sorry."

She'd been grateful to Mitch for helping her with Ben. Paulie was too young to understand, but it was a touchy issue for Ben, his two older brothers, and their parents, who were among the few Italians left in a neighborhood that had become mostly Black and Hispanic. In the year that she and Mitch had lived in their house, she'd never discussed the issue with their mother, Angie, because she knew it would upset her, and she wouldn't dare mention it to Joe, Angie's husband, whose temper was already bad enough when he was sober— though he always seemed to be on his best behavior with the two young graduate students from Burnham.

But now she would be on her own. The university had cut back, and she and Mitch had lost their scholarships. "There aren't any jobs for professors of American history anyway," her advisor said. "With your idealism, maybe you two should try teaching high school." Mitch packed up his idealism, decided to return home, work for a year, and apply to law school. *Law school.* To her, it was the ultimate sell-out, what her parents wanted her to do to make them proud.

Follow in her dad's footsteps. It might have been her advisor's suggestion, or simply a throwaway line meant to soften the impact of her dream crashing, but she believed in her decision to teach. She believed that if she wanted to change the world, she had to change the kids first.

After she left Ben and Paulie that Tuesday morning and went upstairs to help Mitch pack, she found him sitting at the kitchen table eating a bowl of cereal. He pulled her onto his lap. "Come with me to Chicago," he whispered.

"But I have a job here now. I can't quit before it starts." She freed herself from his grasp and stood to face him.

"Sure you can. There are private schools in Chicago too. And if teaching doesn't work, you can always go to grad school there next year."

She bristled. The idea of teaching when she had never done it before made her nervous enough. But Mitch didn't believe in her any more than her professors did. And what if she failed? He'd already bailed her out with Ben. What if none of the kids listened to her?

Cutting yourself off from your past is scary, she thought, and she had already done it twice. She had refused to go with Mitch, even though they had been together for three years, played key roles on three winning co-ed softball teams—he as the pitcher and she as the shortstop—and everything about him had grown as familiar and comfortable as a favorite old glove. And then, when she'd told her parents she'd lost her scholarship and was applying to private schools that didn't require a teaching certificate, they insisted she come home to Albany. But she couldn't see herself back in her old room trying to figure out what she'd do next and dating one of those immature boys from Hebrew school or youth group her mother had picked out for her. When her father said, "This will always be your home, even if you have to come back with your tail tucked between your legs," she slammed down the phone and never called them again. From then on, she corresponded by e-mail, which seemed more distant and a lot safer. She wondered if she'd do the same thing with Mitch or if he'd drift out of her life altogether.

Ben's voice punctured her thoughts. "Are those flowers for us?"

"No. I'm taking them to the family that lost their little boy." She sniffed the flowers' full, sweet aroma, as if trying to draw strength from them. "Would you like to come with me?"

"Nah." Ben laughed.

"I'll come," Paulie piped up.

"You can't. It's dangerous." Ben grabbed Paulie by his t-shirt's collar and pulled him toward the house. "Anyway, Pop'll kill us if he catches us near those sp—." Ben glanced at her. "People."

Her moment of self-congratulation seemed in the next instant more like taking credit for Mitch's action. She asked Ben and Paulie to guard her paper and read it if they wanted, although Paulie, entering third grade, could not yet read.

She waved good-bye to the brothers, the one stocky with short hair and thick features, who already knew too much of the world's meanness, the other small and innocent, with jet-black hair, golden skin, and a delicate face. *Lo siento mucho. I'm sorry your father's an alcoholic and your mother can't do anything about it, and I heard your brother Eddie come home drunk last night, too. I'm sorry about little Luis because I can't bring him back. And I think what I'm feeling is sorry for myself because I'm on my own, truly on my own.*

And as she walked down the broken sidewalk of Wallman Street she remembered her adviser telling her, "You know why there aren't any academic jobs in this field? It's because Americans don't care about their history. We live in the endless present." And she too had cut herself off, even though she would soon be teaching history.

She stopped at the door of the Espadas' tenement and shook her straight shoulder-length brown hair from her face where the wind had blown it. The rusted metal door swung open with her firm push; its hinges groaned. *Ahora es el momento.* Despite the bright sunshine outside, the hallway was almost dark. Next to bare, useless bulbs scorched wiring dangled from the ceiling, becoming sharper and more threatening as her eyes adjusted to the dim light. A rank odor of mold and mildew pressed against her sinuses.

A dust-coated staircase led up into darkness. She tested the first step. The wooden board sagged and creaked under her sneaker. There were no shoe-prints in the dust, no evidence the family lived along that climb into nothingness. She called out, and her voice echoed. Brown water stains created a swirling pattern on the plaster of the downstairs wall, broken only by the hard lines of two gunmetal gray doors. Hesitant to penetrate the grim hallway further, she knocked at the first door. A male voice shouted; she could not make out the words. She raised her voice to carry through the steel door. *"Me llamo Sandy Katz. Soy una vecina de Wallman Street."*

In a few seconds the door opened. A short brown-skinned woman stood next to it. *"Pase,"* she said.

Sandy stepped into a large room with a chipped linoleum floor. The grime that covered the windowpanes made the room almost as dark as the hallway. Inside were a man, the woman, and two boys, the oldest of whom was no bigger than Paulie. On the floor lay two bare mattresses. She noticed three battered suitcases nearby. She held out the vase of flowers and recited the words she had practiced all morning.

"Lo siento mucho."

The father wore a large wooden cross around his neck. Had he been Jewish and lived in a Jewish community, the family would have lit candles and sat *shiva*. Relatives and friends would have come over and together they would have recited the Kaddish, the ancient prayer for the dead in Aramaic that never once mentioned death. Instead, the family's bags were packed.

Luis's mother took the flowers and hugged Sandy. Sandy

had to bend over to put her arms around the woman, who looked so old even though she couldn't have been much more than thirty.

The Espadas thanked her several times. Although her Spanish was rusty—she had placed out of the grad school language requirement and had little opportunity to use the language she'd studied in high school and college—she thought they said they were moving to New York to live with someone's brother. Luis's mother then began to cry.

"Su cuerpo, dígales." His body, tell them. *"Se lo comió el ácido."* Eaten by acid.

Sandy wasn't sure she heard the words right because the newspaper article and the television report had said nothing about acid, only about locating the body and investigating the railing on the bridge. The woman could have been saying something else, maybe about the bridge's condition, and she kept on talking, too quickly for Sandy to follow and too muddled by her tears for Sandy to understand. Her husband put his arm around her and led her toward the back of the desolate room. He turned his head to Sandy. *"Muchas gracias. Que Dios la bendiga."*

May God bless you. Sandy escaped from the tenement into the warm summer sunlight. She closed her eyes against the brightness and stumbled into the chest-high weeds of the vacant lot. They tickled her bare arms and lower legs. She took deep breaths to clear her lungs and sinuses. Like most Jewish people in America, her family had lived in cities, far from nature, but this neglected earth was still God's creation and even the weeds produced oxygen.

Four: Shady Ridge

Streamers in the school colors of purple, silver, and white decorated the teachers' lounge on Sandy's first day at Shady Ridge Country Day School. The students had yet to arrive—classes wouldn't begin until the next day—but this was the opportunity to meet everyone, pick up class lists, get grade books in order, and hear welcoming speeches and last minute instructions from the headmaster and department chairs. Everywhere she went there was food. Coffee and pastries in the auditorium for the opening speech of the headmaster, Dr. Avis. Donuts at the meeting of the history department, where Tim Brownfield, who would be her boss, introduced himself. And lunch in the cafeteria with her fellow teachers, who informed her that the chicken stuffed with bleu cheese would not be the normal fare.

Sandy wondered about the normal fare, and not just the food. So far, the first day at her first real job seemed easy. She found she had much in common with the other teachers, especially Marissa Levine, who would be teaching seventh- and eighth-grade English. In her third year at Shady Ridge, Marissa had received her undergraduate degree from Burnham and decided to stay in the Cold Springs area. She lived near her boyfriend in an apartment complex in Yellow Springs and belonged to a synagogue there that included as members some of the families whose children attended Shady Ridge. "Nice kids," she said. "Good students." It made Sandy hopeful. She envisioned profound discussions with enthusiastic students, children from the large new houses in Yellow Springs Heights that she passed on the way to school, children who this morning rode shiny bicycles through peaceful streets or shot baskets into fancy hoop sets on freshly blacktopped driveways. It was their last day of vacation, and in the quiet breaks between meetings she remembered their joyful shouts. Compared to Paulie, to Ben, to the grieving Espada children, these soon-to-be-students of hers—she imagined them all to be hers even though she knew most attended public school in Yellow Springs—possessed so much life and happiness.

After lunch Tim invited her into his office for a private meeting. The social studies chairman looked no more than thirty, though she figured he had to be older to occupy such a position of responsibility. He had an smooth, clean-shaven face and neatly cropped brown hair, and on this more casual day, he wore a gray polo shirt, pressed khakis, and brown loafers. Of medium height, he appeared trim and athletic, the kind of guy who'd stop at the gym every day after work. Sandy couldn't help but compare him to Mitch, who lived for team sports but would much rather hang out than work out and by the age of twenty-three had developed the love handles to show for it.

Tim pulled a plastic chair up to his desk and motioned for Sandy to sit down, but rather than sitting at his desk, he asked her if she wanted a cup of coffee. Not wanting to offend such a solicitous boss on her first day, she let him bring her yet another cup. While he was gone, she scanned the office.

Tim had arranged his textbooks in alphabetical order by title on the tall gray metal bookcase next to his desk. Following the textbooks came reference books, recently published paperbacks on American history and politics, and finally curriculum kits and videos. He had labeled each section in block letters. Judging from the titles of the paperbacks, he appeared to be a fan of William Bennett and his *Book of Virtues* series. On the desk was a large family photo with him kneeling next to his wife, an athletic-looking woman with thick strawberry blonde hair tied back in a ponytail. In front of the two were a small boy with a thin face, serious-looking dark eyes, and dark brown hair, and his smaller sister, whose frizzy blonde hair framed a sunny face. In the background were trees and part of a swing set.

Alongside the photo Sandy noticed a New Testament with a dark red leather cover, and she made a mental note never to mention her religion or politics.

Tim returned with the single cup of coffee and seated himself in his worn cloth-covered chair. He picked up a manila folder with her name and began telling her how pleased the school was to have her energy and skills as a girls' softball coach in addition to teaching. He had a mournful expression and quiet, almost inaudible voice that Sandy found out of place with his crisp appearance.

He reached into the folder and handed her four class lists. "We had a problem with one of your classes."

She scanned the lists. Two seventh grade and two eleventh grade classes, just as they'd promised. About fifteen kids in each class. She couldn't see the problem.

Tim went on. "In our seventh grade class this year, we have thirty-one kids overall, and only eight girls. I don't know where you're from, but around here, people tend to send their boys to private school and leave their girls in public school. It's a conservative area."

She nodded. It wasn't that different where she'd come from. The private girls' school she'd attended was less than half the size of the boys' school across the street.

"I didn't want the girls to feel intimidated in a class where the boys would outnumber them by so much, so I put all of them in your 7A class and made your 7B class all boys. I thought it would be better for the girls." He paused. "It might be a challenge for you, though."

"I'll be fine." Kids were kids. Besides, she had grown up with two younger brothers and had a whole year of knowing Paulie and Ben and their two older brothers.

"If you have any trouble with the boys' class, Sandy, please see me right away. Don't let things get out of control." He extended his hand. "Good luck."

She shook his hand and left the office.

* * *

She longed to tell Mitch about her classes but felt the impact of his departure as soon as she entered the empty apartment. *E-mail, later*, she said to herself. They had exchanged a few messages since he'd moved back to his parents' house. She knew he was looking for his own place and a job, and she waited for an update on his status while feeling smugly self-sufficient.

Paulie sat in his usual spot on the porch steps. Sandy dropped her school stuff on her desk and went outside to see him.

He'd already had a half-day of school, and she asked him how it had gone.

"Okay." He frowned. "Teacher's mean. I wish I had you."

"Thanks. I wish I had you too." She thought about what Tim had said about her all boys' class being "a challenge." Then she asked, "Paulie, do you think there's any difference between the boys and girls in your class?"

"Yeah. Boys are *bad*." Paulie stared open-mouthed at her.

"How are they bad?"

"Boys are always running around. Teacher's always yelling at them."

Not you, Paulie. She imagined Paulie quiet and glum, his chin on his fists and his elbows on his desk, while the other boys in his class dashed around the room. No wonder he still didn't know how to read. But Shady Ridge wasn't an inner city school, and she wasn't teaching little kids who ran around all the time either.

She wished there were a way she could arrange for Paulie to go to Shady Ridge, so he could have a chance—a chance to do better in the world, to avoid the fate of his alcoholic father and his older brothers. At eighteen, Joey had already dropped out of school, and he and his girlfriend were expecting a baby in January. And just before Labor Day, fifteen-year-old Eddie and a couple of his friends had gotten drunk and stolen a car, which they smashed into a streetlamp. Eddie, sitting in the back seat, escaped unhurt, but Angie, who often called Sandy the daughter she never had, fretted to her about his court date next month and the possibility that they would send him to jail.

As Sandy thought of her new daily commute, her faded and crumbling neighborhood seemed even more decrepit in contrast to the winding tree-lined suburban streets, the large homes with flower gardens and neatly kept front lawns, the three-car garages filled with gleaming late-model minivans and sport utility vehicles. Yellow Springs Heights and Shady Ridge Country Day School seemed to her like paradise— and a world of endless opportunity for the children fortunate enough to be there.

*   *   *

Twenty-four hours later, Sandy sat alone in her study and tried to understand when and how everything had gone wrong. First period the fifteen eleventh graders had filed in as though not quite awake, quieted down when she'd asked, and written their homework assignments in their notebooks. It sounded strange to hear herself called Miss Katz when all anyone had ever called her before was Sandy. She felt even stranger when she realized these almost-grown students would be bringing her pages of written work just because she told them to. The first group of seventh graders, eight girls, seven boys, wrecked the neat semicircle of desks, but after the girls pushed their desks to one side of the room and the boys, their desks to the other, they settled down and let her teach. Still, she wondered if they told their classmates at lunch she was an easy mark, because when she walked into her room after the first bell, a group of the larger boys stood around a pudgy student with glasses and shook his desk until his books clattered to the floor.

"Stop it! Sit down!" she shouted, her voice tinny. She heard snickers, then the second bell. The gangly boys slid into their seats; their victim's cheeks shone with tears. He made her think of Piggy in *Lord of the Flies*.

Several boys switched their names when she called the roll. She knew she would always think of the fat boy as Piggy and it made her even more ashamed of herself for not protecting him, and she remembered another student who wore glasses, a skinny kid with unruly light brown hair. The attendance sheet listed him as Antonio Baran but he went by Tony and he insisted on the pronunciation of his last name— "accent on the first syllable, like the medieval nobleman." When the bell rang at the end of the period, some of the big kids snatched a book out of his arms, held it above their heads, and laughed when he jumped to get it back.

Sandy considered asking Tim for help. But at the end of school he had already gone, and maybe, she thought later, it was best that way. She didn't want to appear so incompetent on her very first day. One more day she would give herself, one more chance to solve her own problems.

One day became one month. She rarely found Tim in his office, and each time she did, she managed to convince herself that things weren't going so badly. By the beginning of October, Columbus had landed, and Spain, France, England, and the Netherlands were fighting over the riches of the New World. The kids' backpacks had been broken in, and the seventh graders' binders already bulged with the worksheets she had given them in her effort to keep them in their seats and busy. The ninth-grade global history teacher said the kids needed routines and gave her some suggestions. Her two eleventh-grade classes soon settled into a familiar, if unexciting, pattern. Fifteen minutes to go over the homework questions. Copying the outline of the day's lesson from the board—another twenty minutes. Then fifteen minutes to discuss the important issues of the day's lesson. The outlines became the multiple-choice portion of the chapter test, while the important issues discussions turned into the essay questions. At least half the kids got A's on the tests, and only one or two in each class ever got below a B.

The seventh-grade boys, however, resisted any attempt to impose a routine on them. Sandy tried a simplified version of the eleventh-grade class but could never turn around to write anything on the board without spitwads flying or a student crying out that someone else was bothering him. She then tried delegating a student to copy the outline on the board. While some of the students eagerly volunteered for the assignment, their spelling and handwriting were atrocious. When Pizarro became Pizzeria and Columbus became Canibus, she realized some of the misspellings weren't accidents either. Discussions were equally futile, as they usually degenerated into a series of silly responses or a bevy of side conversations. Worksheets became her principal teaching tool.

Of her seventh-grade students, Braxton Martineau from the all-boys' class stood out in every way. Over six feet tall, he had short, sand-colored hair and pimples on his cheeks and chin. He seemed to take a particular dislike to the overweight kids, awkward Tony Baran, and Chris Leighton, the only Black student in the class. His tormenting of Chris especially concerned her. The Amatos' prejudice was hard enough to accept, but Braxton's seemed even more incomprehensible. He didn't live in a bleak urban neighborhood but in a peaceful suburb with clean streets, huge lawns, and stately houses set far apart from each other. She wondered about the circumstances of his life, what would make him so hostile and where he would have come into contact with anyone who didn't share his privilege.

One day Braxton shook out a bag of flavored tortilla chips onto Chris's sweater. She called his house that night.

A woman picked up the phone. She sounded woozy.

"May I speak to Mr. or Mrs. Martineau?" Sandy stammered.

"This is Mrs. What do you want?" She had a Southern accent, but contrary to what Sandy had heard about Southerners, her tone was neither friendly nor polite.

The phone clicked, and a man's voice came on. "I've got it, Claudette. You can hang up now." It was Mr. Martineau. He too had an accent, but different from hers. A trace of Southern, a trace of urban, an intonation that reminded Sandy of the French she had taken in elementary school.

Sandy described the incident and mentioned that Chris was the only Black student in the class.

"Miss Katz, I don't think it was racial," Mr. Martineau said. "Whatever you may believe, I didn't raise him like that."

His words made her unsure. Maybe she had jumped to conclusions because of the Amatos, stereotyped Braxton further because of his parents' accents. After all, Chris hadn't been his only victim. She described the other instances of bullying she had witnessed from the first day onward and ended with how Braxton had tripped Tony the day before. Braxton had sent the smaller boy flying, books skidding across the classroom floor.

Mr. Martineau cleared his throat. "I'll talk to Braxton about his disruption of your class. But you're saying some of this occurred before the class period started."

She detected a question, as if he were trying to define his son's infraction in a legal sense. She knew the ploy from the way her father sometimes questioned her and her brothers.

"They were in the room, but the bell hadn't rung yet."

"Look, boys will be boys. It was like that in my day, and your day, and nowadays. They're going to establish their pecking order. It's their nature. How long have you been teaching?"

"This is my first year," she admitted, a catch in her voice.

"That's what I thought. I wish I could help you or give you advice, but my wife is ill and I'm trying to take care of these boys by myself. I don't have family up here to help out."

"I understand," she mumbled.

"I'll do what I can, but you're going to have to find a way to motivate Braxton." She could hear him take a breath before he added, "Those worksheets aren't going to cut it."

After she hung up, she realized she could never call Mr. Martineau again. He didn't support her even though she was the teacher, and she doubted he would do anything to stop Braxton. And what was wrong with Braxton's mother? It sounded serious. Not having children or much time in the world, Sandy only had her parents' experience to draw on. Her mother had been the one to deal with the school, volunteer in the classes, and talk to the teachers at parent-teacher meetings.

She had to get help. She left for school half an hour early the next morning, just after sunrise. It was one of those perfect October days that made her wonder if winter would never come. The beauty of Yellow Springs Heights in the raw sunlight of the new day made her forget her conversation with Braxton's father and the sleepless night that followed. As she crossed the almost-deserted parking lot at Shady Ridge, she savored the mild breeze that rustled the trees in their patchwork of yellows, reds, and greens. Every day before going inside she would pick her favorite tree in this changing mosaic. That day she settled on a tree next to the softball field with one half of its leaves brilliant red and the other half still bright green. For a while she lingered, then felt as if she were dragging her reluctant body inside to knock on the door to Tim's office.

Tim did not rise but called for her to come in. He sat in his desk chair and stared out the window. He was in his shirtsleeves, his suit jacket draped over the back of his chair. The cream had congealed at the top of the coffee mug on his desk, so she knew he had been there a while, neglecting his morning coffee.

Slowly he turned around. His face had a blank expression. "How can I help you?"

She told him about her phone call and what Mr. Martineau had said, though she left out the criticism of her. Tim sighed. "It doesn't do kids any good when their parents make excuses for them," he said. "And that goes for you too. Don't stand between these kids and the consequences of their behavior."

"But I called his house," she protested.

Tim leaned forward in his chair. "You should check with me before calling a student's parents. In this case, there are extenuating circumstances."

"Mrs. Martineau?"

She detected the faintest of nods before Tim changed the subject. "That class giving you a hard time?"

She lowered her eyes without speaking. *You're going to have to find a way to motivate Braxton. Those worksheets aren't going to cut it.* Mr. Martineau's words again stung her.

"I'll come in sometime next week and see what's going on," Tim said. "And if any one of those boys acts up, you send him to me right away."

When she walked into her classroom after lunch that day, the boys greeted her with a chorus of meows. And when she looked at the blackboard, she saw why. One of them had printed in huge block letters, "MISS KATZ HAS KITTENZ."

She dropped her books on her desk and blew out her breath. "So now you've decided to make fun of my name. Well, take out a piece of paper and close your books because you're going to have a surprise quiz."

More meows. Only half the boys reached for their loose-leaf binders. She suspected the prank had to do with her call the night before, because Braxton and his friends whispered to each other and then glared at her.

"Come on, let's go." She paused for a moment. "Question number one."

One of Braxton's friends tore a piece of paper from his

binder. "Guess she doesn't like us making fun of her name." He flashed a nasty grin to his classmates.

Another joined in. "Then maybe she should change her name."

"Yeah, to 'This Class Sucks'!"

She couldn't tell who added that, because the entire class erupted into laughter. Hardly believing that her phone call had led not to an end to Braxton's disruption but rather to a well-planned mutiny, she began to shake with helpless rage. She glanced from student to student, tried to decide who to send to Tim. But she couldn't send most of the class, and she couldn't admit to Tim that her unauthorized attempt at discipline had failed so badly. Without thinking, she screamed, "You people are animals!"

Her outburst silenced the class. Then Tony inched his hand upward.

"Yes, Tony."

"Uh, technically we *are* all animals."

She considered adding Tony to her shit list when someone shouted, "Shut up, dork!" from the back of the room, followed by, "Yeah, fag. Nobody cares what you have to say."

Tony's face crumpled. Sandy folded her arms against her chest. "All right, that's it. If I hear anyone in this class use the word 'fag' you're going straight to Mr. Brownfield."

"Mr. Brownfield? That fag?"

"Braxton, to Mr. Brownfield's office, now!" She wasn't standing in the way of Braxton and the consequences of his behavior any longer. She strode over to his desk and motioned for him to get up. He unfolded himself from his chair.

"What if he's not there?" he asked. His voice, as deep as an adult's, seemed to be mocking her, but she couldn't tell for sure.

"You stay and wait for him. I don't want you back in this class without a note that you've seen him."

After Braxton left, another hush fell over the classroom.

One of his friends blurted out, "I bet Mr. Brownfield's not going to be there."

Quiet Braden Campbell then spoke up, his voice cracking in the throes of puberty. "You guys shouldn't have said what you did about him. You know, his boy died last year."

Sandy sucked in her breath, and so did several of the boys. Finally, Andy Van Camp asked, "How do you know?" The color drained from his thin face.

"My family goes to the same church as the Brownfields."

Sandy stammered the next question. "Was he in some kind of...accident?"

Braden looked down at his desk. "No. I heard it was cancer."

She didn't want to pump Braden for any more information in the middle of class, so she waited for school to end and hurried to the teachers' lounge in search of her friend Marissa. Marissa arrived a few minutes later, a stack of paperback books and student papers in her arms. She unloaded them onto the work table, but most of the books slid off and fell to the floor.

Sandy crouched to pick them up.

"Thanks," Marissa said breathlessly. A strand of her curly black hair had fallen into her face, and she wound it around the scrunchie that held her ponytail.

"Do you have a minute?"

"Sure. I saw our buddy Braxton sitting outside Tim's office today. Did you send him?"

"Uh-huh," Sandy admitted.

"I had to send him to my chair the first week."

"I called his house and spoke to his father last night."

"How did that go?"

"Not too well." Sandy stared at the table. "He was big on the put-downs."

"That's what I've heard. A new teacher last year had Braxton's brother for ninth-grade English, and he and his father made her life so miserable she quit after the December break." Marissa lowered her voice. "The problem is, Mr. Martineau gives a lot of money to the school, so nobody will stand up to him. I guess you have to hope Braxton and his brother don't take a special dislike to you."

Was it already too late, since she'd called his parents? Sandy wondered if a way existed for her to reach out to Braxton, to understand him so he'd work with her and not against her. "Do you know anything about their mother?"

"No. Why?"

"Mr. Martineau said she was ill. And this morning Tim told me there were extenuating circumstances."

"I don't know." Marissa stacked her papers in a neat pile. "But it would explain why those boys are such a pain."

"Did Tim even talk to Braxton?"

"No. I asked Braxton what he was doing, and he told me he got kicked out of class for no reason. Then he sat around the lounge for a while and left when the bell rang."

Great, Sandy muttered under her breath. *Just what I need to show the kids I mean business*. At this rate, she'd have nothing to hold over any of them.

But that wasn't her only reason for seeking Marissa out. Her voice shaky, she asked her friend about Tim and what she'd heard from her class.

"It's true," Marissa said, making that clicking sound some people made when discussing a tragic event. "Kyle died last April of leukemia. Beautiful little boy too. He was in the first grade here, had just turned seven. They diagnosed it last December, and he went through the treatments, but instead of getting better, he only got worse."

"So that's why Tim's never around?"

"That's my guess. It hit his wife and little girl hard. Tim's taking it rough too." She paused. "I suppose it wasn't the greatest time for you to get here, seeing as it's your first teaching job."

Sandy shrugged. Once again, she wasn't going to feel sorry for herself when there were much greater tragedies out there. Compared to someone's child dying, someone else's mother gravely ill, her out-of-control class seemed to fade in the scale of the awful things that could happen to a person.

Five: Exiles

Many of the faculty at Springs Regional Community College were people run out of somewhere else for one reason or another. During faculty meetings, in bars, and at softball games Nicholas collected their stories and shared his own, and it was hard not to think of these people as his family and the college, not Yellow Springs Heights, as his community. The college president had taught political science at the University of Alabama in the early sixties, and for his support of the civil rights movement that "damn yankee" from Boston had gotten on the wrong side of Governor George Wallace. Although he had tenure and a good lawyer, death threats and flaming objects on his lawn drove him back north. Nicholas's closest friends, Larry and Kate—he a Marxist professor of political science and she the college's head librarian—had once worked in Wisconsin. When a conservative faction ambushed his tenure review, she made copies of a picture of Joseph McCarthy and signed notes of thanks in the senator's handwriting to each of the conservative professors. And there was Nicholas's own exile at the hand of a professor of medieval history who'd never reconciled himself to the fact that the mouthy undergraduate had led a massive sit-in at the administration building over the university's investments in South Africa and gotten away with it. Had even graduated *summa*.

Not all of the exiles occurred for political reasons, however. The most egregious case was that of Rich Rankin, a former champion surfer from Southern California who still played tapes of his competitions that appeared on ESPN in the early nineties. Only problem was, Rich was supposed to be in the lab watching his chemistry projects bubble and turn colors. When it came time for his tenure review, the desperate chemist found himself a few samples short, so he interpolated data from the samples he already had to get to the critical number. He didn't get caught right away, so he had several years to enjoy a life of tenured ease with only a few classes standing between him and his surfboard. Afterward came the humiliation of having his tenure stripped, losing his wife and children in the process, and ending up across the country where the waves never exceeded three feet in height.

Nicholas would have expected this collection of Marxists, anarchists, slackers, and assorted troublemakers to have made a lot of noise, but in the prosperous nineties most of them, himself included, managed to tie themselves down pretty well with mortgages, consumer goods, domestic partners, spouses, and children. However, when classes ended, the bars around the college filled with middle-aged professors reminiscing about their wilder days and boasting about what they were going to do when socialism rose again and the kids graduated from college. And every summer the Springs Regional Community College co-ed softball team, the Ship Rats, compensated for what it lacked in ability by developing a reputation for the dirtiest play in the league.

* * *

Rich Rankin, known to opposing batters as Beanball, was leaning against Nicholas's office door when Nicholas returned from his lunchtime departmental meeting. The discredited chemist, now in his late thirties, stood just over six feet tall and wore his shoulder-length dark blond hair in a stubby ponytail, thereby revealing the golden stud that adorned his left ear. His hairline had begun to recede, and a few gray hairs tinged his mustache and beard, but otherwise, he looked as youthful and athletic as he had in his ESPN era. On this chilly mid-October day he dressed in a button-down shirt, baggy sweater, sneakers, and blue jeans, but in a nod to professional decorum his jeans had no holes and only a few frayed spots.

In contrast, Nicholas wore a navy blazer, tie, loafers, freshly ironed gray slacks, and a button-down dress shirt, all of which accentuated his slight build. When he'd taught in the Ivy League, he generally sported something more casual—maybe not dressed down as much as Rich, but a turtleneck instead of the jacket and tie. At the community college, though, he would often point out to Rich that professional attire demonstrated respect for the students, many of whom had to overcome enormous obstacles in order to receive their education. Rich's customary response was that chemistry, unlike European history, often got very messy.

Today Rich carried under his arm a manila folder thick with computer printouts. Like a quarterback making a handoff, he shoved the folder into Nicholas's midsection. Nicholas took it without breaking stride.

"Just arrived from California, dude. The heavy metal report." Rich followed his words with the sound of a Metallica guitar riff.

Nicholas paused to thumb through the printouts, which Rich had sent to a former colleague in California because the single organic chemistry lab at the community college had proven inadequate to identify all the poisons in the river, the soil, and the little boy's sock. Right away, he realized he was out of his element. "Can we go over these tonight?" He stuffed the folder into his black leather shoulder bag.

"Sure. When?"

"Nine." Nicholas knew that, without family obligations, Rich was pretty much free all the time and appreciated company in the evening.

"Okay, but it's Monday Night Football. We can't meet at your hole-in-the-wall bar with no TV," Rich said.

"Shall we do Superchamps then?" The sports bar with the huge-screen TV wasn't Nicholas's favorite, but it was well lighted, which would be an advantage tonight.

"I'm there." Rich clapped Nicholas on the shoulder and left.

* * *

The New York Giants had already kicked off to the Dallas Cowboys by the time Nicholas joined Rich at the back table that Rich had saved. He slipped into a chair and immediately began studying the menu. "What's good here? I'm starved."

"Don't they let you out for dinner?" Rich asked. "Or did half the school come to see you for office hours again?"

"Holly was working late, so I had to pick Tony up from basketball tryouts between classes."

"Did he make the team?"

Nicholas shook his head. "I talked to the coach, though. A lot of kids didn't make it, so they might try to organize a B team." He reached into his shoulder bag and pulled out the manila folder. "Anyway, I got to pick up the enlargement of one of the photos I took last summer."

"Not one of the kid who drowned. Those were gruesome." Rich winced.

"Nope. It's the chemical plant." When Nicholas looked up, the waiter was standing at their table, order pad ready.

The beer arrived right away. Rich poured a glass for each of them. Nicholas put on his reading glasses and opened the folder with the printouts. "So what did you find?"

"The usual suspects." Rich flipped to the second page and pointed to a column of numbers. "Beginning with benzene."

"In which samples did you find it?" The question came out as more a gasp, because the mere mention of benzene, a principal environmental cause of his leukemia, made his chest and throat freeze up. He took a long swallow of beer.

Rich leafed through a few more pages. "All over the place," he said slowly. "The river. The riverbank. The tap water."

"How much in the tap water?"

"Enough to exceed the federal limit." Rich scanned the page and pointed to a column of numbers. "Here."

Nicholas quickly calculated the difference between the federal maximum for benzene and the numbers from the well that served his neighborhood, which left him wondering why the Feds hadn't shut the well down long ago. After he'd gotten sick, the whole family had switched to bottled water, a fact he mentioned to Rich.

"No matter," Rich told him. "Drinking the water is the least of it. When you take your nice long hot shower, you can inhale benzene. Or it penetrates your skin through a cut, even open pores."

Nicholas shook his head in despair. You couldn't protect yourself and your family against that, unless you wanted to adopt the cleanliness standards of Europeans before the twentieth century—the filthiest people in the history of the modern world.

"Oh, and one other thing," Rich added. "The soil samples around your house."

"Yeah, Holly still hasn't forgiven me for digging up the yard. Did you find something?"

"Uh-huh." Rich turned to another page.

This will show her, Nicholas thought in the instant before he realized they weren't supposed to find anything there, that Rich had only suggested collecting the soil samples on the bluff to compare them to the ones next to the river.

"Did the river ever flood in the time you lived there?"

Nicholas filed through eleven years of memories. "Not as far up as the houses. We're on a thirty-foot-high bluff. But there were several times in the spring when we had ice jams and the river rose maybe five to eight feet." He hesitated, the fist of rage again tightening. "Why?"

"I'm trying to figure out how the chemicals got up to the houses then. In the soil next to the river we found traces of about fifteen different chemicals." Rich pointed to the words on the printout as he read. "Chromium, cadmium, arsenic, and mercury, for example. Heavy metals. Real nasty stuff. But in the soil around your house…"

"You found all of those?"

"Not all of them. Mainly benzene and related compounds. But we need to figure out how they got there."

Rich stole a glance at the big-screen TV across the room. The Giants had just evened the score with a field goal. Nicholas sipped his beer and tried to imagine a scenario that could have brought the poison to his very own door. All he could think of were the McDonoughs—his only friends from that neighborhood. What could they have told him, if they were still alive?

* * *

The McDonoughs were one of the first families to move into the new neighborhood, and they were the first to die. Crazy Giants fans from Brooklyn, Roger was a labor organizer and Barbara a peace activist even before the 1960s. In 1982, Burnham University hired him to teach in its school of labor relations. After years of living in cramped apartments with their four kids, they found paradise in the large houses and lawns of a quiet suburban neighborhood. Barbara busied herself in the first garden she ever had, watched over the kids as they passed—virtually unscathed—through adolescence, and founded a local peace group. When Roger wasn't teaching classes or advising various unions in the area, he lay in his hammock, bought during a trip to Nicaragua with the kids, and listened to the tape player he had wedged into the joint of a tree. His singing tree, he called it. Maybe it was the rope from the hammock scraping away the bark, or maybe the tree didn't like Woody Guthrie, Pete Seeger, or Joan Baez, but eventually the singing tree died, and he had to buy a metal frame for the hammock.

By the mid-nineties, all four kids had moved on. The McDonoughs didn't get to enjoy their freedom, though, because right after the youngest graduated from college, Roger was diagnosed with lymphoma. He managed to hang on for three years, but in the meantime, Barbara contracted an unusually aggressive form of the same disease and was gone in six months.

Nicholas kept his own illness a secret from his friends because he didn't want to upset them further. But throughout their mutual ordeal, the idea that these weren't random episodes of bad luck began to form in his consciousness, and by the time both McDonoughs were gone, it had coalesced into an obsession. For the McDonoughs lived only one cul-de-sac away, on Nightingale Court.

* * *

The Cowboys scored a touchdown and now led the Giants by seven. Almost drowned out by the chorus of moans that followed, Nicholas heard himself whisper, "The dirt."

Rich leaned across the table to hear. "What was that?"

"The dirt," Nicholas said, much louder this time. "Was dirt fill added to the bluff? You know, to make it higher, flatter, easier to build on?"

Rich shrugged. "I don't know. I'm the new kid in town."

"And could the dirt have been brought in with the contaminants already there?"

"Sure." The food arrived, and Rich cleared a space for the waiter to set the two plates down.

"So I have to find out where the dirt came from."

Rich picked up a nacho chip loaded with cheese and ground beef. "That might help."

"And take soil samples from around the homes of anyone else who got sick or died."

Rich nodded, his mouth now full.

Nicholas pressed on. "And what about the kid? What did the lab find that could have messed him up like that?"

Rich took the folder from the table and tossed it under his chair. "Later. Eat your dinner before it gets cold."

Though his appetite had vanished, Nicholas forced himself to eat his hamburger and washed it down with another glass of beer. The Cowboys scored a second touchdown just before halftime, and as soon as the two teams left the field, Rich set the folder back on the table. He then poured himself the rest of the beer from the pitcher and signaled the waiter for a fresh one.

"The kid?" Nicholas asked.

Rich turned to one of the back pages of the printout. "That's in your acid group."

"What did you find?"

"Mostly sulfuric acid. But on the fabric sample there were also traces of nitric acid and hydrochloric acid."

Nicholas recognized the last one. "That's the acid in your stomach, right?"

"Congratulations. Professor of European history remembers something from high school biology class." Rich killed the half-glass of beer he had just poured. "But none of the water or soil samples you brought in had significant traces of any acid."

"That's because I took the samples from the Yellow Springs side of the river. Who knows where the kid could have floated?"

"Where did you say he was from again?"

"Dominican Republic. The family was only here for two months. Had no idea they were messing around in a future Superfund site." Nicholas fished in his bag for the envelope. He slipped the enlarged photograph from it and laid it on top. "Here's what I have to show you. The Hometown Chemical Company plant. Or what's left of it." He pushed the photo closer to Rich.

Rich squinted at the eight-by-ten enlargement. "Okay, where's Waldo?"

"Do you need a magnifying glass?"

"Yeah, sure."

Nicholas handed him a small magnifying glass. He waited for Rich to recognize the fifty-five-gallon drums, some of which lay on their sides in the brush just beyond the river's edge.

"You see them?" Nicholas asked.

"Yes."

"You want to go in with me?"

"Tonight?"

"Unless you want to see the rest of the game."

Rich sneaked another glance at the TV. The teams had taken the field for the third quarter, but nothing major had happened yet. "You'll need protective clothing, which we don't happen to have right now," he said.

"Okay, then, Friday afternoon."

Rich reached across the table and put his hand on Nicholas's shoulder. "You know, Nick, you did such a great job collecting those other samples, I'll let you handle this one yourself."

Nicholas shrugged. It wasn't Rich's fight, and he'd already done more than a friend could have expected. But Rich offered to bring over a pair of gloves, a mask, and protective clothing from the lab.

"I'll get you some proper containers for the samples, too. Ones that won't disintegrate no matter what you put in them." Rich paused. "You'll need them."

"Thanks."

"And don't go tasting anything you find in the drums." Rich poured himself a fresh glass from the full pitcher the waiter had dropped off. "Last time you put a bunch of chemicals into your body you were in the hospital for three months."

Nicholas grimaced. After a few beers, his friend could get awfully uninhibited. Nicholas didn't consider his ordeal in California—his bone-marrow transplant with Jake, the brother he hardly knew, as the donor—as anything to joke about, especially by someone who hadn't gone through it. Let Rich lose all his blond hair on his head, his face, his armpits, around his balls, throw up for ten weeks straight, get a mouthful of sores from opportunistic infections, and spend weeks in isolation with no one to look at but his own gaunt, yellow, hairless reflection, and then he could talk.

But this wasn't the time or the place for sensitivity training. And maybe he was just being his usual prickly self. After all, he was in remission, his hair grown back even thicker than before, the collateral physical damage mostly healed. He leaned back in his chair, hands clasped behind his head, and focused on the game.

Despite a Giants touchdown, the Cowboys were still hanging on, playing a game of field position as the third quarter wound down. A punt return for a touchdown at the beginning of the fourth quarter put them ahead by an almost unbeatable margin. Time for the Cowboys to run out the clock. Time for him to go. He collected his various pieces of evidence and left Rich to watch the Giants until the bitter end.

Nicholas did not need a couple of beers in his system to engage in bold and reckless acts. But as he shoved a Wynton Marsalis CD into the stereo of the small car he shared with Rosie, he felt strangely free. After midnight, in the pitch black of a cloudy moonless night, time and space seemed suspended, infinite. Not even Holly would be up waiting for him this late. Turning up the stereo's volume, he took the shortcut home, the rutted road through the abandoned industrial area on the northern edge of Cold Springs that led to the North Springs Bridge. The road passed by the boarded-up Hometown Chemical Company plant.

He paused the CD and switched from the regular headlights to the fog lamps as he turned onto the road leading to the plant. Slowly, he approached the plant, passing brush and stunted trees, rusting vehicles and equipment. He pulled up to a locked gate and got out of the car, leaving the door open.

He took a deep breath and whistled long and loudly. Poised for a quick escape, he waited for the crunch of a night watchman's feet or the bark of a guard dog. Only silence and the steam of his tense breath in the cold damp night greeted him. He reached behind the passenger seat of the car for his flashlight and returned to the gate.

He ran the beam of light along the high chain-link fence. Barbed wire glistened on top. Behind the brush, huge drums in various stages of corrosion littered the factory grounds, tossed carelessly about as if a tornado had blown the whole fucking place apart. A corner of the fence next to the gate had been peeled away, about the size of a small child or a large raccoon. The gate's rustproof chain appeared pristine, but the padlock was dull with dirt and rust.

Suddenly faint, Nicholas gripped the chain link fence to steady himself. The abandoned plant, its windows replaced with faded plywood, rose some thirty feet into the air and stretched almost a city block long, far beyond the beam of his flashlight. He felt the hugeness of it all crushing him.

Make a plan. No different from walking into a library or archive and figuring out how to locate the right documents for your research. After teaching all these years you still remember, don't you? He reasoned that the contents of the drums nearest the river were the most likely to have leached into the water, and those he would sample first. He made a mental note to bring his camera, and he decided to go in Friday morning to give himself more time. The only decision that remained was whether he would pick the lock or cut the fence.

* * *

For escaping detection, Nicholas could not have chosen a better day than that Friday if he'd written the weather report himself. A dense fog had settled over the Cold Springs area in the predawn hours and showed no sign of lifting. After dropping the kids off at their respective schools, he drove over the North Springs Bridge and back down the narrow road toward the plant. He scanned both sides of the road and the parking area for other cars, but saw nothing.

He parked outside the same gate, popped open the trunk, and put the protective clothing and footwear over his street clothes. He pulled on his mask, goggles, and latex gloves but waited with the rubber gloves until he had picked the padlock and unwound the chain.

Inside the fence, Nicholas checked his equipment: his camera, loaded with high-speed film to take pictures in the dim light; glass containers; tools to collect samples from the drums and the soil; marking pen; zippered plastic bags. All inside the black canvas bag. Knowing he could get lost in the fog—the son of a scrap-metal dealer ought to know how to navigate a dumpsite—he had also brought a thick ball of cord that he hitched to one of his belt loops and tied the loose end to the fence.

He walked slowly, gingerly, the fog by the river so thick that when he extended his arm his gloved fingertips appeared as if behind a veil. All was silence except the squishing of his boots in the mud and the occasional squawk of a flock of geese overhead. When he stood still and held his breath in the thick soupy mist, it was like being in his own world, a democratic people's republic of one. The raw chill and drizzle cut through his layers of clothing into his bones. From time to time, an uncontrollable shiver seized him and made every movement shaky and awkward. As he wound his way through the twisted maze of debris, drums and tangles of brush seemed to appear out of nowhere, sending his heart thudding. He broke into a sweat despite the penetrating cold.

His boot caught on a hollow drum, and when he glanced down, he saw a scrap of dark-blue cloth. He crouched to pick it up. It was the remains of a Boston Red Sox cap, crumpled and half-buried in mud, its cardboard bill rotting away. He turned it over, wishing he could salvage this desecrated emblem of his team, thinking someone might have left it there as if expecting him. He stuffed the cap into a plastic bag and then into his canvas bag.

A narrow, slippery path led downhill toward the water. There at the river's edge lay the drums in the worst condition. Many of them had tipped over and spilled their contents long ago, perhaps in one of the spring floods. Nicholas scraped metal and crud from the sides of these, snapped photographs, and labeled each sample's container with the number of the corresponding photo. Other drums in the area remained standing, but without tops, or so corroded that they leaked from their sides and bottoms. The liquid from multiple leaky drums combined with rainwater to form toxic rivulets of white, yellow, orange, blue, and black that Nicholas followed along the bank to the river. Here, he filled his containers with the chemical stew and the river water that had most likely left its mark on Luis Espada, poor kid who came all the way from the Dominican Republic to end like this. He finished a roll of film and then another of the scene: desolation, waste, and death shrouded in a fine mist.

Six: Rookie of the Year

The trophies from the city softball league were ready, and Sandy's next-door neighbors, Monique and Kenny James, were having a team party to celebrate. On her porch, Sandy watched steam rise from the freshly baked apple pie she had set on the railing to cool in the chilly fall air. It was the end of October, her classes had finished fighting the French and Indian War, and the headmaster had asked her to coach the newly created middle-school boys' B basketball team. The team included all the kids who hadn't made the A team, and Tony's father had volunteered to help. She visualized the name on the piece of paper the headmaster had handed her. *Dr. Nicholas Baran.*

She tried to imagine what Tony's father was like, probably some former high-school star worried about his son's lack of athletic ability. Still, she was relieved that she'd kept her job. When Dr. Avis had called her into his office, her only thought was, *I'm going to be fired.* Instead, he had trusted her with an extra responsibility, although she couldn't put out of her mind the way he'd said, "I think it'll help you with your classes if you get to know the boys outside of school," as if he knew how much had gone wrong so far.

While his father and older brother Joey stood talking on the porch, Ben swept leaves from the narrow driveway and stuffed them into a giant orange plastic bag with a Halloween pumpkin face. He flung the plump bag toward the curb, where it faced its shiny grotesque siblings across the street— the bags Ben had filled for Mrs. Calabrese that morning. She had paid him with a stack of worn one-dollar bills that he riffled in front of Sandy before folding and depositing into the back pocket of his too-small jeans. When he bent over, she could see the square outline of the bills, the same shape and dimensions as a pack of cigarettes.

Farther down the street, the remains of the tenement where the Espadas once lived lay in a charred pile of wood, plaster, and ash. The building had burned to the ground two weeks earlier, but the city had yet to cart it away. The fire made Sandy think of the Espadas again, and the day after it happened she did not take her usual route home through Yellow Springs Heights but drove across the bridge from which Luis had fallen. She saw that nothing had been done to replace the two-foot-high railing that separated the roadway from the river below.

She recalled Mrs. Espada's words. *Dígales... Tell them*. The railing was bent and rusted. The rutted two-lane road that took her back home along the northern edge of Cold Springs passed a half dozen abandoned factories—the largest, the boarded-up factory of Hometown Chemical Company. She knew from her study of American history that these factories once drew people from rural areas, Europe, and the South, and when they closed, so many of those people and their communities fell into poverty and despair. She wondered if Global Millennium Bio-Chem, the company that now owned Hometown Chemical Company and sometimes ran ads for various medicines on the sports channels, would abandon the glass-walled office building that dominated the downtown skyline and eliminate those hundreds of jobs as well.

After dropping the second bag at the curb, Ben carried the rake to the small metal shed behind the house and joined his father and brother on the porch. Joe, stooped and slender, with sparse gray hair and leathery skin from years of construction work outdoors, gripped a beer can. Eighteen-year-old Joey, his black hair already thinning but his body tall, hard, and muscular in his long-sleeved t-shirt and jeans, was smoking a cigarette. Ben extended his hand, palm up, to his father.

"Later." Joe sipped from his can. "I'm a little short this week."

Ben frowned and let his arm drop. Joey rubbed the bristly top of his younger brother's head. Across the narrow driveway that separated the Amatos' house from their neighbors', Kenny and another team member brought grocery bags inside. Joe and Joey glared at the two large Black men. Ben glared at his father.

"Where's Paulie?" Sandy asked them, trying to ease the tension.

"Watching TV. He said it was too cold," Joe answered, not taking his eyes off the group setting up the party next door.

"Yeah, I'd be there too, except Mom and Darla kicked me out. Darla says the baby can breathe my cigarette smoke even if he's not born." Joey laughed and shook his head.

Dressed in jeans and a sweatshirt, her hair in stubby dreadlocks, Monique waved at Sandy before lifting the black and gold banner of the Mercy-Flatlands All Stars from the trunk of Kenny's car.

"What's that?" Joey asked. Sandy thought he was referring to Monique's wave, but he pointed with his cigarette to the banner she was holding.

"It's a gang thing," his father muttered. "Coloreds having a party. We're probably gonna have to call the police."

Ben raised his thumb and extended his index finger in the shape of a pistol and made shooting sounds. Joey grinned and slapped him high fives. Sandy wished the boy had gone inside with Paulie.

"Guys, it's for the softball championship," she said. Joe, Joey, and Ben turned to face her. This was the closest she'd ever come to having a talk about the Black neighbors with any of them. Her throat was dry, and her stomach was doing somersaults. "Remember the team Mitch and I were on this summer? The one that went undefeated?"

Joey pointed next door. "Was this the team you tried to get me to join?"

"Yeah. You would have had fun too." Joey eyed her

doubtfully. She went on, as much to keep him from saying something obnoxious as anything else. "Mercy Hospital sponsors the team. Kenny and Monique are nurses, and most of the other people on the team work there too, but they let anyone from the Flatlands try out." She glanced in the direction of the hospital three blocks away, a major employer and stabilizing force in the neighborhood.

"Nurses," Joe said slowly. "You said the guy is a nurse? What is he, a little, you know?"

Sandy stifled a groan as she struggled to think of a point of reference, a way to make them understand neighbors who were so different from them. Her big chance to make peace on Wallman Street. She told Joe, Joey, and Ben how Kenny had received a football scholarship at the state university but quit after his second year to become a physical therapy nurse after his best friend from the team was paralyzed from the neck down in a game.

Joe took a long swallow from his can. "Yeah, I remember that. That big colored lineman. Was gonna go pro." He shook his head. "What a shame."

Joe's remarks encouraged her. That was what she liked about sports. Show some interest and a little actual knowledge, and she could talk to anyone. And being female added an element of surprise. Maybe it would even help her new basketball team win some games.

But Joe had stopped listening. "Joey, do you remember that guy's name? The one that broke his neck?" he asked.

Joey shook his head.

"You, Ben?" His younger son shot him a confused glance. "Nah, you're too young."

Monique approached her porch steps. She held a trophy in each hand. Sandy called her name and motioned her over.

Monique edged toward them. Sandy noted that her light brown skin was not much darker than Joe's. As she introduced them, Sandy wondered how long they had been living next door to each other and never once said hello.

Monique smiled. "Pleased to meet you." Her hands full, she pantomimed a handshake.

"I was wondering if they could see the trophies," Sandy said.

Monique lifted one of the trophies high enough so that Joey could grasp the top of the gilded softball player's head and pull the whole thing over the porch railing. "Whoa," he said under his breath as he turned the trophy. "Yeah, I should have tried out. Maybe this spring, if I'm not too busy with the baby."

"Don't let her hook you into it," his father growled. Sandy didn't know whether he meant taking care of the baby or playing for the team. He surveyed the trophy and handed it back to Monique.

"Nice meeting you all," Monique said.

"You too," Joey replied. "Maybe we'll see you around."

The Amatos went inside, and Sandy joined her friends next door. As soon as she stepped into the Jameses' apartment, Monique lifted the pie from her hands and slammed the door. "I don't know how to say this, but I wish you wouldn't try to make me talk to that landlord of yours. I grew up in the Flatlands, and you're not going to change the way people think around here by pretending we can all be friends."

Monique's words, spoken in the quiet before the guests arrived, almost wrecked the party for Sandy. She began to sputter a protest but recalled the Amatos' equally unenthusiastic response, and her vision of fixing her little corner of the world evaporated into an image of everybody sitting alone in their apartments imprisoned by mistrust and hate. *Lose the self-pity. At least Monique doesn't hold it against you that you live in the Amatos' house.*

The party was crowded, lively, and loud. Monique's youngest sister, Tasha Lockwood, burned the microwave popcorn. The kitchen smelled like the tenement burning, and Sandy decided to help clean up by fanning the smoke toward the window. In the relative quiet of the smoky room, she started talking with Tasha. Smaller, of more delicate build, and lighter-skinned than Monique, Tasha had just turned twenty. Like both sisters before her, she attended Springs Regional Community College.

"So how much longer do you have to graduate?" Sandy asked.

"I finish in May. I quit my job in September so I could concentrate on my classes full-time."

"At the college library?" At the beginning of softball season last May, she'd told Sandy she worked there as a clerk.

"No. I switched to a corporate library downtown. I'm pre-med, and the college couldn't afford to buy the science journals I needed. I thought I could read them in my free time." She laughed.

"I guess it didn't work out."

"Yeah. I could have made more money flipping burgers, and my boss was an idiot." She paused to pry loose a kernel that had stuck to the counter. "Like, he somehow got it into his fool head that we needed to put these little metal clips in the files so that the papers wouldn't fall out. Not that anyone would ever look at the files. I mean, some of them were over thirty years old. But, of course, he wouldn't listen to me. So for two months I took out all the files and put these thingies in. I got about three-quarters done, and then he realized the metal clips caused the files to take up twice as much space. Well, hel-lo! Doofus alert!"

Sandy smiled. Tasha went on, "We didn't have room in the archives for more file cabinets, so I had to go back and take all the metal clips out. That was a waste of three months."

"So what are you going to do now?"

"I took out a loan, and Momma, Monique, and Kenny have offered to help me out. After I graduate, I'm going to UConn. I'll take out all the loans I can so I don't get out of med school when I'm forty."

After the potluck dinner, Kenny handed out the trophies.

In addition to small championship trophies for everyone on the team, a special batting award for Kenny, and a pitching award for Monique, there was an additional trophy for Sandy that she didn't know about—the female Rookie of the Year Award. Soon afterward, people started to leave. Monique stopped Sandy on her way out.

"I'm sorry about what I said to you earlier." She asked Sandy to sit and visit for a while. Before dropping onto the sofa, Sandy set her two trophies side by side on the coffee table with her washed pie plate standing on end between them. Monique crouched on the other side of the table, grabbed a wadded napkin, and pushed crumbs into the palm of her hand. The vacuum hummed in the hallway. Monique raised her voice. "How's the new job?"

Sandy groaned. "I think I'm in way over my head."

"I could have told you the kids are spoiled brats." Monique took out the pie plate and lifted and cleaned under each trophy.

"Not all of them." She thought of Chris and Tony. And even the brats had their problems. "The headmaster just assigned me to coach a boys' basketball team."

"That's a first." Monique tossed the crumbs and napkin into a large black garbage bag on the floor next to the hallway. Kenny pushed the vacuum into the living room and in several quick passes cleaned the worn beige carpet.

Sandy waited until he left. "I don't know whether to be proud I'm a pioneer, or grab the dad who's volunteered to assist me and scream, 'Help!'"

"A student's dad offered to help you?"

"Yeah. Dr. Nicholas Baran. You wouldn't know him from the hospital, would you?"

Monique froze. "He's the Ship Rats' shortstop. Goes by the nickname Mackie the Knife."

Sandy recognized the name of the gangster hero of *The Threepenny Opera* and wondered. Most of the nicknames in the league ran to the raunchy rather than the literary. But the

Ship Rats was the community college team, which might have explained the reference. "Does he teach literature at the college?"

"No, European history. Tasha has him this semester, and my other sister had him too." Monique stepped into the hall and called for Tasha.

The closet door slammed. Kenny came in and laid a huge arm across Monique's shoulders. "She left already." Monique told him the story. "*He's* coaching a team with you?"

"Yes. Why?"

"He's the dirtiest player in the league," Kenny said. "Remember our game with the Rats last summer? He slid into you at second and knocked you clear into the next ballpark." He shook his head and laughed.

The memory came back to her. Covering second base, she caught the throw that forced him out, but before she could flip the ball to first for the double play he slid into her and sent her crashing to the dirt. She rolled over his sweaty body and onto her back like an upended turtle; the ball rolled out of her glove. He scrambled up and helped her up, and she noticed his left wrist wrapped with tape. He grinned and said, "Sorry, I got a little carried away," before jogging off the field to the cheers of his team.

Monique and Kenny, veterans of the softball league, exchanged glances that made Sandy feel even more like a rookie who would never belong. She ran her finger along the smooth back of the batter mounted to her special trophy. It was cold and hard.

"Hey, girl, don't look so low," Monique said. "I never took his class, but my sisters say it's the best. He might be a good coach—as long as you don't go one-on-one against him."

* * *

The Friday before Parents' Day, Amy Reed, a quiet eleventh grader whose average had recently dropped from a B+ to a C, wanted to speak to Sandy after class.

Amy sat at her usual desk, and Sandy pulled up a desk and chair next to her. She was a small, pink-cheeked girl with round deep-blue eyes and wavy shoulder-length light brown hair, streaked blonde in front. She twisted her hands. "My parents can't come to Parents' Day," she began, her voice soft and scared. "It's because of my little brother, Stephen. He's in the hospital, and they have to be there with him."

"I'm sorry. Is he going to be all right?" Her initial thought was not of Amy's brother, but of the phone call she would now have to make to let the Reeds know Amy had stopped doing her homework.

"I don't know. He has leukemia."

Hot blood rushed to Sandy's face, the same wave of shame she'd felt when she'd learned about Kyle. She stammered a question about Stephen's age. Amy told her he was in the sixth grade at Shady Ridge and began to sob.

Sandy hesitated because she had never touched a student before. She reached across the desk and put her hand on Amy's shoulder. She edged Amy toward her and embraced her. The girl's warm tears soaked through Sandy's blouse.

That night Sandy accepted Marissa's standing invitation to attend services at the synagogue in Yellow Springs, Neve Tefillah. The sun had set hours ago, the Shabbat had begun, and the tall stained-glass windows glowed blue, orange, yellow, red, and green from the light within. In the window closest to her parking space a bearded Moses waited for the Commandments. The synagogue was a circular beige brick building, and though the brick was dull with age the stained glass remained brilliant.

Marissa met her inside the two-story lobby that flowed

into the sanctuary. From the synagogue's well-lit interior the windows appeared opaque, the scene hard to interpret. The sanctuary had rounded corners that suggested the circularity of the building, of the seasons, the year, of life.

A middle-aged couple and their gangly Bar Mitzvah, an eighth grader at Shady Ridge and one of Marissa's students, lit a pair of candles and recited the blessings. As she watched the steady flames rise, Sandy recalled her own Bat Mitzvah and the times after that when she had ascended the *bimah*. In high school she had been president of her youth group and won prizes for the community service activities she had organized. What had happened to her that she had become so focused on herself—on the friends and fun, the parties and softball games in college and grad school, and the stresses of her first job?

The boy must have had a small family because no more than two dozen people attended the Friday night service. When Sandy chanted the prayers, which she had not forgotten over the years, she heard her rich alto voice above the congregation. After the Torah had been blessed and returned to the ark, the rabbi read the names of those who were sick and in need of the special prayer, the Mishebeirach. After he finished the list, he asked for people with additional names to stand and announce them.

Sandy gave Marissa the briefest of glances and rose to her feet. He wasn't Jewish and she'd never met him, but it didn't matter. Her voice resonated clear and strong in the nearly empty sanctuary as she called out, "Stephen Reed."

Seven: Parents' Day

Rosie called from the laundry room, "Mom, what do I do about blood?"

Holly left the dust cloth on the bookshelf and hurried into the steamy room. Her sixteen-year-old daughter held up the white button-down shirt of Tony's school uniform. Flecks of dried blood stained the collar, and more blood streaked the right-hand cuff, as if he'd had a nosebleed and wiped it with his sleeve.

"What's going on here?" she muttered, as much to herself as to her daughter. She dug through the pile at Rosie's feet in search of other laundry-day surprises. Tony's khaki pants had another small bloodstain on the thigh. A pair of blue jeans was caked with dirt, and dirt blackened a red and white flannel shirt. Two pale blue towels from the downstairs bathroom were soaked and brown. When she lifted them, she revealed lines of inky mud on the linoleum floor. She glanced over to Nicky's mud-covered boots that sat next to the door to the garage.

He was digging again. He had already torn up their yard, back and front. He'd raked the leaves, then removed the topsoil, leaving gashes around the bushes and trees, in the flower beds, on the ragged lawn where grass and weeds fought a constant turf war, and across the mulch of wood chips where they'd never managed to make anything grow. He'd piled the dirt he didn't need and let the wind carry it away. He didn't listen when she begged him to stop.

She sprayed his shirt and jeans with stain remover, though she wished she could simply throw them away and teach him a lesson. She knew she didn't have the discipline; in the end, she would take pity on Nicky and buy him more clothes to replace the ones he ruined. Then she would worry about the balance on the credit cards and why he never asked her about it.

But the blood on Tony's clothes was new. And not expected.

When she'd asked Tony how school was going, he'd told her, "Okay." When she'd asked him what he'd done in class, he'd said, "Nothing." He hadn't made the basketball team, but according to Nicky the school had promised to organize a B team. So far, he'd brought no friends over and had not gone to anyone else's house. Basically, nothing had changed.

Still, he had never come home bloodied from Yellow Springs Middle School.

She sprayed the pants but took the shirt upstairs to Nicky, who was cleaning the kids' bathroom. He looked up from the bathtub when she entered. "Do you know anything about this?" she asked.

Without taking off his heavy blue gloves, he held the shirt close to his face. "I'd say something happened at school."

"Like an accident? Or a fight?"

He shrugged. "Don't ask me."

Holly imagined him, a public school graduate, thinking how he hadn't wanted to send Tony to Shady Ridge in the first place. It had been her idea, she'd even convinced her parents to pay the tuition before she pitched the proposal to Nicky, and he only agreed after Tony had missed the cut for the tiny honors track at Yellow Springs Middle. A combination of teacher politics and Tony being too busy dodging bullies to concentrate on his schoolwork, she believed, but she reminded Nicky that not accelerating in math and science in seventh grade as Rosie had done would knock their son out of the running for the Ivy League and most other highly selective colleges.

She took the shirt back. "It must have been Friday. Weren't you home then?"

"I had some things to do."

"Mom, I know what happened."

Holly spun around to see Rosie standing at the door. She was a small, slender girl, with a smooth, unblemished face, high cheekbones, shiny shoulder-length dark brown hair, and deep brown, almost black eyes. Nicky's eyes. She stood with her hands on her hips, her thumbs hooked into the belt loops of her low-rise jeans, and motioned with her head for them to follow her out of the bathroom to her room. Downstairs in the living room, Tony shouted rap lyrics over the drone of the vacuum cleaner. Rosie shut her bedroom door.

"Some kids tripped Tony in social studies. I got a ride home from school, so I saw him when he got off the bus. He told me everything." Rosie ran her fingers through her hair to push it back from her forehead, another of Nicky's gestures. They were so alike and yet had nothing in common.

Nicky clenched both fists. "Did he say who did it?"

Holly felt his rage in the pit of her stomach, and she hoped Tony hadn't told Rosie the names of the culprits. Rosie shook her head. "He said it was a bunch of boys."

"Shit."

Nicky, please don't swear in front of the kids. Holly touched his shoulder to calm him. His muscles tensed, resisting her efforts.

"Did he even try to defend himself?" he asked.

"I doubt it." Rosie sniffed. "Maybe you ought to get your money back from that tae kwon do place. It's not like they're teaching him anything."

"They're building his self-esteem. And he has a couple of belts already," Holly said.

"It doesn't do him any good unless he uses it," Nicky murmured. She glanced toward him. They had agreed on the class. She hoped he remembered that.

Rosie continued. "Guys, he begged me not to tell you, but I can't stand to see the little twerp picked on at every school he goes to. When he was at Yellow Springs Middle, I could talk to my friends so their brothers would leave him alone, but I don't know anyone at Shady Ridge."

"That's okay. We'll take care of it." Holly thanked Rosie and left the room, Nicky alongside her. The chemical smell of bathroom cleaner burned her nostrils. She wondered if handling this stuff was any less dangerous than living with the chemicals he'd found in the soil around their house. Or maybe she'd merely imagined the smell; he had been wearing gloves.

In their bedroom, Nicky leaned against the doorway and let out a long breath. "Damn. With the way she treats him, Tony tells her and not us?"

"A lot of times kids tell their older sisters things they won't tell their parents." Holly recalled the secrets she had confessed to Liz and the things Jenny confided in her after Liz left for college. But she didn't mention those to Nicky, and she avoided saying anything about a brother because she didn't want him to think of Jake, who was never there for him during his adolescence. She sometimes thought this was like being the child of Holocaust survivors, the way she avoided talking to him about her family because she never knew what memory of trauma she would unearth in him.

"I need to keep an eye on him," Nicky said after a moment. "I got a call several days ago from the coach who cut Tony, and he said they were thinking of asking that new social studies teacher to coach the B team."

"Why did he call you?"

"He was calling all the fathers to ask if someone could work with her." He pushed his hands through his hair. "First of all, she's a woman coaching a boys' team, so she can't go into the locker room. And then..." He paused. "I don't think they have a lot of confidence in her."

Holly sat on the bed, on Nicky's side, and he came over to sit next to her. "Rosie said those kids tripped Tony in her class. Maybe the school's concerns are justified." She considered the idea of Nicky volunteering. He could watch over Tony. And it would keep him away from the river and from tearing up their yard. "You should help her."

"That's what I was thinking. But I know who she is, and I'm a little surprised she's having so much trouble."

Holly stiffened. If he knew her before, why hadn't he said anything? "Was she a student of yours?"

"She and her boyfriend played softball on another team in our league. She's a tough kid. I spiked her to avoid a double play, and she tagged me out stealing two innings later." He grinned. "Nobody tags *me* out stealing." He tapped his clenched fist on Holly's shoulder. "So when the team captains voted for the awards at the end of the season, I chose her for Rookie of the Year."

"I don't think ballplaying ability and teaching ability are related."

"No, but she's not a quitter. Tony showed me those worksheets she's giving them. They're crap. I'd hate for Tony to have a miserable year because she doesn't know what she's doing and I could help her."

Holly smiled. Nicky didn't manage detail well, and he could focus on only a few things at a time. The more he helped the teacher, she hoped, the less time and attention he'd have to finish his mad crusade.

* * *

Because Nicky had to teach his evening class, Holly came to Shady Ridge alone after work for Parents' Day. She saved the social studies teacher for last, and when she got to the classroom, Marc Martineau was already there. He looked as if he'd arrived from the office as well. He had a trim salt-and-pepper beard, and the neatly cut hair that surrounded the shiny bald crown of his head was only slightly darker than his beard. The beard was new and a good addition. At the neighborhood Christmas party the year before, he had come clean-shaven.

Holly hadn't heard from Marc since the phone message back in August. Perhaps Nicky had erased all the messages since then, or Marc had stopped calling because Nicky had turned his attention to destroying his own yard. She feared the complaints of the neighbors on the cul-de-sac, but maybe they'd become accustomed to the disreputable condition of the lawn at 15 Butternut Court—not that they kept their lawns much better. The people next door had a hyperactive son who stomped through every flower garden his mother put in and crashed his sled into her azalea bushes two winters ago; the bushes never recovered. And the new people on their other side owned a large dog that seemed to have buried an entire skeleton in the front yard. Anyway, Marc might not have known about the destruction of a single lawn so far from his own house or might have considered it a matter unworthy of his attention.

Marc's meeting was finishing up. The two stood and shook hands. Marc towered over the teacher, but when he stepped aside, Holly saw her, a sturdily built young woman with an angular face and shoulder-length brown hair turned under and parted in the middle. She dressed conservatively in a plaid skirt, cardigan sweater, and white blouse.

Marc held the door open for Holly and waited for her to enter. "Your turn," he said, his free hand outstretched.

Holly glanced briefly around the room. The walls were bare except for a lone poster of the Ellis Island museum. She shook the teacher's hand. "I'm Holly Meggett Baran. Tony's mother."

"Sandy Katz. Pleased to meet you." Holly was five four and, in her presence instead of Marc's six and a half feet, Miss Katz seemed more imposing physically. She was at least five eight, maybe five nine. *A big girl*, Holly thought, and pretty in a natural, athletic way.

Miss Katz offered her a seat, and with a sigh Holly dropped into a desk chair. It had been a long day at work, and she had spent the last forty-five minutes meeting with Tony's other teachers. None reported any problem; the smaller classes and more nurturing environment had apparently benefited his schoolwork. But simply remembering the teachers' names and what they'd said took energy.

"I enjoy having Tony in the class," Miss Katz began. Holly noticed that she had hazel eyes and wore no makeup or jewelry, save for a small gold necklace with a Star of David. She went on to describe Tony's work in the class, hardly varying the positive assessment that Holly had already heard from the other teachers. She mentioned nothing about Tony having been a victim of bullies under her supervision.

Holly wondered if she should say anything. Everything about the young woman, from her clothing to her classroom walls, seemed spare, as if she lacked the confidence to speak for herself. Intuitively, Holly recognized the paralyzing self-doubt of her own undergraduate years, and she felt from experience that if she criticized her, the young teacher might be crushed. So when Miss Katz asked how Tony liked his new school, Holly answered, "All he ever tells me is okay."

"Was he in public school before this year?"

Holly nodded and blinked a couple of times. "We took him out because we didn't think he was reaching his potential. There were a lot of..." She paused, searching for the right word, "distractions."

"Distractions?"

Maybe an indirect approach would bring out the truth. "Discipline problems. Teachers spending more time trying to control the class than teaching. He was bored and not doing much work."

Miss Katz stared at the cream-colored desktop. "He's doing all his work for me. He has an A in the class." She flipped a page of her grade book and continued with her effusive praise, as if her compliments could ease the suspicions of a veteran parent.

"Does he have any friends in class?"

The teacher nodded. "A boy named Chris Leighton." Holly had never heard the name, but Miss Katz described how the two boys had become friends of late. But then she digressed, talking more about Chris than Tony. Holly needed to know only that Chris was a good student and not one of the troublemakers. Was the teacher in denial, or covering up her failures?

Miss Katz finished another irrelevant sentence and fell silent. Holly cleared her throat. "Tony was bullied a lot last year. Do you see anything like that happening here?"

"No, no." The teacher shook her head.

It served no purpose to question her further; any help would have to come from Nicky. "I have a message from my husband. He couldn't come because he has to teach tonight and tomorrow. He told me to tell you he didn't forget you or the basketball team, but he can only come on Fridays."

"We have a practice this Friday."

"He'll be there."

Marc was waiting for her in the hallway when she left the classroom. "How did it go?" he asked.

"Fine," she answered, her tone guarded.

"It was a lot better than mine, I'm sure," he said, lightly touching her elbow. "Those boys do get into a bit of trouble." He guided her toward the lobby. "Mainly Pete; he's quite a handful. I guess it's the middle child syndrome."

"You're talking to a middle child."

Marc laughed. He had a quick booming laugh that echoed in the lobby. "Yes, I realize it's a generalization, and I'm sorry if I offended you." He hesitated. "But I'm more worried about Braxton. He has a lot of potential, but that social studies teacher…"

"We're concerned about her too. Nick's agreed to work with the basketball team she's coaching. Will Braxton be on it?"

"He's on the A team. But I think it's great that your husband's helping her out." He readjusted the overcoat on one arm so that it draped neatly over his briefcase and slid his free hand into the pocket of his gray pants. She heard the faint jingle of coins. "I wanted to help her, but I have too much else to do."

She expected him to say good-bye, put on his overcoat, and leave, but after a brief silence he spoke up again. "There's something else I wanted to talk to you about, if you have a minute."

Holly checked her watch. Tony didn't have school the next day, and Rosie had become self-sufficient with her homework as with everything else. That was one of the advantages of older kids, because she couldn't count on Nicky Monday nights. He taught until nine, and he liked to unwind with his friends afterward. She let him have those hours, which often stretched until after midnight, because he needed a lot of unwinding. Sometimes he'd come back from the bar in the middle of the night and then walk the path next to the river until three or four in the morning, walking off the drink or the darkness, she never knew which. She never asked him what drew him to the inky, dead river, even on the coldest nights of winter. *Do I love him enough, now that I don't know his secrets or the way to ease his pain?* Sometimes while lying in bed alone, Nicky down at the river, she replayed how they ended up together in the waning days of their senior year. She thought of that funny Time Bomb game so popular in the early seventies, except in her version whoever held the plastic yellow bomb when time ran out got to keep it.

"I'm free," she said.

"Good. It's about the Community Association."

"Nicky?" she heard herself whisper. It sounded like a betrayal, calling him Nicky to Marc. Nobody since college had used that name. And since they had never attended a reunion and he had lost touch with the last of his college friends after his firing, no one but her ever called him that.

"He never got back to me, but that's not the main reason. I'm looking for someone to take over the vice-president's position. Our vice-president was transferred to Cleveland three years ago. We never replaced him, and I've been overwhelmed with all the work." He leaned against the lobby's red-brick wall. "I have my law practice and with Claudette ill and having to manage everything with the boys." He shook his head. "It's all getting out of control. We're down to the Christmas party and nothing else—no Halloween parade, no Spring Fling, no Fourth of July barbecue, no community garage sale. You must have noticed. I think you were on the garage sale committee."

Holly nodded. The association was falling apart, but she attributed it to the high turnover in the neighborhood—the original residents leaving and younger couples moving in. The Law of Neighborhood Entropy, the friend of hers who had once run the women's club called it.

"I can barely keep up the pool and the clubhouse," Marc continued. "I'm looking for a vice-president to revive the rest."

Holly sighed. His confidence in her tempted her. But Rosie had started to look at colleges, and she would have hardly more than a year before her daughter left. And then, the uncertainty of Nicky's health loomed, no matter how active and energetic he appeared and how much she tried to ignore the memory of his diagnosis and transplant. "Thank you for thinking of me, but I'm afraid I'm too busy right now."

"That's basically what everyone's telling me."

He looked so desperate, as if she had been his last chance. "Why don't you resign? Force some new people to get involved?"

Marc took a deep breath and let it out as he spoke. "If I resign, there won't *be* a Community Association."

He is a generous man, probably too generous for his and his family's own good. Aloud, she tried to reassure him. "Maybe there's something I can do to help."

"Yes. There's one thing you can do to make my life easier." He gazed up at the ceiling and down at her. Her eyes were drawn upward to the gray, black, and brown bristles in his tidy mustache and beard. "I've been trying to get in touch with your husband. I left messages because people saw him taking water samples from the river. Then about a week ago, one of your neighbors complained about your yard."

She tried to swallow, but her mouth had gone dry. "He dug it up. I tried to stop him."

Marc's eyes communicated sympathy. "Do you think you could have him talk to me?"

"I don't know." Maybe another man, someone with an official position in the neighborhood, would convince him when she couldn't. But Nicky had erased the messages and never called Marc back.

"Let me ask you first. What do *you* think of what he's doing?"

Holly sighed. "I wish he wouldn't."

"He's hurting all of us."

He's hurting himself.

"Has he thought about what will happen to the neighborhood's property values if he whips up groundless suspicion into full-fledged hysteria? I mean, you must have a huge investment in your own house."

Does it all come down to the money? Marc didn't know the circumstances surrounding their purchase of the house, that it had been her decision, that she had allowed the realtor to sell her on the community when she hadn't seen the huge crumbling red-brick factory across the river or asked the crucial questions about what the land might have been used for before it became suburb. No, it wasn't even the community he had sold her on but the *idea* of community, as if it could be bought and sold like cars or clothing.

Now, the community had evaporated, leaving Marc to hold up single-handedly what was left of the association, just as he held up what was left of his sad little family transplanted from Louisiana—an alcoholic wife and two of his three boys still at home and getting into trouble. At last year's Christmas party he had confessed his regrets to her, his decision to move away from his large Cajun brood in New Orleans after the oil bust of the early eighties to build a law practice in the just-recovering real estate market of the Northeast. He told her he'd made the fortune he'd sought, but he feared he'd sacrificed too much in the process. Claudette, he said, never adjusted to the coldness of the winters or the people. The boys missed their cousins. They clung to the worst aspects of their culture. At the party Holly noticed the sag in Marc's cheeks and the worry in his pale blue eyes.

The new beard concealed Marc's lined face and gave him a distinguished look, as if he were a man in control of his life. It bothered her that she knew the truth, the vulnerability behind the mask. *A married woman should know only one man's weaknesses.*

"How do you want me to help you?" she said.

"The next time he goes down to the river, please call me. Even if it's the middle of the day, I'll drop everything and get there."

"You won't do anything to him?" Her voice trembled. Nicky was so small. And so combustible.

Marc gave her a reassuring laugh. "I'm not in the business of getting sued for assault. I know how to handle feisty little guys."

"You'll try to talk him out of what he's doing?"

"That's all." Marc fixed his eyes on hers. She believed she could trust him. She would help him. And he would help her.

Behind her Holly heard footsteps. Other people had passed through the school building's double glass doors, but these footsteps seemed to linger, as if the person might have some business with them. Marc saw her first and nodded a greeting. Holly turned around.

It was Sandy Katz, in her Catholic-school-style plaid skirt and simple top. She looked less like a teacher than an oversized, overage student after a hard day, with her wrinkled clothes, her hair out of place, and her books and papers carelessly stuffed into her blue nylon shoulder bag. Her face appeared wan in the lobby's harsh light. She paused in front of them and dug a toe of her loafer into the slick uneven brown tile floor.

Hiding your incompetence must take a lot of energy, Holly thought, her jaw again tightening. She doubted the teacher even remembered their names.

Miss Katz forced her blank face into a smile. "Good night, Mr. Martineau."

Marc gripped her hand and offered a polite farewell.

"Good night, Mrs. Baran."

Holly extended her hand. "You too. Good luck tomorrow."

Holly's eyes followed the teacher as she slipped outside into the darkness. In the corner of her vision, she caught Marc's indulgent smile. She glanced up at him, frowned, and shook her head. Marc was shaking his head too.

Eight: Gardening with Ghosts

In the year and a half since the McDonoughs died, their house on Nightingale Court stood empty, unsold. The "For Sale" sign pitched in the front yard gave way to another sign from another realty company, and eventually the hanging sign that creaked solemnly in the breeze came to sport a companion that read "Price Reduced."

All four McDonough children had moved away, never to return. Fewer tulips and daffodils came up each spring in the garden that Barbara had so lovingly cultivated for so many years. Weeds overran the flower beds, and the once lush lawn was now a homely quilt of rye grass, weeds, and patches of dirt where nothing grew. The vines that snaked along the posts and roof of the trellis and screened-in porch—Roger's "tropical retreat," as he'd called it—had turned brown and brittle. Moss and clover poked through the brick walkway and climbed the house's foundation up to where they almost touched the faded brown cedar siding.

The McDonoughs' house was Nicholas's next destination. But Holly noticed the shovel and red ice chest filled with empty containers in the garage —Nicholas had discarded the canvas shoulder bag after the chemical plant expedition and hadn't yet had time to get another one. She busted him on the Saturday before Thanksgiving, when he had planned to collect samples between dropping Tony off at Chris Leighton's house and picking him up to take him to a guitar lesson.

"Nicky, you are not digging up anyone else's yard."

He shrugged. No point in arguing with her. He doubted he would change her mind, and she wasn't going to change his.

"Excuse, me. You are not going to ignore me and do what you want either." Her voice had dropped an octave, a sign she meant it. After twenty-one years of marriage, they had each other's m.o.s down pretty well. And this one called for a response.

She was standing in the laundry room, folding bath towels. He rested his elbow on a stack and tried to make eye contact. "So what are you worried about?" he finally asked her.

He expected her to say something about being seen or getting arrested for trespassing, but instead she looked away and continued folding. He touched her shoulder. "Holly, look at me."

She didn't move in his direction.

He stepped toward the door. "Okay, I'm leaving. I'll be at the McDonoughs."

Now she whirled toward him, her cheeks flushed. "You're crazy, you know," she screamed in his direction. "First it was the water samples. Then our yard. Now this."

"I thought it was just the water. And bottled water would keep us safe. But the chemicals are everywhere."

"How many yards do you plan to dig up? All of them? Because that's the only way you're going to prove anything."

He swallowed. "If I have to dig up the whole town to prove that the company contaminated this place, I'll do it."

"And what good is that going to do? You know they'll never pay. Even if we find a lawyer to take the case, the company can tie it up in court forever."

"And if we don't do anything, what happens? Who else gets sick?"

Holly bit her lower lip. "People can quietly sell their houses and leave. You know we can do that too, Nicky. There are plenty of other places we can live." She started to name the other middle-class suburbs in the area. Carbon copies of the Heights, but with longer commutes.

"I don't believe in running away. You know that." It was a struggle to keep his voice low and even.

"If you really believe this place is poisoned, you'll move

now for the sake of the kids. Do you want to expose them any longer?"

She had a point, one that he had considered from time to time over the past months and continuously since he'd found out the results of the soil samples. He wondered how long he could hold off before it made a difference for one of the kids. In fourth grade Tony had developed asthma, and it seemed to worsen with every year. Sandy said at the first basketball practice he couldn't get through one wind sprint without dashing for his inhaler. And he was the only one in the family who had it—the poison affected everyone differently.

"Okay." He tapped his clenched fist on the dryer and the hollow impact reverberated through his hand as he tried to stay calm, organize his thoughts. *What kind of father would leave his kids in danger? Any normal person would consider it worse than neglect.* "As soon as I'm done collecting the samples, we go. We'll get an apartment in Cold Springs until the case is resolved because I can't in good conscience sell this house to anyone else."

He waited for her denial. For her to tell him the soil and the water weren't the problem. His leukemia came from the brittle DNA of older parents. Allergies and the stress of unpopularity caused Tony's asthma.

"How do you know the dirt made anyone sick?" she asked.

"I promise you, a year from now I'll have my proof. We'll file the class-action suit, and everyone will be out of here, their houses paid for, if that's all they care about." He spat the last six words because that was all anyone in the Heights ever seemed to care about.

"But you won't win."

He pushed aside the towels. "People have won. What about Woburn?"

"They got $300,000 apiece. Here, that would barely cover the mortgage."

"It's not just the money. The Feds busted their asses and

made them clean it up." He thought of the cases he had read, dozens of them. Communities that won, and communities that lost. Working-class towns and wealthy suburbs. Immigrant neighborhoods and mostly Black areas—textbook cases of environmental racism. Except for those, there wasn't much of a pattern as to who got the pollution and who would succeed in getting it cleaned up. But he had to admit to himself the odds didn't look good, especially in a conservative neighborhood where people had a big incentive to cover things up. Still, he pressed on. "Who knows? If I can prove some top executives ordered the dumping, they could go to prison."

"Is that what you want?" she shouted in his face. "One more person in prison? You—Mr. Amnesty International! You say there are too many people in prison in this country already."

Nicholas slammed his hand on the dryer. Pain shot through his wrist. He was losing it now, hard as he tried to keep control. That was the other thing about twenty-one years of marriage—you got to know your partner's weak spots. His was the white-hot rage he fought to contain behind a veneer of confidence, authority, and civility. Hers was the fear of what she already knew, a fear so strong he sometimes thought he could smell it. And in his blind rage, he was going for her gut this time.

"Okay, Holly," he began. "Who's the criminal here? Who?" No answer. Only her fear, her weakness. "Is it the kid on the street corner selling an ounce of crack to pay the rent, or is it the guys who brought the crack up here to fund right-wing murderers in Central America? We fought that one together, remember?"

She nodded, recalling, he was sure, all the protest marches, teach-ins, pickets, and speeches down in New York.

He took a deep breath. "Is it some guy who fries his brains on drugs, or is it the fat business owners who from their clean office towers order the poisoning of an entire community?"

"People from that company live in this neighborhood," Holly murmured. Her face was pale and her lower lip red where she had bitten it.

"Sure, but not the big ones. And the ones that do, they get transferred every two or three years. Not long enough for them or their kids to get cancer." Holly recoiled at the word. Instinctively, both she and he glanced up to the ceiling, as if to warn each other that Rosie and Tony might hear and learn of their secret, the one thing they had managed to agree on. But neither child was home. "The company buys their house and sells it to the next guy. Yeah, they take care of their own. It's the rest of us they don't give a fuck about."

"Calm down, Nicky." She inched backward toward the wall. He noticed himself breathing hard, blood throbbing, sweat beading on his face and neck. *Count to ten and walk away. That's what the old guys in your neighborhood taught you. That's how you made it through your teens without getting expelled from school, thrown in jail, or even killed.*

Nicholas clenched and unclenched his fists. *Why can't she fucking be on my side?* Frantically, he searched for the right words, for any words. "In my book, you kill people for profit, you're a criminal. And you deserve to go to jail. You knowingly dump chemicals in the water, in the soil, that give people cancer..."

"Stop it!" Holly shrieked, her head between her hands, her ears covered.

"Just say it, Holly. Cancer. Barbara and Roger died of *cancer*. That girl in Rosie's grade died of cancer." He jerked his thumb toward his chest. "I have cancer!"

Tears glistened on her face. Nicholas lowered his voice to a tense growl. "I said, say it. I have cancer."

"Stop torturing me like this," she begged.

"Say it. Don't run away from it."

Trembling, she mouthed the words.

"Louder. So I can hear it."

"You have cancer."

"Say it again."

Why was he putting her through this? Not just to torment her, he told himself. Her fear disgusted him, and if this was the only way to get her over it, he had to do it.

She repeated the words. "Okay. That's enough," he said.

And then, she surprised him. As he stood there, still wound up in his rage, she placed her arms on his shoulders and began to caress the back of his neck. He shivered, but a feeling of calm spread gradually down to his shoulders, through his body. Hesitantly at first, then passionately, he embraced her. She ran her fingers through his hair and whispered in his ear, "I love you, Nicky. Don't you ever, ever leave me."

But he couldn't promise her that. All he could promise her was his passion, his life, on that very day. A day without work responsibilities, without kids. Even the McDonoughs' house could wait. *Carpe diem.*

He slipped a jazz CD into the stereo and turned the volume low. She shut the curtains in the family room, in case unknown voyeurs lived behind them on Riverview Road. And when they finished, they lay next to each other on the carpet with the autumn's afternoon sun slicing through a crack in the curtains across their bare bodies—doing nothing, planning nothing, expecting nothing, just seizing the day.

* * *

Holly may have won the battle, but she lost the war. The next day, while she took Tony to get new basketball shoes—he seemed to be growing out of his clothes every three months now—Nicholas carried his shovel, ice chest, mask, and work gloves across several neighbors' yards to the empty house on Nightingale Court. He surveyed the decaying landscape, vegetation now shutting down for the winter, as more than a decade of memories flooded through him.

Unlike Holly, he had never lived in a suburb before moving here. Or at least not one like Yellow Springs Heights. Suburbs like the Heights were for people who had money, younger parents, two parents. After his mother died, his World War II veteran father had taken him from a working-class neighborhood in Worcester straight to a community of old folks. Without any kids around and his father still running the scrap yard, Nicholas grew accustomed to being alone.

When they moved to the Heights, it became evident that each of them would need a car. Holly couldn't stand the idea of a minivan, with its connotations of dowdy suburban mom tethered to her kids and their soccer schedules. She bought a boxy, macho-looking navy sport utility vehicle that everyone assumed was his. Not being much of a car person, he picked up a secondhand subcompact, upon which he immediately slapped a bumper sticker that read "Friends Don't Let Friends Vote Republican." In the Heights, that guaranteed he wouldn't have any friends.

Except for the McDonoughs.

Being outgoing types with lots of teenage kids, they did manage a cordial if not close relationship with most of their neighbors, who considered the organizers from Brooklyn to be somewhat like aliens that had mistakenly landed their spaceship on the wrong planet. When a next door neighbor, long since moved away, told Roger that another commie had moved to the neighborhood, Roger went looking for inflammatory bumper stickers, and, despite their almost twenty-year age gap, the two families instantly discovered soulmates. Holly appreciated finding other lapsed Catholics with whom to share her overwhelming guilt. At backyard barbecues they chewed over the news of the day, and Nicholas dispensed college and career advice to the McDonough kids like a know-it-all big brother. Barbara and Roger indulged him in this, for they seemed to know intuitively how much it meant to him to belong to a family. A folding chair next to the hammock became "Nick's chair," its woven seat eventually stretching under his weight. And how many times had he told Holly or one of the kids, "I'll be at the McDonoughs' if you need me"?

Now the house was what kids of every generation called a haunted house, the once-familiar landmarks of the large yard—the hammock, the singing tree, the folding chair and mismatched plastic crate footrest, the picnic table, and the gas grill—a geography of memory only. But that geography guided Nicholas as he took his samples and snapped his photographs, and he labeled these according to the things that used to be there. He paid special attention to the area around the rotting stump of the singing tree, because after what happened to Roger, to Barbara, to him, he could assume it wasn't the hammock and it wasn't the music that killed that tree.

After finishing the back yard, he moved his supplies to the front yard. He had just started digging when he heard a car approach. He looked up in time to see a beige Navigator pull to the curb and stop. Marc Martineau stepped out.

Nicholas had occasionally encountered Marc at neighborhood parties and meetings. The president of the Yellow Springs Heights Community Association for as long as anyone could remember, Marc was also a well-known real estate attorney in Cold Springs who represented big commercial developers. That meant, Nicholas joked to Holly after last year's Christmas party, Marc knew precisely whom to bribe and how much in order to get the zoning variances his clients needed. He recalled Holly jumping to Marc's defense, warning him not to make unsubstantiated accusations against the neighbors even in jest.

Nicholas leaned on his shovel, lifted the mask from his nose and mouth, and gave Marc an unenthusiastic wave. He wondered what had brought Marc to the house. Maybe he intended to have it torn down and the property rezoned multi-family or commercial.

"Hi, Nick. Where y'at this fine afternoon?" Marc asked in his politest Cajun accent.

Nicholas did him a not-so-polite Boston accent in return, just to let him know who was closer to his home turf. "What are you doing here?"

"I was fixin' to ask you the same."

Nicholas shrugged. "I asked you first."

Marc took a few steps forward, so that he was standing only at arm's length from Nicholas and looking down at him from a foot above. The typical power play of a bully, just like that kid of his with the odd name who was in Tony's class. Not that Tony had ever said anything, but Nicholas had overheard Chris Leighton talking about it once when he gave Chris a ride home from basketball practice. Chris had also said the kid singled him out because he was Black. That really pissed Nicholas off. Kids picked up that kind of prejudice at home.

Nicholas stood still, not looking up at Marc. Marc slipped his hands inside his jacket pockets and surveyed the cul-de-sac. "As president of the association, I'm going around to see how many houses are for sale."

"And what's the point of that?"

Marc cleared his throat. "Well, we keep all kinds of statistics. The number of houses for sale each month and how long they take to sell. Comparing this year to last year."

"So, are there more houses for sale this year than last year?"

Marc stroked his close-cropped beard. "I don't know. It looks about similar." He glanced down at the shovel and ice chest. "And you, Nick?"

Nicholas was quick with the answer. "Planting bulbs."

"Hmm, that's interesting. Never saw you as the gardening type."

He had that one correct, Nicholas had to admit. On the

scale of suburban infractions, the "Friends Don't Let Friends Vote Republican" bumper sticker was nothing compared to the lawn known as the neighborhood scandal. Holly suffered terribly from allergies—she said it must have been the trees and flowers of New England, because she never had a problem in Minnesota, where everything froze for half the year, and never in Manhattan—so the maintenance of the lawn fell to him. The problem was, despite his halfhearted attempts to weed, water, and reseed, the grass never survived more than a year or two. It didn't help that he scrupulously obeyed summer watering restrictions and refused to hire a lawn service that used chemical pesticides and weed-killers.

For a while, he blamed the kids and banned them from stepping on the grass. But they made poor scapegoats. Rosie always seemed to be at someone else's house, and Tony, who had inherited his mother's allergies, turned out to be an indoor kind of kid. So, lacking any excuse save his own incompetence, Nicholas covered over much of the lawn with wood chips and for the rest discovered some relatively attractive weeds that seemed to thrive in the harsh soil. Barbara disapproved, but on his priority list lawn maintenance fell somewhere between shopping for clothes and taking the car to be serviced.

"So what are you planting?" Marc asked.

Nicholas dimly recalled Barbara's garden conversations. "Tulips. Crocuses. Daffodils."

"Where are they?"

"In the ice chest." He planted one foot on the chest.

Marc peered into the hole. "Aren't you digging a little deep for bulbs?"

Got to get beneath the topsoil for the samples. Even deeper would be better.

He faked it again. "I'm adding some other dirt and fertilizer for a better ph balance. Maybe these guys will live for more than a year or two then."

Marc folded his arms across his chest and drawled,

"Listen, Nick. I know what you're doing. You can't pull the wool over my eyes. I'm asking you quietly to stop before this goes any further."

Nicholas leaned on the shovel again, rocked back and forth. "And why should I?"

"Because your half-baked investigation is going to destroy the property values of the entire neighborhood."

Nicholas stared Marc in the face, into his light blue eyes that were too small for his broad forehead. "So you're saying property values are more important than people who are sick and dying?"

Marc gave him a quizzical look, then recovered. "No, I'm saying your concerns are groundless, and you're going to create a panic. Remember the hysteria over electromagnetic fields? People couldn't sell their homes, and it all turned out to be a hoax."

"Hey, I'd love to be full of shit." With all his strength Nicholas punched the shovel into the dry, hard earth. "But I don't think I am."

Marc sighed. "I don't want neighbor pitted against neighbor, which is what will happen if you have your way. I have to look out for this community as a whole."

"What community, Marc?" Nicholas pointed to the bare ground, partially covered with misshapen leaves from stunted trees. "A community where people get cancer, suffer, and die, and nobody cares? Nobody even knows until the house goes up for sale? Neighbors show up for the open house to snoop around and make sure their own property is still worth what they think it's worth, and the fucking *realtor* tells them what happened?"

Nicholas was thinking of the McDonoughs—he had handled the showing of their house in his usual distracted way for the first few months before their kids took it over. But it could have been him wasting away in lonely agony, Holly a widow selling the house: *Oh, somebody died here? We didn't know.*

"Damn. Why does my life have to be this hard?" he heard Marc mutter under his breath. Louder, Marc said, "Listen, pal. I'm a real estate lawyer, so I know how these things work. It's almost impossible to prove anything. You take your samples to anyone besides some dinky public-interest firm, and they're going to laugh you right out of their office. And if you do find someone to take your case, the judge will laugh you right out of his courtroom." He jabbed his index finger just inches from Nicholas's chest. "And nowadays, if you bring a nuisance suit that's thrown out of court, you're responsible for the defendant's legal fees." He paused and smiled. "You got that kind of money?"

Nicholas swallowed. "You're not going to intimidate me with scare tactics. If we have a cancer cluster here in the Heights, and evidence of chemical contamination—"

Marc interrupted him. "In millions of communities in this country, cancer clusters appear at random. A lousy roll of the dice."

Nicholas gripped the handle of the shovel. His heart pounded. Had his battered work gloves not covered his hands, Marc would have seen his knuckles whiten. Glancing at the McDonoughs' empty house to emphasize his point, he said, "This isn't a riverboat casino, Marc. This is people's lives. Show a little respect."

"I meant no disrespect." Marc enunciated each syllable. He poked his finger into Nicholas's breastbone. "Unlike you."

"Would you care to explain that?" Nicholas sneered. "In words and not by trying to shove me around."

Marc stepped away. His face was red, and Nicholas figured that if he pushed too far, Marc had more than a hundred pounds on him. But it wouldn't contribute to the reputation of one of the city's biggest attorneys to beat some undersized guy to a pulp.

Nicholas cocked his head sideways. "On second thought, why don't you count to ten and walk the hell out of here."

"If I do, I'm getting a restraining order."

Nicholas laughed. "You don't own this house. It belongs to the four McDonough children who lost their parents from cancer within six months of each other, and they're on my side."

Marc backed toward his brawny SUV. He paused for about ten seconds, his hand on the door handle, and glared at Nicholas. Then he yanked the door open and climbed inside.

Nicholas waited for Marc to drive off, then finished collecting the samples. On his way home he cut again through the backyard, the filled ice chest weighing down his right arm, the shovel balanced on his left shoulder. His mask hung from his neck. A stiff chilly autumn wind whistled through bare tree limbs. Dry fallen leaves crunched beneath his boots. He paused and surveyed the scene one last time. He thought he heard a creak in the breeze, like a rusty gate or the old hammock swinging to and fro. And in his mind, inhabiting a hazy, faded tableau of the yard, were the three ghosts. A solid woman with short gray hair, planting flowers and pulling weeds, humming along with the cassette player wedged into the tree. A potbellied man in his late fifties, his thick gray hair in tight curls, rocking in the hammock with a can of root beer in his hand, his heavy body almost touching the ground. A smaller, younger man, seated in the aluminum chair next to the hammock, his legs propped on a milk crate, reading the Sunday *New York Times* before passing it on, section by section, to his friends. And it occurred to Nicholas that what he saw was the ghost of a living person passing a newspaper to the dead.

Nine: The Give and Go

They came to practice wearing jerseys of famous players, dreams of hoop glory Sandy knew they would never attain. Most stood under five feet tall. Three were overweight. Four wore glasses. Nearly half brought doctors' notes for asthma.

Forget jump shots and three-pointers. Most couldn't make a lay-up or a free throw. Only one could dribble with either hand without looking down at the ball. Sandy wondered what the other teams would think when they saw this group of complete non-athletes coached by a girl. She didn't feel like a pioneer any more, and she worried about the kids—her kids—getting teased and discouraged. She recalled when she was their age. Kids took these things so hard. Even now as an adult she hated to lose.

She knew she should have been setting up the passing drills, but instead she stood at center court, her arms folded across her chest, and gazed at Tony's father, who was dealing with a crisis along the sideline. Two laps into a five-lap warm-up run Tony had doubled over in a fit of coughing. Struggling for breath, his neck craned and his lips pursed, the scrawny, pasty-faced youngster reminded her of a featherless baby bird waiting for its mother to feed it. He didn't wear a jersey but a black oversized Rage Against the Machine t-shirt with a picture of Che Guevara on the front. The huge black shirt made him look even smaller, paler, and more pitiful. His father assembled his inhaler, at the same time telling him he should have treated himself five minutes before running laps rather than after he began wheezing. Good advice. Sandy sent the other asthmatic kids over to listen. When he saw the group, he shook his head and frowned. "Sure a lot of kids with asthma around here." He spoke with a Boston accent.

It was his first day to help with the team. She hadn't recognized him when she arrived a few minutes late for practice because she had needed to change in the girls' locker room. Seeing him from behind, she'd mistaken him for one of the students—except he had already organized them into a lay-up drill and was the only one who made all his shots. She had always thought of Mackie the Knife as larger, more imposing. At almost five nine, she had at least three, maybe four, inches on him. White tape covered his left wrist. He wore gray sweats from the community college, and even when standing still emanated a tense energy that kept his young audience mesmerized until she split them up for drills. Close-up, without his helmet or baseball cap, he had a faded look, like a favorite old shirt that had been through the wash too many times. Kind of like Dustin Hoffman somewhere between *The Graduate* and *Rain Man*.

After practice ended and the kids had left to shower and change, he took a couple of jump shots, dribbled the ball back and forth between his legs, and challenged her to a game of one-on-one.

"Sorry, Dr. Baran." She grabbed her gym bag. "I promised a friend I'd go to Friday night services with her." She didn't know why she'd told him this, except that his last name sounded Jewish.

His face brightened, and she knew instantly that she'd guessed right. "Where do you belong?"

"I don't belong anywhere," she stammered. "My friend Marissa—Miss Levine, Tony's in her English class—she belongs to a synagogue in Yellow Springs, and I go with her."

"I see you've mastered the fine art of freeloading." He winked at her. "By the way, you don't have to call me Dr. Baran. Nicholas or Nick would be fine."

Sandy backed toward the door. "Well, thanks again for helping out...Nick."

"No prob. Got to keep in shape for softball season." The gym's yellowish light flashed in his dark brown eyes. "We're going to get your No Mercy All Stars next year."

She suppressed a laugh. The All Stars had gone unbeaten.

The Ship Rats had maybe won three games all season. "Run out, 'cause you're still sinking," she whispered to herself as she pushed her way through the metal door.

*   *   *

Andy Van Camp was one of the quiet kids whom Sandy often forgot in the chaos that was American History 7B. But sometime after Thanksgiving, he stopped coming to class, and two weeks into December a message to call his mother appeared in her box.

As she sat in her living room, Mrs. Van Camp's phone number in front of her, she tried to visualize Andy, a thin, pale boy with long brown hair that fell into his eyes. In a class where the boys ranged from four and a half to more than six feet in height, he was one of the smaller ones, at least a year or two away from puberty. She once overheard the kids saying he was a good soccer player. He played on the middle-school team and carried his books in a brightly colored FIFA bag.

Mrs. Van Camp answered the phone. Andy's mother sounded pleasant, not upset or worried. "I hope he's feeling better," Sandy said, assuming from her tone that he'd had his tonsils out or a bad bout with the flu.

There was a moment of silence before Mrs. Van Camp spoke again. "It's a long story," she began, her voice suddenly weary. "When he was in fifth grade, Andy was diagnosed with leukemia. He went through the treatments. The doctors said his prognosis was excellent, and in fact there's been no sign of the cancer since."

Sandy thought of the less-fortunate Kyle Brownfield and of Stephen Reed, in the hospital and, according to his sister, not getting better. Every Friday night, Sandy recited the Mishebeirach prayer for Stephen, and even though she'd learned that she couldn't expect God to reverse the laws of nature, it still bothered her that her prayers had not been answered. And now a third child had appeared like a divine taunt.

"But there were other problems," Mrs. Van Camp continued. "Ever since his illness, Andy's been afraid to do things. We transferred him to Shady Ridge in sixth grade because the public school in Yellow Springs seemed too rough for him. But he loves soccer, and my husband and I pushed him to play. He's good, and we thought it would build his confidence." Mrs. Van Camp then described how Andy had become ill during a game at a Thanksgiving weekend tournament in Syracuse. "It was probably a stomach bug or something he ate. You know how it is, traveling."

"Oh, yes," Sandy said, trying to remain calm.

"Andy became hysterical and refused to go to school. He mentioned some kids who were bothering him." Her words caused Sandy to sigh in shame and frustration. Even the quiet, unnoticed kids suffered because she couldn't control her class. "Every morning he says his stomach hurts, and I guess maybe I've been too quick to indulge him, but after everything he's had to deal with…"

"Oh, I understand." An automatic response, for Sandy knew she couldn't truly understand.

"He's seeing a psychologist, and I hope after Christmas we can get him back to Shady Ridge. If not, we might have to transfer him to another private school." She finished by asking for all Andy's assignments so that he could salvage the semester.

Sandy promised to leave the assignments from Thanksgiving to Christmas at the main office and hung up the phone. She took the Cold Springs directory from her bookshelf and began looking up names. Brownfield, Timothy J. and Christine R. 3 Canary Court, Yellow Springs Heights. Van Camp, Andrew T. 33 Sparrow Bush Road, Yellow Springs Heights. There were too many Reeds, so she retrieved her Shady Ridge directory from under a pile of yet-to-be-marked homework papers and found Amy and Stephen's family at 48

Eagle Street, also in Yellow Springs Heights. She dashed downstairs to her car and pulled her local map from the glove compartment. She located the streets, all within a six-block radius.

* * *

Despite practice twice a week, Sandy's basketball team remained hopeless. By mid-December, its record stood at zero wins and four losses. The kids were starting to lose heart, the parents complained after every game, and she feared for her job. Only Nick remained unconcerned.

"Most of these kids have never played on a team before. Some of them haven't played basketball, ever," he explained to a group of fathers who joined them at a fast-food restaurant after an away loss. Grownups at one table. Kids at a table across the room, throwing French fries at each other, just as in her day. Nick continued, "Maybe they'll learn from the better teams and come to enjoy the game. If they get bigger and improve, they might make varsity."

"I don't think any of them are having fun now," one father grumped.

"The first thing they have to learn is to play together. Even if they never win another game, that'll make it more fun," Nick said. Sandy thought of how much the boys looked forward to Friday practices, when he showed up. His enthusiasm motivated them to work hard, and his presence raised Tony's prestige on the team. *Your dad's cool*, they'd say, and Tony would smile the way she'd never seen him smile in class, even when he got an A plus on a test.

But the other dads looked doubtful. The father of one of Braxton's friends turned to Sandy and said, "You need to have a winning attitude, Miss Katz. This touchy-feely 'everyone plays equal time and learns' crap isn't going to work. Let the best players play, so at least we win some games."

Sandy felt herself wither and shrink into her plastic chair.

But Nick leaned forward and glared at the father. "Here's what. I've got a deal for you, and anyone else who has a problem with the way we run this team. Sandy and I will challenge you to a game of two-on-two." Nick tapped the table with his index finger. "Any takers?"

The dads glanced at each other. A few of them squirmed. Finally, the father who'd started it, a large, heavy bald man, asked, "Do you run the team our way if we win?"

"No," Nick answered. "You just get the pleasure of kicking our asses."

Sandy stared down at her French fries. She heard someone say, "Yeah, I'm in. Where do we meet?" and her chest tightened.

Nick suggested his college. The two dads hesitated, argued that it was located in a dangerous neighborhood. Nick clenched his jaw and stared at the ceiling. Sandy wondered what they'd think of the neighborhood where she lived. Whispering between themselves, the dads discussed the guest policy of the health club where both belonged.

"I don't do private clubs. And it's my challenge." Nick slammed his empty soda cup on the table. Their whispers stopped. "River Rock State Park. The court closest to the river."

"Are you crazy? It's forty degrees outside," the heavy, bald dad blurted out.

Nick shrugged. "Take it or leave it."

The other dad, a younger man with brown hair and glasses, said, "We'll meet you in an hour." The two dads smiled at each other and dug into their burgers and fries.

Sandy picked up several of her fries, now cold, but their smell turned her stomach. She offered the rest of her lunch to Nick, who'd ordered nothing except the soda. He waved it away.

After the other dads had left with their boys and Tony had gone home with Chris to work on a science project, she and Nick transferred the scorebook and balls to her car. She asked him why he had challenged the dads like that.

"Because the parents are the ones who care so much about winning and losing. The kids, they're grateful to have the chance to play. So when these guys shot off their mouths, I thought this isn't the kids' problem, it's their problem. I gave them the opportunity to deal with their problem themselves. I'm surprised any of them took me up on it."

"Yeah, but now we're screwed. Those guys are way bigger than we are."

Nick slammed the hatchback shut. "We do our best, play our hardest. Trip them, hold them, elbow them in the face." He grinned. "If we lose, we lose. History is filled with losers who gave everything they had in them to the struggle."

"I'm surprised you haven't taught the kids to play dirty."

"That's because they're kids. When they grow up, they'll figure out for themselves what it's worth to them." Sandy caught his piercing stare. "What anything is worth to them."

At that moment he frightened her. And when she drove back to her apartment, she dreaded meeting him at the park. His reckless and stupid playground challenge, into which he'd drawn her, didn't strike her as a fundamental quest for justice. *Who does he think he is, Malcolm X? By any means necessary?* And she was supposed to be the coach. She made the decisions. Not him.

But she saw the kids, all twelve of them, as if they had lined up before her, expecting her to choose for them. Kids like Tony—clumsy, weak, nearsighted kids with asthma who still had every right to play. Did they show up on time to every practice, wheeze and gasp through ninety minutes of drills, go home exhausted, their chests aching, only to spend the entire game on the bench? How many times in her school career had she stood on the sidelines with the ball, waiting for the referee's whistle so she could make the inbound pass, and from behind listened to the tiny, pleading voice of another girl, *Coach, please put me in?*

Yes, this was her decision, and this was principle. Inside her apartment, she yanked off her skirt, blouse, and sweater, kicked her loafers across the bedroom, and pulled her hair into a tight ponytail. She dressed in layers—her lucky Cornell t-shirt and matching shorts, gray sweats like Nick's, a windbreaker, and a wool cap. She laced her high-top sneakers in a double knot. On her way out, she grabbed a basketball.

Nick was already at the court. He was wearing sweats and a cap but no jacket. He was practicing three-pointers, but the stiff wind seemed to carry every shot away from the hoop. Sandy called out to him.

He tucked his ball under his arm and approached her. "We should warm up and work on some plays. With this wind, we're not going to get very far on outside shooting, and those guys are big."

They sat on the court and began their warm-up stretches, but the chill from the concrete rose through Sandy's layers of clothing and tightened her muscles. It was a cloudy day, and the damp, icy December wind blew dirt and dry leaves across the court and made her shiver. *Relax. At least we'll be prepared.*

They jogged around the court until Sandy felt warm enough to remove her windbreaker, which she tied to a bench overlooking the Yellow River. Across the river the tree limbs were bare, and she could see the homes of Yellow Springs Heights—large boxy colonials all beige, gray, light blue, brown, and white with identical charcoal-gray roofs, all set amid tidy lawns.

They practiced setting screens, the pick-and-roll, and the give-and-go. Nick dribbled near her and slipped her the ball. It was cold and rock hard in her hands. She envisioned her two opponents drawn to her and without looking at him fed Nick the bounce pass. He finished the play with a soft lay-in.

"Perfect," he said and tapped her shoulder. They switched; she led off the play and finished it. By four, the sky began to darken, and the lights came on along the streets and in some of the houses across the river.

Nick walked over to the bench and squinted as he gazed eastward into the night. "Holly's upstairs in the bedroom," he said softly.

Sandy stepped toward him. "What?"

He pointed to the houses, arranged on curved streets and cul-de-sacs like a connect-the-dots of lights amid a drab patchwork. "Our house. Just past that first row of streetlamps across the river." He counted off. "Eighth cul-de-sac from your left."

Sandy boosted herself onto the backrest of the bench, planted her feet on the seat, and leaned forward. She imagined Nick's wife as she remembered her from Parents' Day. Beige business suit. Light brown hair short and teased up. Steel gray eyes. But above all, she remembered Holly's dangling earrings, carved animals in shades of brown and black, that swayed as she talked. She'd been tempted to ask Holly where she'd found them, but she'd felt too intimidated. She believed that Tony's mother, like Braxton's father, could see through her clumsy efforts to teach their boys, and when she passed them on the way out of the school that night, she sensed they'd been talking about her.

Now she pictured Holly taking off her earrings and setting them on her dresser. Waiting for Nick to return home. "I don't think those guys are coming."

"I didn't think they would."

"Why?"

"I know one of them from the softball league. His law firm sponsors a team, the Sharks. Does he get off his can and play? Hell no."

Sandy climbed down from the bench and untied her windbreaker. "I guess I'll head home then."

Nick sat on the back of the bench, next to the spot that Sandy had left, and stared across the river. More lights had come on, enough that she noticed the blank spaces, dark houses where no one was home.

"Go ahead. I'm going to stay here a while," he said.

Sandy set her ball next to Nick's and put on her windbreaker. She could see why Nick wanted to stay. From the park, Yellow Springs Heights seemed so still and peaceful. She thought that her own neighborhood would look just as peaceful from above and afar, and she told Nick that. He asked her where she lived.

"Flatlands."

He jerked up straight. "You really live there? I thought you and your boyfriend were ringers from Burnham." He seemed shocked that a teacher at a school like Shady Ridge could live in such a run-down neighborhood.

"No, we lost our scholarships and we didn't want to play for the Grad Student Association team, given the circumstances. Our next-door neighbors are the captains of the All Stars, and they recruited us."

"Kenny James and Mo' Lockwood? The ex-football player and the former all-city girls' pitcher—talk about ringers."

Sandy smiled. "Yeah. You know them?"

"I'm the Ship Rats' captain. So you must live on Wallman Street." She nodded and picked up her ball. "Did you ever see the kid who drowned in the river last summer? He lived on your street, you know."

"I never saw him, but I knew about him. After he died, I took flowers to his family." She told Nick about the family moving away, and the tenement burning down a month later. She didn't tell him she suspected that her landlord's son Eddie and his drunken friends had had something to do with the fire.

"That was a nice thing to do, bringing the flowers." Nick glanced in the direction of his neighborhood. "The kid only had five years of life. At least you acknowledged his existence."

"Yeah, but it felt really strange at the time because they only spoke Spanish, and my Spanish is so rusty." Thinking about it now, she could still hear the words of Luis's sobbing mother: *Digales. Tell them. Was it his body eaten by acid or the bridge?* She said good-bye to Nick and turned to leave.

"One other thing," Nick called to her. She turned back toward him. "I want to apologize for dragging you out here. And you probably think I'm a jerk for volunteering you against those guys." He cleared his throat. "I was so pissed at them for questioning your coaching. I guess I got carried away."

"It's okay. You made me realize why it was important to have everyone play equal time. It was my decision, but I need to be able to defend it." A gust of wind blew across the empty court. Sandy shuddered, dropped the ball, and buried her hands in her jacket's deep pockets. The ball bounced at her feet and rolled away. "Tony works his heart out in practice and he deserves to play. So do the others. And it's meant a lot to him to have you there."

Nick didn't respond for a long while, and when he did, he didn't look at Sandy but at the distant lights on the opposite side of the river. "That's why I offered to coach with you. I hadn't paid a lot of attention to Tony recently, and then I realized he's going through a pretty rough patch." She thought he'd go on to tell her about the bullying or about Tony's asthma or about his lack of athletic ability and self-confidence, and she feared that Nick also lacked confidence in her. Instead, he pushed up the left sleeve of his sweatshirt and motioned for her to come closer.

"Four summers ago, I fractured my wrist in a softball game."

Sandy shuddered again, but this time from apprehension. She didn't know where his remark—seemingly unrelated to Tony—was coming from and where it was going. The moonless sky was now almost completely dark, and she wanted to get home.

Nick clutched his taped wrist. "The thing kept on bleeding internally. The next day I had a massive bruise and my hand and wrist swelled to twice their size. They diagnosed me with leukemia, which was why the bleeding didn't stop. After a few weeks at Burnham Medical Center getting chemo, I flew out to California for a bone-marrow transplant from my brother. Holly stayed back with the kids because we didn't want to tell them. Unless we had to, that is."

"Do they know now?" Sandy asked. Inside the pockets of her windbreaker, her hands were sweaty and trembling.

Nick shook his head. "The transplant was successful, and I've been in remission ever since. But I don't know how much longer I'll be alive. My daughter, Rosie, she's practically grown up, and she's going to be fine, but Tony..." He stared down at his arms, which now rested across his knees. "You see he really needs me."

I am not hearing this, Sandy said to herself. Her first concern was for Tony. He had enough problems without a father who had cancer and wouldn't tell the truth. Her second concern was for Nick. Would he even make it through the season? He looked healthy enough, but he hadn't eaten anything at the restaurant.

The words she had once rehearsed came to mind. *Lo siento mucho.* But when she began to speak, she couldn't translate them into English. She sputtered and fell silent.

Nick leaned forward and grabbed her left arm, just above her elbow. "Listen, Sandy," he said, his voice hoarse. "I didn't plan to tell you this about me. I know Tony is in your class. I expect you won't say anything and you'll treat him like you would any other student." He let go. Her muscle hurt where he'd squeezed it.

She had felt cold all afternoon, but now the blood rushed to her face, making her dizzy and flushed. *What the hell is going on in that town? Three kids and now Nick. With the same kind of cancer. And what about Braxton's mother? Mr. Martineau said she was ill, but with what?* Sandy wondered

103

if Nick even knew about the others and whether she should tell him. But her arm still ached. She dreaded navigating the winding road out of the park at night. And she felt the same fury as when he'd volunteered her against those dads. *Why did he dump this news on me? Did he just get carried away— again?* Her voice wavered when she answered him. "I won't treat him any differently, I promise. And I really have to go."

"Okay. See you next week." She stumbled along the dirt path toward the parking lot and rubbed her upper arm to get rid of the creepy sensation of his fingers pressing into her skin. Then she heard him call her name. She turned around. He hadn't moved from his perch on the back of the bench, and she thought he might stay there all night, staring down into the thick velvet black ribbon that was the Yellow River and beyond it the lights of his neighborhood. "You forgot your ball."

She scanned the windswept court and the path next to it in vain. Perhaps a gust had blown her ball into the stand of trees and she would never find it.

"Take mine." He lobbed his ball toward her, as though flipping a give-and-go pass over the heads of defenders. Though she could barely see, she caught it with both hands.

Ten: Rage

Now that Tony had found a basketball team that would take him—and he actually got to play—he began to watch basketball on television. He'd come back from Saturday's game and sprawl in front of the set in the family room for the rest of the afternoon, much of the evening, and most of Sunday too. College, pro, it didn't matter to the kid, but he absorbed the commentary the way he absorbed everything he learned in school, and within weeks he talked like he should have been the assistant coach as the backdoor cut, the 2-1-2 zone defense, and the crossover dribble became part of his vocabulary.

"Hey, Dad, check out that sweet reverse lay-up," he called out one Sunday afternoon. Nicholas missed the play, but they showed it on replay. Twice. In slow motion.

Nicholas dropped onto the floor and leaned against the sofa. Dinner would have to wait. In fact, a pizza delivery sounded perfect. He would have preferred to be in the gym with his own crossover dribble and reverse lay-up because seeing the moves on television made his muscles twitch. He imagined the smell of sweat and leather, the sound of heavy breathing and sneakers squeaking on waxed hardwood, the feel of the ball in his hands in the seconds before he let it fly.

The day before, he'd looked forward to challenging those two blowhards who'd complained about Sandy's coaching. Bunch of cowards, standing them up. He and Sandy would have made a great team. She claimed—most likely with false modesty—that she hadn't played basketball since high school, but she knew the precise places to stand, to move, to pass the ball. She caught the ball in total darkness. The young woman had an athletic gift, one that he'd noticed the first time he'd seen her on the softball field.

That said, Nicholas hadn't meant to reveal his secret to

her, and every time he thought about it, the hot rush of shame filled him. He detested the empty spaces in his life—time spent waiting, things supposed to happen that didn't happen, moments of silence—because eventually they would force him to contemplate his weakness. Alone, down at the river long after midnight, he fought it, a silent, protracted battle in his heart, in his gut, inside his bones. But he hadn't been alone as darkness approached then, and she was a person who cared about Tony and remembered the dead.

But he needed to be stronger. He couldn't let his secret get out any more. That his friends at the college, his department head, and the college president knew was one thing. They'd had to cover his classes when he went out to California. Rich and some others were helping him now with his clandestine research. The college librarians had ordered back issues of the *Cold Springs Post-Examiner* on microfilm and requested on interlibrary loan dozens of documents that pertained to Hometown Chemical Company. Even though he brought Tony to the college from time to time, no one would say anything about the illness that, if the kids found out, would change their lives forever.

But Sandy was merely Tony's social studies teacher— and not a very good one either. Nicholas chided himself: *You've forgotten your own lessons.* The boy remained engrossed in the basketball game, oblivious. Nicholas knew no better way of learning a lesson than teaching it to someone else.

He waited for halftime. Then, before Tony could flip the input switch to his video game, Nicholas asked him, "Is there a boy with the last name of Martineau in your class?"

"Yeah, Braxton." Tony returned to his place on the rug. He didn't look upset about having to talk to his father instead of playing the game.

"Is he one of the boys who picks on you?"

Tony's eyes fixed on his knees. "He's an asshole. He picks on a lot of kids."

"But you're one of them?"

Tony mumbled, "Yeah."

"We need to talk about how to deal with people like him."

Tony scooted a few feet away and raised his voice. "I told you and Mom it's okay. You guys make me take tae kwon do. That's enough."

His college students never resisted like this. Nicholas pushed on. "I was the smallest guy in my class. How do you think I survived?"

Tony didn't hesitate. "You were good at sports. You already told me."

Nicholas closed his eyes and tried to conjure the image of the vicious little punk he used to be, the one everyone called the Junkyard Dog.

* * *

They said his own father feared him. Feared the anger that would explode in a fiery rain of expletives: *What do you mean you have no food in the house? You got the truck. All I got's this fucking bicycle.* Feared the rocks he threw with perfect aim into car windows and inches from birds and small animals in the woods behind the trailer park. Feared when he came home high and drunk with a girl and walk straight to his bedroom, daring the old man to stop him.

Some of the stories were true, and some were fiction. He never drank much, smoked much weed, or tried hard drugs because he rode his ten-speed bicycle everywhere, and with the occasional drivers who liked to run hippie cyclists off the road, he would never have survived riding while impaired. He did bring home a series of Catholic girlfriends, usually when his father was away—out of consideration for the girls, not his father. Catholic boys were in the Dark Ages when it came to using contraception, so the girls flocked to the local Jewish atheist, who harbored no such qualms. And there was the story that made his reputation right before he entered high school, and it happened just the way they told it.

He was thirteen and pissed-off on that cold, wet December day. His father had forgotten to buy cereal for breakfast five days in a row and to top that had run out of cash. *Why don't I say I'm an orphan and apply for the free fucking lunch?* Nicholas had shouted in his prematurely grown-up voice before he slammed the trailer's door. Riding his bike to school, he pulled up to a stop light next to a bright red sports car. The guy had a bumper sticker, a peace sign with the words "footprint of the American chicken." One more militaristic bully, he thought. *I'll show him who's chicken.*

Nicholas flipped the guy the middle finger and said a few things too, loud enough that the guy could hear him through the glass window. That released the rage and made him feel calm for about ten seconds until the light changed. The guy in the sports car hung back, then gunned his engine and slammed broadside into him. His leg caught in the chrome bumper; he heard the ripping of clothing and flesh in the instant he flew off the bike. The handlebar jabbing into his left side broke his fall. He skidded on his knees and elbows on the gravel shoulder and would have had his skin shredded had it not been for his heavy parka. The guy yelled something back before speeding off, but Nicholas didn't hear; though unable to take in air, pain searing his leg and side, he picked up a nearby rock and hurled it through the car's back window.

He had three cracked ribs and needed two dozen stitches in his leg. He still hurt by the time baseball season started in April, but he had his best season ever. The rock through the window failed to quell the rage that continued to tear at him like a badger trapped inside his body, and he swore that if the car and his baseball bat were ever in the same place, the guy would be sorry he messed with him. Nicholas spent his next summer riding all over central Massachusetts in search of a red sports car with a certain bumper sticker.

He found it outside a movie theater. He left it unrecognizable. Two days later, the guy brought his once prized, now battered, wreck of a car to his father's scrap yard. Nicholas was there, his hair cut short for the summer; the asshole didn't know who he was. He waited on him and charged him double for the parts.

Soon after, he started high school. He was an honor student, member of the varsity baseball and cross-country teams, president of the student council, defender of the weak and the weird against the powerful. He even gave advice to other screwed-up teenagers as a counselor for a youth hotline. But everyone, save most of the adults who claimed to run the school, knew Nicky Baran was major league psycho. And nobody ever messed with him.

* * *

Nicholas sighed. Thirty years later, remembering the experience still made his ribs ache. "It was more than that. You have to use your head. Attack them when they don't expect it and in their weak spots."

"Like how?" The kid's tone of voice challenged him: *Convince me anything you say will make a difference.*

A Teacher of the Year should be able to teach his own son. Nicholas buried his fingers in his hair. "The idea of confronting these guys is scary, right?"

Tony nodded.

"Have you seen them bother anyone else?"

"Yeah, like Chris. And they're really bad to Miss Katz."

"So what do you do?"

"Be glad it's not me." It was the response Nicholas expected; Tony couldn't defend someone else until he had stood up for himself first.

"What if you looked at what they've done to you as if it

weren't happening to you? As if it were happening to someone else, like Chris or Miss Katz. So that way you could sit down calmly, take it apart, and analyze it."

An expression of confusion crossed Tony's face. Nicholas wondered if his lesson was beyond the comprehension of a twelve-year-old in the bottom half of the maturity range. Perhaps he and Holly had made a mistake sheltering Tony, trying to preserve his innocence. He hadn't wanted his son to grow up the way he had, at age ten suddenly becoming the adult, fending for himself and often responsible for the house and the scrap yard as well. He used to say his Bar Mitzvah, his official initiation into the grown-up world, came three years too late. But because of the choices he and Holly had made, Tony might never grow up.

Or maybe I don't have enough patience. Nicholas tried again, explained in another way his plan for confronting the scary things in life. A good teacher could do that, explain things in however many different ways it took for a student to understand. He used the example of the teen hotline he once staffed. Callers often began with "my friend" or "this kid I know" before they described what was clearly their own problem. In those cases, the words "thinks she's pregnant" generally followed, but he didn't tell Tony that. He didn't tell him about the ten-year-old boy who discovered his dying mother and called the ambulance himself, only to watch her take her last breath before it arrived. And he didn't tell Tony the secret he should never have told Sandy, although the desperate pregnant teenagers who called his hotline with numbing regularity made him realize how often people told strangers things they hid from their own families.

Tony looked up, his eyes bright and a smile across his face. He was beginning to comprehend the first step. Nicholas went on. "Once you observe the situation, as though it's happening to someone else, think about every aspect. What are your strengths? What are his weaknesses? Take the tae kwon do, for example. It's not going to help you if Braxton sticks his foot out and trips you, but if he attacks you head-on, you can defend yourself."

"Yeah." Tony sat up straight and faced him. Now he was listening.

"So you do something to him that causes him to rush at you. It has to be so outrageous he can't even think straight. You kick—"

Tony interrupted him. "I'll get in trouble for fighting. Chris's brother was suspended two weeks just for threatening Braxton after Braxton messed up Chris's clothes."

"It's self-defense. If anyone sees, he went at you first. If there aren't any witnesses, who's to get you in trouble?" Nicholas leaned forward and met his son's eyes. "So you have to use your intelligence to figure out where he's weak and how you'll get to him." He paused for emphasis. "The final step is to attack. Attack the source of your fear. But be smart about it."

Tony recited the three steps, so Nicholas knew he'd understood. But he didn't have any ideas for an attack yet. That was fine; he was only at the first step. He needed to observe. Then would come the analysis, and finally the action.

After the basketball game ended, Tony had some questions on his homework. He ran up the stairs to fetch his books. His steps seemed lighter, as if he no longer dreaded returning to school the next day but rather looked forward to the challenge he had been given.

While waiting for him, Nicholas reached for the remote and punched in the channel for the sports news station. He read aloud the final scores for the first round of football games, absorbing the numbers and rearranging the standings in his mind. Most of the late games were already in the third quarter. The ads came on, and he would have gotten up for a snack and soda were it not for the before-and-after images that froze him in place.

An ad pictured cancer survivors—bald children lying in

bed and then running on a soccer field, a young woman getting up from the sofa to ride a bicycle, and an older man playing with his grandchildren. Three people brought back to life by chemotherapy and immune system boosters, one of which he recognized because he had received it to stave off infections after his bone-marrow transplant. From particles of blue and green graphics the company's logo solidified on the television screen, and it too looked familiar. A globe that comprised the letter G and a futuristic M, it represented Global Millennium Bio-Chem, the company that had purchased Hometown Chemical Company a year ago almost to the day.

Rage scalded his entire body, as if he had spiked a one-hundred-five-plus-degree fever that threatened to destroy his vital organs. He saw himself again, the forty-year-old community college professor with a wife and two children, lying wasted, curled in fetal position in a hospital bed in California, near death from the chemo and radiation that had annihilated his diseased marrow and hollowed out his bones. He drifted in and out of consciousness as a liquid the color of dirty rainwater dripped into him from a thick plastic bag that hung three feet above his bed. The bag could have been three hundred feet above him for all he could do to touch it. At the time he'd pleaded with his body not to reject his brother's donated marrow, which in retrospect resembled some of the samples he'd dredged from the river.

"Damn them," he muttered. "They dump the shit that gives people cancer, and now they're making money off the cure." He remembered he couldn't speak back then, couldn't eat or drink, for his mouth was a massive burning open sore.

"What was that you said, Dad?" Tony stood behind him with a math book and binder under his arm. Nicholas took a deep, painful breath and felt the sweat bead on his face and soak into his shirt.

His rage, kindled by the ad, had punctured his objectivity and compromised his secrets, and he suspected that what he had just taught Tony was a lie or at least a theory he could not put into practice. He couldn't draw Tony into his world because he loved Tony too much to destroy the only world the boy knew. He could not tell of the assault on his body perpetrated by Hometown Chemical Company, the stew of rage and vengeance and fear that simmered inside him, and the energy it took to keep it there. He had to continue teaching, both of them had to go on living, and neither he nor Tony was ready for the truth. So he turned off the television and fished for yet another lie.

"They were showing a documentary on some crooked company that's trying to make money off people's suffering. I caught the end of it."

"I'll watch it with you," Tony offered.

"It's over." But in his mind Nicholas recorded the words: *I am the documentary.*

Eleven: A Cul-de-sac Is a Dead-end Street

Around the time of Nicky's diagnosis, Holly read an article in the *New York Times* about two young men who rescued an elderly woman from a burning building in Queens. The men had never seen each other before, one spoke little English, and they had no emergency training. But when they saw the smoke and heard the woman's screams from the fourth-floor window, they scaled the fire escape and brought her to safety, injuring themselves in the process. After she read the story, Holly pictured these strong, energetic young men and the wordless glance exchanged between them in the moment before they dashed toward the building.

That glance was a sign she could never truly understand, for a fraternity she would never be able to join. She knew Nicky would have gone up that fire escape in an instant, not thinking of her, the kids, all his other responsibilities. Not thinking of what could happen to him. She realized she had pledged her life to a man who had never quite lost his adolescent belief in his own invulnerability. And every day he cheated death, that conviction hardened to the point that he was standing up and daring God or the devil to take him.

Nicky should have known better than to expose himself to more toxic waste, especially if he believed it had sickened him in the first place. Though she begged him to stop taking samples from their yard, the only difference her words made was that he wore a mask and gloves. So after their fight the weekend before Thanksgiving, after they had reconciled— or so he thought—with passionate sex on the floor in the family room, after he had left to drive Tony to his guitar lesson, she called Marc.

Marc thanked her and promised he'd take care of everything. But Nicky mentioned nothing about an encounter when she returned from the mall with Tony the next day, and

Marc called her shortly after she arrived at her office on Monday.

"I have bad news for you," he said after some nervous small talk and the question she'd dreaded to ask. "He wouldn't listen to me, even when I explained to him how this will impact the neighborhood and what the consequences are of filing a nuisance suit."

"What consequences?" She had no legal training; she believed when the judge threw a suit out of court, that was the end of the matter. Marc's explanation terrified her, for Nicky didn't know how little they had in savings and how much she owed on the credit cards. She thought of the expensive basketball sneakers that Tony had convinced her to buy, as if the one hundred twenty dollars would make a difference. She twisted the thick phone cord. "So what can I do now?"

"Do you have any documents, photos, or a list of contacts that he may have left lying around? At least that'll give us an idea of the damage he can do to this community."

"Damage?"

"How real the threat is of him trying to expose something."

She read in Marc's words the possibility that he too knew a horrible truth that had to be covered up. The truth she didn't know the summer she bought the house, the truth she didn't want to know. "I'm sure he doesn't have anything," she stammered. But her denial was a defensive action, not a statement of fact. Ever since Nicky had lost his job in New York and had to give up research for full-time teaching, he had kept all his papers and notes in his office at the college. Sometimes he brought Tony there to play on the computer, but rifling through his files wasn't the kind of thing she could ask a twelve-year-old to do. "Do you think there really is—"

"No," Marc cut in. "Whatever he has is unscientific, cannot be proven. We don't know the lab where he's taking the samples, how qualified it is to analyze them. Most likely, he or some glorified high-school chemistry teacher is testing them at his college." Holly's mind flashed to Rich Rankin, one of Nicky's friends at the college. One of those people you could look at and guess "pothead." Marc continued. "I've talked to some people at the company, and they've assured me there's nothing out there."

"You didn't tell them about Nick?"

"No, and I won't. I simply inquired as president of the association. I'd like to keep the folks at Hometown—I suppose now we're to say Global Millennium—from discovering what he's doing and blowing it out of proportion on their end." She heard his exasperated sigh. "The problem is, in my position I have to balance everyone's interests. It does us no good to have anything end up in the newspapers or the courts, because soon enough some journalist who has nothing better to do is going to create a panic."

Panic. Holly's mind caught on the word. It was what she often felt contemplating that infinite emptiness of life without Nicky. They had met so young; she had never loved any of the ones before him in the same way. But spoken in Marc's accent, the word reassured her. It meant a groundless fear, Nicky's illness in remission a curable misfortune caused by nothing—not God's wrath, not bad genes, not chemicals with scary names. "I guess I need to talk to Nick again. Thanks for trying."

"I'm sorry I couldn't be more successful." His tone softened into a sympathetic murmur. "Now that the weather's getting cold, I think you should hold off confronting him. He can't dig if the ground is too hard or covered in snow, and if it's cold enough the river will freeze along the shore." He cleared his throat. Holly said a silent prayer for a long, frigid winter. "I can't tell you how much I admire you for your courage. Most wives wouldn't have spoken out the way you have. And believe me, Nick can be intimidating." He hesitated. "I'm concerned for you. I hope he treats you right."

"He does." She raised her voice, the conviction as much for herself as for Marc.

"He did his best to provoke me into hitting him yesterday."

She bit her lower lip. *Thank you for not hitting him*, she thought, but all she could say was, "I'm sorry." She had tangled the phone cord; it was no longer perfectly coiled. With nervous fingers she tried to fix it.

"I worry that he acts this way with you."

"I'm fine." *I'm used to bad marriages. It could be worse; I could feel nothing for him.* She remembered the way Marc had talked about Claudette at the Christmas party a year ago. And while they wouldn't mention it in front of the kids, Holly always had the impression her parents disgusted each other.

"Does he hurt you?"

"No." But hurting wasn't only physical, she knew and couldn't tell Marc; she couldn't tell him that when Nicky felt like hurting someone he never left any mark people could see.

After an early December cold snap the ground froze. Nicky pursued the far safer activity of coaching Tony's basketball team along with the young social studies teacher who according to Marc had made scant progress in controlling her class or motivating Braxton. Marc even phoned Holly at her office—not to complain about Nicky's digging but to see if Nicky could recommend a tutor for Braxton. She called Nicky at the college, and he gave her the phone number of a student, Tasha Lockwood. She called Marc back.

"Thanks for checking, Holly," he said. "But I'm looking more for a teacher. I don't think a student will have the background."

"Nick said she's pre-med, at the top of her class. He recommends her highly."

"A community college is not what I want Braxton to

aspire to. I'll check the association's records to see if someone from Burnham can help me."

Was this what Nicky meant when he said Marc taught his kids prejudice? Holly couldn't let it pass, knowing how Nicky dedicated his life to these students. "I think you're being a bit narrow-minded. I've met some of the students, and they're bright and hard working. They haven't had a lot of the advantages we take for granted."

"But do they have the preparation?"

"I'm sure they can handle seventh grade American history." She paused for emphasis. "And it might be a good experience for Braxton."

"I'll have to think about it." She repeated the name and phone number and heard the scratching of a pencil or pen on the other end of the line. "By the way, is Nick keeping out of trouble?"

"He's not collecting samples."

"Everything else all right?"

"Yes." Her voice rose in question, for she wondered how much Marc suspected.

"You're sure?"

"I'm sure."

Growing up with her parents' marriage, Holly had learned to accept things rather than fight. So she said nothing when Nicky stayed out half a chilly night playing basketball with some guys he'd met while coaching the team. Two days later he had a sore throat that soon became a nasty cold. She suggested he call in sick. He refused; she chose not to nag. As a result he dragged his sniffling, coughing, feverish body around town all week and then to the neighborhood Christmas party.

Red and green lights hung from the eaves of the Yellow Springs Heights clubhouse on the Saturday night before Christmas. Holly commented on the new icicle-style lights, but Nicky merely grunted, about the only noise she'd gotten from him except hacking since he'd returned from an afternoon reception at the college.

"I know you don't like these neighborhood things," she said to him. "But try not to be such a bear." He responded with another grunt.

The clubhouse was already packed when they arrived. Claudette Martineau greeted them at the door. Her shimmering blonde hair was combed under rather than teased up as she had it done last year. She stood tall in her high heels, drink in hand, her face flushed. She touched Holly's shoulder and planted a wet bourbon kiss on her cheek. "So nice to see you." She reached for Nicky, who stepped backward and raised his hands.

"You don't want my cold."

"No, I don't. Thank you." She pointed toward the three tables with the potluck dishes. Holly dropped off her pumpkin pie at the dessert table and surveyed the guests.

The party appeared lively, upbeat. She remembered some of the parties in the early nineties, when recession and corporate downsizing devastated the neighborhood. In those days, the guys hit the bar first thing and stayed there, congregated in morose solidarity while the women fretted over who had been laid off and who would have to move. In recent years, though, conversations turned to fat bonuses, new cars, swimming pools, vacations. With Nicky tenured and her civil service job as an editor with the state office of economic development also secure, they missed both the bad times and the good. Holly asked herself if she would have traded it. *No, not after what happened in New York*. Still, she couldn't help but feel envious.

Nicky handed her a gin and tonic while she stood with the mother of one of Rosie's friends. Both their daughters had gone to a party, and she carried the cell phone in case Rosie's boyfriend of the week had too much to drink and Rosie needed a ride home. She supposed she would have liked it if no one drank liquor at a party of high-school students, but who was she kidding? Better to be safe than sorry.

Nicky had drifted off by this time. She felt relief, for she knew how much he missed Roger at events like these. As she helped herself to a second drink, she spotted Nicky standing with a trio of men who had their backs to her. He held a plate of food and a fresh drink. He seemed fine, so she turned to the food table.

Marc appeared beside her. A tie with Santas and candy canes stood out against his muted gray suit. "Don't leave without us having a chat. And don't pass up the jambalaya. I made it myself." He pointed to a large enamel dish in the center of the table that had seen few takers.

She tried Marc's dish. It was too hot for her Midwestern palate, but she smiled at him as she formulated a strategy to dispose of it discreetly.

"If you like it, do you want to take some home? We're leaving tomorrow for Louisiana, and we're never going to eat it before then. I guess it wasn't a best-seller."

She agreed to take a container, even though she knew she'd have to toss it the minute she got home, lest it sit at the back of the refrigerator and become a science project on the mold-retardant properties of cayenne pepper.

Marc thanked her and added, "A lot of people up North don't appreciate our cuisine. You should come down to New Orleans and get some real food." He pronounced the city's name "Nahlins."

When she didn't reply right away, he said, "Mardi Gras is coming up in just a few months."

"So we can drink the most polluted water in America." She whirled around to see Nicky standing at her other side, his face red.

"Well, if it isn't our neighborhood do-gooder. What's Saint Nicholas up to these days?" Marc said. Holly gasped. If this was the way Marc had talked to Nicky, no wonder he had failed. Nicky did not use ridicule as a weapon, nor did he tolerate it in others.

"Now that you mention it, I'm giving you a lump of coal for your part in this cover-up." Nicky rubbed the back of his neck. "By the way, I got the preliminary results from the samples I collected at the McDonoughs' before Thanksgiving. The ones you tried to stop me from getting. You want to know what the lab in California found?"

Marc just stared, his mouth open. "Nick!" Holly hissed.

If he heard her, it made no difference. "Benzene, which is a principal cause of leukemia. And it leached into the well, because I got the results of water samples from the county. The lab also identified related compounds and traces of mercury." He recited a host of cancers and birth defects the chemicals caused and finished by asking Marc, "Do you want me to fax the results to your office or your home?"

Marc excused himself. Holly slammed her plate and drink down on the table. Gin and tonic splashed on her sleeve; the cold, fizzy liquid tickled her wrist. She grabbed Nicky's forearm and dragged him into the hallway leading to the restrooms.

"What do you think you're doing?" She was trying not to scream and make more of a spectacle than he'd already made.

"Telling the truth." He twisted out of her grasp and paced the narrow hallway. "I was talking to some guys who work for Hometown. The parent company's going to shut the office here and transfer them all to New York or Atlanta." He glared at her, jaw clenched. It made her feel as though she had done something wrong. "Typical of them to make a mess and then leave town."

"Can you relax and try to enjoy yourself? This is a Christmas party, not an EPA hearing."

"We don't have much time. They said by next Christmas the entire office will be gone. History." He sliced the air with his hand.

"What does that matter? The river will still be here." Despite her effort, she felt him once again pulling her into his obsession.

"Documents. I've already gotten some on interlibrary loan from their corporate library. Nothing incriminating, but they're pointing in the right direction." He pushed his fingers through his hair. "But they'll be harder to get once the company's gone."

Holly grasped both his hands to slow his pacing, which was driving her crazy. Again, he had embarrassed her in front of the neighbors, the reason why except for the McDonoughs, they had never in eleven years invited another couple from Yellow Springs Heights over for dinner or eaten as a couple at another house. And, unlike Claudette, he didn't have the excuse of being drunk. For a moment he stood still, and she squeezed his shoulders and leaned into him as if to pin him to the wall. He bounced the back of his head against the sheetrock. She eased him toward her, extended her arms across his shoulders, and massaged the rock hard muscles of his neck and upper back. The problem was, from the very first time she met him at the South Africa sit-in, she had found his crazy intensity profoundly erotic, and it took all the willpower she had not to attack him right in the hallway.

"You are wired tonight, Nicky baby," she whispered instead.

"I was on my way to get another drink, to see if that would help."

"How many have you had?"

"Two." His usual limit. At one hundred twenty-five pounds, with a liver weakened by the chemo, he couldn't take much more.

She pushed his hair, damp with perspiration, back from his face and felt his forehead. It was a bit warm, and she recalled her earlier suggestion that he come home and nap rather than spending the afternoon at his college. At that moment, he pulled her to him and kissed her on the mouth.

122

She wrapped her arms around his neck and inhaled a subtle mixture of soap, alcohol, and sweat.

"All right, kids, let's keep it decent."

They glanced up at the same time to see a large older man waddling toward the men's room. "Eat dogshit," they mouthed in unison as he passed through the door. Their laughter ended for Nicky in a fit of coughing.

Afterward, he sagged against the wall. He pulled a crumpled, filthy handkerchief from the side pocket of his slacks and spat into it. She felt herself go cold. "You look like you're going to crash," she said.

"Yeah." Nicky cleared his throat. The man came out of the bathroom and brushed by them. "I'm not having that great a time either."

"Let's go then."

"You stay. I need to walk." He shoved his hands into his pockets and kicked the wall with his heel.

It was less than half a mile to the house, but she didn't want to send him out in the cold in his condition, especially since she wasn't sure he'd go straight home. She brought him a cup of hot tea.

"I'll tape that Branford Marsalis concert on PBS for you, so you don't have to rush back," he promised. "Just call Tony and tell him I'm on my way so he doesn't freak out when I ring the doorbell."

* * *

Later, Holly would tell herself she should have left with Nicky. She should never have made that promise to talk to Marc, and she should never have kept it.

Claudette was stone drunk. By ten she lay sprawled on the couch like a homeless person on the subway, everybody staying a safe distance from her. From time to time Marc glanced in her direction with such an expression of pain and disgust that Holly offered to drive Claudette home, even though she'd finished two more gin and tonics herself to unwind from her fight with Nicky.

Marc thanked her but declined. Through the thick fuzz penetrating her brain she reasoned that he wanted to bring Claudette to bed without his boys seeing her. "But if you want to go, Holly, I'll get the jambalaya for you right now," he said.

"I think I'll stay a while." She realized she would need some time to sober up before she drove anywhere. A poor example she'd be setting for Rosie if she didn't.

"I'll get it for you anyway. I might forget later." His eyes met hers. The flesh sagged around his small blue eyes like the eyelids of a Basset Hound. She let his melodic accent hold her spellbound, so different as it was from Nicky's flat, rapid-fire speech.

The crowd had thinned at this late hour; about twenty people remained. Marc picked up his still-full serving dish, and Holly followed him into the clubhouse's roomy kitchen. Plastic containers and platters of all shapes, sizes, and colors lay piled up on the counters like a Tupperware party gone berserk.

He selected a quart plastic container and started to fill it. The scent of cayenne wafted toward her. "I haven't seen Nick for a while. Is everything all right?"

"He left a couple of hours ago. He had a cold and was out of sorts." She took a deep breath. "I'm sorry for what he said."

Marc smiled. "No need to apologize. He's the one who should be sorry."

Marc's words should have made her feel better, but they didn't. He laid his huge hand on her shoulder. "I've been worried about you for a while."

"I know. I'm really okay." She tried to sound perky, convincing, but it was hard to get her tongue around the words.

"You're not in any danger?"

"No." The act of shaking her head made her dizzy, and she leaned against the counter for support.

"I care about you, Holly. You can be honest with me."

"He doesn't abuse me."

"Abuse can be emotional. I've heard his language, and I can't imagine how a polite, cultivated woman like you can take it all these years."

She stared at her silver pumps. "I tune it out." She added, "As best I can." She visualized Nicky in mid-argument, his fists clenched, his face red, his words spiked with profanities, and her heart raced as it did at those times. *How did I come to marry someone so scarred and angry?*

Marc touched his chest with his free hand. "As the husband of an alcoholic, I understand how you must feel."

She felt compelled to tell him. "Nick doesn't drink much."

"You can't blame yourself for his actions. You aren't responsible for what he does; he is." Marc lowered his head and drummed his fingers on her shoulder. "Believe me. It's taken me a long time to get there. At first I denied Claudette's drinking problem, and then I blamed myself. Finally, I got help and realized I couldn't do anything about her. The only thing I could do was be the best father I could be to my boys."

She listened, because what he said made a lot of sense even if the problem wasn't the same.

Marc added, "I've got a good Al-Anon group. You know, for family members. You should come with me one evening."

Holly clenched her teeth; Marc hadn't paid attention to her words. Rage sizzled inside her, and all the ignorant comments she'd heard when Nicky had lost his job came back to mind. But she wasn't going to swallow or rationalize it or fantasize revenge against a real or imagined culprit. That's what Nicky did, and now he was the neighborhood nut case.

"Nick's not an alcoholic. He has cancer." She couldn't believe how easily the words had slipped out. All the times Nicky had forced her to say the C-word had taken away her fear, and now her own family's secret was revealed. "He thinks he got leukemia from either the water or the dirt fill they used when they built the neighborhood. Or both. That's why he's collecting those samples."

She watched Marc's expression turn to complete shock. "I-I don't know what to say, Holly. I am so sorry."

"Please don't say anything to anyone else. Not Claudette, not the boys, not anyone." She lowered her voice to a whisper. "We didn't tell our kids."

Marc laid his free hand on her other shoulder. "I'm not going to say anything, I promise." He hesitated a moment. "I'm not telling you how to run your family, but don't you think your kids should know?"

How many times had she and Nicky asked the same question? *But once you tell the first lie, all the other lies come easier. Telling the truth is what gets harder and more complicated.*

"Nick received a bone-marrow transplant three years ago. The doctors said he had a fifty-fifty chance for a total cure. Under those circumstances, we didn't want to worry the kids if we didn't have to."

"So how's he doing?" Marc sounded genuinely concerned.

"So far, so good." She crossed her fingers. "But Nick's convinced he's not going to make it. He says he's done research, and people who have been exposed to certain toxic chemicals have a much poorer prognosis than others with his type of leukemia."

"Well, I hope he's going to be all right. For his sake and all of ours." Marc stroked his beard. "That explains a lot." He shook his head and after a moment said, "I can't help but think of our conversation at the McDonoughs' house. I compared cancer clusters to a lousy roll of the dice, and he didn't take the remark too kindly. Now I know why."

"It's not your fault. Most people can't fathom what he's gone through." She sighed. "And it's made him so much harder, so..." She paused, searched her foggy mind for the right word. "Unforgiving."

This time, Marc stroked the top of her hand. "But it's a terrible burden for you."

"Yes," she whispered. He leaned forward, and she embraced him. He had a solid build and hardly more body fat than Nicky had. *He could have crushed Nicky.* Her arms went all the way around Nicky, but her hands just reached the back of Marc's rib cage. Everything about him felt powerful yet comforting.

"Did I tell you that you look beautiful in that dress?" he whispered in her ear.

She had bought the long, slinky silver dress the week before the party. Nicky hadn't said a word about it. She'd learned early on in their relationship that she had to look good for herself because he never noticed those things.

"Thank you," she murmured.

He stepped back and touched her chin. "It hurts me to see you so sad."

Her face felt hot. She flashed back to earlier in the evening, her argument with Nicky and their passionate embrace and kiss. The same bristling excitement came over her again. But this time she was with another man, one whose secrets she already knew and who now knew hers. He'd listened to her and valued her opinions. She'd changed his mind. *Nothing I say ever changes Nicky's mind.* Marc had worried about her, and they'd helped each other, protected their neighborhood and the lives they'd made there even if it meant betraying Nicky's cause. *One lie leads to another. One betrayal can lead to another, if you let it.* In the kitchen, empty except for the two of them, the discarded containers, and the too-hot jambalaya, their mouths met in a long, gentle, sweet kiss.

"I wish you didn't have to go tomorrow," she said.

"I have something to show you tonight." He put his arm

around her shoulders and pulled her to him. "Tell me where your coat is."

On impulse—the only way it seemed she and Nicky ever did these things—she gave Marc a wicked smile. "I don't need a coat. I'm from Minnesota."

He ducked out for a moment, and when he returned, his wool overcoat was draped over his forearm. "Take mine. Please."

With exaggerated chivalry he hung the massive coat on her shoulders. Before guiding her out of the kitchen, he fished in one of the pockets and pulled out a ring of keys, attached to a red enamel crawfish. Outdoors as the frigid night air closed in on her like a tightening net, it occurred to her that, as president of the Community Association, he would have the keys to the clubhouse and all the other common buildings.

Even more than the bitter chill, the thought of where she was headed made her shiver, and she wrapped his coat around her. The sleeves dangled empty beyond her fingertips, but her hands were sheltered from the wind. She sniffed the faint aroma of spice and sausage, of jambalaya, penetrating everything in Marc's house. Marc stroked the back of her neck. The current from his touch spread through her.

They passed the half-drained pool, covered by a sheet of thick blue plastic, and came to the pool house. It was a short cinder-block building about a third the size of the clubhouse. He sorted through the keys and opened the door.

Nicky would have picked the lock.

The pool house was freezing cold. Marc felt for the dial on the baseboard heater. "It'll take a few minutes to heat through," he said.

He turned on a small lamp and rummaged through the pool house for a mat and some towels. Cleaned up for the new season, they smelled of chlorine and detergent.

As the warmth from the heater pervaded the room, Marc massaged her shoulders, then her back. She rubbed his neck and buried her face in his soft beard. Finally, he unzipped the back of her dress. She held her breath.

I am getting into this with my eyes open. Maybe I've had too much to drink, but I want this. One night—nobody will have to know.

Naked except for his dark socks, Marc laid a towel over the mat and dropped to his knees. He rubbed her hips. "Do you like this?"

"Yes." Silently, she thanked him for asking. Nicky never asked but acted on whatever inspired him in a wordless, passionate improvisation. She shivered when Marc brought his hands toward her crotch, and she squeezed his shoulders in rhythm with the squeezing sensation inside her when his finger tickled her. Her vagina turned soft and wet and achy. She knelt next to him, and they kissed. She extended her tongue and touched his. He touched hers back, and it surprised her that he didn't press his tongue into the inside of her mouth first or shove it toward her throat. Marc tasted of sausage and shrimp and red wine, and the flavor made her stomach sizzle. Blood rushed to her ears. They kissed and stroked each other for a long time in the semidarkness, then he lay back and put on a condom he took from his wallet. She eased herself on top of him and let him slide into her. Her orgasm preceded his and rocked her again the instant he came with a shudder beneath her.

For one night, Marc offered strength, stability. She savored his gentleness. From the first time she saw him, nothing about Nicky was gentle. They tore each other's hearts out and then had great sex. One moment she would be so mad at him that she could kill him and the next so madly in love with him that she wanted to live with him for all eternity. Tonight's wild ride was just one more episode in Life with Nicky Baran.

She needed a vacation.

*   *   *

How to face Nicky, after I've betrayed him in so many ways?
She asked herself that question as she drove home in the
frozen darkness, her eyes filled with tears.

She entered the house through the garage and had to walk
through the family room. Nicky lay on the sofa under a woven
blanket, a half-full mug of tea on the carpet. She didn't like
him leaving drinks there, but she let it go. The concert was
winding up, the credits rolling. His eyelids fluttered.

"I taped it," he mumbled.

"Thanks."

"You can stop the tape if you want. It's over."

"How are you feeling?" More through habit than desire,
she ran her fingers through his hair. Compared to Marc, he
seemed old, worn out, even though Marc had at least five
years on him.

"Okay. I'm going to bed."

She offered to check on Tony and ease him off to bed,
after which she would wait up for Rosie. She found Tony in
his room, practicing the guitar.

"Hi, Mom. Have fun at the party?" His voice cracked.

She asked him if he'd had a chance to talk with his father.

Tony's face brightened. "Yeah, we watched *American
History X* together. It was wicked good."

"The movie about the Nazi skinheads?" She wasn't sure
Tony was ready for it, but he seemed okay.

"Uh-huh. Dad told me more stuff too. About the Nazis in
Europe and how they came to power. You know, people
actually voted for them. That's, like, sick."

"We can talk about it in the morning. You'd better get to
bed." She rubbed the top of Tony's head. Her little man. He
had changed so much in just a few months. She remembered
Marc's words, that all he could do was be the best father he
could be to his boys.

130

Amid all the craziness, she sensed something beautiful happening between Nicky and Tony. And she had to risk it all by throwing herself into Marc's arms.

* * *

She awoke the next morning with a crushing headache, a churning stomach, and an overwhelming sense of dread. Nicky brought her a glass of water and two aspirin tablets and apologized for passing his cold to her. He stroked her back, but in her misery she had no intention of reciprocating his passion. She still felt nothing for him, just a vague longing for Marc's gentle hands and huge body enveloping her, protecting her where Nicky could not. And she realized then that if Marc returned and asked for what they both seemed to want and need, she would not be able to resist.

That afternoon, as soon as her head and stomach settled, she drove to the mall and bought Nicky a new shoulder bag to replace the one he had destroyed collecting samples at the abandoned factory. It was a burnt red color with navy trim. Made from a heavy waterproof—but probably not toxic chemical-proof—nylon, it had a shoulder strap, a carrying strap if he wanted to use it as a briefcase, and a webbed pocket on each side for his water bottles. To ease her conscience further, she hiked up a flight of stairs to the boy's section—Nicky often fit in boy's clothes, which cost less—and selected the cargo pants, t-shirt, button-down shirt, and vest displayed on a mannequin. As she handed her charge card to the handsome young store clerk with the dyed-blond hair, she imagined Nicky in the new outfit and at that moment convinced herself she would make it through the holidays without obsessing about Marc.

But the Monday morning after New Year's Marc called her at her office. He said he had something to show her. Something he'd "picked up" in Louisiana, as if it might have been a seashell from a Gulf Coast beach.

"Can you meet me for lunch tomorrow?" he asked.

Her hand trembled as she held the receiver. With her other hand, she flipped the page of her date book in the hope that an appointment would make the decision for her. She peered at the row of blank lines. *Your choice. The right thing, or the thing you want to do.* She took a deep breath. All he wanted was to show her something, she reasoned. And share a lunch, nothing more. "I think so. When and where?"

By the end of the conversation, she had penciled onto one of the blank lines: *Les Trois Canards. Noon.*

All night long she couldn't sleep. Nicky mumbled next to her, but the pillow muffled his words. It used to amuse her; she'd tell her friends it wasn't enough he talked all day long, he had to talk in his sleep too. Lately she'd started to listen for some clue in his incoherent syllables, some way of getting through to him to stop his crusade. Now she blamed him for keeping her awake and resented him for sleeping so soundly. As usual, she couldn't make out his words. One word ran through her mind: *cancel*. She tiptoed downstairs and fixed herself a mug of peppermint tea. She'd look terrible in the morning, and Marc would notice the bags under her eyes and ask her again if everything was all right.

Nicky noticed nothing. Not her wan complexion nor the circles under her eyes that she covered up with an extra layer of foundation. While she dressed in her nicest business suit— the one she saved for meetings with the governor—he sat in bed reading the *Times*, listening to "Morning Edition," and commenting on the news. *Doing three things at once, and he can't even bother to look at me.*

When she arrived at the restaurant, Marc kissed her on the cheek. "You look wonderful," he said. He took a step backward, and she thought she saw a touch of awe in his expression even though she felt heavy and slow from lack of sleep. At their table he handed her a green velvet jewelry box.

"You didn't have to." Her hands shook as she opened it. She hoped to find something small, a token of friendship that carried no obligation. Inside was a pair of emerald and diamond earrings that matched her outfit.

Marc smiled. "I picked these out in New Orleans, but I didn't know you'd wear this dress today. It must be telepathy."

She tried on the earrings and felt hot blood course though her ears and face. She slipped the small mirror from her purse and observed herself. Her cheeks were red, but the color gave life to her face. The earrings, delicate dangling teardrops, sparkled in the reflected light. *They are perfect, and they make me feel beautiful.*

"I can't accept these," she whispered. She set the mirror on the white linen tablecloth.

"Why don't you wear them for lunch. They look so good on you."

She left the box on the table, promised herself she would return the earrings.

Les Trois Canards was located on the ground floor of the shiny new Grand Springs Hotel, built several years earlier on the ruins of a dilapidated, drug-infested, and ultimately boarded-up downtown shopping mall. Over dessert, after refilling her wine glass for the second time, Marc told her he had represented the developer of the hotel complex. He described how the hotel and convention business had revived downtown Cold Springs after increasingly larger suburban malls—whose developers he also represented—had wiped out most of the retailers. His power and his understanding of how the city worked astounded her. Nicky might have made some great speeches in his day, but Marc had a vision and accomplished so much.

She asked him if he'd represented the developer of Yellow Springs Heights. He laughed and said that he couldn't serve as the president of the Community Association if he did. "I don't handle residential development anyway, only commercial. And contrary to what Nick probably believes, I never did any work for that chemical company. Big as they are, they have their own people in-house."

Holly shivered at her husband's name. Marc took her hand and slipped a small plastic card into it. Peering between her fingers, she recognized a coded room key for the hotel.

"I have a suite, 1512, that I sometimes use for meetings." Marc stroked his beard.

Even after three glasses of wine, Holly knew he didn't use a hotel room to meet clients. And she probably wasn't his first tryst either. Her eyes downcast, she pushed the key toward him.

He reached across the table, placed his thumb and index finger under her chin, and slowly raised her head until she was gazing into his face.

"I need you, Holly," he said. "And you deserve to treat yourself."

"I don't know. I have to get back," she whispered. Her hand moved toward the side of her face, to remove the earrings.

"What we had that night was beautiful."

She shook her head. "I was drunk. And Nick and I'd had an argument."

"You argue a lot."

She nodded. "But I can't do this to him."

"You have to think of yourself. What do *you* want?"

Holly held her breath to control her racing heart. Marc had treated her well and would genuinely care if she enjoyed their lovemaking. Pleasurable memories of the night in the pool house rose up in her and pushed aside the guilt that would later consume her. "I'll go upstairs now and freshen up." She reached for her purse and the key.

By the time she got off the elevator at the fifteenth floor, she already had a throbbing headache. Alcohol never agreed with her, a fact she learned in her wilder days when she and Nicky were first married and living in New York. She awoke hung over from her reckless nights, leaving Nicky to nurse her with the bemused smugness only one with a strong stomach and high tolerance could muster. He suffered from a different alcohol-related problem: his self-control, tenuous when sober, vanished completely after about two drinks. When they became parents and felt it necessary to adopt a more responsible lifestyle, she and Nicky began to watch out for each other at parties, to remind each other to slow down.

But no one had warned her to slow down as she stood alone in Marc's private suite, surveying the striped damask eighteenth-century French reproduction furniture and feeling like Marie Antoinette with the world in turmoil all around her. Waiting for her King Louis to come upstairs for an afternoon of dissolute pleasure, she was prepared to betray once again the crazy idealistic Marat she had married, whose words unleashed a fury that destroyed everything in the end.

Damn European history. For the rest of the afternoon she would see the image of Nicky as Jean-Paul Marat, the assassinated leader of the French Revolution, in her mind.

The lock clicked, and Marc strode into the room. They embraced for a long wine-flavored kiss. Afterward, Marc removed her earrings and necklace and set them on the table in the sitting room. "I just changed my meeting. Let's not rush this," he said.

Smiling up at him, she took off her watch and laid it on the table next to her jewelry. As Marc undressed her, he stared at her body with a dreamy expression, caressed her breasts, stomach, and thighs as though seeing her naked for the first time. She realized it would be the first time too, because the small dim lamp inside the pool house had transformed them into surreal, shadowy figures, and they'd had to navigate each other primarily by voice and touch.

He knelt in front of her and ran his index finger along the dark pitted line from her navel to her crotch, the visible evidence of her two pregnancies. His warm fingers sent shivers and a liquid sensation through her insides at the point where he stroked her. He kissed her belly near the top of the line, then shook his head. "Don't let anyone make you feel ordinary. You are a rare jewel."

Her mind flashed to Nicky. Sex seemed to render him speechless. She used to believe it was because his intense physical performance took all his concentration, but maybe it was because nothing else—not even she—meant that much to him.

Once again, she felt slender and strong, as if twenty-one years and two children hadn't changed her at all. And now she saw herself as if from above—a vibrant, desirable, seductive woman, unbuttoning Marc's dress shirt and unzipping his slacks, stripping one of the city's most distinguished attorneys down to his pink core.

Marc opened the French doors that led into the bedroom. He threw back the quilt on the king-size bed and held out his hand.

In the light of day Marc was the same gentle lover he had been in the pool house, but she observed in his huge, firm, almost hairless body his power and stature and the respect he commanded from those around him. She spread her arms around his waist, buried her face in his belly, and savored the contrast between this delicious human easy chair and the hard life that was all Nicky could give her.

* * *

Marc lived on Elk Court, in a section of five-plus-bedroom houses with stone façades and three-car garages, set on large wooded lots. Yet Holly never saw the inside of his house, only his hotel suite in what had become, by the end of January, a twice-a-week event.

She found herself falling behind at work, rearranging meetings to accommodate her long lunches, and staying late to catch up. It wasn't just the time she spent with Marc. The way he refilled her wine glass made her suspect more than she ever wanted to know about the origins of Claudette's problem, but it also took several hours for her to sober up, get rid of her headache, and concentrate on her work.

"I don't know how often I can see you," she confessed over dessert a couple of weeks after their first meeting. "I'm having money problems." She explained that several years earlier she had begun to take on freelance editing. The insurance failed to cover many of the expenses from Nicky's transplant, and their austere budget left her feeling deprived and depressed as though on a starvation diet. She usually did the work at her office after hours, when she had some quiet. But she no longer had time to take on extra projects, and the bills were still coming in from her latest shopping spree.

Marc smiled and clasped her hand. "I can help you." At their next meeting he gave her the name of one of his clients, the head of an advertising agency who needed an experienced copywriter. The job paid twice as much as her current one, and the agency head offered it to her on the spot even though she had never worked in the field.

That night, while they sat next to each other on the edge of the bed, she told Nicky about the offer. He congratulated her, then embraced her. She felt numb in his arms, and when he tried to kiss her, she shrank back.

"Do you want the job?" he asked

"Sure," she replied, even though the way she'd gotten the position made her feel dirty. "Why?"

"Because no job is worth the money if you're sitting around Sunday afternoon dreading Monday morning."

"I've always wanted something more creative. Like what I had in New York." A hurt expression crossed Nicky's face. He stood and left the room.

She took the offer, to start as soon as the kids returned to school from February vacation, and she gave notice to her boss that she would leave just before the break. That gave her a week of uninterrupted time with Rosie and Tony, since Nicky had to teach. She promised the kids a trip to the Mall of America and booked three tickets from LaGuardia to Minneapolis-St. Paul.

After calling her parents about her new job and unexpected visit, she realized how desperate to get away she must have been. *Who goes on vacation to Minnesota in the middle of February?* And with her parents, she had merely traded one icy conflict-ridden relationship for another, though she figured they'd behave for their grandkids.

At their next lunch meeting she told Marc she'd taken the job and thanked him. Again, they made love. While she relaxed with a warm bath afterward, he came into the room and asked if she could meet him on Saturday morning, the third time that week. "I hope you don't mind. I get so lonely. I can't talk to Claudette the way I can with you." He gave her a desperate, pleading look.

She forced herself to smile, but inside she trembled. He had gotten her the job. He had made her feel good about herself. When she was with him, all the disappointments and hideous uncertainty vanished, and all the promise of her life in New York seemed once again attainable. She had admired Marc's power, but now he'd turned that power against her.

"What time do you want to meet?" she stammered.

"Can you be here at ten?"

She agreed, though she had less than forty-eight hours to give Nicky and the kids a reason for why she had to slip away on a Saturday morning. Before she left, Marc handed her a small wrapped gift. Not another necklace, she thought, her throat tight.

"Open it," he urged.

She removed the wrapping paper with shaking hands to reveal a pair of compact discs. She strained to read the titles.

Marc put his arm around her shoulders. "You've heard of Beausoleil, haven't you?"

She hadn't, but she nodded her thanks anyway.

"They're my favorite Cajun group. Listen to them. You'll love them." He kissed her good-bye. "See you Saturday."

"Yes," she mumbled, her eyes lowered.

In the elevator she jammed the CDs into her purse. She had drunk even more wine than usual at lunch, and her head and stomach swirled in reaction to the alcohol, the sex, and her emotional turmoil. Before she could stop them, the tears began to flow. Wobbling on her high heels, she rushed from the elevator to the bathroom. *What have I done?* She asked herself, Nicky, God. A punishment awaited her; that much she knew. Fifteen minutes later, with her freshly applied mascara gone and her eyelids rubbed raw and dry, she still felt unsteady but better for having had a good cry.

She got lucky on Saturday morning. A soft, powdery snow had fallen during the night, and eight inches blanketed the ground by sunrise. By nine, Nicky had already cleared the driveway and awakened the kids and was mustering them out for a morning of sledding at a steep, rocky hill in North Springs. She warned them to be careful, kissed all three good-bye, and left in Nicky's car as soon as the station wagon had vanished from her sight.

Although Marc disliked rushing, she pushed him to finish. For the first time, she took no pleasure in their intimacy. She felt in his gentleness a lack of resistance that bored her. Her immediate concern was that Nicky and the kids would return first, and she would have to invent a trip to the mall to cover up her absence. After a quick shower in Marc's suite, she put on a new perfume, prepared to tell Nicky she'd tried a sample at Nordstrom's in case he noticed.

She raced home and beat them by half an hour. She heard a rattling in the garage, and Tony tore through the door.

"Hey, Mom, it was wicked fun!" he shouted, unaware he was indoors and not on an icy, windy hill. "We had a race to see which was fastest—the sled, a cafeteria tray, or the metal trash can lid without its handle."

She wondered where Nicky had pilfered the tray and if he had ruined the lid to the new garbage can. "Okay, what won?"

"The tray." Tony examined the wadded-up piece of paper that he'd pulled from the pocket of his soaking wet jeans. "By one point eight seconds. But you should have seen that trash can lid spin!"

Rosie followed Tony. She carried the victorious tray above her head. "Yeah, right. You should see Dad." She waited for her father to come in and yanked off his black wool cap.

Holly screamed. Nicky's hair on the right side was matted with blood, which streaked his forehead and the side of his face. He and the kids laughed at her reaction, which made her more furious. "What on earth happened?"

"A live test of centrifugal force. Nothing to worry about," Nicky said.

"Did you get knocked out? Are you okay?" Thoughts of a concussion or more serious brain damage raced through her mind as she waited for a coherent response.

"I'm fine. I was wearing a helmet." He eyed Rosie and Tony. "A good lesson for you guys." In a perfectly straight line he walked over to the kitchen and handed Holly the helmet. She fingered the deep dent on the right side, most likely made by a sharp rock.

Nicky snatched his own car keys from the counter and lifted the mangled helmet from her hands. He dangled the keys in front of Rosie. "Guys, would you do me a favor and take the helmet back to the bike shop in North Springs? It has a warranty, so make them give you the same model."

"Why don't you do it, Dad?" Rosie asked.

"Because I brought them one back in July, and they don't want to see me again."

Rosie sniffed. "You are so cheap!"

Nicky ignored her. "Tony, you go with her and look at the bikes. You've outgrown your old one."

"All right!" Tony punched his fist in the air. His sister glared at him.

"Can't Mom do it? I'm supposed to go with friends to the mall," she moaned.

"She has to stay here and clean me up." Nicky gazed into Holly's eyes with an expression of intense desire. She noticed his pupils were the same size, another positive sign. "You'll be gone less than an hour if you leave now." He gestured for them to go.

After the kids left, Holly felt Nicky's head for the source of the blood. She stopped on a sticky gash a couple of inches above his hairline. He flinched.

"It's a scalp wound. They bleed like crazy," he said between gritted teeth. He poured a glass of water from the jug in the refrigerator and drank it in one gulp.

"Do you want me to wash it off for you?" she asked him.

"No, it can wait."

He held her in his arms and pressed his lips to hers. After Marc, who stood so much taller, it startled her to be with someone her own size, someone so thin she could wrap her arms all the way around him and feel his chest and abdomen move with each breath. She inhaled his sweat and the faint odor of dried blood. His warmth penetrated her body, pierced her numbness. She was no longer ice but liquid.

Nicky had gone silent, but she could imagine the words running through his mind: *Right now. The floor in the family room. Put on something different, how about some West African music. And then a good hard fuck, forget about everything else.*

"Nicky, say something," she pleaded as he pulled her to the floor next to him, Ismael Lo playing softly in the background.

"What do you want me to say?"

"Whatever comes into your mind."

Please tell me I'm still beautiful. Please.

"Damn, I wish we could do this forever," he whispered in her ear.

"I do too, Nicky."

It was the best she could have hoped from him. And when they reached climax, it felt as if he ripped her in two. In her confusion she saw herself again as Marie Antoinette while two men battled for her heart and her world collapsed around her.

In one corner stood the decadent king with his wine, his too-rich food, his jewelry, and his elegant hotel suite. All his power could not make up for the hollow loneliness that he felt and the refuge that he found in her. But she didn't know how much longer she could stand the pressure, as he demanded more and more of her time, loosened her up with liquor, presented her with gifts she couldn't easily hide.

In the other corner stood her bloody Marat, her little revolutionary—five foot five, still skinny as nothing, Nicky Baran, who'd come back from the dead and believed himself invulnerable. He'd lived a hard life long before he'd met her, and it only got easier for a while, but he never complained. Perhaps his raw courage, his willingness to throw his fragile body at whoever or whatever threatened his idea of a perfect world, was his way of confronting despair. But he had dragged her with him, this doomed champion of lost causes, and pushed her beyond her capacity to endure. Now she needed him to protect her not just from herself but also from a man who hated him and held power over her. Nicky would do it in an instant; her problem was that she could never ask him. For as much as he tried to deny it, she knew Nicky could feel pain, and she suspected that to get out of this situation she had created, she'd have to hurt him far worse than he could possibly imagine.

Twelve: The Battle Flag

Christmas vacation ended too soon. It was that way when Sandy was a student and no different now that she'd become the teacher. She stuffed that bit of knowledge into her mental file of things she'd always wondered about teachers. Yes, they did talk about students and their families in the teachers' lounge. Yes, they hated to come back from vacation as much as the students did.

Her students returned to class with new clothes, new shoes, and the same old attitudes. Her eleventh graders, who had grown listless and apathetic in the weeks before Christmas, seemed mired in their stupor. At least two, often more, failed to hand in their homework assignments, and the rest took less and less care with those they did complete. Her seventh graders hadn't forgotten her surname over the break and continued to interrupt her class with annoying meows. Her basketball team lost all its games.

She did notice some changes. Tony got braces and grew at least an inch. Andy did not return, and a note to his teachers explained that he'd transferred to another private school. Marissa, who'd broken up with her boyfriend in the fall, found a new one and took a second job as the synagogue youth group advisor to work with him. Nick hardly spoke to Sandy at practice anymore. With Marissa prattling on about her latest guy, Sandy longed for Nick's adult conversation, however strange it could turn, because he was someone to talk to besides sixteen-year-olds, twelve-year-olds, and Paulie.

And Braxton brought the binder.

He told his friends he got it as a gift from one of his cousins in Louisiana. It was a regular cloth-covered three-ring loose-leaf binder, but the entire cover sported the design of a Confederate battle flag, the stars and bars. To her surprise, none of her students complained to her, but Sandy felt she should discuss the matter with her chairman, especially since Braxton—who ordinarily did just enough work to pass—turned in a quiz blank and stopped bringing in his homework altogether.

"It's not our business," Tim said when she told him about the binder. His voice was stern. She realized she should have told him first about Braxton's failing work, a far less controversial issue. But she and Marissa had discussed the binder in the teacher's lounge, and Marissa had pledged to go to her chair as well. As Tim spoke, Sandy twisted her Star of David necklace around her index finger. Braxton and his family would call the flag their heritage, she told herself, just as the Star of David was hers. But when did pride in heritage end and the hurting of others begin? Were the stars and bars the same as the swastika? Tim went on, "As offensive as the flag may be, we have no right to infringe on a student's freedom of expression."

He was wrong, Sandy knew. Schoolchildren did not have the same Constitutional rights as adults, and schools had the right to censor. But she didn't want to argue with him, given the students' lack of concern and the generally chaotic state of the class. Instead, she told him about the decline in Braxton's work.

Tim shifted in his chair. "I'm aware of the situation. Mr. Martineau called and asked me to recommend a tutor, but by the time I got back to him, he'd already found one. I suggest you get the tutor's name from Braxton and try to coordinate your efforts so you don't work at cross purposes."

But when Sandy approached Braxton for the tutor's name, he refused to give it to her. "My dad's going to fire her soon anyway."

"I guess she's not doing a good job."

"She sucks. Dad said she's a science major, and she's supposed to tutor me in that subject too." He hesitated. In that instant his boldness seemed to evaporate, and he appeared before her another confused, unsure preadolescent. "She came to the house to get paid. My mom saw she was Black and slapped my dad right across the face."

"In front of the tutor?"

"No. That night at dinner. They had a huge fight."

"How did you feel about that?"

Braxton shrugged. Twice—on the phone and at the parent-teacher meetings—Mr. Martineau had said his wife was ill, and Sandy wondered how ill she could be if they'd fought and she'd hit him. And she remembered also how Braxton's father had criticized her for implying racism on his part when it turned out not to be him but his wife. In her inexperience she'd jumped to conclusions. Maybe Tim was right, and she shouldn't have called parents without his permission. She decided not to mention the binder at all, since it seemed she and Marissa were the only ones who cared.

"Can I go now?" Braxton asked. His defiance had returned; she saw it in the hardness of his stare. His face reddened to a shade not much lighter than his acne.

"Okay. But your father said your mother wasn't feeling well. I hope she's better now."

Braxton looked away and muttered under his breath, "Stay out of my life, okay?" He slid his books into his backpack and stalked out of the room.

* * *

In the three weeks since the break, the student council president, a senior named Kwame Ellsworth, had not returned to school. Now teachers in the lounge whispered the words "Hodgkin's disease." Sandy had never met Kwame, but from the other teachers' descriptions of him, she wished she had.

"You know, he was admitted early to Harvard," one said.

Overheard conversations mentioned other people with the same illness. Cousins. Uncles. Friends. Another high-school student at Shady Ridge several years earlier. Sandy slipped into Tim's office while he was out and pulled from the shelf one of his Shady Ridge directories to look up Kwame's address. The directory was two years out of date, but it didn't matter. She found the address—38 Nightingale Street in Yellow Springs Heights.

Child number four. One adult. Maybe two.

Before the break, before Kwame, she had asked herself what she was going to do about it. Now she had her answer.

Nick. Why had he told her his secret?

Afraid to call him, she had to wait two days until Friday practice. Both nights she woke in the early hours and fantasized about a monster that snatched the lives of children as they slept in their beds. She couldn't get back to sleep again; by morning, her head buzzed and her hands shook. On Friday morning she saw two fresh pimples on her neck. She took off her button-down shirt and replaced it with a turtleneck. The girls in her third-period class had already commented several times on her acne, which had flared up miserably since she'd started teaching.

Somehow she got through the day without flipping out at every little annoyance, from the pop quiz in first period that a third of the students flunked to Braxton waving his binder before class and shouting, "Save your Dixie cups; the South will rise again!"

And then came basketball practice. Her heart was pumping so hard she had to sit on the bleachers to catch her breath. Nick ran the practice in her stead, and when he jogged to the sideline to take a drink from his water bottle, she gasped, "I have to talk to you. Today. It's really, really important."

He looked at her with a mixture of disdain and suspicion. He probably thought she was going to quit because she was doing such a rotten job coaching the team.

"Not today. I've got to take Tony and Chris home, and

it's my night to cook dinner." He squirted some of the water on his head and let it stream down the back of his neck.

She wondered what more she could do to persuade him. He was a parent of a child in her class. He had a wife and another kid too. He had a life.

His case was no different from Braxton's. She had no right to stick herself and her concerns into his life just because he had told her he had cancer. If there was anything she should have been worried about, it was that he'd told her and hadn't even told his own kids, though if she compared Tony, an A student with a small but good circle of friends, with Braxton, a bully who was failing the class, she could understand the wisdom of parents hiding their problems from their children. Regardless of what she had imagined as Nick's reason for telling her, none of this was her business anyway.

Realizing that calmed her down, and she rejoined the practice. She'd almost forgotten her urgent message when Nick dismissed the kids and approached her as she was putting the balls back on the metal rack.

"So what did you want to tell me about?" he asked.

She avoided his eyes. "Nothing important."

"You said 'it's really, really important.' Did I get that quote correct?"

"Yes," she mumbled, her head still lowered.

"Listen, Sandy. I heard you've had a tough time with that class of boys. You're talking to someone with sixteen years of teaching experience. When I started teaching, you were how old?"

"Seven."

"I'm a nine-time winner of a 'teacher of the year' award. I can help you if you want me to."

She looked across the rack at Nick, at his lined face and deep brown eyes. He folded his arms on the row of basketballs and drummed the fingers of his left hand on a ball. She noticed that he had started to unwrap the tape on his wrist but hadn't gotten far. Again, her heart pounded.

Tell him about the four kids and Mrs. Martineau? Or just say I need teaching tips, which I do, big time.

The grotesque kid snatchers, visions of her sleepless nights, blocked out all other thoughts. She opened her mouth to speak, but no words came out at first. Finally, she sputtered, "You live in the Heights, don't you?"

"Yes." He sounded confused. She glanced at the gym door to make sure no kids were there.

She took a deep breath. "Four students at this school from the Heights either had cancer or have it now. The son of my department chair passed away last year."

Nick glanced at the door too, then leaned over the balls until his face was less than a foot from hers.

"All from the Heights?" He almost mouthed the words, but from that close she could hear him clearly. His breath was warm and sweet with a hint of cinnamon.

She nodded. "I looked them all up."

Nick drew back a step and sighed. "Can you meet me tonight at nine?"

"Tell me where."

He gave her directions to a bar named Cliff's near the community college and said, "Can you bring names, ages, addresses, and any other information you have about their illnesses?" As he mentioned them, he ticked off the items on his fingers.

"I'll have them."

On her way out of the gym she passed Tony and Chris, dressed in their school uniforms, their packs hanging from their shoulders by a single strap. Two boys, probably thinking of a weekend of video games and late-night horror movies, innocent of the horror going on all around them. Tony grinned at her with his mouthful of braces and said, "Bye, Miss Katz. See you at the game tomorrow."

"Yeah, see you," his friend added.

"We're going to win tomorrow. I can feel it." Tony said.

Chris let out a snort. "You're crazy. We totally suck."

Tony laid his hand on Chris's free shoulder and looked at him with the same intensity Sandy recognized in his father. "Christopher, dude. You gotta believe."

* * *

All the booths were taken when Sandy arrived at Cliff's at nine, the paper with the four students' names, addresses, and ages tucked in her purse. She scanned the place for Nick but recognized no one. She did notice on the dark paneled walls just above the heads of the bar's graying clientele an exhibit of photos of Cold Springs, taken by students at the community college. Nick showed up ten minutes later. He greeted some people he knew and apologized to Sandy.

"I had to drop Rosie at the movies. It was the only way I could get out without Holly accusing me of going to dig holes in someone's yard," he said.

"Dig holes?" Sandy could understand a wife worried about a possible affair, but holes?

"I'll explain later." As he too surveyed the place for a table, Sandy admired his red shoulder bag. She had seen one like it at the mall in Albany, but it was out of her price range.

Several people scooted over to give Nick a pair of seats at the end of the bar. After ordering two beers, he hung his jacket and Sandy's on a nearby peg and took a spiral notebook and pen out of the shoulder bag.

"Nice bag," she remarked.

"Holly got it for me for Christmas. She thought if she got me something nice, I wouldn't mess it up."

The uncomfortable silence that had characterized their relationship ever since he'd told her his secret descended over them once again. Sandy's eyes were drawn to his black and white checked shirt, which he wore tails out over a black t-shirt, like a college student. When the beers arrived, he drank about a quarter of his tall glass in one gulp and reached for the notebook. "So did you bring the information?"

She handed him the piece of paper. He lifted a pair of reading glasses from his shirt pocket and studied the list. She sipped her beer.

He shifted in his bar stool and locked his eyes on her. A chill passed through her, as if someone on his way out had left the door open. "Okay, here's the deal. Since last summer I've been collecting water samples from the Yellow River and from every house I can get myself into, samples of the soil next to the river, at my own house, and at the house of my best friends, who died a couple of years ago."

"Both of them?" she asked.

He nodded. "From lymphoma. It's a type of cancer." Though she had a basic idea of what it was, he described in clinical detail this more deadly cousin of the Hodgkin's disease that Kwame had contracted. "That boy we talked about before, who drowned in the river in August?"

"Luis Espada?"

"I saw him when they pulled him out of the water, half-eaten by acid. I swiped some of his clothing to be tested and took photos."

Sandy jerked up straight. "His mother said something about acid. When I took the flowers to them."

"What did she say?" He pushed the hair from his face.

"I didn't understand her too well. I thought she referred to the bridge, because it was in pretty bad shape."

"Yeah, and so was his body." He swallowed some more beer. "Then I broke into the abandoned plant and found all kinds of things they were storing there, in leaking and corroding drums. Some of the drums probably washed into the river with the spring floods." He stopped for a moment and took a deep breath. "The point is, Sandy, Yellow Springs Heights is one big fucking toxic waste dump, and I'm going to nail the company that did it."

Sandy's mind shifted to the large new houses, the green lawns now covered by a blanket of pure white snow. She thought of her own neighborhood, where the snowbanks turned gray and garbage-strewn within a day. But the ground beneath her neighborhood was safe, at least as far as she could tell. "Who do you think is responsible?" she asked.

"Hometown Chemical Company. They got bought out less than a year ago for big bucks. They still have a headquarters in Cold Springs, though they moved most of their manufacturing to the Third World, where they can poison their workers and only pay them eleven cents an hour. And if anyone complains there..." He made a gesture as if firing a pistol.

"Global Millennium bought them out, right? They run all the ads..."

He finished her sentence. "How they make the drugs that fight cancer. The cancer they caused in the first place."

"So you knew about the kids all along?"

"Actually, no. Besides my two friends, I know of one other person, a girl who was in my daughter's grade. She died of bone cancer last year. Fifteen years old. She'd been sick for two and a half years."

Nick finished his beer and leaned back on his bar stool, as if trying to find a comfortable position. Then, before Sandy could think of anything helpful to say, he kept on talking. "I don't know where you're from, but the Heights is the kind of suburb where people don't generally talk to their neighbors. And even if they do, we're not the kind of people they'd talk to." He paused and motioned for the bartender. She ordered another beer; he switched to club soda. "Also, a lot of people move in and out, on a two-year cycle. Reduces their exposure, makes them more concerned about the resale value of their house, and keeps the neighborhood from becoming too friendly and cozy. By the way, where *are* you from?"

"Near Albany. A suburb called Delmar."

He pushed his hair back from his face again and leaned over the bar. Trying to tune out the rising noise level, she listened to him describe the working-class community where he grew up. He said that his family was one of a minority of Jewish families in a Catholic area of people of Italian, Irish, and French-Canadian heritage. The close-knit Catholic community revolved around the parish, and the priest always knew who was sick and where they lived and what they had. It made her think of the way that her father used to describe the Albany of his childhood.

Nick tapped his fingers on the bar. "In the Heights, you have people of all religions and lots of people who don't belong to any religious group. The churches and synagogues are scattered throughout the entire Cold Springs area. So where do you get information on people who are sick? Nowhere." He held up the list. "So this is really helpful information. Now if you could just give me details on their illnesses. Anything you can think of." He flipped open his notebook and uncapped his pen.

For the next forty-five minutes she told him everything she knew about the four kids. Dates, to the best of her knowledge, their specific conditions and progress, and how their illnesses affected them and other people around them. She described Andy's psychological problems and Tim's neglect of his work after Kyle's death. Nick listened and filled several pages with his tight angular printing.

"This is great stuff," he told her when she finished. "I'm ready to start the next stage of my research."

"And what's that?"

"Cluster mapping. You know what a cancer cluster is?"

She nodded. Just what she'd found. A lot of people in an area with the same disease.

"If I can get permission from the families or sneak in when they move away and the house is for sale, I'll take soil samples as well. But I have to wait until spring. The ground is too hard now."

"Maybe I can help. You know, get permissions," Sandy offered.

"We'll see. That's a tough one. People in the Heights are

real private, and I've already got the president of the Community Association riding my ass." He returned his glasses to his shirt pocket. "You know him, by the way."

"Who?"

"Marc Martineau."

"Him?" She watched Nick nod, his jaw clenched. "But his wife is sick."

Nick snorted. "You think *she* has cancer?"

"I don't know. He says she's ill, and he has to take care of everything."

"She's an alcoholic."

His words and the way he spoke them made Sandy feel foolish, as if she had wasted her concern on the Martineaus all these months. "Is he in with the chemical company?"

"Not directly. Most of the time things aren't so tidy. He's mainly looking out for the property values. And like a lot of people, he believes giant corporations can do no wrong." Nick finished his club soda and crunched an ice cube between his teeth, all the while staring at her. "I've got to pick Rosie up soon. But there's one other thing I need to know."

"O-kay." There was a hitch of doubt in Sandy's voice. She'd told him everything she knew, and if he wanted more, she didn't think she could help him.

"Why are you doing this? Giving me this information?"

What kind of question is that?

He pressed on. "You don't live in the Heights. It's not your issue."

"I was worried about all those kids who were sick and dying. Not that I go to services regularly or even light candles, but it's part of how I feel I'm Jewish. Ever since my Bat Mitzvah I've always been interested in the idea of *tikkun*."

"*Tikkun olam*. Repair of the world," he said, his words barely audible amid the surrounding conversations. He touched the Star of David that she had intentionally worn outside her sweater as a reminder to her of why she had gone there. "You're talking to a soulless liar, because I was an atheist when I went up for my Bar Mitzvah to profess my faith, and I never set foot in a synagogue again."

"I take it you still don't believe."

He shook his head. She recalled what she had read about bone-marrow transplants at the library over vacation and the words a guest speaker at her youth group had once suggested they use when someone told them a sad story. The words she should have used when Nick told her his story at the park. *I'm sorry you had to go through this.* It amazed her that he appeared so strong, so physically whole, after the devastation he must have endured. *Nobody should have to experience what you've been through.* She heard herself say those words out loud, above the din all around her.

Nick dropped his notebook and pen into his shoulder bag. "Yeah, nobody should. Especially those kids." He threw a ten on the bar and reached for their jackets. "But don't do this because you feel sorry for me. Understand?"

* * *

In keeping with her promise to Nick, Sandy tried to treat Tony like any other student, but she often found it hard to look at him directly. He seemed not to notice and continued to participate in class with his usual enthusiasm, which attracted the derision of Braxton and his fellow bullies. One day at the end of January, Tony appeared in her classroom at the beginning of the middle-school lunch period, which was her lunch period as well. He slid into his desk chair and dropped his red backpack on the floor with a thud. She noticed a new Rage Against the Machine patch ironed on the front.

"Miss Katz, may I use your classroom this period to do my math homework?"

Again, she tried to avoid his gaze. "Don't you have lunch?"

"Yeah, but Mrs. C. said if I miss another homework assignment, I'm screwed." He paused, his expression sheepish. "Well, she didn't exactly say it that way. But you get the idea."

"Okay."

Tony dug his binder and math book out of his backpack, which still appeared stuffed. He arranged the two books neatly on the desk but didn't open them.

"Don't you get lunch this period too?" he asked in his awkward manner.

"Yes." There was the hint of a question in her voice.

"Why do the teachers buy their lunch in the cafeteria but then don't eat there?"

"We usually eat in the teachers' lounge with the other teachers. When you're with kids most of the day, you like to spend time with other adults." Were he not Nick's boy, she realized, she probably would not have told him this.

"Is there a soda machine in the teachers' lounge?"

All his talk was starting to make her hungry. She took her brown bag lunch from the desk drawer and gathered her books. Tony still smiled as he waited for her answer.

"Yes, there is." She hesitated, not knowing the school rules on this one. "Do you want me to get you a soda?"

He pulled a brown paper bag out of his backpack. "No, I got one here. I just wanted to know."

She warned him not to spill anything and left him alone in her classroom.

Half an hour later, she heard a commotion outside the teachers' lounge. The first thing she recognized was Tony's voice. "I gotta hide. He's going to kick my ass."

She rushed to the door, along with a half dozen other teachers in the lounge. Tony waved Braxton's binder in the air. Braxton stood ten feet away, his face bright red and his fists clenched.

"Here, take this." Tony handed Sandy the binder and

crouched in a defensive stance she recognized from her brothers' tae kwon do classes.

"Okay, okay, what's going on here?" Tim rushed down the stairs into the hallway where the two boys faced off.

Without taking his eyes from his adversary, Tony spoke first. "Mr. Brownfield, he's going to beat me up. He's been bothering me all year, and now he's going to kill me. Look at him."

Braxton still had the mad bull look. He began to sputter, "He took my notebook, and…"

At that moment, the teachers around Sandy began to laugh. She glanced down at the binder and saw why. She also understood why Tony's backpack had been so full and why he had been so eager for her to go to lunch.

He had used a blue marking pen to fill in the thirteen white stars on the crossed bars. Then, with typewriter correction fluid and most likely a stencil because the letters were so neatly printed, he had written in the place of the stars, beginning with the bottom left bar, "I AM," "RACIST," "WHITE," and "TRASH" for each of the four quadrants.

"This is great," someone behind her whispered.

Tim stalked into the lounge; the two boys trailed him. "What's this about a notebook?"

Braxton was still smoldering. And stammering. "M-my b-binder. He wrote on it and showed it to everyone at lunch."

"Mr. Baran, what do you have to say?" Tim glanced around the lounge for the binder, but one of the other teachers had spirited it away.

Sandy expected Tony to wither in the face of authority, but he stood straight and looked the chairman in the eye. "I'm sorry it had to come to this, Mr. Brownfield, but that binder was offensive. Braxton was sticking it in Chris Leighton's face all the time, and nobody did anything."

"Where is this binder anyway?" Tim asked.

All the teachers shrugged. The bell rang, and Tim sent Tony and Braxton to class. "I'll get to the bottom of this." He turned to Sandy. "If you'd kept your class in line, Miss Katz, none of this would have happened."

Tim's words crushed her. Because he was seldom around when she needed his help. Because Braxton had brought the binder to all his classes, not just hers. Because no adult had done anything about the binder, leaving a twelve-year-old kid to take matters into his own hands. Because Tony hadn't defaced Braxton's binder during her class but rather swiped it during gym class and altered it during lunch.

Because, at the bottom of it, Tim was right. Had she put a stop to the bullying the first week of class, none of this would have happened.

She expected Braxton's father to complain about her and Tony to get suspended for destroying another student's property. To her surprise, neither of these took place. Tim never saw Tony's handiwork and therefore couldn't punish him. In short, no evidence, no crime. The ninth grade social studies teacher took the binder home to add to his private collection. He told the other teachers he planned to give Tony an automatic A-plus in his class in two years.

Even more surprising, Mr. Martineau never complained. Braxton returned to school the next day with a plain binder. Sandy overheard him telling one of his friends that his father said it was his own fault for bringing in something so important to him and not keeping track of it.

But Sandy had to say something, if only to let Tim know she didn't condone the destruction of property and was taking action to resolve the discipline problems in her class. So she mentioned the incident to Nick after Friday basketball practice.

"We talked about it before he did it. How did it look?" Nick grinned.

"You jerk," she whispered under her breath. She dropped her arms to her sides in frustration and added, louder, "You almost got me fired." Her words echoed in the gym.

"You didn't have anything to do with it."

"But they blamed me anyway. Tim Brownfield said none of this would have happened if I'd kept my class in line."

Tony appeared at the gym door and called for his dad. Nick twisted around. "Tony, can you wait in the locker room a minute? I need to talk with Miss Katz," he said sharply. Tony scurried off. Nick reached into his gym bag for his water bottle and towel. "Brownfield. Isn't he the one who lost his little boy last year?"

"Yes. He's Kyle's father."

"That's rough." He stood, the towel around his neck, and took a long drink. Then he wiped his face and said, "We've got to talk about that teaching situation, though. You're dying out there. You know it. I know it. The kids know it." He sprayed the top of his head and shook the water from his hair like a dog. Droplets clung to the ends, making it appear as if he had gone completely gray. His voice softened. "I hope you don't mind my being so blunt."

Sandy's lower lip trembled. She bit it to keep it steady. "What are you going to do? Come to my class?" she blurted out. Tim had already been to her class once. The kids behaved perfectly that day, and shocked, she finished her lesson in half an hour, which left her to improvise a review session for the final twenty minutes.

"No, but I'm inviting you to my class."

"You teach college. How's that going to help?"

"I teach history. I get the students involved. You really ought to see." He drank the rest of the water and threw the bottle and towel back into his bag. In white lettering along the side of the small red duffel were the words "Property of Springs Regional Community College Athletic Department."

"How's February break? I have some free time then," she answered after a while.

"Sounds good. We're not off that week." He zipped up the bag. As he started to leave, he stopped and turned toward her. "On another subject, Sandy, we got a notice that they closed the well for the western half of Yellow Springs Heights as of January third."

"So you were right!"

"They didn't give a reason. But our buddy Martineau called me up and accused me of all kinds of terrible things. Communism, Satanism, you name it.

"But don't they want safer water?"

"Not if their rates go up. And get this." He backed toward the door and pointed at her. "I didn't even report it. The Feds did it on their own."

Thirteen: Otherside

Nicholas didn't tell Sandy what else Marc Martineau said after the Feds shut the well down: "I'm going to fuck you over so badly you'll be sorry you ever started this."

I'd love to see you try, Nicholas wanted to say. But he had never heard Marc use profanity before, and that worried him. Marc was a dignified sort, a Southern gentleman who kept his hands and his language clean. Not some undersized, undersocialized trailer rat with a list of scores to settle.

A restraining order came to mind. Or a lawsuit. But Marc couldn't do either of those alone, in spite of being one of the most powerful attorneys in the area. The Community Association had no money for legal fees, because no one ever paid the annual dues. If Marc convinced the lawyers from the chemical company to take action, the damage would be done because the press would be all over the story. With the lab results, the shut-down well, and the pictures of the drowned boy, Nicholas already had enough information to make the front page of the local paper for at least a couple of days. If he got lucky, a muckraking journalist would take it from there.

He had nothing to fear.

Holly had arranged a trip to Minnesota with the kids for the vacation, and he had accepted an invitation to speak at a teaching workshop in New York City over the Presidents' Day weekend. He looked forward to seeing old friends and returning to help Sandy. She had helped him with the information on the kids; it was the least he could do for her. And although he didn't say it, he felt guilty that Tony's action against the bully Braxton, which they'd plotted together, could have cost Sandy her job.

He drove back to Cold Springs on Monday evening weary and suffering from a monster headache. He didn't have the tolerance for liquor he used to have, and it had caught up with him. He'd stayed awake most of two nights talking and drinking, reconnecting with the friends who'd shared their lives and stories through graduate school and those early, vulnerable years as junior faculty, before lost tenure decisions scattered them up and down the East Coast. The Radical Diaspora, he called it. About half of them had been forced out of academia and now taught high school.

He yawned and dug into the storage compartment between the two front seats in search of a CD to keep himself awake. He had turned the heat off in Holly's silver station wagon because the Volvo's efficient heating system would have lulled him to sleep. He pulled out a jewel case expecting jazz or maybe earnest rock like U2 or R.E.M.

Michael Doucet and Beausoleil. What is this shit? He glanced back and forth from the CD case to the road. He first thought bluegrass—a lot of guys with guitars, fiddles, a banjo, and an accordion, and leafy trees all around. He shoved the CD into the slot and vaguely familiar music filled the station wagon. It occurred to him that this was the Cajun group they sometimes played between segments on "Prairie Home Companion," which should have been Holly's favorite nostalgia program except he listened to it more than she did. But when did she suddenly become a fan of Cajun music?

The fiddle's whine made his head pound even harder, and he pressed the eject button. Where was Miles Davis when he needed him? Holly had left none of their jazz CDs in the car, but he drew yet another Beausoleil along with the U2s and a Lilith Fair. That concerned him because she always planted the Lilith Fair when she was mad at him about something.

Okay, I'm an insensitive prick, so what's new? He wished she'd just come out and tell him rather than leaving these encoded messages. Even on a good day he had trouble deciphering the code. He felt bewildered when dealing with women's emotions and what they expected of him; maybe not having a mother had left him this way. And today wasn't a good day. His raw, unmedicated pain coupled with his exhaustion made it impossible for him to think straight.

Arriving home, he unpacked, threw his dirty clothes into the washing machine, and fixed himself a bowl of corn flakes, something easy that his depleted system could handle. He could go to bed early and sleep all morning; he didn't teach a class until three in the afternoon.

The phone rang. It was Holly. She asked him how the conference had gone.

"Great." He told her about their old friends from New York, what had happened to them. He'd been fortunate in comparison to most of them even though he hadn't become the bigshot Ivy League professor she'd hoped. He had to make her see that. "How's Minnesota?"

"Cold."

"It's cold here too. Kids having a good time?"

"Rosie's been out with her cousins and their friends every night."

"And Tony?"

"He misses you."

"Let me talk to him."

Tony came on the line. He asked if any of his friends had called while he was away.

Nicholas checked the list of messages he had written down. He read off the names of several boys from the team. "And a girl. Megan Kiefer?"

"Yes!" Tony hesitated, then said, "It's not what you think, Dad. She's just a friend." Nicholas noticed a harsh edge to Tony's voice, more easily distinguished over the phone without the distractions. The change had begun, and within a year the kid would look and sound like a man, even though he had such a long way to go.

"Are you having fun out there?"

"Not really. I wanted to hang out with my friends at home. But Mom's taking us to the mall tomorrow. At least

I'll get something out of this trip." So the kid didn't miss him; he missed his friends. But a year ago, Tony wouldn't have missed anyone, and Nicholas knew he should have been grateful for that.

Afterward, Nicholas called Sandy. He gave her directions to his office and told her to meet him at five thirty the next day, an hour before his evening class. He wanted her to see the evening class because he found keeping students awake and interested after a day of work to be the ultimate challenge.

"Should we go somewhere for dinner afterward?" she asked.

"Sure. I know some decent places near the college that aren't too expensive. By the way, if your boyfriend's around, have him come too." He hadn't heard her mention her boyfriend, who played for the softball team, except that he'd also lost his scholarship. Maybe like Sandy, he'd found some other job in the area.

"Boyfriend?"

"That guy on the team. You two were a couple, weren't you?"

"We broke up at the end of the summer. He went back to Chicago and applied to law school."

"That's a shame." Nicholas thought of those few friends who enrolled in law school when they couldn't find jobs or didn't get tenure. They all ended up on the corporate side; not a single one he could turn to for a class-action suit. As long as I'm doing work I hate I might as well take the money, one of them had explained. "We already have enough lawyers," Nicholas told Sandy. "What we need are good teachers." She agreed, and he hoped he could make her one of them.

* * *

Nicholas awoke refreshed the next morning, his headache gone, but the silence and emptiness of the house disturbed him. Twenty-one years of marriage and two kids had spoiled him, he who had spent so many years of his youth in solitude. He opened the window shades to let in the weak winter sunlight. The light glinted off the jewelry Holly had left on her dresser in her haste. He remembered how she couldn't decide what to take and Rosie picking through the remains. There seemed to be a lot more jewelry lying around; Holly had done some shopping recently, he guessed. He picked up a pair of earrings with diamonds and some green stones. Emeralds. The bright red stones in one of her necklaces were rubies, and the darker reds garnets. Garnet was Holly's birthstone. He knew that because he bought her a wedding ring made of garnets. He couldn't afford diamonds, and, besides, when they got married back in the late 1970s they were boycotting South African goods. He'd bought her diamond earrings nine years ago after the end of apartheid, and he didn't find them on her dresser. She must have taken those, he thought, smiling. He searched through her jewelry box, lined the pieces up by stones, and tried to identify all of them, as if taking a quiz in earth science.

When he was done—with about a C-minus in precious stone identification—he dropped the pieces back into the box, but they no longer fit. He picked up the box to shake them down, and he noticed an envelope with a rip at the top and Holly's name on the front. He slipped a card out. It had a picture of a flower, imitation Mapplethorpe. He opened it and read:

To Holly, my rare jewel. Love, Marc.

He read the message again. His hand trembled, and then the trembling seized the rest of his body. He broke out into a sweat that chilled him in the next moment. The note explained it all. The Cajun CDs. The extra jewelry. Marc's words replayed in his mind: *I'm going to fuck you over so badly you'll be sorry you ever started this*. He'd never expected Marc to mean it literally.

He wanted to call Holly but he knew her mother would

answer and he would explode. He wanted to smash the dresser or punch the wall but a broken hand wouldn't do. He had to teach. The lesson called for his students to be thinking about Gramsci's hands, not their teacher's.

He clenched his right fist and pounded the fleshy part against the wall in a tense rhythm, tried to count to ten and regain control of himself so he wouldn't bust everything up. He couldn't get beyond the count of seven before visions of Marc humping Holly and thoughts of blind destruction intruded and he had to start over again. He had awakened hungry but his stomach was now in a tight knot, and the idea of food revolted him. His genitals burned the exact way they'd burned from the radiation to his testicles before his transplant, which left him sterile but far from impotent.

He pulled on a sweatshirt and sweatpants, laced his sneakers, yanked a wool cap over his head, and left the house without locking the door. He grabbed the two Beausoleil CDs from Holly's car and threw them into the garbage can.

In the fifteen degrees of a February morning he ran. He ran the way he'd run as an angry teenager—straight ahead and at full speed, with no thought of the cold or where he was going, until he collapsed breathless on the ground, doubled over with dry heaves, then he picked himself up and ran some more. He'd built up such endurance in those days he could have run all the way from Worcester to Boston and he'd gotten himself ranked in the top ten in Massachusetts in boys' cross-country.

He ran two miles up to the North Springs Bridge and turned right. He passed the spot where Luis had fallen into the river, where the low guardrail was rusted and split and a little boy could have slipped through. On the Cold Springs side he wove between the passing cars and the snowbanks until he found himself at the intersection of the two-lane road that led to the abandoned chemical plant.

Someone had plowed the pot-holed asphalt. *What's the point of plowing a road that leads to nothing?* His breath grew tense and labored as he pushed himself in the direction of the hulking red brick factory with weathered plywood nailed to the windows, a monster that rose above the snow.

They were still bringing in drums. As the old ones disintegrated and leached into the river, new ones took their place. It had snowed three days earlier, and as he approached the factory grounds he saw puffy white mounds atop most of the drums and some with no snow at all, brought in, he guessed, within the past forty-eight hours.

He ran toward the fence, stumbled over chunks of ice churned up by the plow, and dropped to his knees in the snow. His bare fingers clung to the chain links. The enemy was massive and ugly. Dark red like blood. Pink like Marc Martineau's face. Littered with fifty-five-gallon cylinders that lay amid the brush and snowdrifts, each one a bomb that contained its own deadly poison. He imagined Marc entering Holly, contaminating her with the filth of every other woman he had slept with. His vision clouded over; in his parched mouth he tasted bile. His heart thrashed against his ribs and sent waves of pain down his left arm. The dumpsite spun around him. He felt his fingers weaken, and he willed them to hang onto the cold metal, to hold him upright until the dizziness left him.

The shut-down chemical company reeked of decay. The smell took him back to his father's scrap yard in the years before the old man died. The yard was killing him, his father used to say, and Nicholas would tell him he ought to give it up if he felt that way.

* * *

Everything was killing Sam Baran. Widowhood. His rotten kid. His ungrateful other kid, who never called from California for months at a time. The scrap yard. Life. Chronic depression made it difficult for him to get out of bed in the morning and to see an alternative to the routine he detested.

Nicholas considered it his duty to give life to the business. Alone in the office he played acid rock until the windows shook. He made up stories about the cars and the places they'd been and the unplanned children conceived in their back seats. He gave unauthorized discounts on parts to his neighbors who took him in as if he were their own grandchild, fed him breakfast, taught him to play chess, and turned him on to *The Daily Worker*. Old socialists had ratty cars that broke down all the time and needed spare parts. The old men and their wives taught him to live in society, to live with himself, to control his anger, and not to let his pain control him. He came to them a feral child and they tamed him, one of them remarked, to which he responded, "I wasn't feral, only a stray. If I'd knocked up another stray, our kids would have been feral."

The summer after his senior year in high school he worked at the scrap yard by himself almost every day. His father seemed more serious than usual about selling it—he said he needed the money to pay the college tuition—but no one came forward to buy it. Three weeks before he was supposed to leave for college, Nicholas came home from closing the office for the night to find his father passed out on the floor next to a spilled bottle of scotch and an empty container of sleeping pills.

For the second time in his life, Nicholas dialed the rescue squad. At the hospital the doctor put an arm around his shoulder as if he were a little kid and praised him for his courage and clear thinking. And Nicholas did not say aloud the words running through his head: *My dad pulls this shit, and in three weeks he's going to turn someone like me loose on the world*.

Two summers later, Sam Baran sold the scrap yard to a developer who shut it down the next day. And at the beginning of Nicholas's junior year, he finally got the fatal pills-and-booze combination right because there was no one at home to stop him. Nicholas told his friends and professors his father died of a heart attack. He told Holly the same thing when he started going out with her a year and a half later, and he never bothered to amend the story once they married. Sometimes he caught himself believing his own lie. He could believe it because it always astounded him how someone as damaged as himself could marry, have children, raise his own children, hold a job, and keep his marriage more or less intact, at least until this day.

* * *

For two hours Nicholas ran. Upon returning to his deserted house shortly after noon he stripped off his clothes that were soaked with sweat and snow. He forced himself to drink a glass of juice and went upstairs to shave and shower. He dressed by the steamy bathroom mirror to avoid the place where he had discovered Holly's secret. He would have to confront her with the evidence when she called that night. He could not predict what would happen afterward.

But he had to compartmentalize, erase from his mind what he had found, because he had two classes to teach and Sandy observing him. As he put on his pants and dress shirt, tied his tie, and combed his hair, his lesson coalesced in his mind. He stared at his hands and rehearsed the culmination of his lesson. He wiped the mirror clean with a bath towel. His throat was sore, his stomach still churned, and his chest, ribs, knees, and calves ached. He felt completely broken inside, but he looked all right. His classes would be brilliant.

Fourteen: Teaching Lessons

In her twenty-three years, Sandy believed she had learned a few things about the world and people in it, and one thing she'd learned was that those who bragged the most often had the least to show for it. Enough of her rivals in softball and basketball—those on her own team as well as opponents— substituted boasting for hard work while she preferred to say nothing and let her game speak for her.

Still, she didn't doubt Nick, and she trusted that his class would prove the exception to her rule, even if she didn't know what to expect. She had considered asking Monique to contact one of her sisters for a sneak preview, but Monique and Kenny, like her landlords' boys, stayed indoors during these cold, dark, depressing days. She hated the way friendships withered in the winter, but she felt too drained and burdened with work to call or drop in. And now that Nick had started talking to her again, she didn't feel as starved for adult company.

Nick had invited her to a Tuesday evening class and given her directions to meet him at his office at five thirty. Almost two months after the shortest day of the year, the overcast sky had already begun to transform to dusk as she parked her car outside the drab yellow-brick administration building.

To her left was the humanities building. It was the same design but three stories instead of two. Just outside the glass door, Nick stood under a weak orange light, his hands in the pockets of his unzipped down jacket. Underneath, he wore a coat and tie, with a pressed shirt and pants. It surprised Sandy to see him in something besides the sweatshirt and sweatpants he wore to practice and games, or the casual clothes she saw him in at Cliff's. He looked as if he'd stepped outside for a cigarette, though she didn't think he smoked. She asked him anyway.

"I needed some air after class." He shivered. "I can show you around a bit if you want."

His face seemed oddly grim, his thin lips pressed together. She suggested that he zip up his jacket.

"Yeah," he mumbled as though the idea had never occurred to him. He struggled with the zipper of the faded and tattered jacket.

He took her along the shoveled walkway through a campus that looked like the grounds of a factory. He pointed out the business and science buildings, identical siblings of the humanities building, and the gymnasium that bordered College Park Field, where she'd collided with him months before she'd gotten to know him.

The inside of the humanities building was as unadorned as the outside, but the dim lighting made it appear even sparer. Sandy attributed the low-wattage bulbs to budget cuts. As she imagined Monique and her two sisters walking these corridors, she contrasted the Spartan conditions endured by the community college students with the luxury enjoyed by her students at Shady Ridge. But the students she knew at the college seemed so serious, so proud of their accomplishments, while those at her own school took their privilege for granted.

Nick, more cheerful by this time, pointed out the various departments on his way up the stairs to the third floor. They passed the elevator. She didn't bother asking if it worked. She guessed Nick liked the exercise and didn't have the patience to wait for a slow elevator anyway. As they continued toward his office, teachers and students slapped his hand or paused to say a few words, but he didn't introduce her to them.

His office door was open. He plucked from the floor what looked like a note attached to a flyer, then hung his jacket on a peg attached to the back of the door and motioned for her to enter. He stood in the middle of the room, reading the papers.

Nick's office looked like the kind of place where people spent a lot of time hanging out. He had covered most of the grimy gray tile floor with a multicolored rag rug. Against the wall was a beige cotton canvas sofa that sat between the door and a tall black file cabinet. An old camp trunk in front of the sofa still bore his name in small white stenciled letters and a partially worn-off street address. Across the room from the sofa, below a bank of windows, was a long dark-stained plywood desk supported by file cabinets and a small refrigerator. Sandy noted the collection of Boston Red Sox mugs and the large family photo.

Nick's bookshelves were filled not only with books about European history but also with works of literature, world history, U.S. history, and current events. The shelf next to his desk held four trophies, all from the softball league. She drifted over for a closer look. Alongside the trophies were photos of various incarnations of the Ship Rats.

She examined the posters on the walls. Most were prints of paintings from museums in Europe, and others depicted subjects in European history. The largest was a print of Jacques-Louis David's "The Death of Marat," showing the French revolutionary leader stabbed and bleeding to death in a bathtub. And taped to the side of the file cabinet next to the sofa was a reserved-parking sign for Red Sox fans only.

She hung her jacket next to Nick's. He dropped the papers on his desk and offered her a seat on the sofa. The daughter of New York Yankees fanatics, she asked, "You aren't going to tow me if I sit here?"

Nick flipped his desk chair around to face her and sat. "Did you bring a notebook?"

"No."

He yanked a couple of sheets of paper from his printer and handed them to her along with a pencil. "Okay, principle number one. Dress appropriately. It shows respect for your students." He straightened his tie. She glanced down at her frayed jeans and began to write.

"Principle number two." He checked his watch. "Arrive early, before the students. That way, you have time to organize your materials, set up your classroom, and greet your students as they come in." He waited to let her finish. She thought about the mayhem that occurred in her classroom every morning before she even arrived. "Always greet your students by name. Let them know you care about them and their lives. Got it?"

She nodded.

"Principle number three. Have your materials organized, whatever they are. Teaching is a performance. You're the director, lead actor, *and* stage manager."

He checked his watch again. "Principle number four. And this will be the last one until after class because I have to get ready." He leaned forward. "Absolute concentration. It's just you, the students, the classroom, and the lesson. Nothing else." He swept his right hand in an arc as he spoke. "Whatever other shit is going on in your life, do not bring it into class." He detached his gaze from her and stood. "Now if you can just step outside for a minute, I need to get ready."

Sandy watched from the hallway while he gathered his books, his notes, and the water bottle that he seemed to carry everywhere. For a long moment, he stared out the window into the darkness. Though his back was turned, she could see his slender shoulders rise and fall with his deep breaths. Then he strode quickly down the hall to the classroom. She eased into a jog to keep up with him. "What's this class?" she asked.

"Twentieth-century European history," he shot back. "Today, the rise of fascism in Italy."

Before the students trickled in, Nick wrote on the board the homework assignments for the following two weeks and the date of the next test. As he'd suggested, he greeted each student as he or she came through the door. By six thirty, all the students were seated, notebooks open and pens ready. Nick stood in front of the class, looking trim in his coat, tie, and slacks. Sandy's eyes paused on the firm, tight center of his body from where he seemed to draw his energy. He had not an ounce of fat on him, she observed, and, even in the classroom wearing his nice clothes, he looked like a runner getting ready for a big race.

Nick shed his coat and draped it over a chair in the corner of the room. "All right, who's going to set the scene for me?" he called out. A dozen hands rose into the air. "Raúl." The student named Raúl described Italy's loss in the First World War and the collapse of the country's economy.

"Everyone blamed each other," a young woman named Crystal added.

Seated on the edge of the desk, Nick leaned forward and gazed at each of the students who responded. "Yeah, that's what usually happens when things go wrong. So who blamed who and why?" He slid off the desk and walked up and down the rows, calling out names. As students raised their hands and answered, Sandy studied the class—a diverse group ranging in age from teenagers to seniors. From their enthusiastic participation and the depth of their answers, she could tell they had done their homework. Throughout the lesson, Nick stopped to make eye contact with individual students when they spoke or he made a key point. Sandy recalled the modern European history course she had taken in college with a professor who'd stood behind a podium and read from tattered notes, but Nick's voice kept pulling her back to him as if in this class of forty students plus one he was addressing her directly. *A great teacher can do that, stand before a group and make it seem as though he's speaking only to you.* She realized all along she had been speaking to no one in her classes—looking down, glancing from student to student, avoiding their eyes.

Nick taught as if possessed with perfect faith in his students, himself, and his lesson. His words flowed in rapid succession; his voice changed to express every nuance of his story. When he detailed the chaos in Italy following the First World War, he made it seem as though chaos reigned just outside the classroom door and they could hear the Blackshirts marching. His mesmerized audience came to understand why the terrorized people turned to the fascists, their tormentors, for protection, just as many of Sandy's own students stuck to the bullies to avoid becoming their victims. And finally, they heard of the courageous but doomed resistance of the social democrats and communists, many of whom were assassinated or found themselves rotting away in Mussolini's squalid prisons.

Nick paused for a moment. He stared at his shoes, his hands in his pockets, his shoulders hunched. For a second, he appeared even smaller—frail, lost, and alone. He raised his head to face the class. "One of those who resisted the rise of fascism was a personal hero of mine, Antonio Gramsci." He wrote the name on the board. "This giant of the political scene stood less than five feet tall. I would have looked tall standing next to him." Sandy and several of the students laughed. "Like you and me, he grew up in a working-class family and struggled against all kinds of odds to get an education." He described Gramsci's frail health, his tireless work as a journalist and political theorist, his eleven years in prison separated from family and comrades, the international campaign to win his release, and his death just one week after attaining his freedom.

Nick continued. "Eleven years he spent in prison, serving what amounted to a death sentence. Eleven years without seeing his two children grow up. Eleven years with no one to talk to except his jailers. Imagine it. What would you do?" Nick waited for his words to sink in. "Now imagine every organ in his fragile body slowly deteriorating from the filthy conditions, rotten food, and lack of medical attention."

Nick held out his hands for the class to see. Sandy realized how tiny his hands were compared to those of his students. She focused on the pale scar across the top of his left wrist, the only visible sign of the devastation he had endured. "He suffered an almost unbearable burning in his hands and lost much of the use of them. But despite this, he managed to fill thirty-three notebooks, almost three thousand pages in his tiny handwriting, with brilliant political theory and discussions of literature and culture that can guide us today in our struggle for justice."

As he finished his story with a summary of Gramsci's ideas, it struck Sandy how thoroughly Nick had transformed himself into the quixotic Italian communist, his own lonely crusade against Hometown Chemical Company perhaps left at the classroom door but providing the fuel for an explosive dramatization. Sandy had read Gramsci in college, before she was expected to forget those useless and unfashionable theories and pursue a lucrative career. Nick's lesson reminded her why, for instance, Marc Martineau could do the chemical company's enforcing when nobody paid him. Why everyone else in Yellow Springs Heights despised Nick for taking a stand to protect them. Why people everywhere supported powerful corporations or governments that deceived and harmed them and in this way consented to their own oppression. And when Nick held his arms outstretched and said quietly, "I'm done. See you Thursday night," the class of forty students and she, too, applauded.

After the last of the students left, he dropped into a chair and closed his eyes. His hair fell onto his forehead, which was beaded with perspiration. A moment later he sat up straight. "Okay. Let's get out of here," he said.

Walking back to Nick's office, Sandy asked him, "How many times a week do you do this?"

"Ten. Twelve. Depending on my schedule."

"Where did you learn to teach like this?"

"Basically, I taught myself." He unlocked his office door, and she followed him inside. "In college, when I decided I wanted to teach at that level, I started watching my professors to see what worked and what didn't. I also did a lot of public speaking back then."

"Like debates?"

Nick grinned. "Not exactly. More like demonstrations, marches, and sit-ins." He went on to describe the various protests he had led, and she thought of the marches against sweatshops that she and Mitch had attended in college and graduate school. She was about to tell Nick how they'd signed a pledge not to buy certain athletic labels when he switched the subject back to teaching. "Do you have your notes?" he asked.

Embarrassed, she picked up the paper and pencil he had given her. He frowned.

"Make sure your students are prepared." He leaned against his long desk. "As you saw, my lesson had a structure. The discussion we had for the first hour was based on their homework assignment. Their job is to read their textbook and to come to class ready to talk about it. My job is to make the reading come alive by evoking the setting, the events, and the people."

She sat on the edge of the sofa and wrote down the two additional points.

"Finally, you get to the essence of history—the story. Have you ever heard a good storyteller?"

"We used to have them in elementary school. And at the public library."

Nick shook his head, probably thinking this graduate of Cornell had less sense than a first-year community-college student.

"If your students aren't paying attention, it's because you're teaching history as a dry collection of facts and dates. Tell the story and tell it well, in the language of the students' lives." He clenched his fist. "Hit them with the emotion, the drama. Don't be afraid to use words that are vivid and powerful." He waited again for her to finish writing. "Do you ever read literature? Poetry?"

"No." She wondered when, between teaching, coaching, and worrying about her job, she'd ever have time to read.

"I'll send you a reading list. Forget about the textbooks.

The writers are the real historians." He tossed her jacket to her. "My goal one of these days, if I'm still alive, is to teach a class in literature."

And at that moment she wanted to be the first to sign up.

* * *

Sandy and Nick had arranged to eat dinner together that night, but he backed out, saying he had to get home for his wife's phone call from Minnesota. He invited Sandy to come to some of his other classes that week, and she left his office feeling like a slow learner who needed to attend every single one.

His first class the next day started at ten. Sandy set her alarm for eight thirty but turned it off and went back to sleep, figuring she could make his eleven o'clock class and another half dozen after that. She awoke again after ten and wondered what had happened to her sense of urgency of the night before. She quickly dressed and drove to the college. Finding the lot full, she parked on the street next to the ball fields and followed the ski tracks that crossed the sprawling snow-covered fields. She found the humanities building and took the stairs to the third floor.

Nick's office was locked, and in the classroom where he'd taught the night before a bearded professor with glasses was sitting on the teacher's desk and lecturing to a room of bored-looking students. She peered through the little windows in the doors of the other classrooms and spied Nick at the end of the hall. As energetic as always, he was working his magic on another group.

A few minutes before noon the class ended. She waited for the students to file out and tried to catch snatches of their conversations as they left. Nick stopped short when he saw her, a look of surprise on his face.

"Come back for more?" He gave her a crooked smile. His lips were dry and cracked, and she noticed dark circles under his eyes. "I have another class at one-thirty if you want to wait."

"Thanks." She walked with him to his office. Inside, he dropped his notes on the trunk, tossed his coat on his desk chair, and fell back onto the sofa with a deep groan.

"I'm supposed to meet a friend for lunch, but I'm really not up to it. Some twenty-four-hour thing, hope you don't catch it."

She hung his coat on the back of the chair so it wouldn't get wrinkled. Maybe he hadn't been feeling well the night before and used his wife's call as an excuse to get out of dinner. She imagined the dire possibilities, and her throat ached from worry.

She heard a knock on the open door, and a tall, bearded, well-built man in his late thirties strolled in. He wore a gold hoop earring and his dark blond hair in a ponytail, along with jeans and a sweatshirt from a company that made snowboards. He surveyed Nick lying on the sofa.

"What's with you? You look awful."

"Upset stomach." Nick lifted his right arm and clasped his friend's hand in greeting.

The man with the ponytail turned to Sandy. "Haven't I seen you somewhere before?"

Nick pulled himself upright. He introduced her, recited her accomplishments in the infield, then added, "Sandy, this is Rich Rankin. He teaches organic chemistry here. You probably know him as Beanball."

She nodded. On the mound, the guy was known to send the hardiest of batters running for cover.

"So what are you doing, hanging with a member of the opposition?" Rich winked at her. "Okay, let me guess. She's helping you play the field."

"Tony's in her class at Shady Ridge. It's her first year, and I was giving her pointers on how to teach." Nick sagged back on the sofa and closed his eyes.

Rich paced the rug. "Now how does that line go? Those

who do, do; those who can't, teach; those who..." He waved his hand. "Forget it. You don't even make that joke around Nick Baran. The dude's a freaking legend around here."

She smiled. "I observed his class last night. It was awesome."

Rich scanned the office. He snatched a bag of gingersnaps from the corner of Nick's desk and offered her one. She shook her head and thanked him. He shoved two into his mouth, one after the other, and flipped the bag back onto the desk.

"You want to get a sandwich?" he asked her after finishing the cookies. "I can show you how to teach, too. You know, give you a different perspective."

She glanced toward Nick for a signal that he wanted her to go. Or stay. He lay still, his eyes closed.

"I've seen him like this before. He won't be much for conversation," Rich said.

But lunch with Beanball wasn't the reason she'd come. "Maybe another time."

He looked disappointed. "Okay. See you opening day." He said good-bye to Nick and left.

Would Nick say she should have gone too? She leaned against his desk; her hands trembled behind her back.

But the first thing he said was, "Don't ever show up to class looking like Rich. Nobody will take you seriously."

"I understand." She hesitated. "Is there anything I can do for you?"

He asked her to fill his water bottle and make some tea. She opened his compact refrigerator to look for bottled water, which she'd been using ever since he'd told her about the contaminated water samples. "You can use the regular tap water," he said. "Cold Springs water is from reservoirs up in the mountains. It's safe. It's these little towns and suburbs, each with their own wells, that you have to worry about."

When she returned, he told her to close the door. He drank some of the water and leaned back. His head rested against the bottom edge of the reserved parking sign. "Yesterday morning I found a note to Holly from Marc Martineau and some jewelry he had given her. I confronted her over the phone." He shook his head. "She told me that she and he have been screwing each other ever since the neighborhood Christmas party."

Sandy sucked in her breath. *Why are you telling me this? I'd thought better of Holly. And of all people, to be having an affair with him?* Sandy wondered if Marc had given Holly the earrings she'd worn on Parents' Day. Then she thought of the other strange things she had noticed over the past weeks. Braxton revealing how his mother had struck his father. Braxton's father not complaining when Tony defaced the binder. Nick's grim expression the day before. The cancelation of their dinner.

He swallowed another mouthful of water. When he spoke again, his voice sounded strangled, as if someone had yanked his tie too tight. "She had to know it would tear me up inside, after all we've been through together. And with that swamp snake. She might as well have shoved her hand down my throat and ripped my guts out."

Sandy lowered her eyes. She sat on the edge of the trunk and pushed his hair from his forehead to the side. She expected him to say more or to start crying, which she would have done if it had been her, but he simply took another drink and closed his eyes again.

"I think the hot water's ready," she said.

"I'll take harvest spice, not too strong, lots of sugar." He sighed. "I have an eighty-minute class I've got to get through."

She sat next to him on the sofa. As they drank their tea, he told her about the class. The same twentieth century European history, different group of students. Today's topic: Weimar Germany and Hitler's rise to power.

"So you're definitely coming?" he asked.

"Yes. Though if I watched you every day for the next year I could never teach like you."

He rested his left hand on her shoulder, which surprised her, but she didn't move away. "Don't be so pessimistic. I can show you the basics, but if you care enough you'll find your own style." With his free hand he stirred the remains of his tea. She surveyed the office and observed in his objects and posters his attraction to the sides that never won, and she asked herself if she wasn't simply another losing cause.

"I want to apologize for crapping out on you last night." He was tapping her shoulder now.

"That's okay. You had a good reason." She stared into her mug. When he didn't say anything for a while, she raised her head to face him, to see in his ragged appearance the impact of Holly's betrayal. She wanted to tell him she was sorry for what Holly had done to him, but she didn't want him to think she pitied him. This wasn't like getting cancer or falling into a river, an accident of nature for which she should feel sorry.

He removed his hand from her shoulder and pushed back his hair with both hands. He folded his arms across his knees. "You want to come to my house tomorrow night?" he asked. "We can watch a movie, have a beer and some popcorn."

She had reached for her mug, but her hand froze in mid-air. She glanced over at Nick again. His eyes met hers with a frightening certainty that assured her this wasn't an innocent invitation.

And she accepted. She wanted to spend time with him. She did feel sorry for him, although he'd asked her not to. Besides, it was winter, and she was lonely. *Admit it. You were hot for him the minute you saw him in the gym back in November.*

"I'll give you directions to my house. Come by tomorrow around nine." He ripped a page from his notebook and wrote out directions next to a rough map that he sketched.

"That's kind of late if we want to start a movie."

"I don't get done teaching until almost eight. And

students might have questions afterward." He gulped the rest of his tea and cleared his throat. "If you don't want to drive home that late, we have a spare room and a sofa. Holly and the kids don't get back until Saturday."

She didn't know what she really wanted, how far she wanted to go. But she couldn't banish the idea of retaliation from her mind. "You're not going to tell her, are you?" she asked, then added, "If anyone finds out, I could lose my job."

He held both her hands in his. "You can trust me, Sandy. Unlike someone else, I know how to keep a secret." She squeezed his hands the way she used to do when she and her girl friends made promises intended to last forever.

He pulled his hands away and glanced at his watch. "I've got to go." He handed her the water bottle. "Can you fill this up and bring it to the classroom? Same one as this morning."

He jumped up from the sofa, and what little color he had drained from his face. He grabbed the tall file cabinet to steady himself. She touched his shoulder. "Are you going to be okay for your class?"

He smiled, and his color started to come back. "Just watch me."

Fifteen: Two Step

Sandy stared into her duffel bag, piles of clothing next to it on the bed. Pack for one night or two? Sweatpants and hoodies, or tight jeans and the skinny stretch top her ex-boyfriend used to like so much? Her hands shook when she rolled her flannel pajamas into a ball and stuffed them in a corner at the bottom of the bag

So who are you—Florence Nightingale?

While Nick taught his classes, Sandy paced her apartment and asked herself that question. She hadn't gone to observe him because she didn't want to attract any more attention from his students or colleagues. She left for his house that night without the map and trusted her familiarity with the suburb to get her there. And the street signs were good, not a given in neighborhoods designed to keep strangers out. She noticed the themed street names, mostly bushes and trees in this part of the Heights: Cedar Avenue, Azalea Court, Ivy Court, Birch Lane, Walnut Court, Butternut Court.

Nick had left the lights on, so she had no problem finding his house on the dark cul-de-sac. A few bushes and stunted, bare-limbed trees appeared like shadowy statues of a family frozen in the front yard. Snow blanketed the yard on both sides of a cleared brick path, but she could see wood chips poking through. The house itself was a stately colonial, dark blue with pale yellow shutters and a black door.

She rang the doorbell, then heard Nick's voice from the direction of the garage. Even though it was well below freezing, he had on jeans, sneakers, a faded rugby shirt, and an unzipped fleece vest. She thought that for someone getting over a virus he should have dressed more warmly.

He pulled her to him, and they embraced. His body felt wiry and hard and small. She asked him how he was doing.

"Better. I slept for sixteen hours straight last night. But the house is a mess, and I didn't make it to the video store."

"That's okay. There's always ESPN." She noticed his smile when he picked up her duffel.

Nick moved his car into the driveway so Sandy could put hers in the garage, hidden from nosy neighbors. They went inside.

A pile of laundry on top of the washing machine greeted her. *Don't tell me he expects me to clean up after him.* But as she followed him into the family room, she was relieved to see a modest amount of clutter, no worse than her place: A couple of CDs scattered on the carpet and a few days of mail and newspapers piled on the kitchen counter. She picked up the CDs. Jazz.

"You don't have to put those away." He returned to the laundry room and stuffed the dirty laundry into the machine. As soon as he finished, the phone rang. He dashed past her to the wall phone next to the refrigerator and picked it up.

"Hello." He signaled for quiet. "Holly, calm down. I didn't answer because I was sleeping. How are the kids?"

Nick slipped out of the kitchen. The phone cord curled around the doorway. His voice was hushed, inaudible. Sandy tiptoed to the CD rack and started to read the titles.

"I'm not whispering," she heard Nick say from another room. There was a slight echo, as if he were standing in an open entry hall. The next time he spoke, his tone hardened. "Look, I told you before. He doesn't care about you. He's doing this to get back at me, since he can't stop me any other way. Not that this is going to stop me either." Nick appeared in the doorway for a moment, the fingers of his free hand buried in the graying hair behind his ear. "I'm not telling you to say fifty Hail Marys and all is forgiven. Go to a priest for that. You're going to have to show me you're sorry and you won't do it again."

Sandy felt guilty listening; by stepping out, he obviously hadn't meant for her to hear. But he was shouting, and there was no way she couldn't hear. "You say that, but do you mean it? Because if I ever see you with that swamp snake, I'm going to kill him. I'm ready to take him down with me." A hand slammed against the wall; across two rooms, Sandy felt the vibration. A moment later, he said, "No, I didn't punch any holes in your goddamn wall." He paused. "You don't have to come back early. I'm fine."

Sandy heard a deep sigh. "Okay, I'm surviving. I'm trying to get through it. It's not the first time I've had to deal with some heavy shit by myself." For a long while there was silence, then he said, "I know you're sorry. Just prove it, okay." He returned to the kitchen. "Yeah, good-bye." He lowered the phone into its cradle.

He poured three fingers of scotch into a regular drinking glass and muttered, "She doesn't get it. It's not intentions that matter. It's what you do." He turned to Sandy. "You want a drink? Beer, wine, the hard stuff?" He drank a third of the scotch in one gulp.

She stared at him. In her mind she replayed the phone call she had just overheard and tried to reconstruct Holly's words. *She's sorry. She wants him to forgive her. Thou shalt not commit adultery. Thou shalt not covet.* For her this wasn't adultery. And when they taught covetousness it always involved things, like toys or television sets. Sandy recalled the retreats she'd helped to organize, ethical dilemmas she had devised for her fellow youth-group members: turning off life support to comatose patients, resisting peer pressure to try drugs, reporting a friend who copied a test paper. Back then, she couldn't have anticipated this. *If I sleep with him, or even stay overnight to keep him company, he won't be doing anything different from what Holly did, except that she cheated on him first.*

Nick waited by the refrigerator, drummed his fingers on its beige door. Marc had only seduced Holly to get back at him, he'd said. *Am I doing this to help him get back at her?* Sandy imagined herself becoming a player in Nick's macho contest of power and vengeance—like a prized young lioness, swift and muscular, her sand-colored coat shining. She flipped her freshly washed hair from her face.

Nick shrugged. "I guess you don't want anything." He poured another shot of liquor on top of what remained in his glass.

"I'll have a beer."

He took a bottle from the refrigerator, twisted off the cap, and set it on the counter in front of her. He sipped his own drink while pacing the floor, on his way to getting extremely inebriated, which at his size she figured wouldn't take long. He'd mentioned nothing about the popcorn he'd promised the day before. She asked him if he'd eaten.

"Yeah. You hungry?"

She nodded even though she wasn't.

"I don't have a lot here. I didn't have a chance to go shopping." He opened the louvered door to the pantry and pointed to a box of corn flakes. "How's cereal?"

"What about the popcorn?

"I didn't pick it up."

"You're the prepared host," she mumbled. She took out the box with the red and green rooster and said, louder, "I hope this wasn't your dinner."

He leaned against the counter. "Listen, Sandy, I didn't really think this through when I asked you over here. I'm not sure it's going to work out."

She shifted to face him. Her chest ached. "What will you do if I leave?"

Nick grimaced. "When Holly told me about her and Marc, I went down to the path along the river and walked all night. I'll probably go there again."

The thought of him staggering drunk and disoriented next to a contaminated river where several people had already drowned made her shudder. "I don't want you to be alone."

He returned the cereal box to the pantry shelf. "Fine. I'll show you to the guest room. You can leave your things there."

She picked up her beer bottle and duffel and followed him up the stairs. The liquor had started to work on him; he held his hand to the wall to steady himself. His glass was nearly empty.

He offered her a tour of the house. After dropping her bag on the daybed in a room furnished in matching beige canvas and white pine, she lingered in Rosie's room, then Tony's. Rosie's room looked immaculate, hardly lived in. Sandy smiled at the Dave Matthews Band posters and the CDs stacked neatly in a storage rack next to her desk.

Tony lived in total chaos—books and magazines scattered all over the place, clothes lying on the floor, an electric and an acoustic guitar leaning against the wall, a lime-green computer with a scanner, CD burner, game joystick, and printer crowded onto a desk made for a far simpler hardware configuration. She guessed from its unmade state that he slept on the top bunk of a black metal bunk bed and used the bottom bunk as a sitting area. His walls were almost entirely covered with posters of punk and rap stars. Nick stayed far from the mess and had an embarrassed look when he closed the door behind him, as if to say "he doesn't get his organizational habits from me."

He led her into the master bedroom, a room almost half the size of her entire apartment. It looked like something from a magazine, decorated in blue, green, and yellow pastels. A pale yellow down quilt lay in a heap on the rug, and the sheets and blanket were partially tucked in. Sandy left her bottle on the nightstand and peered into the walk-in closet and a bathroom larger than her living room.

After setting his glass down, Nick dropped onto the bed, kicked off his sneakers, leaned back against the headboard, and closed his eyes. Sandy couldn't tell if he was inviting her to join him or on the verge of passing out. Again, her chest ached, and her stomach fluttered.

"I'm going to start unpacking, okay?" She thought he might fall asleep and make the next decision for her. After a while in the guest room, she began to shiver and was about to put on her sweatshirt when she heard footsteps. Nick leaned against the doorframe, his head resting on his forearm.

"Is this all right for you?" he asked. His words were slurred.

"It's kind of cold." She patted the inside of the empty duffel in search of her wool cap, even though she remembered leaving it downstairs with her jacket and gloves.

"Yeah, we shut off the heat to this room. We don't get a lot of guests." He took a step inside. His fingers grazed the wall. "We could have gotten by with a smaller house."

She saw his weak smile and struggled for a cheery tone. "It's really okay. I'll be fine with an extra blanket."

"I'll get the quilt from my room. You can fold it over."

Sandy glanced at the narrow daybed, neatly made, perhaps by Holly for a visitor she never expected. On his way out, Nick tripped and stumbled into the door. *Forget the quilt—you're going to need help just walking.* Sandy followed him, her outstretched hand inches from his back.

In his bedroom an upbeat jazz tune was playing from speakers across the room. Nick sat at the edge of the bed and drained his glass. "Have you ever heard Ornette Coleman?" he asked.

"No. I'm more a rock person."

"He's worth a listen."

Sandy sat next to Nick. He rested his hand on hers. She squeezed his shoulders, beginning under his hairline. He didn't seem wound up and hyper, the way he'd been earlier, but his muscles were still tense. "You look like a guy who could use a good back rub," she said. Jock that she was, she considered herself an expert on the subject.

Nick stripped off his vest, shirt, and undershirt and rolled onto his stomach. Right away, Sandy knew his back was going to need a lot of work. After a while, he reached up and drew her to him. He pressed his mouth to hers, and she relaxed in his arms. He stroked her hair. She tasted the smooth bitterness of undiluted scotch in his mouth and began to feel flushed, overheated. When their lips separated, she pulled off her long-sleeved t-shirt.

"Do you want this? I don't want you to do something you won't feel good about later," he said. His wet lips glistened.

"What about you?" she asked, thinking about their conversation in the kitchen.

He grinned crookedly. "I'm too far gone to give a shit."

She held him close and pressed her fingers into his ribs, fitting them into the soft spaces between the bones and feeling each breath. One thing she'd learned from wild college parties: loosened inhibitions were contagious, even for the cold sober. "Yes, I want your sodden little body," she said.

"Okay, you got it."

They were new to each other, and they explored each other's bodies like kids set loose in a toy store. She stroked the firm muscles of his legs and arms and ran her hands along the straight line of his waist and hips. She paused just below his ribs and rested her hand lightly on his flat belly because he said it felt so good, so relaxing. She admired guys who were in shape, and this one worked at it. She smoothed the curly salt-and-pepper hairs on his chest and around his navel and caressed the lined skin of his narrow, angular face, feeling under her fingers the stiff bristles of his upper lip and jaw. And when he squeezed her breasts, her entire body tingled.

In the silence between songs she could hear the hollow groan of his stomach, as if he hadn't eaten in days. She rested her head there, her ear to his skin, and listened while he ran his fingers along her shoulders and backbone. She inched up and pressed her ear to his heart. She heard not the clear thump she expected but the sound of a solid object beating against small waves, like a paddle cutting through a fast-flowing river.

"Hold on a minute." He wriggled out from under her and dug through his nightstand drawer. He pulled out a box of condoms. The small cardboard box was squashed and yellowed with age. "I hope you don't mind," he said. "I can't get you pregnant, but I don't know where you've been, and to be honest, I don't know where she's been."

Sandy shook her head. At that moment she saw herself in the hands of a responsible adult male, even though he was drunk and she had let one thing lead to another.

Her heart pounded. He kissed her again, pressed his tongue against her tongue and the side of her mouth. He twisted his firm body around hers and smothered her in his wild energy. She pushed herself into him, matching his physical strength with her own. His silence enveloped her. When he entered her, two things raced through her mind—the memory of falling on his hot, hard body in the game last summer and the refrain from the Dave Matthews Band song "Two Step."

Their passion chased everything from her except raw physical sensation. And only after he drifted off to sleep did she remember he was twenty years older than she, he might be dying, the house they were in might have been built on a toxic waste dump, he was married and the father of her student, and sometime between Christmas and that day his wife had broken his heart by sleeping with his nemesis.

And she was going to make it all right.

Sixteen: Thirty Feet High and Hanging

Nicholas woke to "Morning Edition" on the clock radio. He opened his eyes and rolled from his stomach onto his left side. Sandy was still there, asleep with her back to him. He pieced together the sensations of the night before—her hands massaging his back, her mouth against his, the room spinning, the climax that convulsed him all the way to his toes and fingertips, that drained his tensions away. Was this just *"An eye for an eye. An affair for an affair?"* He wasn't sure, but for the first time since discovering Marc's note, his muscles unclenched, and he felt relaxed and powerful.

Sandy stirred. He kissed her on her head. "Sleep well?" he asked.

"Yes."

"Was it good?" He rubbed her naked back. He hadn't forced her into anything, he told himself. He had given her the option of leaving, and she hadn't. He recalled his words: *I don't want you to do something you won't feel good about later.*

She turned to him and grinned. Her face was round, smooth, and unblemished. An innocent face, even if she hadn't acted that way. She'd been as lively as Holly but more of a physical challenge because of her greater size and strength. "You want to do it again?" she asked.

"Not before class. I'll be too mellow to teach."

Her grin faded. "Should I just let myself out after you leave?"

"No. Stay." He reached for her hand. "Holly and the kids don't get back until tomorrow evening, and I'm the one picking them up from the airport."

"Okay, cool." She squeezed his fingers.

"I only have morning classes, so I'll be back by lunchtime." When he rolled onto his other side to turn off the radio, he winced. The right side of his abdomen felt full, hot, and tender. He remembered his appointment with the oncologist after class. With his heavy drinking this week, he would certainly fail his liver function test. He sensed his vital organs deteriorating, but this time it was his own damn fault. Holly's call had left him shaken and more conflicted than he wanted to be about asking Sandy over. He'd needed to obliterate the conflict, the ambiguity, before it weakened him. The familiar tension oozed through him. He lifted strands of Sandy's hair from her face. "I forgot about a doctor's appointment, so I might not be back until one thirty. Don't answer the phone or doorbell while I'm gone."

Sandy dozed off. Nicholas padded to the kitchen and choked down a bowl of cereal. He had to force himself to eat in the mornings before his medical appointments. He needed the energy to teach, and his classes in turn kept him distracted. His shower must have awakened Sandy, because in the bedroom he could sense her eyes on him as he tied his tie and combed his hair in front of the mirror above Holly's dresser.

He turned to Sandy. She had a pensive expression. "What are you thinking?" he asked her.

"The way you teach. It's like someone winds you up and sets you loose, and magic happens. It's incredible."

Nicholas rubbed his right side, where his enlarged liver felt like a foreign object beneath his skin. He thought about what she'd said. He was wound to breaking, trying to keep himself together with the shit in his life—Holly's sleeping with Marc, his sleeping with Sandy, his doctor's appointment, the poison in the soil and the river, and the next step in his investigation: Mapping the cluster. He made a mental note to stop at the office supply place near the hospital to pick up markers, pushpins, and poster paper.

Sandy spoke again, her voice dreamy. "I guess someday I'll live in a big house in the 'burbs and watch my husband get ready for work."

"Yeah, and you better make sure the dirt your house is built on is clean." He adjusted his slacks so his belt wouldn't press into his upper abdomen when he bent over.

Approaching Burnham Medical Center after class made him sweat and his heart race. The adrenaline that coursed through his bloodstream when he taught seemed to double in potency now, as if his struggle for survival had distilled the fight-or-flight chemical to its purest state. He stopped at the basement lab for his blood work, then checked in at the reception area and took his customary seat farthest from but facing the main door. He picked up *The New Yorker* and, unable to concentrate, threw it back on the table. The waiting room had posters of art exhibits and a jazz concert. He'd noticed that about oncologists. Maybe because they dealt constantly with the life-and-death issues of patients whom they got to know over a long period of time, they had taken a literature course or two, read books, and occasionally visited museums or attended concerts. Showed some humanity, in other words. Or maybe he had generalized on the basis of his own doctor, located as he was in a medical center affiliated with an Ivy League university.

By the time Nicholas got to the examination room, his nerves quivered on the edge of exploding, and his mouth was parched. He yanked his water bottle from the outside pocket of his shoulder bag. After taking a long swig, he poked his head outside. Nobody was coming down the gray-carpeted hall. He shoved his hand into the latex glove dispenser and pulled glove after glove from the cardboard box. He rolled his booty into a thick ball and dropped it into the main compartment of his bag. He checked the hallway again, slipped into the adjoining bathroom, and rooted through the cabinet under the sink for individually wrapped specimen cups. He counted out twenty. After leaving his own urine specimen and washing his hands, he fitted the remaining cups into the bag. He cased the examination room for more treasure that he could use. Tongue depressors. An all-purpose tool. Gauze. Good for a makeshift mask. A black marking pen. Bingo. Too bad they didn't have pushpins and poster paper; it would have saved him a trip to the office supply store. The act of liberating useful objects helped to calm him. He patted his full bag and stowed it under a chair in an out-of-the-way corner.

The doctor came in, still reading his chart. They exchanged pleasantries. "Your blood count's the same as last month," the doctor announced. That was good. "But your liver enzymes are off." He gently pushed Nicholas backward onto the examination table, lifted the cotton print hospital gown, and pressed his abdomen.

"It's been a crazy week. But starting today I'll lay off the booze and stick to the diet. Oh yeah, and no contact or extreme sports."

The doctor glared at Nicholas. "I wish you'd move far away, like Oregon, and give me a break," he muttered.

"I hear the whitewater rafting's good there in the spring. Lots of rapids," Nicholas snapped. He knew he wasn't behaving, but this doctor liked patients with fight in them.

He returned to the house around one thirty with the groceries and supplies. Sandy was in the kitchen waiting for him. She wore tight jeans and a stretch top with the sleeves pushed up. She had found some chocolate chip cookies; the empty bag lay on the counter.

"Hope you like fish. I stopped at the City Market after my appointment and picked up some sea bass." He took a bunch of coriander, three tomatoes, a head of purple cabbage, and a package of soft tacos from the paper bag along with the fish. "I was in Texas once for a conference and had some great grilled fish tacos. I'll try to do a reasonable imitation for dinner."

She smiled. "I'm glad you're cooking. I'm not a kitchen superstar." She looked away, and her voice wavered when she asked him how his appointment had gone.

"I'm alive." He paused to listen to the jazz-inspired soft rock coming from the stereo. "What is this music?"

"Oh, I borrowed some CDs from Rosie's room. I'll put them back."

"No, it's nice. I've never heard it before."

She looked shocked. "Doesn't she blast her stereo all day and night?"

He leaned over the kitchen counter, his elbows on the Formica and his arms folded. The knot on his right side seemed smaller, less intrusive. "You've got to understand Rosie. She's gone and found other families to live with. She comes here to do her laundry."

"You mean she's moved out?"

He laughed bitterly. "Not exactly. She's usually here on school nights." He glanced down at the counter and pushed his fingers through his hair. "I think she knows about me, though she doesn't say anything. She was thirteen when I went out to California for my bone-marrow transplant, and even though she didn't know him well, I don't think she believed for a minute that it was her Uncle Jake who was in the hospital for three months." He stood up straight. "You can't really fool kids when they're that age. It was after I got back that she started to drift away."

"Do you miss her?"

"I think it's been harder on Holly. She's the middle of three girls; I just had a brother twelve years older. And no mother. I wouldn't know what to do with a teenage girl."

"No mother?"

"She died suddenly when I was ten. My father fell apart after that." He turned away from her. He had revealed too much already. At this rate Sandy, whom he hardly knew and seemed never to have had a crisis in her young life, would know more about him than Holly did. All Sandy had ever told him was that her parents were alive and healthy and too involved in her life, at least until this year when she had started to distance herself from them.

She came up behind him and squeezed his shoulders. His insides twisted; his physical attraction to her tugged against his guilt. Sandy was Tony's teacher and not much older than Rosie.

"Maybe we should break for lunch. I'm starved," she said.

He searched through the shelves of canned goods he'd just put away and picked out a can of black bean soup and one of tuna fish. He yanked a couple of stalks of celery from the bunch in the refrigerator and took out the mayonnaise. He still wasn't hungry, but he needed to put something healthy and nutritionally balanced into his system, for he'd eaten nothing but cereal since Monday. He asked Sandy to massage his shoulders and back while he fixed lunch. Maybe it was wrong to keep their relationship going on this level, but it was the only way he knew to wind down.

* * *

He was five years old when he heard his brother say, "Mom, there's something wrong with Nicky."

He had already decimated Jake's model plane collection that hung from the ceiling. He'd piled up chairs and books to climb up to them, swung from their strings, and crashed the fighters and the passenger jets against each other until fragments of downed planes covered the carpet in the room they shared. Spectacular rollovers and cataclysmic multi-car collisions chipped the paint from Jake's prized Matchbox and Corgi cars. Once he jumped from the top bunk into his brother's chemistry project, scattering colorful Styrofoam balls—carbon and hydrogen and oxygen—across the room. Little did he know chemistry would someday return to take revenge on him.

He threw violent tantrums. Only when his mother held him tight in her arms did he settle down. His struggle against her was token. The softness and warmth of her body and her firm pressure against him made him relax instantaneously, instinctively. And when she died, he didn't want anyone else to touch him.

Years later he discovered girls. With each of them he tried to recreate what he'd felt in the arms of his mother. None came close, not even shy Holly Meggett who, her roommates assured him, lavished unlimited affection on her boyfriends. Actually, "after about a year or so she wore them out," was the way Cindy and Gwen had put it. Gary concurred, in fact cut Holly from the sit-in list so he could prowl for someone less demanding.

Nobody wore Nicky Baran out. And that was why he sent for Holly that evening the way his co-organizers would have sent for pizza. And for eighteen years they matched each other's sexual drive, fed the fire that had first brought together two such disparate personalities. But he never found the same peace when she held him because it wasn't something he could control and he figured that the instinct must have left him when his mother did.

Then came the transplant, the weeks in isolation when no one could touch him. Afterwards, he craved physical contact, not just sex but Holly's arms on his shoulders, brushing against his neck as she kneaded his taut muscles. Sometimes he would think of his mother as his rage dissipated and his muscles turned to jelly. Sometimes he would contemplate Jake's appraisal of him and the irony of his genius big brother hospitalized for the same depression that had plagued their father while he remained incredibly, certifiably, sane. But while his new-found hunger for touch was elemental, it was also insatiable and indiscriminate. Sandy had soothed him as effectively as Holly did, and he sensed that, despite his guilt and his better judgment, his need for her was growing.

*   *   *

They ate. They enjoyed another round of energetic sex. They killed half a bottle of white wine that had been sitting in the refrigerator, didn't bother to pour it into glasses but passed it back and forth while they lay naked in bed and listened to music. Feeling much better by then, Nicholas pledged to himself that he'd stop drinking tomorrow; one more day wouldn't matter. Then, as the sun was getting low over the rooftops, he asked her to go with him to the river.

Bundled up, they walked out into the late afternoon chill. They followed Riverview Road up to the end, past the large mock Tudor and Victorian homes known as McMansions because, as he explained to Sandy, they had the same floor plans throughout the country and oft-transferred executives could be guaranteed that their furniture and area rugs would fit. Where the road dead-ended, they picked their way down icy and crumbling concrete steps, evidence of the Community Association's neglect, to a snow-covered dirt and asphalt trail along the river. He pointed out the closed Hometown Chemical Company plant and the drums of toxic waste that lay in the dirt and weeds on the opposite bank. He described the chemicals he had scraped from the sides of the drums and dug from the damp ground on that foggy October morning. She knew he'd broken into the abandoned factory site, but she had to see for herself the total desolation and danger of the place. They followed the slow-moving river downstream. On its surface, chunks of ice floated, and outcroppings of ice clung to the banks on both sides, coming close but never quite meeting in the middle. He showed her the spots where he had collected the water and soil samples, and the inlet where the recovery team had brought Luis Espada's drowned body ashore.

Sandy nodded. He sensed her drawing toward him. She reminded him of so many students who had done the homework and participated in class but maintained a distance from the material until the moment they saw for the first time that something happening in Europe a hundred years ago had meaning for their lives. It happened for most of them eventually, and when it did, he knew he had them.

The path ended at the Yellow Springs town line, and he led her back the way they'd come. About halfway on the return trip, he stopped. It was time for the test. He gazed up at the top of the bluff, already dark in the shadow of the setting sun.

"Let's climb it," he said. The thirty-foot climb was not especially difficult because of the jagged rocks and tree roots that protruded from the dirt. He'd done it alone many times with ropes. But with ice covering some of the rocks and no ropes, it could be treacherous.

Sandy looked doubtful. He gave her a pleading stare. "Okay, sure," she said.

Getting up to the first ledge, about six feet from the ground was the initial challenge. He explained how the spring floods from ice jams had washed out the dirt underneath. She took her gloves off for a better grip. He didn't have any to begin with. He boosted her to the ledge, and she pulled him up. The stab of pain in his side reminded him of the doctor's orders he had once again ignored.

"Have you ever done this before?" she asked him as they stood on the ledge, their hands in their pockets. He exhaled a deep breath and watched the steam vanish into the still winter air.

"All the time." He locked onto her hazel eyes, the blues and greens a complex mosaic in contrast to Holly's pure gray. "I need to see how we work together."

"Shouldn't we have helmets?" She was more experienced at this, had probably done an outdoor adventure course in high school or college.

"Not if we're careful. I know the way." She nodded, willing. If he hadn't already intimidated her into this test, she might have also pointed out the contradiction of his insistence on safe sex. But the condom was less for her benefit than to prove a point about where Holly had been.

The next part was the easiest. The bank was not sheer but a forty-five degree angle with rocks and chunks of ice. He suggested, as the smaller of the two, that he go first and she steady him; then she would follow and use his body for support while he clung to the lowest of the tree roots. He lingered on his part of the climb, savored her hand on his back. He stood straight, gripped the damp root, and stifled his arousal as her hands moved up his body as though he were a very thick rope.

She pointed to the twisted roots overhead that protruded from the top part of the bluff. "These should be no problem. We'll climb them like a ladder."

"Won't support us." He pulled himself onto his left knee on the lowest one and balanced himself with his right foot on her shoulder. He shifted part of his weight to a slender root, grabbed a large one near the top of the bluff, and climbed onto it by digging his boots into a succession of tiny crevices. The effort made him gasp for air, and the cold air then chilled him from the inside out. He clenched his jaw to stop the shivering that threatened to loosen his grip.

When the chill passed, he hung by his legs from the thick root and slowly lowered his body, upside down and facing the river. He extended his arms and called, "Now grab on to me and climb up. We're almost there."

"Glad you like hanging off that thing," Sandy shouted. He gazed down at the riverbank and the sluggish, almost frozen river. His chest tightened, and a wave of dizziness almost overwhelmed him before the adrenaline kicked in and his senses sharpened. The cold that penetrated him made him strong, as if he had become as solid as the ice. As she clung to him she dragged his jacket and layers of clothing downward and exposed the bare skin of his middle, but he hardly felt it. He squeezed his muscles tight and lifted her toward the large root. She scrambled up. The root shook, and his head spun from the sudden motion. He tasted wine. She offered her outstretched hand.

He knelt on the root and waited for everything to settle into place. "Good job." He tapped her shoulder with his fist. They climbed the rest of the way to the top and stood next to a row of bushes and a chain-link fence that separated the bluff from Riverview Road. The fresh breeze blew underneath his jacket and tickled his skin, and he tucked in his shirttail. They paused there for a while, arm in arm, and watched in silence as the setting sun cast its pink, orange, and purple reflection over the water.

"I love this place. Even if it had something to do with my cancer," he murmured, not quite loud enough, he thought, for Sandy to hear him. He squeezed his eyes shut and envisioned everything he had seen along the path: the crumbling steps, the jagged rocks, the dirt bank hollowed out by the spring floods, the torn, twisted, and exposed roots of living trees, the sturdy bushes growing in toxic soil, the poisoned river that was at the same time so very beautiful. He felt them in his own body, his visceral, all-too-intimate connection to the nature from which he had come and to which he would one day return.

Later, as he washed his hands at the kitchen sink, he gazed out the window into the darkness and asked Sandy, "Have you ever had a secret place that was all yours? Not that you owned it, but it was there and nobody else wanted it because nobody else saw what you saw in it."

She shook her head, but he knew she understood.

* * *

"I have something else to show you," he told her after dinner. He took her into the dining room, where he unrolled a long sheet of poster paper to cover the table. He set down a folded

Cold Springs regional street map with the Yellow Springs Heights section facing them.

"This is what's called a cluster map. We use it to find patterns in the occurrence of cancers around here." He pointed to the poster paper. "We'll take the street map and enlarge it using a grid. The grid is twelve times larger than the original."

"Can't you do this easier on a computer?"

He shrugged. "Sure, but the only person with a computer and scanner who knows how to use it is Tony, and I don't want to get him involved."

He drew the grid lightly in pencil, and for hours the two of them drew and labeled the streets of the Heights. He let her do most of the labeling because he liked her handwriting, her tall, rounded, neatly formed letters printed close together, the lower case ones hardly smaller than the capitals. An egalitarian script, it occurred to him. The street names seemed to amuse her, and he would have been amused too except that he already knew of too many people who had died and he'd just started to search the obituaries.

She wrote the name of the final street. "So what do we do now?"

"I'd like you to take the map home. Put it on your wall." He handed her a package of pushpins. "Each color corresponds to a disease. Red for leukemias. Green for lymphomas. Yellow for multiple myeloma. Blue for other types of cancer. Then you take a black marking pen and color the top of the pin if the sick person is under eighteen years old. Like here, your boss, Brownfield." He pointed to a spot on Canary Court. "Put a red pin in here and color the top black because Kyle was only six when he fell ill." He pointed to where they stood, on the west side of the Butternut Court cul-de-sac. His throat closed, and his vision blurred. "Here you stick in a red pin. Don't color it."

Seventeen: The Sneakers on the Phone Line

The map covered one wall of Sandy's study, eight feet long and four feet high, two sheets of poster paper that Nick had taped together. Even though he had stretched the thick masking tape onto the back of the map rather than the front, when the sun came through the window at certain times of the day she could see a dark horizontal band through the thin paper. It cut Yellow Springs Heights in half just below the street where the Barans lived.

She picked out the otherwise useless clear pushpins to attach the map to her wall. The wallboard was stiff but penetrable. If she ever moved out, she'd have to fill in the pinholes with toothpaste or risk her landlord's wrath. She ran the palm of her hand across the smooth paper, traced her finger southeast to northwest along the black-lined streets from Shady Ridge toward the river to Butternut Court, the route Tony followed every day. Everything seemed so simple, so flat and colorless, without the real houses, trees, streets, cars, and people that gave the neighborhood life, without the pins that marked the neighborhood's deaths. In the stillness of her study, all of the voices had disappeared: the din of her classroom, the birds chirping in the trees, Nick's rapid Boston-accented speech.

Her hand shook when she reopened the plastic box and dipped in her fingers. She counted, her lips moving in silent recitation: One. Baran. Red. Two and three. McDonough. Both green. Four. Brownfield. Red. She colored the tip black. Five. Reed. Red, black tip. Six. Van Camp. Red, black tip. Seven. Ellsworth. Green, black tip. Nick had given her five other names before she left yesterday morning, before he drove to New York to pick up Holly and the kids. She placed a blue pin with a black tip for the girl in Rosie's school who had died of bone cancer. There was a yellow pin a block away and three blue pins in distant spots further east.

She stepped back, surveyed the first pins, and tried to find a pattern. Four blues, four reds, three greens, one yellow, twelve in all. Seven were on the top side of the thick tape line; a blue pin with a black tip was on the line itself. The river seemed to draw them like a magnet, but Nick lived near the river, and he'd probably heard about more people on the streets closest to him.

She knew already which pins stood for people who had died: all the blue ones, the two greens that shared the pinhole on Nightingale Court, the red for Kyle Brownfield. She had never met any of them but she conjured Kyle's face from the picture on Tim's desk as she whispered the Kaddish. *Yisgadal v'yiskadash sh'mei raba...* One was supposed to have a *minyan*, a gathering of ten Jewish adults, to recite the Kaddish. She didn't even know ten Jewish adults in the Cold Springs area, had never joined the synagogue because of the dues. She thought of the Heights where Nick said people didn't talk to their neighbors, didn't find out who had cancer. Without a community she prayed alone. Without a community they got poisoned.

School resumed the next day, and Sandy could tell which kids had gone away for the vacation because they looked different when they returned. Those who had gone to the Caribbean came back with faces fully tanned, but those who had gone skiing had pale raccoon eyes from their goggles. Tony showed up with a brand-new navy blue canvas jacket. On entering the class, he whipped out a pair of expensive designer sunglasses.

A couple of his friends exclaimed, "Wow!" Others just looked surprised. One of Braxton's crowd blurted out, "Looks like you ditched the Wal-Mart, geek-boy."

Tony grinned. "Yeah, and Target too." He pronounced the store "Tar-*zhay*."

"So where did you go?" someone asked.

Tony stowed his shades and shoved his hands into the jacket's roomy pockets. "The Mall of America. Biggest mall in the world."

Braxton's eyes hardened. He stood and reached his fist under Tony's chin, as if he were going to chuck him. Sandy readied herself to break up a fight, but Tony didn't even flinch.

"Oh, did your hootchie mama drop you off at Camp Snoopy while she tramped around?" Braxton taunted.

A few kids sucked in their breath, but most simply looked confused. Sandy froze, uncertain. Due to his parents' talent for hiding their problems, marital and otherwise, from him, Tony had apparently missed the reference. After a moment, he looked up at Braxton, a cruel smile on his face. "Yeah, I actually did go to Camp Snoopy. And it was fun. A lot more fun than Camp Stay at Home Because My Mother's Too Drunk to Give a Fuck."

Scattered murmurs escaped from the boys. Sandy feared Braxton would punch Tony, but before he could react, Tony staggered off, pretending to drink from a bottle. He bumped up against his desk, flipped over it, and landed sprawled on the floor, to the laughter of every boy except Braxton.

The bell rang for the start of class. Tony leapt into his chair, ready to go. Braxton's face was scarlet. Sandy took a deep breath and tried to come up with the right thing to say, knowing what she did about the two boys' parents. "Tony, I don't approve of profanity in class," she began.

Braxton interrupted. "But he used the f-word. Send him to Mr. Brownfield."

And you called his mother a hootchie and a tramp. She wondered if Braxton had found out about his father's affair, or if Mr. Martineau merely spread malicious gossip without mentioning his key role. "I'll see both of you after school."

"I have basketball practice," Braxton protested.

"You can be late."

Braxton muttered something under his breath. Tony cried out, "I'll miss the bus!"

Sandy's mind flashed to the map and how many blocks separated the school from his house. It was quite a few. "You can walk home."

After school she made Braxton and Tony apologize to each other. Braxton was eager to leave for practice, but Tony lingered. His basketball season had already ended without a single win. Still, he had made new friends who after his defacing of Braxton's binder sat next to him in class as if they saw him as their protector. His voice had almost completely changed, his hair had darkened to a medium brown, and the skin on his face had become rough like Braxton's though not yet pimply.

"Can you give me a ride?" he asked.

"No. You can go to the office and call your mom or dad to pick you up."

"But they don't get off work till five."

"Tough." She paused. "You know things aren't easy for Braxton, and you don't make it better for him, the rest of the class, or me when you go at him all the time."

"But he pushes everyone around. Someone has to stop him."

Sandy sighed. In Tony's words she heard Nick. And she had let her student take advantage of her because of her attachment to his father. She reflected on how the balance of power had passed from Braxton to Tony. Under Tony's reign the class had become somewhat more productive, but the first five or ten minutes were devoted to everyone's opinions on punk, rap, and rock music and the trading and sale of bootleg CDs. And Tony ruled discussions. If Braxton or one of his friends reverted to the kind of silly comments that had dominated in the fall, he'd shout out, "Shut up, loser. You'll be serving my French fries."

One week after the end of the vacation, on a dreary, raw Tuesday in March, the headmaster asked her to come to his office after school. She crossed the brick walkway in the drizzle, past the muddy garden where flowers would soon grow, already suspecting why he wanted to see her. While chaos ruled in only one of her four classes, none was what she would consider inspiring—at least after she'd seen what a truly inspiring class looked like. Her basketball team had set a school record for futility. And then, there was what Dr. Avis didn't know, what he couldn't possibly know: how she had spent her February vacation.

Dr. Avis offered her a leather chair and sat behind his huge mahogany desk. He didn't even bother with the small talk.

"Sandy, I called you here to tell you as soon as possible so you can make other plans. We've decided not to renew your contract for next year."

Just like that, he fires me. So quickly, so coldly. Sitting behind his barricade of a desk. His words didn't shock her, but until she heard them, she could hold onto hope of mercy, of understanding.

Dr. Avis went on. "We felt that you haven't shown enough leadership either in the classroom or with the basketball team."

Who were "we," she wondered. Tim for sure, but who else?

"Did you talk to the parent who helped me with the team?"

He shifted in his chair. She avoided his eyes, focused on his white-blond hair combed over his bald crown. "I didn't feel we needed to. The team's record stood for itself."

So was this all about winning? What did he expect, with that group of kids and the first time they'd had a B team? For all she knew, the A team coach had placed them in too high a division. And then, there was that nightmare class of all boys.

She felt her face getting hot. "I think you gave me an impossible situation. I wish I had a second chance."

Dr. Avis cleared his throat. "Someone else may see it

that way, but I can't offer you another chance here. We lost a student from your class in the middle of the year. As a small independent school dependent on tuition, we can't risk letting that happen again." He stood and picked a book from the shelf behind his desk. "This is a directory of all the private schools in the United States. You're welcome to borrow it for your job search. I'll have a letter of recommendation for you by the end of next week."

After leaving the headmaster's office, she rushed to the teachers' lounge to collect her things. Only a handful of teachers remained, none she knew well. Tim's office door was open. As she peered in, she felt a hand on her shoulder.

She whirled around to face Tim. "I'm sorry," he said. "It was my decision to give you that class. I don't know how many teachers could have handled it."

She shook off his hand. Tim tried again to put his hand on her shoulder. "I think you did the best you could with those boys, and I'm going to write that in my recommendation."

"Thanks. Dr. Avis didn't even bother to see how much better things are going now. And he blamed me for Andy leaving. I had nothing to do with it." She wiped her eyes on the sleeve of her sweater. Several strands of hair clung to her face.

"I realize it's not fair, Sandy. But sometimes life isn't fair. You have to trust in the will of God, for it's all part of His higher plan."

She nodded, though she didn't believe him. She didn't want to make him angry because she needed his support. But what did God have to do with the unfairness of her being fired? What higher plan required Him to put Andy and the other kids through their suffering and to take the life of Tim's seven-year-old boy?

"If there's anything you need, please let me know." With those words Tim went into his office and shut the door.

When she got home, she called Nick at work and caught him between classes. She told him what happened.

"You want me to come by tonight after class?"

"Could you?"

"Sure. I have a few more names to add to the map."

When he rang the doorbell, juggling two milkshakes and a colorful bouquet, Sandy was already in her bathrobe. She answered the door with her head hung in shame. He had spent two days showing her how to teach, for all the good it did her now. Upstairs, she stuck the directory of private schools in his face and spat the words out. "This is all he did, give me a book and tell me to get fucked."

Nick lifted the directory from her hands and guided her toward the kitchen, where he set his bundles down and began to massage the back of her neck. "You know, you're not the first person who's been fired. You want to talk about it?"

She got his meaning right away. "You?"

He nodded.

"But you're the best," she gasped.

"That doesn't always matter."

While they sat at the kitchen table and drank their milkshakes, he told her how he'd been fired from a prestigious university in New York City for a handful of misplaced footnotes. She asked him why.

"It was personal. In my student radical days I pissed off a professor who later became head of a right-wing scholars' group. They singled me out as their first target."

"Couldn't you have sued? What about academic freedom?"

Nick leaned back in his chair and stretched his arms behind his head. His dress shirt tightened across his chest. "I could have, but it would have dragged on for years, and I didn't have much grounds for winning. In this country you can be fired for any reason unless you've been discriminated against on the basis of a handful of categories, and you probably still won't win." He jerked his head back, as if to toss his hair out of his face. He needed a haircut. "In the meantime, everyone in the profession would have seen me as the victim of this group. I don't like being a victim. I'd rather be known for what I did than for what was done to me."

He pitched his empty cup into the garbage can, banking it off the kitchen wall. "Of course, if I had, say, two weeks to live, I'd be tempted to stop in on that guy and blow his brains out."

Sandy laughed, though Nick's ever-growing hit list was starting to scare her. "So that's how you ended up in Cold Springs?"

"You got it." He paused. "And it wasn't such a bad move. I love teaching here. I like my colleagues and playing for the Ship Rats. The way I see it, you make your own choices. If you want to keep teaching, do it. Don't let someone else decide."

Nick's advice made sense. She wanted to start writing application letters that evening. But then she began to think of all the other things she had to worry about. Like money. Her nine-year-old car with a hundred fifty thousand miles. Her gym membership. Forget about joining the synagogue. She couldn't afford it now and would probably have to move anyway. Nick listened. He offered tips on saving money. He told her on which shifts the staff never checked IDs at the community college gym.

He said she needed a good back rub, and he gave her an outstanding one. After they made love, she thanked him for stopping by and caring so much. He sat on the edge of her bed and played with her hair.

"Holly and I had a long talk last weekend."

Her heart sped up, but when she opened her mouth to ask what happened, no words came out.

"She promised she wouldn't have anything to do with Marc." He paused, held his breath, then let it out slowly. "I thought about it and decided separation wasn't an option. Holly felt the same."

"So is this the end for us?" Her mouth was dry, her chest tight. But she was prepared to live with their decision.

"She doesn't know about us. She agreed never to see Marc again, and I agreed to be more sensitive." He tapped her shoulder with his fist. "I don't make promises I can't keep."

"Does it bother you that we're still sleeping together?" she asked after a moment because it had started to bother her now that he'd mentioned Holly. But on another level she hoped it didn't bother him because she couldn't stand the idea of losing her job and her relationship with him on the same day.

"Some." He yanked his undershirt over his head and reached for his shirt. "Day to day, I don't know how I feel. If my soul is as hopelessly polluted as that river, which most of the time I think it is, it doesn't matter at this point as long as no one finds out and no one gets hurt." He started to button the shirt. "We're still working on the cluster map here whether or not we sleep together. And if we do sleep together, it's your decision too, and I'll expect you to keep it a secret just as I do."

Sandy nodded. Suddenly ashamed of her nakedness, she untangled the sheet and blanket and covered her bare shoulders with them.

"And there's one other thing." He stood and pulled his slacks over his boxers. "It's not love. We're friends, intimates, *compañeros* in a war. Can you accept that?"

Looking down at her bare knees, she mumbled yes. She had entered this relationship with no illusions, and she still couldn't say she loved him though she admired him for his teaching and cared about him very much. He was trying hard to be sensitive, practicing for Holly maybe. Tears stung her eyelids. *It's not love. It's not love.*

After they finished dressing, he inspected the map in her

study and added four more pushpins. Three blues, one green, none with black tips. He promised he would visit her again after class on Thursday, and he kissed her on her forehead. "Take care of yourself, kiddo," he said before he left.

* * *

In mid-March Kwame Ellsworth finished his first round of radiation and chemotherapy and returned to school. He dropped by the teachers' lounge at the end of the day. The fluorescent light reflected off the top of his bald head. Sandy could see the veins sticking out like narrow rivulets of rainwater. The bones of his face, wrists, and hands protruded. And instead of light brown, his skin was a sickly orangeish hue. She didn't know Kwame personally, so she didn't stop to talk with him, but she flashed him an encouraging smile.

Nick had made Kwame's acquaintance, though. On a Saturday afternoon toward the end of March, Nick showed up unannounced at Sandy's apartment with a small red picnic cooler. When she asked what was inside—expecting something he had cooked and wanted her to try—he showed her two dozen plastic specimen containers, the kind found at doctors' offices, filled with dirt.

"Soil samples," he explained. "I wanted you to see them before I took them to my office."

"Where are they from?" She had been surfing the Internet for information on other private schools before Nick arrived. Now she flushed the web site to pay attention to him. He leaned against the cluster map, to which they had added another half dozen pins, one with a black tip.

"The Ellsworths. Kwame's family on Nightingale Street. They gave me permission to dig."

"No kidding!" She added, "You know he's back at school."

"Yeah. He's a courageous kid. He helped me collect the samples."

"How's he doing?"

"He'll be okay, I think." Nick pushed his hand through his hair, a reflexive action at this point, because he'd cut his hair to about two inches on top and even shorter on the sides. "He got into Harvard, but he'll have to take next year off." Nick shook his head. "He said if there was any way he could contribute to exposing this mess and preventing anyone else from having to go through what he's gone through, he wanted to be part of it."

Nick asked her to help him make labels on the computer for the soil samples. He stood behind her, leaned over her shoulders, wrapped his arms around her body, squeezed her tight. She kissed him on the cheek. He smelled of freshly dug soil, of spring, and at that moment she thought, *it is love*. She wanted him to stay forever, even though she knew he would eventually have to go.

Beginning with the samples from the Ellsworths, dirt started coming in and going out of her apartment. Most of the pushpins were concentrated in the northwest part of the Heights within five blocks of the river, in what Nick called the bird neighborhood and the tree neighborhood. They'd placed only two blue pushpins in the southeast quadrant, below the tape and east of Yellow Springs Heights Boulevard, the wide street that divided the eastern part of the town from the western part. Nick also took control samples from the southern and eastern parts of the town, on higher ground and farther away from the river, in what he called the spice neighborhood, the mammal neighborhood where she knew the Martineaus lived, and the bush neighborhood. He brought in samples from undeveloped land near Shady Ridge and along the northern and eastern borders of the town. The Leightons, who lived on Curry Court, gave him permission to take samples from their yard, and Sandy was relieved to find out that at least this student was safe.

*　*　*

By the end of March the weather turned warmer and breezy, and Paulie came out again to take his place on the porch steps. After Sandy got home and changed out of her school clothes into jeans and a sweatshirt, she joined him. Though the tree limbs remained bare, the hard little buds that grew bigger by the week promised pink blossoms and delicate new yellow-green leaves. They sat next to each other and watched children ride their bikes up and down the street, young mothers push babies in their strollers, men old before their time drink from bottles in paper bags, and dogs walk themselves. They waved at neighbors coming home from work and at the retired people rocking on their porches. Mrs. Calabrese, who lived across the street, spoke some Italian, and if Nick stopped by while she was outside, they would speak Italian to each other, because Nick remembered a little from his years as a graduate student and assistant professor. Paulie would perk up when he heard Nick talking with Mrs. Calabrese. He didn't understand what they were saying, but he said it reminded him of his great-grandmother.

Paulie asked Sandy if Nick was her new boyfriend.

"No, we're just friends," she told him. "We're working on a project together."

Paulie seemed to accept that. "What kind of project?"

Nick had told her not to tell anyone what they were doing. He still had a lot of information to collect, and he didn't want a restraining order placed on him or incriminating files to disappear because the wrong people found out. She didn't think Paulie would tell anyone, but she had to trust Nick's judgment, for he had been working on this a long time with a lot of people opposed to him.

"There's a town far away from here where children are getting sick," she said to Paulie, in a voice she would use to tell him a fairy tale. "We're trying to help the children and fight this monster that's making them sick."

Paulie's eyes grew wide. "Is it a big monster?"

"Yeah, it's big."

"What does it look like?"

Sandy recalled the sprawling abandoned chemical factory she'd seen on the other side of the river when she took her icy walk with Nick. And just a few days ago she'd heard on the six o'clock news that Global Millennium Bio-Chem was planning to move the office of the Hometown Chemical Company division from Cold Springs in stages beginning in the fall. First the research and development department would transfer to a facility near Atlanta, then management would move to the main headquarters in New York City, and finally the skeleton staff that maintained the buildings would be let go. She'd seen the outside of the office building, fifteen stories of steel and glass, almost a twin of the Grand Springs Hotel, the two of them all that passed for high-rises in downtown Cold Springs. In little more than a year one of those tall buildings would be as empty as the factory, the company fleeing its responsibility to clean up the mess it had made and transferring or laying off another five hundred people.

But as she contrasted the crumbling factory with the shiny office building she realized the dilemma she'd created for herself. If she described the monster as if it were real, Paulie might get scared and tell someone. If she said it wasn't a real monster, he might get confused and start to ask questions. In the end she stammered, "Well, it isn't the kind of monster you can see. It's in a building far away."

"There aren't any kids around here getting sick?" Paulie asked. "The monster's not going to come here?"

She shook her head. "Do buildings move?"

"No."

But their companies do. Trash the place and start over somewhere else.

Paulie smiled, and she said, "Then it's not coming here. There are no monsters here. Everybody's just fine."

Later that week she noticed Ben's old sneakers hanging from the phone line to the house. Paulie knew nothing about them, so she waited for Ben to ride by on his bike and waved him over.

"What's up, Sandy?" He bumped his fist against hers. Over the winter he hadn't grown much taller, but he'd gained another ten pounds or so from sitting around the house and eating his mother's cooking. His gut overhung new baggy jeans and a leather belt.

"What happened to your sneakers?" She pointed to the line.

Ben shifted from one foot to another. "Oh, it's nothing. Eddie and I were fooling around, and he threw my old sneaks up there."

"Do you want me to try and get them down?" She then realized she didn't have a pole or any other way to retrieve them.

"Naw, that's okay. They don't fit me no more anyway."

Eighteen: Sleep of the Just

In her old job Holly had her own office, but the advertising agency gave her a cubicle in the middle of a large room. A maze of other cubicles surrounded hers. Her new boss explained that open space encouraged creativity in his copywriters. He also told her casual Fridays had morphed into casual everyday, and she could wear anything she wanted as long as she didn't have a meeting with a client.

She picked up the phone and dialed Nicky's office number. In the middle of her report to him on the new job, heads appeared over the partition. One of them wore a baseball cap backwards. She wanted to tell them, *don't you have better things to do than listen to other people's conversations?*

They joked about her calling him Nicky. She brought in a large photo of him holding a baseball bat. Though she didn't make any friends, they left her alone.

But Marc continued to call her at the office even after she returned the gifts and told him she could no longer see him. He didn't believe she had ended the affair of her own free will and kept asking if Nick had harmed her in some way. She routed her calls to voice mail. His messages dwindled from one a day to one a week. Toward the end of March he left a final recording, "I realize that for whatever reason this won't work out. I need to move on."

She switched her voice mail from two rings to six, relieved to be able to answer her phone again. She knew she had hurt him with her silence. While she ate her brown-bag lunch at her desk, she remembered the afternoons they'd spent together. Her belly went liquid, then her face grew hot with shame. She imagined that her co-workers could see her through the cubicle's fabric-covered walls, figure out how she had gotten her job and how with zero experience she could earn almost as much as they did. And she still had the job; Marc had not retaliated against her. If she'd been married to Marc and rejected Nicky, he would have had her fired within a day. The thought made her shudder.

The first week in April her boss asked her to join him for lunch to meet a new account, the manager of a declining suburban mall who thought a name change and a new ad campaign would revive its business. He made reservations at Les Trois Canards.

She and her boss arrived first. She tensed the moment she stepped inside. The restaurant's dim lighting and dark wood paneling made her feel trapped once again; the aroma of pepper and rich food turned her stomach. The waiter seated them at a table for four next to the wine rack. "Try the duck. It's the specialty," her boss said after the waiter handed them the menus.

Her boss ordered a glass of Cabernet. With her low tolerance she didn't want to start drinking during work hours again, but she knew she wouldn't be able to eat without a buzz. She asked for the same. Soon after the drinks arrived, a slim woman in her early thirties approached the table. The woman wore a navy blue pantsuit with a red and white pinstripe blouse and her dark brown hair done up with ringlets around her ears. She didn't come alone. Behind her, towering over her, Marc stood in his gray three-piece suit.

"Hello, Holly," he said. He shook hands and exchanged greetings with her boss. The woman introduced herself as the mall's manager. Her name was Brenda, but Holly didn't catch her long surname. Marc cut in as soon as she finished. "I'm handling her application for a green space variance so we can get a major department store in there. By next Christmas you won't even recognize the place." He pulled out Brenda's chair. She smiled up at him, and he squeezed her hand.

Holly gulped her drink. Her eyes were drawn to Brenda's dangling earrings, rubies with diamonds, and a matching ruby and diamond necklace. They complemented her business suit perfectly, and Holly suspected they were a gift from Marc. She tried to track Brenda's left hand in search of a wedding band. Questions raced through her mind, and she could no longer focus on what Brenda was saying about the mall and the ad campaign she envisioned. *Does Brenda have a husband she can hurt? Does she also meet Marc in his hotel room upstairs? Does Marc think she is more beautiful than I am?*

Brenda had an unwrinkled face and no gray hairs. She wore several rings but none that resembled an engagement ring or a wedding band. *No husband, no kids, no physical imperfections, no reason to hide or worry, no need to feel guilty.* Brenda spoke with confidence and ate with enthusiasm, probably knowing she had time to go to the gym afterward and work off the heavy meal. Marc told a raunchy joke, and she laughed without inhibition or shame. Holly stared at the lipstick-smeared napkin in her own lap. She'd heard nothing of the woman's presentation, and she would soon have to develop an ad campaign for a downscale mall she wouldn't be caught anywhere near.

Outside the restaurant Marc shook her hand but said nothing more. Nothing about them, nothing about Nicky, nothing about how he worried for her. *Don't let anyone make you feel ordinary, because you are a rare jewel*, he'd told her while kissing her stretch-marked belly in the middle of a hotel room filled with reproduction eighteenth century French furniture. *Ancien régime*—ancient history. Now it was Brenda's turn, and Holly had become ordinary, one more in a line of conquests.

The ad agency office was two blocks away. Holly and her boss started walking. Marc and Brenda lingered at the restaurant entrance. Holly glanced over her shoulder and checked on them at the first crosswalk.

"How do you feel about handling this account by yourself?" her boss asked.

Why did Marc even have to come? What does a green space variance have to do with the ad campaign? She pressed her hand to her chest to rub out the stabbing pain. "I-I think I can do it."

"Good. I'll need you to work up a proposal and timeline. Give it to me tomorrow, and if it's okay, we'll present it to the client and you'll take it from there."

At the next crosswalk she turned away from him and gazed down the street toward the fifteen-story building that dominated the skyline.

"Holly?"

"Yes." She twisted her head to face her boss. Her throat tightened.

He stepped toward her. His lips curved upward into a smile. "I'm impressed by the work you've done on the other projects. You're smart. You've picked up the business quickly." His body blocked her view of Marc. She forced herself to look into her boss's face, not over his shoulder and two blocks away. "I took you on as a favor for my buddy Marc, but you've done such a good job, I'm grateful." He glanced at the "Walk. Don't Walk" sign. It clicked to "Walk," and he started toward the office, but she stood frozen in place. "Are you coming?" he called.

She squinted in the sunlight. Her mind raced. "I just got an idea. I'll be back in a minute."

"Sure. Take your time." He smiled again before he crossed the street. In the distance she spied Marc. He was a head taller than the rest of the pedestrians who walked by him and the slender, attractive woman who stood beside him. With his back to Holly and his arm around Brenda, he and Brenda passed together through the hotel entrance.

Holly stayed late at the office that afternoon to work on the proposal, but open space inspired no creativity. Having missed everything Brenda had said, she didn't know where to begin. Her boss's praise echoed in her head, hollow words that betrayed no awareness of how stupid she'd really been.

At seven thirty she packed up her work to take home in the hope that a change of scenery would help her.

Nicky had fed the kids and sent them off to do their homework, and he offered to reheat the eggplant Parmesan for her. She took it cold. He sat across from her at the kitchen table and, although he said he'd already eaten, he dug into another plateful of his creation. She picked at her portion.

"Did I put in too much garlic?" he asked.

"It's fine. I'm not hungry."

"Rough day at work?"

When she didn't answer right away he got up and poured each of them a glass of Chianti. She noticed a tomato-sauce stain the size of a quarter on his Red Sox t-shirt just above where he'd tucked it into his jeans. She sipped the wine, held it in her mouth, allowed its astringency to blot out the taste of duck that had stayed with her since lunch.

He slid into his chair and drank from his own glass. "So what happened?"

"Nothing." She bowed her head. She could feel his eyes on her, as if he knew of the humiliation that she could never describe to him. "Just a new account that's going to be a huge pain."

"They wanted everything yesterday?"

"No, tomorrow. But it's that old mall in Yellow Springs they're trying to revive."

"What mall?"

"Didn't you read about it in the *Post-Examiner*?" She had spent all afternoon checking the newspaper's online archive, trying to reconstruct the mall's history, its changes of ownership, and the town's efforts to save it from closing. But her and Nicky's roots in Cold Springs were still so shallow that they paid more attention to the *New York Times* than to their hometown daily.

He stared at her, open-mouthed.

Desperation is asking your socialist husband for advice on how to resuscitate a failing shopping mall. She saw herself losing her job, a job in which after a year she would have earned more than Nicky, after two and a little fiscal discipline been able to pay off all their debts without him knowing how much she had run up. Maybe she could take a general approach, she figured, recycle some of the material she had created for the state over the eleven-plus years she'd worked there.

Her plight made her think of Miss Katz, whom Nicky had tried to help. Poor incompetent thing, lying to cover up her failures. They had fired her last month, Tony said. He also said he liked her; she knew a lot about American history and was trying to make her class more interesting. Still, it didn't surprise Holly that the teacher had lost her job, and she hadn't sympathized at the time. *You suck, you lose.* One of his friends in the class told Tony that when he tried to defend Miss Katz. And now Holly herself was sinking, overwhelmed, about to lose.

Nicky swallowed the last bite of his eggplant Parmesan and the rest of his wine. She had already finished her glass but could only force a quarter of the small portion of cold eggplant past her constricted throat. "You done?" He reached for her plate.

"Yes, sorry. The dinner was good. I'm just really tense."

Nicky shoveled the remains of her dinner into his mouth. He stacked her plate on top of his, carried them to the sink, rinsed them off with the sprayer, and loaded them into the dishwasher. Then he went into the laundry room and took off his t-shirt. He squirted stain remover on the orange splotch and tossed the shirt into the washing machine. His full stomach strained the size thirty waistband of his jeans. Curly hairs, a few of them gray, climbed from his navel up well-defined muscles to his chest, where they formed a forest of salt and pepper. Even at the end of a long, cold winter his skin was a light tan that revealed his Mediterranean heritage, Jewish and some Italian from his maternal grandfather.

Marc's chest and stomach were pink and almost hairless,

she remembered. Her insides shuddered, and she took a deep breath in a futile attempt to calm herself. She envisioned Marc again, this time with Brenda, his arm around her as they passed through the hotel lobby and up to the room where he received his concubines. *He acted as if I were special and then he dragged me through the dirt with my boss sitting there.* She felt Nicky's small, strong hands massaging her shoulders. After a while he pressed his bare chest to her back and wrapped his arms around her. His hands and breath smelled of garlic, and the swirling inside her now was not fear or disgust but arousal. He kissed her on the side of her neck, little vampire nibbles that made her shiver.

"I need to finish this proposal," she whispered.

"You need to relax, honey, or you're wasting your time."

Two points, professor. She blinked back tears. Nicky still wanted her; he had begun to forgive her. She would have been satisfied had they merely resumed their old intimacy, which they'd done within a couple of weeks after her return from Minnesota. From Marc. But Nicky had promised to pay more attention to her feelings, and he had kept that promise. She turned to face him, lowered her eyes to the hairy center of his waist and below to the bulge in his jeans. He smiled and with his index finger gently wiped an escaped tear from her cheek. Then he motioned upstairs with a jerk of his head, his usual silence descending like a fog that surrounded him alone.

She locked the bedroom door. He put on Coltrane. She slipped off her pumps and stockings and waited for him to undress her. He opened the drawer of his nightstand and took out a condom.

Oh, no, you're not going to do that again. Her breath caught in her throat. After she'd returned, he started using condoms whenever they had intercourse. *You might as well have had sex in a dumpster full of used syringes the way that guy's been around*, he'd said about Marc. And he'd proven to be right, even though Marc had used protection.

She didn't want to argue with Nicky. He needed to express his hurt. But it took the edge off her pleasure and left her only a little less tense when they finished. She soaked in the bathtub for half an hour, which helped to relax her some more, and then she brought her work to bed.

Nicky sat in bed next to her, grading papers. From time to time he reached out his left hand and stroked her neck and shoulders. Done with his work by eleven, he switched off the lamp on his nightstand. He fell asleep almost immediately.

She worked until after midnight on a first draft and then couldn't sleep. She had set her alarm an hour ahead so she could arrive at her office early to edit and type the proposal. She counted the hours of sleep she could at best get. *Six. Five. Four. Three and a half. Two.* She would look dreadful at work and feel dull and slow on her feet, not the way she wanted to appear for her first solo project. Beside her in the darkness, Nicky mumbled. She thought she should have talked him out of that extra helping of eggplant; the more he ate at night the more noise he made in his sleep.

But he had a healthy appetite, and he seemed to be sleeping better than usual these days. When he taught in the evenings, he now came home before midnight and went right to bed instead of walking the path by the river. It was as if their fates had reversed and she had become the tormented one whose pain he could not fathom, while he slept the sleep of the just.

Pale light began to filter through the curtains around five thirty, and she gave up all pretense of getting any rest. She turned off the alarm clock. Nicky, now quiet, breathed in a soft rhythm. She pushed away the sheet and blanket and with her index finger traced his knobby spine under his soft gray community college t-shirt. Then she noticed the box of condoms on his nightstand. It cast a long shadow, and she leaned over him to push it into the drawer but only succeeded in knocking it to the floor. She raised her eyes to the ceiling and whispered to Nicky, to Marc, to God, *I know I did wrong, but please stop torturing me because I'm tired of paying.*

Nineteen: Death Certificate

"Where do you get all this information?" Sandy asked Nick one evening in early April. He crouched in front of the map. He had a blue pushpin between his teeth and was sticking another one in a spot on Deer Run Avenue.

"Newspapers. Obituaries. Five years' worth," he mumbled. He located Azalea Court and found a home for the pushpin in his mouth.

A pattern was starting to take shape, a multicolored oval with jagged edges. Red, green, and yellow pushpins, many with black dots, crowded into the bird and tree neighborhoods on the left side of the map, top and center, next to the blue-lined river. A few red and green pins appeared in the bush neighborhood at the bottom left, with one or two greens in each of the other neighborhoods, as if flung out of the cluster by centrifugal force. Blue pushpins were scattered throughout the map, with the exception of the two with black dots, which were both located in the top left-hand corner.

She tried not to notice the black dots interspersed among the others, so many children with cancer.

"Here's my theory," Nick explained. "You have three zones. Zone one consists of the five blocks west of the river, from the North Springs line down to Spruce Street. You have contaminated soil and contaminated water." With his finger, he drew a ring around the jagged oval. "You also have the highest incidence of leukemia, lymphoma, and multiple myeloma, and the most children with cancer."

"And zone two?"

"Zone two is the area of the Heights served by the well the Feds closed in January. I haven't taken soil samples there yet, but I suspect the dirt is clean; only the water was contaminated. The incidence of cancer is lower but still above normal."

He took a deep breath and swept his hand over the rest of the map. "Zone three is clean, according to the samples I've taken so far. No problem with the water either. And we have no leukemia or myeloma. Just a few people with lymphoma and the rest solid tumors." He stepped back. "The blue pins are what you'd expect from a random distribution of cancer. Since the chemicals identified in the soil and water are major causes of leukemia and multiple myeloma and, to a lesser extent, lymphoma, that's where you have the cluster."

Nick surveyed his handiwork and punched his right fist into the palm of his left hand. "We're getting them, Sandy. We're getting them."

"So where do we go from here?" She smoothed down a corner of the map that had curled around the pushpin holding it to the wall.

He took several folded pieces of paper from the side pocket of his slacks. "I have about seventy obituaries without a cause of death except 'long illness' or 'brief illness.' I need to go down to the Vital Records office at Cold Springs City Hall for more information. And I have to track down more kids with leukemia or Hodgkin's who are currently in treatment or who were treated and cured."

"How will you do that?"

Nick pushed his hair back. "The easiest would be to file a class-action lawsuit. That would bring the families forward. But I'm not ready for that step yet."

"Why not?" She thought a suit was supposed to be the goal, a big payout to cover the medical bills and the value of the houses.

"I'm still searching for documents that link company officials to the dumping." He sat on the edge of her desk, on top of a folder of job application letters. "If we file a lawsuit now, the company has a chance to hide or destroy those papers. But if I have the papers in hand, I can file the suit later and still get the information on the kids." He jumped off the desk. "You have to do everything in the right order."

"As far as I'm concerned," he added, his teeth clenched, "the money's only the beginning. I want the place cleaned up and the company's officers punished. What they did goes beyond money." He pressed his index finger into the map until his skin turned white all the way up to the second joint, and he stared at her so hard she shivered. "Each of these pins is a life interrupted, or a life destroyed. I'd like to see those bastards' lives fucked up the way these people's lives have been."

"You know they're moving," she said, although reluctant to make him angrier. "I saw it on the news."

"Yeah, in about six months. It doesn't give us much time."

She tried to sound hopeful. "That's only research and development. The others don't go until after the first of the year."

"Doesn't matter," he snapped. "I need the research documents too. And they're not exactly forthcoming with the interlibrary loan requests. It'll be a lot harder to get those documents when they're in Atlanta."

"I'm going to have to leave soon too. If I find another teaching job," she said after a moment.

He squeezed her shoulder, and she felt the current spread from his fingers through her body. "I know. That's why I want to get the map done."

Time had begun to torment her. Two evenings a week after his classes and the occasional Saturday, Nick came to her apartment to work on the map and make labels for soil samples. At the end of March, she began coaching the varsity softball team and didn't get home from school until six each day. On Thursdays, her game days, she didn't get home until eight and arrived only minutes ahead of Nick. He noticed her frazzled state, and she told him about her new assignment.

"They didn't renew your contract and you're letting them exploit you like that?"

"I need their recommendation," she answered, her eyes

averted. She realized that if she let it, the unfairness of her situation would consume her, the way Nick's anger consumed him. And she had come to believe, as he had, that sex kept them both sane even if it wasn't love.

Using the Internet as well as the directory Dr. Avis had loaned her, she sent out over ninety letters of application to private schools from Maine to Maryland. By mid-April she had a stack of rejection letters and not one interview. Tim had still not given her his letter, in fact had not talked to her in weeks. She felt as if she were teaching Immigration, Progressivism, and the First World War in a trance, halfheartedly applying Nick's lessons. With little time to prepare classes or grade papers, untidy piles soon covered her desk.

The third week in April her vacation coincided with his. He had arranged through one of his former students, now the supervisor at the Vital Records Office, to search death records on Monday. But the Leightons had invited Tony to join them for their annual trip to Jamaica, and Nick had driven them to Kennedy Airport over the weekend, an all-night journey for him. He returned exhausted, so he postponed the project until Tuesday.

At eight thirty in the morning, with the sun shining brightly on City Hall, Sandy and Nick walked through the double doors and down a wide marble staircase. A set of glass doors separated the Vital Records office from the rest of the basement corridor. A man about thirty years old with glasses and a medium brown complexion met them inside. He shook hands with Nick, and the two embraced. They were about the same height. Sandy looked down at the desk and read the nameplate: Edwin Rodríguez.

"So you won Teacher of the Year again," Edwin said. "I saw your name in the alumni newsletter. Congratulations, man."

Sandy wondered why Nick hadn't told her. Maybe he

was so used to winning, or maybe he didn't want her to feel bad about getting fired for her teaching.

Nick introduced her as his research assistant. She calculated that when Edwin took Nick's class, she'd just started high school. Edwin led them to a private conference room, and they settled down to work. She fetched files. Nick took notes.

As she dug through the gray metal cabinets, Sandy tried not to think of what was inside: death certificates, the cold paper records of lives shortened, of pain and loss. She saw the names of children like her students, young adults like her, mothers and fathers like Nick. And there was his running commentary on people he'd known or met.

He passed a couple of files across the table to her. She read the names on the official certificates: Barbara McDonough, Roger McDonough. She knew how they'd died, but here were the hard facts, in a doctor's scribbled handwriting. Cause of death. Date. The seal of Burnham University Medical Center.

"My best friends," he whispered. Behind his reading glasses, his eyes grew watery. He stripped off his glasses and buried his head in his hands. He didn't make a sound, but his entire body was quivering.

"Nick, are you all right?" She reached over and touched his shoulder. She realized this was the first time she'd ever seen him cry. And she didn't understand why he was torturing himself by looking up his friends' death certificates anyway. They already had that information.

But whatever reason Nick had, she wasn't going to find out. After a few minutes, he raised his head. His face was blotchy and damp. Without another word, he opened the next folder and began writing in his notebook.

She knew Nick well enough to know he couldn't stay silent for long. Fifteen minutes later he was telling her how to read between the lines for cause of death, because people often died of other problems related to the cancer, such as infection, internal bleeding, or multiple organ failure. And there was the file he sent her way for an eight-year-old girl with leukemia.

"She was one of the kids you could sponsor from those 'last wish' groups," he said. "Rosie was in student council that year, and she got involved."

Sandy recalled that her Temple youth group had had a booth at the mall for the holidays. She always looked forward to it. Do good, and do some shopping too. "So what did this girl want?"

"Disney World." He glanced at his notes. "Kids' wishes are so simple. Disney World, a new computer, a day with a basketball star."

Not "get bastards that poisoned neighborhood." She imagined Nick's face and story on one of those flyers.

At twelve thirty Edwin stuck his head into the conference room. He asked if they planned to break for lunch.

"Awesome idea," she said.

Nick finished writing and slid his notebook into his shoulder bag. Edwin seemed a little nervous in the presence of his old professor. "Could I please ask you to put all the files away?" he finally said. "We're going to need the conference room for the next hour or so."

They divided the files and replaced them in the tall file cabinets. As they were putting the last ones away, Edwin showed up again. He asked them to stop in the conference room on their way out.

Inside, Edwin stood along with two other young men and four women of various ages. A young Black man carried two large pizza boxes, and a pale woman with dark, frizzy hair and big earrings was putting out large bottles of soda, cups, and plates. All seven, Sandy soon found out, were Nick's former students. All worked at City Hall.

Nick appeared stunned for a moment, then a smile spread across his face. Each one of his students embraced him in turn. They settled down to a lunch of clam pizza, the local specialty, while the students told Nick about their jobs, their families, and other people from the same class. Five had gone on to earn four-year degrees, and one, an animal control officer, was starting veterinary school in the fall.

While they talked, Sandy did the math in her head. If Nick had taught twelve years, five classes a semester and one or two in summer school, forty students in each class, it meant around five thousand people in the Cold Springs area had passed through his classroom. The number amazed her. How many lives could a great teacher change? How many people would remember him or her?

And in this office, where all the births and deaths of Cold Springs were recorded, she thought of how people could go through life and leave their footprints, but soon all that would be left of them were pieces of paper in file cabinets. Or a person could leave footprints that other people followed, and over time those footprints would become a path, a chain of people he or she had touched, the origin of a legend.

Because of the impromptu party, Sandy and Nick only got through forty of the seventy names they needed to check. She wanted to finish the next day, but he had plans to go mountain biking with Rich and another friend, whom she knew as Leapin' Larry, the Ship Rats' first baseman. So they set their meeting for Thursday morning at ten, which was fine with her because Nick needed a lot more fun in his life.

* * *

Nick showed up fifteen minutes late on Thursday, and he walked stiffly, as if he'd suffered a major wipeout the day before. Sandy thought he must have overslept too, because he looked like he hadn't shaved in at least a day. She noticed a number of gray hairs among the dark bristles on his cheeks and chin.

He eased himself into a chair in the conference room.

"How was your bike trip yesterday?" she asked him.

He grinned. "The best. I'm not feeling too good today, though." He reached into his bag for the spiral notebook. "I thought I was in shape, but..." His voice trailed off as he shook his head.

"Did you crash?"

"No. That's Larry's department." He picked up the top file folder and glanced inside. "Something about turning forty-four. These old bones can't be shaken, rattled, and rolled the way they used to."

Having just turned twenty-four two weeks earlier, Sandy felt a new appreciation for her youth. She couldn't imagine what it would be like to be old. Nick was so full of energy and enthusiasm that she often thought of him as her age or, at most, ten years older. Her father, on the other hand, was old. He had a potbelly, wrinkles, and thinning hair that was almost all gray. Even more ancient were his attitudes. But he'd hit the big five-oh the year before, so maybe that was where the difference lay, the line between young and cool and old and washed up.

They finished the files by one in the afternoon, all except for twelve that they couldn't find. Nick called Edwin over. Edwin explained that only people who died in Cold Springs had records at City Hall. Yellow Springs Heights residents who died at home would be filed at Yellow Springs Town Hall, along with anyone else who was pronounced dead within the limits of the Town of Yellow Springs, which included the Heights.

Edwin called the clerk at Yellow Springs Town Hall and arranged for photocopies of the missing records to be sent over the next week. Nick said he would pick them up and drop by her place after his Tuesday and Thursday evening classes for as long as it took to finish the map. She calculated that they had more than thirty names to add. Eight of them were children.

They put the files away. At one point, a folder from Nick's stack slid off and fell through the back of the drawer.

Wincing, he dug through the drawer until he pulled out the wayward folder. He smiled, triumphant, but both sleeves of his sweatshirt had been pushed back, and she noticed the dark bruises that dotted his forearms.

She clutched his left hand and leaned forward for a closer look. "Are you sure you didn't fall yesterday?" she asked him, because the bruises looked nasty. She thought he might have broken something.

Nick pushed up his sleeves to his elbows and gazed at his arms as if he were seeing them for the first time. His eyes grew wide, his mouth dropped open, and the color drained from his face.

"Oh, shit," he whispered and shook his head. "This is definitely not good."

Twenty: A Tree Marked

Lying in the hospital bed Nicholas saw himself, a tree marked with an X. Or maybe just a slash, as if the cosmic surveyor with the bucket and paintbrush, the one he visualized as the younger searcher who pulled Luis Espada's body ashore, was in a hurry. The mark signified a tree scheduled to be cut down to a stump and the stump ripped from the earth, its legacy— in fact, all evidence of its existence—to fade away with the winter snow and the spring rain.

The X-marked tree does not have consciousness. It does not know whether it will be cut down because it stands in the way of a highway or a house, or because its wood is needed for furniture or boats. Or if it is already sick and dying, infected with a plague or simply rotting from the inside. The tree does not know what will happen to it after it falls, if part of itself will persist in the form of other objects or if it will be left to decompose, burned in a bonfire, or ground to mulch in a chipper.

The tree cannot grieve for itself. But Nicholas could, and while he looked the same on the outside as long as the bedsheets covered his bruises, he felt inside the red X that marked him for destruction. The mark didn't hurt, didn't make him dizzy or tired or weak or sick to his stomach— though he knew in time he would experience all those, especially if he tried to fight—and he didn't curse God for marking him because he didn't believe in God. But the bruises on his arms and the X-mark in his consciousness led to the same conclusion—he was destined to be cut down before his time.

* * *

While he waited for Holly and his doctors to gather in his room, his mind returned to City Hall, to the moment when he realized he would have to set his emergency plan in motion. He retraced his path home, trying to stay calm and pay attention to the road, too stunned to play the CD he had listened to that morning, a lifetime ago. Once at the house, he punched in Holly's number and extension.

"The kids are okay," he began, because that would be her first worry. "But I need you to come home."

She sighed. "I have a meeting with a client in an hour. Can it wait?" The kids safe, maybe she thought something in the house had broken. Something that made a huge mess, like the plumbing. Something not worth risking her ill-gotten job with the ad agency.

It's not the goddamn plumbing. "Cancel the meeting," he told her.

She must have sensed the urgency in his voice because she said, "Okay," and hung up the phone. And when she came through the door from the garage to the laundry room, her face was pale and her eyes wide. He met her there and without a word pushed up his sleeves. He showed her the bruises Sandy had seen, on the arms Sandy had held. The thought of his lover noticing before his wife made him shudder.

Holly embraced him. Her fingers clawed his back, and she pressed her head into his shoulder. Later he would notice new bruises where her nails had dug into his skin.

They decided to tell the kids together, which required three more days of lies until Tony got back from Jamaica. The doctor admitted him to Burnham University Medical Center that Thursday afternoon; they told Rosie only that he'd gotten hurt while mountain biking and needed further tests. And Sunday night Holly brought the kids to his room.

Nicholas remembered Tony's deep brown tan, his hair in

dreadlocks, the Bob Marley t-shirt that he wore. Marley—another tree cut down too soon. Tony pushed himself up against the door while Rosie sat in one of the two worn blue chairs at the foot of his bed. She took the one in the best condition. The seat of its mate had begun to unravel at the edges, where the fabric was stapled to the scratched wooden armrest. Confusion twisted both kids' faces.

Holly stood behind him then, the way Hillary stood behind Bill when he swore on national television he hadn't had sex with "that woman." The long-suffering wife backing up her prevaricator of a husband, perhaps in on the lie for her own reasons.

Rosie pushed back her shiny dark brown hair. He noticed the fear in her eyes, her reaction so much like Holly's. Rosie had visited him in the hospital when he'd broken his wrist. Then he'd gone away. As he told Sandy, Rosie suspected something, and he guessed it was that he and not Jake had spent months in a California hospital fighting for his life.

"I had hoped we wouldn't have to tell you this," he finally said. "That September, when I went out to California for several months…"

Rosie nodded. Tony shrank farther into the shadowy corner.

"We told you your Uncle Jake was in the hospital." He took a deep breath in the hope that Holly would extricate him before his lungs stretched to their limit. Pain shot through his chest and shoulder from the port the doctors had implanted that morning. Holly kept silent, and he reminded himself he was the one who'd gotten them into this situation by believing himself indestructible and them too fragile to endure the truth.

Rosie glanced at the tiled ceiling. "I never believed you. I thought you guys just had a shitty marriage." She grimaced. "I told my friends you might be getting divorced and were trying to hide it from us in case you changed your minds."

Holly moaned softly. This wasn't the reaction he'd

expected either. "I *was* there. I had leukemia. Jake served as the donor for my bone-marrow transplant." He reached up, clasped Holly's hand, and felt her braided gold wedding band cold, hard, and rough against his fingertips. "I guess you could say our marriage is in better shape than you thought. But the cancer has returned, and I'm going to have to stay here for tests for a few days and then get treatments."

Rosie's mouth was wide open and silent. He gestured for her to come closer and grasped her hand. He turned his arm so she could see his bruises, know he was not lying to her and would no longer lie to her. She gasped when she saw the dark blotches that marked him. "Are you going to die?"

He cleared his throat. "I hope not. I've got too much in my life to leave it." He motioned Tony toward him, but the boy didn't move. Tony seemed to be staring not at him but at the IV tube that carried platelets from the hanging bag to the needle in his chest. "I promise you I'm going to fight with everything I have to beat this thing. And I'm going to get out of here as soon as possible so I can come home and be a father to you two."

"Don't even bother." Tony took a step away from the corner. "What kind of father would hide something like this from his kids?"

Rosie turned her head. "Shut up, twerp. Can't you see he's sick?"

Tony yanked the door open and stalked out. The door slammed shut. Holly rushed after him. Nicholas's legs quivered. He wanted to run to the boy, but the IV held him in place.

Rosie shrugged and dropped back into her chair. Nicholas looked at her, tried to think of something to say by way of apology or explanation, but nothing seemed right. In the fecund darkness his secret created, there grew a malignant suspicion—not the one he'd feared but another far more hurtful. The secret had caused his daughter to drift away from him in her loyalty to her mother, and now three and a half years were lost.

"I should go," Rosie said, fracturing the silence. "Mom's probably waiting downstairs."

"I'm sorry."

Rosie stood and put on her yellow varsity jacket, which sported the crimson emblems of the field hockey and track teams and the student council. She pushed her hair from her face and jacket collar. "I guess you guys must have had your reasons."

"I hoped I'd be cured and we'd never need to tell you." He thought of all the shit he'd done and lied about throughout his life and never gotten caught, none of which mattered anymore.

She inched toward the door. She reached out to open it, then dropped her hand to her side and approached the bed instead. She gripped the metal railing and leaned over to kiss him on his forehead. "Bye, Daddy. Feel better." She ran her fingers through his hair. "You're going to look really weird with no hair, you know."

He reached up and touched a sprig above his ear. "Yeah, last time I wore a wig so you wouldn't notice."

Her gaze remained fixed on the top of his head as if she were trying to memorize what he looked like *before*, before the treatments transformed his body into something no one would want to see. Would he scare them? He wondered because two days after telling them, Tony still wouldn't visit him or speak to him by phone. Rosie had shown up once, briefly, to copy a file from his laptop; she said schoolwork, track, and friends were keeping her busy.

And now Holly had arrived, and the doctors would soon be there to give him his prognosis and treatment plan. His head throbbed from a lumbar puncture the previous morning, and he felt drained from five days of poking, prodding, and inactivity. Holly told him she had spoken with the guidance counselors at both kids' schools. He made a mental note to call Sandy as soon as the doctor discharged him and he could get to his office, where he kept her number. She would have to pick up the vital records from Yellow Springs Town Hall, and he wanted her to keep an eye on Tony.

He checked his watch. The doctor was late. He asked Holly to search through the clothes in his duffel bag for his best shirt and the khaki pants he had worn to the hospital on Thursday. He slipped the hospital gown over his head, stuffed it underneath his pillow, and sat at the end of the bed to put on his pants. Holly showed him the shirt choices: a wrinkled button-down, a Red Sox tee, his college sweats, a white sleeveless tee with bloodstains from a needle taken out prematurely during a transfusion. All of them smelled of antiseptic. He'd requested the shirts the first evening; the skimpy johnny with its faded gray flower pattern offered no dignity. Were he to get out of bed and walk around, his former students who worked as nurses and orderlies would see his fluorescent orange boxers or worse, his hairy off-white Jewish-Italian ass.

But the transfusion convinced him of the Johnny's practicality, and by the third day he had become accustomed to institutional life—passively wearing the hospital clothing, eating the hospital food, watching the NBA playoffs on the tiny wall-mounted television, ready to give up his freedom and forget the things he still had to do.

He had just finished buttoning his shirt when the doctor came through the door. He hadn't knocked, which left Nicholas no time to tuck in his shirttail or comb his hair. And he came alone; his partner, he said, was called to another case.

"Someone else with leukemia?" Nicholas prodded, hoping to ask him next where the guy lived.

"Can't say," the doctor responded sharply.

"So do I go home tomorrow?" Nicholas thought of Tony holed up in his room, the cluster map missing thirty-two pins, and his classes mishandled by the substitute, and he figured if he could get himself discharged by seven in the morning he could drive Tony to school, get to the college in time to teach his full schedule, and call Sandy.

"We'll see," the doctor said in the same tone Holly used when one of the kids asked the impossible. Without looking up from his clipboard he read a series of numbers and scientific terms. Having already used his laptop to search the Internet, Nicholas knew what the data meant. He had caught the recurrence at an early stage, but the disease would advance quickly without immediate treatment. The doctor praised his alertness, and Nicholas wondered what would have happened had he not pounded his body on the bike trails, had waited the ten days until his regular appointment. But he said nothing to the doctor about his fondness for extreme mountain biking; the guy was still smarting from his crack about riding the rapids on the upper Columbia River with a bellyful of enlarged vital organs.

"We'd like you to stay in the hospital for the initial round of treatments," the doctor said.

"No fucking way," Nicholas shot back. A volcano of pain erupted into his skull from the puncture site in his spine. His neck muscles tightened. Standard treatment, he knew, meant four to six weeks caged up in the hospital, a two-to-three-week break, and then another four to six weeks with a different drug combination.

The doctor set his clipboard on the bed and shoved his hands into the pockets of his white lab coat. He described the treatment and its side effects and warned of the risk of infection from both the disease and the cure. Nicholas reminded him that hospitals harbored antibiotic-resistant bacteria but his house was sanitary. He even cleaned the bathrooms himself.

The doctor was bald and had a chubby face, and he turned red all the way to the crown of his head. Nicholas imagined the words going through his mind: *Are you really that stupid and reckless, or is this just an act?*

Holly squeezed his shoulders, signaling that he had pushed too far. He needed her to massage his neck, but she lowered her arms. The doctor picked up the clipboard and jabbed it at Nicholas as he spoke. "I don't think you understand. You're going to need platelets and possibly whole blood transfusions several times a week—"

"I'll stop by and pick them up after class."

"I'd appreciate it if you kept your mouth shut and listened."

Holly gripped the metal railing of the bed. Her knuckles were white and her jaw set. He was not impressing her with his bravado, he realized, and not helping his cause if he needed her to drive him to the outpatient clinic.

The doctor continued. "With the drugs you're getting, it's likely you'll also need intravenous fluids and nutrition. If you choose to undergo chemotherapy as an outpatient, I want you to think of the burden this places on your wife and children." He motioned Holly away from the bed and whispered something to her.

"Will I have to give him an IV?" Holly asked.

"At some point, yes," the doctor replied, louder but with his back to Nicholas. "We could set you up with a visiting nurse to get you started. But he needs extensive supportive care that is easier to provide in an inpatient setting."

"You said easier?" Nicholas cut in.

The doctor shot him a "didn't I tell you to shut up" look. "Yes."

"Maybe for you."

"And for your family too. Think about it."

Nicholas slid off the edge of the bed and faced Holly, implored her with his eyes. The floor seemed to rock beneath his bare feet, and his head pounded in time with his heartbeat. It all came down to her. His ability to teach the rest of his classes for the semester. His work on the cluster map. His freedom. Everything depended on whether she would stay home from her high-powered job to take care of him.

He thought of his former students who worked at the hospital. They would come seeking one last bit of wisdom, an inspiring story, an opinion on the news, a recommendation. He knew he would have limited energy to devote to anyone else, and as much as he valued his students, he wanted to save what little he had for his own kids.

He wondered if it wasn't already too late. Rosie and Tony hadn't come to see him in the hospital. Was it anger, fear, or something else? All week long he'd believed the worst thing about his lie was getting caught. But perhaps the months he spent in California separated from them had enabled his kids to get along without him and he had become as superfluous as his father.

Holly slipped her hand into his. "I understand your concern, but I think my husband needs to be home with his family."

Though she didn't know of his affair, he felt as if she had taken him back, just as he had taken her back after her betrayal. He vowed to throw away the condoms with which he tortured her and to stop sleeping with Sandy. With his relapse, only one target of his vengeance mattered anymore.

After Holly left for home, he packed his things. As he worked, he thought of his mountain bike ride the week before, when he and Rich and Larry did the killer trail at Hamilton Hills, the one that began at the cell tower. They'd dropped Larry off at the top, but he and Rich rode up the switchbacks and walked around some of the creeks and side trails so they could get a feel for the downhill ride. Three trails led from the tower—two wide intermediates and the challenging single-track, which was steep, rocky, winding, and scary beyond imagination.

When he closed his eyes and held his breath to avoid absorbing the hospital smell, Nicholas felt himself flying down that trail. The trees spun around him in a blur. The impact of his tires crashing against roots and rocks reverberated in his arms, his legs, his spine. His mouth was dry. He sensed the icy water splashing his face from creeks swollen with melted snow.

All night long he replayed those moments in his mind. He wanted to burn them into his memory because he knew he would never again feel so free or so alive.

But as he recalled those moments, he realized he could slow them down. Each tree, each protruding root, each fallen pine needle had also become part of his memory.

He thought of the sturdy old trees along the trail, trees that hadn't yet been cut down. Trees that had resisted storms and floods and fire. He wanted to steal the shiny rustproof chain, the one he had unwound when he picked the lock to break into the abandoned chemical plant. He wanted to feel its heaviness in his hands, wind it tight around his body, find the largest and strongest tree. There were radical environmentalists out west who chained themselves to ancient redwoods to save them from clear-cutting. To stop devastation and death. And for a moment, with his eyes squeezed shut and his breath suspended, Nicholas imagined he could chain himself to the tree and by doing so chain himself to life.

Twenty-one: The Return

It took just enough time for Sandy to drive home and heat some Ramen noodle soup for lunch to realize the significance of her discovery, the dark bruises on Nick's arms. And she felt in the pit of her stomach what he must have felt at that instant of terrible recognition—a huge hole, as if she had gone into a free fall but did not know yet when, and how, she would land.

In her study she stared at his red pushpin without a black dot and the number that she had penciled next to it. *One. Baran. Two and three. McDonough. Four. Brownfield...* The numbers followed an order neither alphabetical nor chronological but according to the moment it occurred to her or Nick that these illnesses were no accident. Nothing on the map indicated which pins stood for living people and which ones marked the last location of the dead. Only Nick's information forms revealed who had passed from one to the other.

Would they finish the map, or leave it frozen in place at the moment of his relapse, the red, green, yellow, and black mosaic of a jagged-edged oval with the mostly blue pins scattered outside? And how would Nick tell Tony after keeping the truth from him so long?

The next evening she returned to synagogue for the Shabbat evening service. She'd never joined, hadn't gone to services since Marissa had found her new boyfriend there. Although he and Marissa had invited her to a Passover Seder at the beginning of April, she instead drove the three hours to Albany and spent the weekend with her family. *The job is great*, she'd told them while wondering how she'd managed to get herself fired and entangled in a relationship with a married man.

The affair, she guessed, was over.

In the synagogue lobby she saw Marissa. No boyfriend. "Welcome back," Marissa said.

Sandy almost told Marissa why she'd come but caught herself. And she remained silent when the rabbi called for the names of those who were ill and in need of prayer, though she repeated Nick's name in her mind and prayed with *kavanah*.

On Monday Tony returned to school but sat in a corner at the back of the room. When his bewildered friends tried to draw him out, he ignored them.

At lunch on Tuesday the school counselor called a meeting of the seventh-grade teachers and the department chairs. The counselor loaned Sandy a book on how to talk to teens about death and dying. It was not a hopeful sign.

On Wednesday afternoon Nick called from his office. He asked her to stop by City Hall after school the next day to pick up the photocopies of the Yellow Springs death records that Edwin had requested. She had to coach a softball game after school, so she dashed out during her lunch period. And when she got home after the game, Nick was already there, seated in Paulie's place on the steps.

Despite his ordeal, he didn't look much different from the way he had the week before. By the way he was dressed, she assumed he'd come directly from class. Not caring if people in the neighborhood saw her or what they would think, she hugged Nick as though she hadn't seen him in months.

"I'm sorry I'm late. I had to coach," she said, prepared to hear another lecture about the school's exploitation of her.

Nick gazed up at the telephone line, where Ben's old sneakers continued to dangle. "It's okay. I just got here myself. Did you win?" She detected the weariness in his voice.

"Yes. Six-zero."

"That's what happens when I don't coach with you."

They went upstairs and into her study. She asked him how he was feeling. "I really don't want to talk about it right now, okay?" He shut the door. "We've got a lot of work to do."

The normally talkative Nick spoke only to give instructions. They finished sticking the pins on the map, which looked even clearer and more ominous with the latest round of victims. Inside the rough oval were patches of red, green, blue, yellow, and black nestled together. Some streets had several people with cancer while others, even inside the cluster line, remained untouched. Sandy numbered the spaces next to the pins while Nick filled in the detailed forms that described what had happened to the people. He had only finished a few of those forms by ten when he had to leave.

"I don't know when I'll be able to come back." He rested his clenched fist on her shoulder. "I start chemo tomorrow, so we'll see how it goes. Check your e-mail."

"Will you be taking the week off from teaching?"

"No. It's the last week before exams." He took a deep breath and let it out slowly. "I've never taught classes while in treatment before. This should be an adventure," he said, with not even a hint of sarcasm in his voice. She couldn't imagine his looking forward to it, but, brilliant teacher and general lunatic that he was, he might have relished the challenge of teaching under the worst circumstances possible.

"You'll be around for opening day, won't you?" She had already checked the schedule, and the Ship Rats played the game right after hers at Southside Field.

"Next Saturday?" He picked up his shoulder bag and started down the stairs. "I'm still the captain. If they have to carry me in, I'll be there."

* * *

Mayor Sonny Dellacagna threw the initial pitch at Southside Field the first Saturday in May, and another city co-ed fast-pitch softball league season began. Sandy and the rest of the All Stars sat in the dugout of their home field, in their black and gold uniforms with their banner hanging from the roof. Across the field were their opponents, the Owls from the Burnham University Graduate Student Association. She saw a few members of the two teams that would play the second game. She waved to Beanball—Rich Rankin—and he waved back but didn't come down from the top bleacher, where he sat with several of his teammates. She didn't see Nick.

As soon as their game ended in a 16-8 win over the disorganized Owls, Monique suggested they go to the adjacent field so she could watch her cousin play. Sandy went with her because his team was playing the Ship Rats. A man with the name Maldonado took the field at Nick's position.

Has this guy replaced Nick?

After Maldonado led off in the batting order, Monique elbowed Sandy. "I don't see Mackie the Knife."

Sandy shrugged. He'd said he'd never miss the season opener, even if they had to carry him in. But she hadn't heard from him since the day before his first treatment, and now he'd missed the opening ceremony, warm-ups, and the start of his game.

By the middle of the second inning the other team led 4-0. And then she saw Nick. He wore an olive green army jacket, a black t-shirt, jeans, and sneakers. Only his red baseball cap indicated he might have been a player rather than a spectator. Before his teammates took the field, they embraced him. He shouted words of encouragement to them and raised a defiant fist to the opposing team.

"He must be injured," Monique remarked.

Nick strolled over and sat beside Sandy on the bleachers. His skin was ashen and his hair beneath his cap dull, as if someone had shaken a fine powder all over him. When he squinted in the bright sunlight, she noticed his sunken eyes and cheeks. His lips were dry and cracked, with a white crust.

"Hey, how'd you do?" he asked in a hoarse voice.

"We slaughtered them," Monique answered.

It's easy to slaughter a team of transients, probably what those guys at Hometown Chemical Company were thinking. Sandy's throat tightened. She glanced at her friend and wondered if she noticed anything unusual about Nick, since she worked as a nurse. Monique called out to the batter on her cousin's team and turned toward Nick. "Looks like your team could use you."

He shrugged and gripped the next bleacher up as if to steady himself. "Maybe tomorrow if I'm feeling better."

Monique reached behind Sandy and felt Nick's forehead, first with her palm and then with the back of her hand. "You get on home to bed, Mackie. You have a fever. Low grade, about a hundred."

"Thanks, Mo' Lockwood. I owe you." He tapped Sandy's shoulder. She drew back from his rotten breath. "Sandy, I need to talk with you for a minute."

Monique gave her a confused look. Sandy figured it had to do with the map. She left her bat and glove and walked slowly with Nick down a gravel path to a small and decrepit children's playground. She sat in a swing. He lowered himself cautiously to the ground and leaned against one of the wooden posts that supported the swing set. He burrowed a hand inside his jacket. She swung gently back and forth. Her feet dragged in the dirt.

"Can you stop that swinging? You're making me dizzy," he snapped.

She jumped out of the swing and sat next to him. After apologizing, she waited for him to say something about why he'd called her over. But he remained silent, and she thought best not to push it. She glanced at the game going on at the other end of Southside Field and surveyed the rest of the neighborhood, a collection of warehouses and empty factories beyond which lay the small port and Cold Springs Harbor. The whole place had an overgrown, abandoned feel that she'd always liked because it was her team's home field and about as far away from the pretensions of Burnham University as one could get. But now the utter desolation made her think of the chemical factory at the opposite end of town, and she couldn't shake the sense of dread that overcame her.

Nick took his water bottle from the pocket of his jacket. He squirted in a mouthful, swished it around, and spat it out. He removed his cap and ran his fingers through his hair. A greasy gel, like what her boy students wore to spike up their hair, covered his head, but his hair appeared dull and matted.

"I need to ask you a major favor," he finally said.

"Anything." She figured, how much more major could this favor be? She'd already slept with him, many times. She guessed he wanted her to do more on the cluster map because of his illness.

"Anything?"

She nodded yes. He clutched her arm, and she could feel his fingers dig into her skin. "One of the kids downstairs from you is a drug dealer."

Her mouth dropped open, and she could feel the shock all the way to the pit of her stomach. "How do you know?"

"The sneakers hanging from the line."

She whispered Ben's name under her breath. He had just turned up with a brand-new mountain bike too. How could she have been so stupid? So out of it?

Nick cleared his throat. "I need some weed from him. This first round of chemo is intense, and I haven't eaten a whole lot that's stayed in me." He flipped the water bottle and caught it in his free hand. "Right now, I'm not handling liquids or the antibiotics I have to take too well either." He went on to tell her that if he didn't do something soon, his kidneys would start to shut down and he would end up in the hospital on an IV.

"So what did you do about your classes?"

"Taught them. They were the only times I felt good all week." He punched his fist into his open palm. "Look, I don't do drugs, haven't done them since high school, but the legal stuff's useless."

Though she could not conceive of his agony, she nodded. Still, he had asked her to commit a crime that involved the son of her landlord, and he didn't give her the option of backing out, as he had when she'd slept with him at his house. Instead he'd described the dire consequences if she didn't help him, and she knew he had a lot to do—his final week of classes, the cluster map, his team's game. And being a father to Tony, who in two weeks hadn't emerged from his silent place at the back of the room.

"When do you need it?"

He sighed. His face had turned a weird shade of green. "Now."

"Okay, let's go."

He pressed his hand to his stomach and held out his other arm for her to pull him to his feet. His hand was hot and dry and his grip weak. He leaned on her for several steps, then shuffled toward the parking lot under his own power. She jogged the rest of the way to the field.

Sandy grabbed her equipment and gave Monique an excuse for why she had to leave so suddenly. On her way out she glanced at the score. The Ship Rats were behind by twelve runs, and in the slow-pitch league they would have already invoked the ten-run mercy rule. When she got back to her apartment, Nick was sitting on the steps. She didn't see either Ben or Paulie.

Paulie, she remembered, was at a Little League game, and Ben had gone with him because their mother had recently taken a job at the garage where Joey worked. Sandy told Nick about Ben having to watch his brother. It made Ben seem less sleazy, though Sandy knew she would never regard him the same way again.

"I'll wait inside. I should lie down, and maybe I'll do a little work on the map." Nick took her bat and glove with him and left her alone on the steps.

She didn't have to wait long. First Ben sped around the

corner on his new red, yellow, and silver double-suspension bike, and Paulie followed on his old one-speed.

"How'd it go?" she shouted to them.

"Great!" Ben flashed her a grin. She now wondered if he referred to the game or to the other business that he might have conducted at the park.

"We won! I got a hit!" Paulie shrieked.

She swallowed nervously. Her mouth was dry. "Ben, can I talk to you?"

"Sure. What's up?" Despite his confident manner, he seemed a little surprised, even scared, though it could have just been her imagination.

She went out to the street, where he straddled his bike. Paulie remained on the steps.

"A friend of mine needs your help," she whispered.

Ben laughed. "That old guy? What is he, like some hippie dude from the sixties?" He raised his fingers in a peace sign. "Grateful Dead, man!"

"Cut it out, Ben," she said between clenched teeth. "He has leukemia. It's a form of cancer. He's in treatment, but the treatment makes him really sick."

"Yeah. So?"

"Marijuana makes him better. So he can eat and get stronger."

"And what does that have to do with me?"

Her gaze bounced from the sneakers above her to the fancy bike. She hoped Nick knew what he was talking about. "He told me about your 'open for business' sign."

Ben pulled up on the handlebars, lifting the front wheel. "Yeah, yeah. It's getting a little old if people like him figure it out." He lowered his voice. "So how much do you need?"

"Whatever you have." Never having bought marijuana before, she had no idea how it came or how much she needed.

Ben patted the cargo pockets of his drawstring pants, also new and fashionable. "I'm a little low right now, but I can get you started." His eyes zeroed in on Nick's car parked across the street. "Where is he?"

"Upstairs. Do you want to meet him?"

"Nah. I believe you." He scooted his bike to the curb and rubbed his thumb and forefinger together.

"How much?"

He held out all ten fingers. She patted the empty pockets of her uniform pants.

"Pay me later. I know where you live."

Ben left his bike in the garage, sent Paulie to bring him a soda, and met Sandy just inside the downstairs door of her apartment. He handed her a small baggie with a wad of dried green leaves and a package of rolling papers. He slipped out the door, and she ran upstairs, two steps at a time. "I got it!" she called.

When she heard no response, she checked the living room, expecting Nick to be crashed on her sofa. It was empty except for the army jacket that hung from the back of a chair. Her bat and glove lay propped against the wall between the bathroom and the kitchen, and the door to her study was open. Inside, Nick crouched in front of the map, filling out some information forms and mumbling to himself as he wrote.

He glanced up when she entered. "I found out about two more kids when I was getting my chemo. Might as well have been the public library, charts sitting out for anyone to read." He tapped the notebook with his pen. "A nine-year-old boy with leukemia on Cedar Avenue, and a seventeen-year-old girl with Hodgkin's on Woodpecker Way. Rosie said she had a class with her last year."

Sandy massaged his shoulders. "You know, you might feel better if you rested instead of pushing yourself all the time."

He gave her an irritated glare, dropped his notebook and papers on the worn green carpet, and extended his hand toward her. "Just give me the dope and can the advice."

The harshness of his words and tone stung her. She

handed him the plastic bag. "You owe Ben ten bucks," she said as she walked out the door.

She opened the windows in the living room and straightened up a little. She considered for a moment going through the pockets of Nick's jacket just to be nosy. After all, given his penchant for picking up strange and worthless objects that weren't his, he probably would have gone through hers. She heard him rummage through the kitchen cabinets and decided to let him keep looking for whatever he wanted.

After a while he joined her in the living room. He had a full liter bottle of club soda under his arm and a lit joint between his lips. He inhaled deeply, then fished through one of his jacket pockets for an orange pill bottle and plopped down on the sofa as if he lived there.

"An antibiotic," he explained. "This chemo regimen makes me vulnerable to infection. I'm trying to stay out of the hospital because that's where the nasty bugs are."

After a few more hits, he offered her the joint. She took it to be polite—she didn't smoke much, even in college. He drank from the bottle of club soda, swallowed a pill, and wiped his mouth on the back of his wrist.

She handed back the joint and started toward the kitchen. "Sit down, Sandy," he said quietly. Suddenly, he seemed so much older that it intimidated her. She dropped into a chair.

Nick went on. "Listen, I want to apologize for snapping at you before. You were right to be upset. Guys tend to get real crabby when they're hungry, tired, or feel like a sack of shit." He inhaled again and held his breath for a while. She took her turn. "The problem with you is that you're too nice. And you expect everyone else to be the same way. But the world isn't nice. It's cold and hard and it doesn't care about you. You have to push back, and you can't be afraid to use the power you have to break a few balls." His eyes met hers. "A jock like you ought to know how to break balls."

She laughed. He continued. "Like that class of boys you have. If you'd busted their butts on day one, things would have been a lot easier. And that includes one loudmouthed little twit with the name of Antonio Walter Baran."

"Lay off Tony. He's a good kid," she said, still laughing, stoned already.

"That's because you don't have to live with him." Nick took another long drink of club soda. The greenish tint had faded from his skin, and he seemed relaxed, almost comfortable. "Twelve days he doesn't speak a word to me, and then I'm walking out this morning and he says, 'What's with the hair? It totally sucks.'" Nick did an imitation of Tony's cracking voice.

Sandy lifted Nick's red cap from his head and rubbed off some of the gel. "Yeah, what is this stuff?"

He grinned. "It's supposed to keep my hair from falling out. I leave it on for twenty-four hours after a treatment." He replaced his cap. "They're doing a study at Burnham Med, and I signed up. Of course, I could be in the control group, and this could just be the stuff Tony uses to look like a punk rocker." He went on to tell her about all the other experimental therapies he'd found on the Internet, some of which could be lifesaving rather than merely cosmetic. But he might have to travel somewhere else in the country on short notice if one of those medical centers accepted him for their trial. So far, he said, he'd contacted fifteen medical centers and sent follow-up records to one. The whole process reminded her of her job search, even though she hadn't gotten one call.

"So I'm not doing this just because I'm vain," he said. "I figure if I behave myself, somebody else with the cure for my type of leukemia might take me on."

He got up to leave about two hours later, having finished off the club soda and a bowl of Ramen noodle soup. He seemed to have his wits about him, which was more than Sandy could say for herself. Her lips felt numb and her mouth like cotton, and every time she stood, she had the sensation of floating about three inches above the floor. He took a ten-dollar bill from his wallet and stuck it inside a copy of *The Outsiders* that he pulled from her shelf.

She followed him downstairs. Ben popped out of his house, and Nick handed him the book.

"What's this?" Ben snapped.

"Look inside," Nick replied. "And thanks, Ben."

Twenty-two: Closing Day

Stephen Reed died just before Mother's Day. Sandy found out from a note in her mailbox, three lines typed on Shady Ridge letterhead sent to all the teachers in the school. She already suspected the worst; Amy had missed a week's worth of classes and softball practices. During her free period Sandy stopped at the teachers' lounge in search of some way to share her grief for a child she had prayed for but never met. One teacher offered her advice on how to excuse Amy from assignments without the rest of the students finding out and taking advantage of her. That was all her colleagues thought of her; she couldn't control her students and needed their advice.

And now she prayed for Nick.

He still came to her once a week after his classes ended. He had meetings at the college and would soon begin teaching a summer school class on Monday, Wednesday, and Friday mornings. He'd also initiated a Monday afternoon workshop for local professors and grad students and a follow-up discussion over lunch on Friday. She asked him about it when he first told her, the day after she heard about Stephen, because she worried that he drove himself too hard and at the same time wished she could attend.

"I need the distraction. Call it denial, a coping strategy, whatever. I don't want to think about what's going to happen later." He lay on the floor in her study, on top of a foam pad and her sleeping bag, his head and shoulders propped up by a pillow wedged vertically between his body and the bottom shelves of her bookcase. A blanket covered him because it was a damp, cool day and she'd turned the heat off in her apartment to save money. Between the charcoal gray blanket and his dark hair his face appeared ghostly pale without his shadow of a beard. The experimental gel had preserved the hair on his head, but his facial hair had fallen out, leaving him without eyebrows or eyelashes and with his chin smooth and his cheeks already hollow. She brought him a mug of hot tea with honey and lemon, which he sipped as he worked. Several times she refilled his mug. He wouldn't eat any of the food she offered.

She sat at her desk and typed into her computer the information he read aloud from his notes. They had almost finished the forms that corresponded to the pushpins, and that was all he'd asked her to do even though she knew he'd recently sneaked onto a vacant property in the cluster and dug up its yard.

"What happens when we're done?" she asked him. She estimated the week after Memorial Day as their last for this phase.

He cupped his hands around the steaming mug. It should have burned him, but he seemed not to notice. "I'll photograph the map in sections. We can break it down for storage then." The words she dreaded. The map going meant he would have no reason to return. "But I'd like to leave it up as long as possible for any new cases."

"As long as you're updating, I found out Stephen Reed died."

Nick set down the mug and reached for his spiral notebook. "Add that to the computer record."

Sandy searched for the file on her database. She could hardly believe Nick's callous reaction, not much different from that of the teacher who'd advised her on how to give Stephen's bereaved sister an extension. She told herself that Nick had never met Stephen either and dismissing the death of someone with the same illness might have been his way of protecting himself. But she needed someone to talk to, someone who would understand her sense of betrayal. Someone who had more serious things to think about than Marissa with her second breakup in six months.

Sandy took a deep breath. "I prayed that Stephen would get better."

Nick made a notation and flipped back to his original page near the end of the notebook. "Can we finish the next two people? I need to get home."

"Sure," she mumbled. She knew she shouldn't have even bothered him. He didn't believe, and he had more important things to worry about than her and her prayers.

* * *

"Girl, I gotta talk to you," Monique told Sandy after their evening game the next week. "Give me a ride home and let Kenny stay and celebrate with the team."

Four weeks into the season the All Stars had not yet lost a game. Sandy had never thought winning would get old, but now she barely followed the standings. Monique's lack of enthusiasm surprised her, though.

As they got out of her car, she saw Ben rocking back and forth on his new bike, reading *The Outsiders* in the fading light. She waved to Paulie on the steps before going into Monique's apartment.

Monique shut the door and glared out her living room window at Ben. "I wish someone would do something about that low-life kid. One day the cops are going to come busting in here thinking we're the dealers because we're Black."

Sandy nodded. Guilt swept through her for her role in supporting Ben and endangering her friends.

Monique sat heavily on the sofa. "I'll start with the good news." She flashed Sandy a brief smile before her face turned serious again. "I'm pregnant."

Sandy congratulated her and asked when the baby was due.

"End of December," she answered. "We're looking for a house because we'd like to move out of here by the end of the summer. This neighborhood is no place to raise a child."

Sandy glanced toward the window. In a few months Monique and Kenny would be leaving. In a few weeks she would no longer have a job. The All Stars would have one final winning season before they scattered. And the player they all knew as Mackie the Knife would have one final season, if even that. As Monique described the house near College Park that she and Kenny had chosen, Sandy realized how much all this mattered to her.

"So will you join another team?" she asked.

"Not if I have to work full-time and take care of the baby," Monique answered. "I'd like to cut back except I promised to help Tasha through school."

"That's very generous of you." Sandy wondered if she'd ever give up something she enjoyed so much to help one of her brothers, not that they'd need her help. She'd read about young Jewish immigrants who quit school and went to work in sweatshops so that their little brothers could get a diploma, but not even her own immigrant great-grandparents had made such sacrifices, as far as she knew. And for her and her brothers, the college fund had always been there. No need for this big sister to put her life on hold.

Monique ignored the compliment and instead sighed loudly. "That brings me to something else. Tasha's professor. The Ship Rats' captain. The father of your student, I believe."

Sandy nodded, anxious about where this was going.

"He's been coming around here all the time. What's that about?"

"We're coaching a team."

"Basketball season's over." Monique drummed her fingers on the armrest of the sofa.

"He was helping me with my teaching. And we're working on something."

"Like breaking up his marriage?" Monique leaned forward. "Don't think I don't know what you're doing. He's been showing up at your place for at least two months now. I see it out my window just as I see that sorry Amato punk dealing his smoke. It makes me sick, thinking how much Tasha and Diane admired him."

Sandy's mouth moved to protest, but Monique kept talking. "So are you two just knockin' boots, or do you really think he's going to leave his wife and kids and marry you?"

"It's kind of complicated," Sandy managed to say.

"Go on, girl. I got all night. I'm working second shift tomorrow," Monique snapped.

Tears came to Sandy's eyes. She had disillusioned her friend, helped Nick do the same. She had endangered Monique by buying drugs for Nick. Did Monique also know he now bought his weed directly from Ben and had even toured the plot of land deep within the vacant lot where Ben grew his own? Did she know Nick regularly got high right next door? What would she say if she knew her sisters' professor was a user of illegal drugs?

"Maybe you should start at the beginning, like how you two went from coaches to players." Monique's tone was as sarcastic as her words. Sandy quickly wiped her eyes with the back of her hand. Monique inched yet closer, and Sandy began to think that perhaps her friend didn't want to scold her as much as listen to every juicy detail.

Sandy stared at her interlocked fingers, her hands on her knee. Silence would be her response.

Monique sighed. "Okay, I guess I'm a little hard on you, but I grew up with a player for a dad. He'd mess around, and my mom would take him back, and one day he left and didn't come back."

Sandy detected the different tack—bad cop, good cop. But she also felt herself open up, Monique's sympathy, false though it may have been, like a single lighted candle on a frozen night. "We did have sex, but not anymore. And that's not why he still comes around."

"So what's up? I'm your friend, Sandy. You know that." Monique touched Sandy's hand.

Sandy gulped and wiped her eyes with a tissue from the

box Monique handed her. "He lives in the Heights and he figured out that his neighborhood is built on a toxic waste landfill. The government just closed a contaminated well there."

Monique sat up straight. "The Heights? You mean that fancy neighborhood is on a toxic *dump*? Usually it's us poor folks they do this to." She blew her breath out between her pursed lips.

Sandy nodded. "Yeah. He says people hush it up to protect the value of their houses. I offered to help him because some students at my school had come down with leukemia." She held her breath. "Like him."

"You mean Mackie the Knife has leukemia?"

"I think he's dying, Mo. He was in remission for three years, but it came back last month." She glanced out the window. It was completely dark outside now, and under the streetlamp there was no Ben, only a parked car that seemed to glow like an ember in the dim light. "Remember when you saw him at that game and he looked so bad."

"When I told him to go home?"

"He'd been in and out of the hospital all week." She added, for Nick's reputation remained at stake, "He taught every one of his classes."

Monique whistled under her breath. "I gotta tell Tasha. When she quit that awful job, he found her some tutoring and a scholarship so she could go full-time."

Sandy thought back to the party, when Tasha burned the popcorn and she helped her clean it up. Tasha said she'd worked for a corporate library downtown that had science journals. How many corporations in Cold Springs had to do with science? How many corporations *were* there in Cold Springs? "That job she quit? Where was it?"

Monique pondered for a moment. "It was in that big office building. Used to be Hometown Chemical Company. They changed their name."

"To Global Millennium Bio-Chem. They got bought out."

"Yeah. They have the ads on TV. All those people with cancer playing sports." She paused. "I've seen those drugs work. Maybe they can help Mackie."

"Maybe not. That's the company that poisoned the Heights."

Monique gasped. Despite Nick's warning not to let anyone know what they had done, Sandy told Monique about the soil and water samples he had collected over the past year and the cluster map they had assembled. She realized Monique would probably call her sisters, and she feared how far all this information would go.

"It's okay if you tell Diane and Tasha about Nick's cancer. But please don't tell them about the toxic waste. The company might try to stop Nick, and he doesn't need that right now."

"How's he doing with the chemo?"

"He doesn't tell me much." *But he's buying plenty of dope from Ben*. She wondered how long she'd be able to keep that secret from snoopy Monique. For the first time, she looked forward to finishing the cluster map.

"Don't worry, Sandy. You can trust me."

* * *

June ninth was the last day of school. The last day of work for Sandy. When the Closing Day assembly ended, she returned to her empty classroom to clean out her desk and take down Tim's poster. She found a note on her blackboard. In the left-hand corner, where she always wrote it, was the date in another handwriting and below it a message, "Today is my birthday. I expect a present. Signed, Tony Baran." She smiled; she missed him already.

Tim tapped at her open door and stepped inside. "I wanted to give this to you," he began. He handed her a typed letter on school letterhead. The recommendation, which she had despaired of receiving ever since she heard he'd accepted a position as the assistant director of a private Christian school in Virginia, beginning in the fall. She skimmed the letter. "I'm sorry I didn't get it to you earlier, but you know how busy I was. And frankly, I wanted you to deserve it." He held out his hand. "Congratulations."

Mechanically, she shook his hand. The letter described her difficulties at the beginning of the year and her improvement in the spring. She hoped it would be good enough to get her another teaching job. She told Tim she hadn't found one yet.

"Something will turn up. A lot of these private school positions aren't filled until the summer." On his way out of the room, he paused at the door. "I'm sorry I wasn't available to help you this year. I hope you understand the circumstances and find it in your heart to forgive me."

Sandy's first thought was, how many teaching awards had Nick won after being diagnosed with cancer? But then she remembered the innocent boy in the picture on Tim's desk, the dark-haired child with the serious eyes. Nick had shown again and again that he was an adult who could take care of himself. Kyle was a helpless child, and she couldn't imagine anything worse than having a young child—who expected his parents to protect him—waste away and die and there was nothing his parents or anyone else could do.

She tucked the recommendation into her shoulder bag and handed Tim his rolled-up Ellis Island poster. Then she picked up her stack of lesson plans and worksheets and joined him in the hallway. "I'm sorry about Kyle. I wish I could have known him," she said.

He thanked her and added, "I think you'll find what happened here to be a blessing in disguise. Sometimes you have to make a fresh start."

Sandy tightened her grip on the papers. "Is that why you're moving?"

Tim nodded. But she wondered if he knew about the soil

under his house, for even after they moved Kyle's legacy would remain as pushpin number four, red, black tip, the number penciled beside it in her own hand. Tim had prayed for Kyle, and his prayers hadn't been answered, but somehow he hadn't stopped believing. Not like Nick, an atheist by thirteen, who'd stepped up to the *bimah* for his Bar Mitzvah to proclaim what he had long before forsaken. *How do you manage to keep your faith?* She wanted to ask Tim, but she couldn't bring herself to cross the divide between her liberal Judaism and his fundamentalist Christianity, and anyway, Marissa and Tony were standing in the crowded teacher's lounge, on the way to Tim's office.

Sandy stopped. The room buzzed with farewells. Tim glanced around the room, nodded a hasty greeting, and brushed past Tony.

"I think Mr. Brownfield's still mad over the binder," Tony said. Sandy's eyes followed Tim, who paused briefly to speak with another social studies teacher in the corner near his open office door. He strode into his office and shut the door.

"Don't worry about it. He's leaving anyway," she said.

"Where's he going?"

"Virginia." She straightened the papers under her arm. "By the way, happy birthday."

Marissa laughed. "Did you get one of those notes too?"

"Yeah." Sandy peered down at Tony. He clutched a trophy for winning the middle school geography bee. He had gotten his ear pierced the day before, and his left earlobe was red and swollen around the small gold stud. His stained backpack sagged as if deflated, the iron-on Rage patch peeling off. "'I expect a present,' huh?"

Tony flashed them an embarrassed smile. "Sorry."

"Are you doing something special tonight?" Sandy asked.

"We had the party last night. I got a mountain bike from my mom and a baseball bat signed by Nomar Garciaparra from my dad. My sister gave me some new CDs because she hates my music."

"How's your dad doing?" Marissa asked.

"Okay. He's picking me up soon. You want to see him?"

"Sure. I always like telling parents good things about their kids," Marissa said.

"Be back in a minute," Tony shouted as he ran out the door.

They had to wait more than a minute for Tony to return with his father. Nick wore his teaching clothes, though he had left his coat behind on this warm summer day. He put his arm around Tony's shoulders. At that point, no more than an inch or two separated them in height.

"So my boy did us proud." He grinned and gave Tony a little shake.

"He's an exceptional young man, as a student and a person," Marissa said. "We've been amazed how he has matured over the past year."

Nick nodded. Tony beamed.

"So what do you have planned for the summer, Tony?" she asked.

Tony glanced over to his father, and a look of apprehension crossed his face. "Dad needs me to help out at home. Mom can't take any more time off work, and now that school's out, I have to start doing my share."

"His sister has two more weeks to go," Nick said. "So this afternoon, I'm taking this big guy to lunch to celebrate the end of school, and then he's going to accompany me to the hospital for my treatment. While I'm getting it, he'll meet with the nurse to learn how to take care of me afterward. And we're going to give the girls the night off."

As his father spoke, Tony buried his hands deep in the pockets of his khaki pants and stared at the floor. His dashing out to get his father, which seemed at first a natural expression of pride, now appeared to Sandy as a stalling maneuver.

And one doomed to fail, for Nick glanced at his wristwatch and said, "We've got to get moving, champ. We have a busy afternoon."

He gestured for Sandy to follow him. She lingered for a moment; she wanted to talk to Marissa about Tony. Worry twisted Marissa's face, and Sandy guessed that she, too, had never accompanied a family member to the hospital, never come face to face with sickness and death. If Tony had been raised Jewish, like his father, Marissa, and her, rather than nothing, the child of a mixed marriage of nonbelievers, he would be having his Bar Mitzvah. In the eyes of the community, he would be a man. But instead of a public ceremony, Tony would have to find his own way to manhood through an intimate trial that would test every bit of courage and caring he could muster.

Sandy turned to Marissa and then to Nick, unsure whether to follow him. She didn't want to let Marissa get away, her only link to the school, to the students she would miss, to the synagogue *Neve Tefillah*, her oasis of prayer. Marissa had remained her friend despite her failure, but so had Nick, who had never given up trying to teach her to teach. And he probably needed her to take down the map, which they'd finished and he'd photographed the week before.

"Go on. I'll call you tonight," Marissa said, as if she understood her dilemma and how to be a good friend. Sandy adjusted the books and papers under her arm, smiled, and waved good-bye. She caught up to Nick and Tony on the stairs.

Nick handed Tony the car keys and let him run ahead. At the landing Nick paused and leaned on the handrail to catch his breath. Sandy asked if he was all right.

He nodded weakly, his face ashen. "Red blood count's a bit low. I started a new drug cycle, and I'm waiting for it to kick in." He closed his eyes, rocked back and forth, pushed off with his elbows when his back touched the wall. "Any news on your job?"

"Nothing. But Tim finally gave me the recommendation."

"Was it a positive one?"

"He talked about how much I improved. I have you to thank for that." She felt some papers—old lesson plans and worksheets—slip from her grasp. He sat on the landing, picked up the pages, and leafed through them. "I can keep the map up all summer if you need it. I don't think I'll be going anywhere," she said.

"Let's leave it then." Nick examined a page, handwritten on loose-leaf paper. Squinting, Sandy made out a lesson plan. Eleventh grade, Andrew Jackson and the Indian Removal Act, taught sometime around Christmas. Without looking up at her, he continued, "If you've got nothing else for the summer, Holly and Tony had the idea for you to watch him once or twice a week. Give him a break from me for a while."

Sandy's knees wobbled at the mention of Holly's name, even though it involved Tony and had nothing to do with the affair. She thought of Monique spying from her living room, Ben dealing his crop, and Tony getting drawn into a lot of things he had no business knowing.

"We'll pay you and cover your expenses," Nick added, his voice emotionless.

"Was this your idea?"

"No, but for some reason, Holly didn't want to call you."

Sandy gripped the handrail, her knees again weak. "Does she know about us?"

He shook his head. "She has a lot of other things to worry about. Job from hell, husband from hell…"

"Okay. I'll do it." She owed him, big time. He was the only reason she had a decent recommendation and a chance to teach again. All year long, Tim had never helped her and no one else had believed in her. Still carrying her papers, he shuffled up the stairs. She trailed him, half-expecting him to stumble and need her to catch him even though his dizzy spell seemed to have passed. When they reached the trashcan in the lobby, he raised his hand above his head and dropped the papers into the can. She protested. She would need the lesson plans and worksheets for her next job.

He pointed to the pages under her arm. "Are those the rest of them?" She nodded. He slid them out and tossed them too. "Listen, they were shit. Don't even think about using them again."

Twenty-three: Orders of Protection

As a child Holly encountered death through stories of the martyrdom of Jesus and as a teenager through the literature she devoured. Her tastes, the textures of her dreams, ran to the Romantics: wan poets or their frail lovers who wasted away with consumption. Sanitariums were places of beauty and of insights revealed to doomed geniuses, and she imagined herself tending a fading Keats, the quintessential Romantic, author of odes otherworldly in their beauty, the youngest of the poets to die.

Books portrayed dying as noble and heroic, and she didn't have the experience of anything else. From the printed page she couldn't smell the blood her tubercular heroes coughed up or hear their groans. Their physical agony had been edited out even if their tears of despair had not.

She had no idea what a messy, frightening, and tedious business it was until she stood alone between Nicky and death. Unaccustomed to the reality—the sounds and odors, the waiting and fear—she longed to pass the responsibility to someone else, as when he flew to California and she stayed back to maintain the normalcy they'd fabricated for the kids. Nicky was much better at handling these things. He had experience.

Rosie offered to help. She said she knew what it entailed. One of her friends had a mother diagnosed with breast cancer the year before. But Holly could already hear Nicky grilling his daughter in the seemingly endless nights they would spend together, with nothing else but her, him, and his pain: *How old is she? Where does she live? How long has she lived there? Did she do the gardening? Did she drink the tap water? Would they mind if I took soil samples from their property?*

No, Rosie would have to get a summer job to earn money

for college. And Tony was too young, too innocent. Too helpless. Bullies locked their sights on him. So she filled out the application for him to return to computer camp, but the deadline came and went without her sending it in.

She still believed she could save Nicky, but not if she had to do it alone. From the moment he phoned her at her office and told her to cancel her presentation, she had gone in only to drop off the copy and press releases she'd put together at home while he rested. But the boss needed her for a big campaign, even bigger than the mall, and she needed the job.

The tug of war. Nicky. The job. Choices the Romantic poets never had to face. Choices she never thought she would have to face when she moved in with Nicky after they graduated.

His firing ended her bohemian fantasy. Just as he kept meticulous records of the myriad transgressions of Hometown Chemical Company, Holly kept meticulous records of her own transgressions, her succumbing to the temptations of the material world, her gradual drifting away from the intellectualism of their days in New York. In the suburbs, so close to the values of her parents that she thought she'd rejected, she found herself making the little decisions that seemed so automatic, so accepted, so much a part of a comfortable life in the Heights. The stereo system with which she soothed herself after she overheard the student suggest she get an abortion. Another stereo for the family room of their brand-new house, later joined by the big-screen TV and the VCR and DVD players. Stereos and computers for both kids and the laptop for Nicky that he didn't ask for and that Rosie eventually appropriated. The new Trooper was followed by the Lexus sedan, then the Volvo station wagon. But those decisions all added up to one huge bill, a bill she could pay only by betraying Nicky.

The job came out of a betrayal. And she felt as though she would betray him again if she returned to it.

She wanted Nicky to tell her not to go back. To find another sleep-away camp for Tony since she'd already missed the computer camp's deadline. She asked him on the Saturday before Tony's last week of school because her boss needed a decision and she needed to make plans for Tony.

"Do you want to go back?" Nicky said.

"I feel I have to."

"Not if you hate it."

"I don't hate it."

Nicky squeezed his eyes shut, as if to fight a wave of pain. He had just eaten his first solid meal after his treatment the day before, and he lay on the sofa in the family room watching a video, catching up, he said, on all the movies he'd missed and all the ones he'd ever wanted to see again. Digestion took all his energy and hurt him as well, since chemo destroyed the lining of his stomach and intestines, exposing the sensitive tissue beneath to the caustic enzymes and abrasive food that he needed to regain his strength. He compared himself to a snake that had swallowed a huge animal whole; he could feel his insides stretch and burn as the mass made its way through him.

She sat on the carpet beside the sofa and lightly massaged his stomach. She felt the muscle churn to the beating of his abdominal artery and imagined she could soothe his pain from the outside, work the chicken and rice and applesauce down for him. After a while he answered, "Don't stay back for me. Tony can take care of me once he's done with school. He's a big boy."

"I don't think he's ready for this." She thought of Tony's reaction to the revelation of Nicky's illness, the almost two weeks when he spoke to no one.

Nicky hit the pause button. *Mission Impossible*. She was surprised at his recent interest in mindless action flicks. "I've seen him grow up a lot this year. I'm willing to give him a chance, and I'm the one who has to deal with it if he can't."

He let his breath out slowly. She heard his insides groan. "If the job means that much to you, I don't want you to lose it. And Tony will learn what's really important in life." He paused. "Anyway, I need to spend more time with him."

Did he see this as a last chance to connect with his son? How much had doubt crept into his consciousness? Would he accept his prognosis, stop fighting? She had never spoken to him about it, but these questions hung over her when they were together. And she too doubted.

She recognized the doubt in her gestures. Ever since his relapse, she had needed to touch him, to feel the warmth of his body and his quivering muscles because in death a body turns cold and still. Sometimes he turned hot and restless with fever. As she sponged him down and fed him acetaminophen and antibiotics with lots of ice water she wondered if she should let the hospital take him for a time and if she was risking his life by keeping him and his too-warm body with her. When he sat motionless, which he did so much more than usual now, she would press herself to him. She rubbed his back in wide circles while he ate, praying silently to God to let whatever he ate stay down, and when he huddled over the toilet to expel his stomach's contents, pleading silently for him to do it gently and not tear anything.

She knew he craved her touch by the way he relaxed beneath it. And she wondered if Tony could calm him in the same way and if Tony could tend him without carrying a raw wound for the rest of his life. *No child should see what I've seen.* But Nicky wanted him there, and because of her choices, she needed him there.

She told Tony later that night while helping him organize his notes for his English exam. He didn't protest, but in the incomprehension of childhood he asked if he would have to stay home every day or whether he could play with his friends. It took her a minute to realize he now had friends he might want to see over the summer. And who would drive him, with her and Rosie working and Nicky still teaching and arranging his treatment schedule around his classes? She explained the problem.

Tony's face brightened. "I got an idea." She nodded, listening. "You know Miss Katz?"

"Your social studies teacher? The one who won't be back next year?"

"Totally unfair," he pronounced. "I mean, she's really cool. Maybe she can drive me." Holly gave him a dubious glance, though she knew she should have been more charitable. "Or I can ask Dad to talk to Rich."

"That's okay," Holly said quickly. "I'll see what your father thinks about Miss Katz."

She suspected Tony had a crush on Miss Katz. Ever since Nicky's relapse Tony had talked about her constantly, how she helped him make up his work and spent extra time with him during lunch or after school. He believed she'd become his friend. Holly knew how easily kind intentions could be misunderstood, especially among the young, inexperienced, or desperate.

When she returned, Nicky had finished *Mission Impossible* and was watching the eleven o'clock news. He reached up and clasped her hand, then asked her to bring him some apple juice and a package of gingersnaps. Clinging to him was a distinct pot aroma, rich and verdant like freshly cut summer grass. He must have visited Rich recently, she thought with satisfaction, for the more dope he smoked the less he talked about the chemical company.

She knelt next to him and handed him a plastic cup with a straw. "Tony said he'd stay with you. But he wanted some time to be with his friends."

"He should have a break," Nicky sipped the juice. "I won't need him on Mondays because I teach all day. And Wednesdays if I'm feeling all right..." He was pushing it, teaching on Wednesdays, hardly twenty-four hours after his chemo. "Should I have Rich take him out biking?"

"He suggested that social studies teacher. The one you coached with."

Nicky glanced back and forth between her and the baseball scores. "Oh, yeah, sure. Do you want to ask her?"

"Not really."

"Why not?" He bit into a cookie and stared at the half that remained, as if mesmerized by its jagged edge.

"She lied to me when I asked her about Tony getting bullied in her class. On Parents' Day…" She stopped because Nicky was laughing, not even listening to her. He had crushed the piece of cookie in his fist and was dropping crumbs all over himself and the sofa. "What's so funny?" she said between clenched teeth.

"She lied?" He had an incredulous expression in the moment before he started to laugh again. It came out more like a squeal, and she thought he could get so silly and obnoxious when stoned. "You think nobody lies in this world?"

"No. It just bothered me." It was no use talking to him further in his condition, and she didn't know what she wanted anyway, except maybe for him to reassure her that her maternal instinct was wrong and Miss Katz would be a very good babysitter. "Tony wants her, so I suppose I'll call her tomorrow."

The sports segment ended and Nicky pressed the remote. The color image blinked once and vanished. She got up to leave, but he grabbed her arm. His hand was damp and sticky from the cookie. "Listen, I'm not helpless. I'm picking Tony up from school on Friday. If it's too much for you to ask her, I'll do it," he said.

* * *

Holly detested softball. It conjured memories of hunting four-leaf clovers in right field and sitting at the end of the bench in cold dugouts, hoping that rain or the mercy rule would send her home. None of the Meggett girls possessed athletic gifts—she least of all—but their father, perhaps disappointed at not having had a boy, pushed them to play.

Now she had to go each Sunday in case Nicky became ill or exhausted and needed her to drive him home. He shouldn't have played at all—the risk of infection or injury was so great. The impact of sliding into base, even on his back, could have ruptured his spleen. He insisted that as team captain he had to be there to keep score, but whenever she glanced toward the dugout she always saw the scorebook abandoned on the bench, its keeper in the field or the batter's box.

The day Tony's school finished, a feeling of dread descended upon her. Even before his treatment Nicky had seemed weak and tired, and while there, had received a transfusion that turned his left forearm an ugly purple. The color matched her mood; despite looking forward to her break, she was too preoccupied that evening to enjoy her time with Rosie at the mall and the movie.

Tony stayed with Nicky through the night but said nothing about it the next day. He slept all day and only woke to eat dinner, watch a video with his father, and fall asleep again. Nicky too dozed on and off. Sick for much of the morning, he recovered enough by nightfall to eat a small solid meal and get a full night's rest. She noted all these in the journal and its accompanying chart—intake, output, temperature, sleep patterns, unusual symptoms—just as she, an anxious first-time mother, once recorded when and how much Rosie napped, nursed, excreted, and spat up.

But Tony had forgotten to keep the detailed journal, which Nicky's doctor required as a condition of his staying out of the hospital. "Make up the numbers and times. You can start with last week's and take away a few hundred mils on each side because he didn't force me to drink the way you do," Nicky told her in bed Saturday night. He grinned. "If Rich can fake data, so can you."

She found her copy of the previous week's chart,

subtracted three hundred milliliters from his fluid intake the night before, and adjusted the output categories to remain consistent. She didn't know if the transfusion would make a difference, but when she turned to Nicky to ask him, he was already asleep. He breathed in a soft rhythm; he no longer mumbled the incoherent syllables that used to keep her up at night.

A steady rain drummed on the roof when she awoke in the morning. It gave her hope that the game would be canceled. Over the next hour she listened to its beat slowing, then stopping altogether. Nicky stirred. She propped herself up on one arm and stroked the back of his neck. He nuzzled his head into her shoulder.

"It's raining," she said.

He pushed back the covers, padded to the window, and peered through the blinds. "Not anymore. We'll play the Mud Series today, should be fun."

"Are you up for this?" she asked in her most discouraging tone.

He eased himself onto the bed and caressed her face. "I'm up for a lot of things."

She shivered as he embraced her. His recuperative powers astonished her, and for a time while they made love, sweet and gentle with a long, slow buildup that let him save his strength and her savor her pleasure, she believed without a doubt that he could beat the cancer and stay with her forever.

Nicky's game was scheduled for the early afternoon. The kids were already waiting in the car, and they all would have left, except he couldn't find one aluminum bat he wanted. Dressed in his jersey and stretch pants that reminded her of how emaciated he had become, he rummaged through the hall closet while muttering to himself that his mind had gone to hell from the chemo and the dope.

The phone's ring startled her. She picked up the receiver. "Hello."

"Holly?"

Marc's plaintive tone made her tremble and her throat close. She turned her back to Nicky, no more than fifteen feet from her. "I can't talk. I'm just walking out the door," she whispered.

"Don't say anything. Don't hang up on me. Just listen."

"Please make it quick."

"I've been trying to get you for the past month. I've called your office, and they say you're not there. Then I heard from your boss he loves your work. Are you avoiding me?"

Her voice shook. "I've been working at home."

"Oh." He cleared his throat. "What happened with the mall campaign?"

"I had to give it up. Personal reasons."

"It doesn't have anything to do with Brenda and me?" His voice rose an octave.

"No."

"Because I wanted us to get back together. You were the one who broke it off."

Holly cupped her hand around the receiver. "You know it's over. Why are you calling?"

"Ever since that lunch, I've wanted to apologize. I was wrong to go there with Brenda. I let my disappointment get in the way of my better judgment."

Holly felt her face grow hot. Nicky would see her flushed appearance and suspect something. "It's okay. I understand."

"Holly, come back to me. I'll take care of you."

For a moment she imagined he could bail her out of a hundred thousand dollars of debt on top of the mortgage, a contaminated house, and the exhausting routine of Nicky's struggle. Restore the life she had before, as in some kind of postmodern fairy tale. "I can't. I have to go."

"Can you call me later? When it's safe for you."

"No."

Marc sighed. "Okay, I can't beg any longer. But somebody saw your husband digging again. Are you aware of this?" All the sweetness drained from his voice.

"Yes." She hadn't tried to stop Nicky this time. It would make no difference; the most she could do was urge him to listen to his body.

"You were supposed to keep me informed. I thought we were together at least on that." He paused. "Even if he made you stop seeing me."

"These weeks have been really rough, Marc." She gasped after his name slipped out. She couldn't take it back. She could only hope Nicky was too deeply buried in the closet to hear. She glanced in his direction and saw his legs behind the louvered door. Again, she lowered her voice to a whisper. "Nick's cancer came back at the end of April."

"I'm sorry to hear that." Though he pronounced the words in his most sympathetic tone, she heard the falseness of a man who had convinced himself that her husband abused and dominated her and probably believed that in a few months she would be freed from his oppression and come crawling back. She again recalled with shame Marc's hotel room and the eight weeks of their affair, for she knew Marc had never truly cared about her. Even in those days, she had no illusions that he would leave Claudette and marry her. He was a devout Catholic and, like her, believed in holy matrimony for better and for worse even if, as Nicky said, two of the Ten Commandments peeled off his wall. But the more she thought about it, the more she came to believe Nicky and his primitive calculus of justice and revenge— that in spite of his affection, in spite of his loneliness, in spite of his efforts to find her a better-paying job to cover up her addiction, Marc had simply used her to attack Nicky where it hurt the most since he couldn't stop Nicky any other way. "How long does he have?" Marc asked.

"We don't know. He's going through chemotherapy, and…" Her voice trailed off when she heard footsteps behind her and felt Nicky's warm, metallic breath on her neck.

"Is that Marc Martineau?" Nicky's voice sounded strangled.

She nodded. Nicky sucked in air. His words rose from deep within him, "Marc, if I ever catch you calling here again, I'm going to burn your fucking house down."

"Is he threatening me?" Marc bellowed.

"With you in it."

Holly's hand trembled, and she was almost in tears. "Please don't call again, Marc. Just leave us alone." She set down the receiver and clutched Nicky's shoulder. He shook her off. In his right hand was the baseball bat. "He wanted you to stop digging."

Nicky whirled around and started toward the door. Without looking back at her, he snapped, "To hell with him. I'll dig up every yard I want."

From time to time at the game, Holly glanced at Nicky to see how he was doing. He played well in his anger, and in the fifth inning hit an infield home run that put his team ahead for good. He said nothing to her about the call either before or after, and she suspected it was one of those things that would eat at him for a while. For the moment, though, he seemed happy about winning the game.

Miss Katz began work the next day. And when Holly returned from the office, Tony, the Mac fanatic, was in the den with the Windows computer playing a game his new babysitter had downloaded for him. Beside him Rosie complained that the Windows machine was hers and he had no right to use it.

Holly sighed. "Where's your father?"

"I don't know. Try upstairs," Rosie said.

Holly raced up to the master bedroom, two steps at a time. Nicky sat on his side of the bed holding a metal picture frame with both hands. He glanced up, smiling, but didn't move toward her for their usual embrace.

He flashed the frame at her. "Look." The overhead light reflected from the shiny glass surface but she could discern a sheet of white paper with small black print. "I got home today with Tony, and a sheriff's deputy was parked in our driveway.

He asked if I was Nicholas Baran, and when I said I was, he handed me this."

She took it from him. Inside the glass was an order of protection that prohibited Nicky from going within five hundred feet of Marc Martineau's house. She gazed at the signatures, Marc's loopy script and a judge's scrawl, and she felt the room spin.

"I framed it, and I'm going to hang it up here," he boasted. "That guy has more than a foot and a hundred-fifty pounds on me, he's in perfect health, and he's scared of me." He rose from the bed and lifted the frame from her hands, which felt dirty as if she'd touched a criminal. She wiped her palms on her skirt.

"Please don't do anything reckless, Nicky. He knows the law and all the judges around here. He can hurt us."

"Yeah, that's how he got the order in a day and some poor woman whose husband or boyfriend is beating the shit out of her has to wait until the scumbag kills her."

He tossed the frame face-up on the bed, sat, and dropped his head into his hands. Guttural moans rose from him.

"Nicky, are you crying?" she asked, surprised. He shook his head, still buried in his hands. Through long nights of pain and fear, he had never cried. She sat next to him and put her arm around his shoulders. The mattress sagged at the edge under the weight of both of them.

"He's going to call again," Nicky finally said. "After I die."

You're never going to die. You promised me. Maybe you thought you were asleep, but you promised me. Or maybe she had repeated the words so often as he slept that she only believed he'd promised her, because Nicky wasn't one to make promises he couldn't keep.

"Tell me," Nicky continued. "If I die…" *If.* That was better. "You won't end up with someone like Marc." He took a deep breath. "You'll stay strong and take care of Tony."

Like your father never took care of you. But Nicky was

right. There were a lot of ways Tony could end up alone in the world, and what Nicky's father did to him was only one of them. And she knew how much wealth and power and professions of sympathy had already tempted her.

The next Sunday she awoke early and put on a dark cotton dress. Something long, down to the middle of her calf, and she found a woven white shawl to throw over her shoulders. She left a note for Nicky, still asleep, his body, she hoped, repairing the damage from Friday's chemo. She skipped breakfast. For a few minutes she sat in her car in the garage and thought about where she could go. St. Joseph's on the border of Yellow Springs and the Heights was where the Martineaus and many others in the neighborhood went, though some attended St. Brigid's in North Springs. Some of Nicky's colleagues might have belonged to Our Lady of Peace in Cold Springs.

She remembered one of Rosie's friends taking her to a church at the southern end of Yellow Springs, near the harbor. The girl lived deep within Yellow Springs in a modest neighborhood of two- and three-bedroom Cape Cods with one-car garages, sidewalks, and tiny, well-trimmed lawns. Corpus Christi was the church's name.

Holly drove southward toward the harbor. She passed strip centers with deserted parking lots, new and used car dealers whose polished offerings gleamed in the morning sun, and the dying mall that Marc and Brenda were trying to revive. She arrived at the two-story gray stone church just as the nine o'clock Mass began. The building appeared to be from the early twentieth century and somewhat older than the restaurants, insurance offices, and repair shops surrounding it, and she wondered about the cycles of construction and destruction that had placed this anachronism in the midst of a sprawling commercial strip.

She pushed open one of the church's dark brown wooden doors. It was heavy and scarred. She slipped into a rear pew and laid her purse beside her. The sanctuary was half full;

she knew no one. Rosie's friend's family, she recalled, attended the later Mass, so they wouldn't see her.

In twenty-two years she had not entered a church, except for an occasional wedding or First Communion. How many sins had she committed in that time? How long could she keep the priest in confession? She would have to edit, she who had spent so much of her life as an editor. She could start at the beginning, pick up where she had left off in a life story gone astray. Sex before marriage, with a Jewish boy who had paced a folding table in battered canvas high-tops and captivated her with a speech. Or she could start with the worst sin: Was it adultery, committed against that same Jewish boy? Or greed, that she needed to indulge herself with the house after losing the lifestyle she loved? She couldn't decide, and she couldn't decide either whether her first prayer should be for forgiveness, for an end to her beautiful Nicky's suffering, or for him never to finish and never to die.

Twenty-four: Tony's Summer

Tony stood open-mouthed and silent in front of the map. His finger traced the black-line streets of his neighborhood and grazed the side of red, green, yellow, blue, and black-tipped pushpins that rose like tiny plateaus within the cluster. Sandy imagined him thinking, *as I walk through the shadow of the Valley of Death*, but in the rap of Coolio rather than the Psalm of David. From time to time, he stopped and squinted at a line and a blank space—the imaginary lot of an imaginary safe house—where one of his friends lived. He motioned Sandy over.

"Dad told me not to tell Mom about the map. He says she's against what we're doing."

"Did he say why?" *We should have taken the map down last week. Why didn't Nick think of that?*

"She has friends in the neighborhood and she's afraid of what they'll think." Tony tugged at his earlobe. Sandy guessed it still itched because the piercing hadn't healed. If he kept pulling, it might never heal. He continued after a moment. "I can understand that. I wouldn't want to do anything to make my friends mad."

"What did your Dad tell you about the map?" Her voice shook.

"He said to look at it. That you helped him put it together because you knew of all the kids at school who were sick. Like Andy." He stepped backward and surveyed the entire map. "Do you know what happened to Andy? I mean, is he okay?"

Sandy nodded. "His parents transferred him." She hesitated. But school was out, and she would never be going back. She had a right to express her opinions. "On account of Braxton and some of the others."

Tony grinned. "Yeah, he didn't know how to handle them. But he was nice. I miss him."

Tony grew quiet and after a moment turned away from her and left the room. She found him in the living room. He had pushed up the screen and now leaned out the open window, his forearms on the sill. He was letting the bugs in and could have fallen out. A faint odor of uncollected garbage filled the room.

Sandy had agreed to Nick and Holly's offer without considering all its implications: that she would be drawn further into this family's secret life, that she might have to witness the deterioration and death of a man she'd loved, that she would have to comfort his son and conceal her own grief. Her bad judgment had already made her unworthy, no matter what Tim's recommendation said.

"Do you want to call a friend?" she asked Tony after a while.

"No, they're probably still sleeping." He pulled himself inside. "I wish I could sleep late."

In the next weeks Sandy saw how much Tony's responsibilities weighed on him. It was almost impossible to sustain a conversation. He reminded her of Paulie, the way he would rest his chin on his fist and stare into space, hardly ever saying a word. The second Monday she only had him after noon. He had gone with his mother in the morning to get contact lenses, and all afternoon he kept feeling his face and reaching at glasses that weren't there. Along with his baggy cargo shorts, he wore a faded t-shirt, a wrinkled plaid button-down shirt with the sleeves ripped out and little threads hanging down, and a hemp necklace and matching bracelet. He had a good tan, and muscles had begun to appear on his arms. She thought of how remarkable his physical transformation had been since the beginning of the school year. He had grown about five inches, gotten braces, an earring, and contact lenses, wore fashionable clothes and his hair spiked up, and spoke in almost a man's voice. She commented on all the changes. He just shrugged, though his shy smile told her he was pleased that she'd noticed.

Two days later she picked him up at Nick's office. She hadn't seen Nick since the end of school. On Memorial Day weekend he'd bought a full month's supply from Ben and delivered the payment inside a boxed set of the collected works of Edgar Allan Poe. Ben told her he had given Nick his best merchandise because it was for a just cause and they all ought to write letters to the state legislature to get the laws changed. She suggested he write one to start but never heard another word about it after that. She knew that in a week or two, though, Nick would need more, and she would have to hide his business from Tony.

In her car Tony was fooling with the cassette player, trying to find a song on a tape he'd made. She asked him how his father was doing.

"Okay," Tony mumbled without looking up.

She figured if he didn't want to volunteer anything she'd have to respect that. She asked him where he wanted to go next.

"Riverview Drive-In. I'm supposed to meet someone there."

She turned toward Yellow Springs Heights. Just south of the town line, on Riverview Road in Yellow Springs, sat the Riverview Drive-In, a favorite summer spot known for its hamburgers, French fries, and ice cream. After it opened for the season, she'd gone there a couple of times after school with Marissa, and every time they were there, Marissa saw at least one person she knew.

Whomever Tony wanted to meet—she guessed it was Chris—hadn't arrived by the time they drove up. Tony perched atop one of the picnic tables beneath a huge red and blue umbrella. The umbrella had several tears through which one could see the bright sunshine on this early summer day. He surveyed the cars parked in front of the outdoor dining area and commented on a shiny Beemer and a rugged-looking bright yellow sport utility vehicle.

He pointed to the SUV. "Rich has one just like that. He said he'd sell it to me cheap when I get my license."

Sandy glanced at the long line of people waiting to order. "Do you want to eat?"

"No. I'll wait."

As soon as he answered, a group of four girls piled out of a car, all of them her former students. They seemed shocked at the sight of her. Two of them waved and said hello. One asked what she was doing this summer and where she would be teaching next year.

The smallest of them, Megan Kiefer, ran up to Tony and gave him a hug. The other girls drifted to him. Tony listened as the girls talked about their summer, and they asked him about some of the other boys.

"So what are *you* doing this summer, Tony B?" one of them said.

"He's dating Miss Katz," another giggled.

Megan frowned. "Will you all shut up? She's helping out because his dad's sick."

The girls grew silent and returned to their conversation. Sandy herded them to the food line, and Tony slipped behind her.

"Thanks, Sandy," he said in a low voice so the girls wouldn't hear. "I didn't think Megan would bring her friends."

Megan stepped toward them. "It was the only way I could get a ride. I'm really, really sorry, Tony." She twisted the small ring on her finger, the kind of ring Tony might have given her if they were going out. "So how is he?"

Tony stared at the ground. "About the same. I'm the one in trouble."

"What happened?" Megan's voice squeaked.

"He caught me getting into his weed."

Megan's eyes grew wide. "Your dad smokes pot?"

Tony buried his hands in his pockets and dug his toe into the gravel. He explained to Megan the way his father must have explained to him how marijuana controlled the nausea of chemotherapy. Finally, he said, "I was watching him smoke and wondering what it would be like to get high. So when he fell asleep, I swiped some of his stash and started rolling a joint. Except he wasn't asleep."

Megan blew out her breath. "Wow! Are you grounded?"

Tony fingered his necklace. "I wish. He gave me this speech about responsibility and trust, and how hard it is to earn back someone's trust if you break it."

"Well, maybe he shouldn't have been smoking in front of you."

"That's what he said too, and he wouldn't do it anymore. But I don't want him hurting himself because I fucked up."

Tony stepped away for a few minutes, and although she didn't see him, Sandy knew he was crying. Anger welled up in her. Not that she wanted Tony smoking pot, but Nick had laid a heavy guilt trip on the kid for giving in to temptation, for doing what plenty of thirteen-year-olds would have done under normal circumstances.

And she didn't want Nick to end up the way she had seen him at Southside that day—desperately ill, too weak to teach, to pursue his campaign against the chemical company, or to be of much use to anyone. She vowed to talk to him, to get him to change his mind.

She offered to take Tony and Megan to play miniature golf and then to Tony's house, where Megan could keep Tony busy and she could talk to Nick in private. Megan whipped out her cell phone and called her mother for permission, which was reluctantly granted. Megan explained that her mother believed leukemia might be contagious and she could get it from hanging around the Barans' house. Ironic, Sandy thought. She had looked up the Kiefers' address once and found they lived on Hummingbird Circle, a block away from where a child had died.

They returned from miniature golf around three thirty, and Tony and Megan settled down in front of the TV in the family room to watch a video. Nick arrived shortly after. He greeted the kids and dropped his shoulder bag and coat on the back of the sofa.

"How'd it go?" he asked Sandy.

"I have to talk to you."

"Okay." He opened the refrigerator and asked if she wanted anything. She shook her head. He took out a can of ginger ale and suggested they talk on the back porch. "I could use the fresh air."

The last time Sandy had been inside the house was in February, and because of the weather then, she hadn't seen the screened-in porch. It was a large, airy space, with a ceiling fan, window seats along two sides, a bay window, and doors to the kitchen and to an open deck. Two mountain bikes, one shiny yellow and silver, the other red and scratched, leaned against the far wall. In the center of the porch were a glass-top table and two chairs. On the wooden floor lay a bare mattress with a folded blanket, a pillow, and a rolled-up sleeping bag on top. A black guitar case rested against the window seat. Sandy noticed several paperbacks and a small desk lamp. She guessed that this was Tony's getaway spot, since he'd once told her he'd gone to sleep-away camp for several years and probably missed it this year.

She pulled up one of the chairs. Nick sat on the window seat and leaned against the side of the house. He loosened his tie, unbuttoned the top of his shirt, and took a couple of deep breaths. "What's up?"

"I heard about Tony getting into your weed," she began.

"What did he tell you?"

"He didn't say anything to me. I heard him tell Megan."

Nick twisted around and glanced in the direction of the house. Through the glass door, one could see the glow of the television and the two children in silhouette. "So?"

"He's really sorry about what he did. I saw he was

crying." She added after a moment, "And he feels really guilty, because he knows this is going to hurt you more than it hurts him."

Nick's upper lip curled. "Good."

She fished for the right words. *Don't you have better things to do with your summer than wreck your health to prove a point?* Far too provocative for a guy who had already shown his testiness. So was anything with the words "guilt" and "trip" in the same sentence.

Nick popped the top of his soda can and took a swallow. "Tony has to learn that his actions have consequences for others. I don't smoke pot for fun, and I'd never teach stoned under any circumstances."

"But don't you think it would make more sense to punish *him*? He's the one who made the mistake." She thought about all the things that were important to Nick. "You've got your classes and the soil samples to collect. Just because he's thirteen and does stupid teenage stuff doesn't mean you should sacrifice what you're doing."

Nick pushed the back of his head against the wall, stared up at the ceiling, and exhaled a long, measured breath. His face had a greenish tint, as though the sunlight had thrown the soda can's reflection onto him. "I think I've been at this parenting thing a lot longer than you, Sandy. I'll do what I have to do, and nothing you or Tony says will change anything. End of discussion." He glanced in her direction. She averted her eyes.

Then she thought of Tony inside with Megan—his very first girlfriend—and something in her snapped. "No, it's not ended," she said, her voice breaking. "Tony's going to have to live with what you did to him for the rest of his life. I may not be a parent, but I know what it's like to be a kid. And…" She drew in her breath and lowered her voice. "I know what it's like to be doing your best, putting your heart into something that's really hard for you to do, and you make one mistake—that's it." She slashed the air with her hand. "Is that the way you want Tony to feel?"

An expression of wide-mouthed shock crossed Nick's face, as if she'd punched him rather than merely challenged the wisdom of his childrearing techniques. His jaw twitched, and guilt at disturbing him swept through her. This was the man she had slept with. She still cared about him, and like Tony, she didn't want him to suffer more because of her. His sallow skin and the dark circles under his eyes showed his exhaustion; he could not answer her outburst. He sipped his ginger ale.

"You can fire me if you want." Her voice shook with her spent emotion. "I'm used to it."

"I would in a minute."

His words and the bitterness of his tone stabbed her. "Then go ahead. I'll bring the cluster map to your office. You can figure out how to explain my absence to Tony."

He released a wet burp and wiped his mouth with a handkerchief he pulled from his pocket. "That's the problem. Along with our history, and the fact that I don't have the energy to sit here all night and argue with you."

"So are you going to tell Tony instead that your health comes first and he'd better stay out of your medical marijuana because you need it?"

"Now that you've pounded me into submission, yeah. Thanks for putting it that way." Nick sagged into the padded window seat.

She scooted her chair closer to him. Her hand trembled as she felt his forehead. He was a bit warm. He took another sip of soda and closed his eyes. "I don't sleep much on Tuesday nights, so I'm pretty fried," he mumbled. "And the acid that disintegrated that little boy's skin."

"Yes?" *What about it?* She touched the back of his neck. He was starting to relax. Without opening his eyes, he handed her the can and tapped her forearm with his fist.

"Imagine having something like that dripped into your

bloodstream twice a week. Then try to think rationally." He sighed. "So if you hang around me, be prepared to listen to some crazy shit."

Before she could say anything else, he had drifted off to sleep. She maneuvered him onto his stomach because that was the way he usually slept, placed the pillow under his head, and went inside. Tony turned from his movie. "How did it go?"

"I think I talked him out of it."

"Yes!" Tony exclaimed, as if cheering on a winning basketball team and not worrying about a sick parent.

"You know what you have to do, though?"

His expression grew serious, and he nodded. "Should I talk to him now?"

"He's pretty wiped." She pointed to the back porch. "You'll need to check on him from time to time. If it gets cool out there, throw a blanket over him. He was a little feverish, so I left him uncovered."

Megan looked concerned and a little frightened. "Should I go?" she asked Tony.

Sandy saw Tony's face darken. "No. It's not contagious," she said.

* * *

The following Monday the heat wave began. When Tony arrived at nine, it was already eighty degrees outside. And Tony didn't want to do anything except sit in her apartment and play with the computer. By noon Sandy suggested they see a movie. At least it would be air-conditioned in the theater.

"You could take me home," Tony said. "My house is air conditioned."

She thought about how little fun he was having so far and the long hot weeks that stretched in front of him. "You know, maybe you should talk to your parents about going back to summer camp, now that Rosie's out of school."

"Been there, done that. Mom says Rosie has to earn money for college." He typed in a web address and hit the enter key. "But she said I could copy some of her CDs."

"Does she have a job yet?" Sandy hoped Rosie didn't, so he'd have an excuse for at least a little break.

"Yeah, she's working at a music store, so it's a good deal for me. By the way, do you want any CDs burned? I sell them cheap."

"Cheap's not low enough for my budget." Sandy wondered how much Tony made from his business. He was in the process of ordering a box of blank CDs and a computer game, using his father's credit card number. She asked him about it, and he told her he had permission. Suffering from the heat and still stinging from their argument, she didn't call Nick to verify.

She heard a knock at the downstairs door. She opened it, and her first thought was, *here comes trouble*. Ben stood at the door. He twirled a bike lock around his index finger. "Is Tony here?"

"How do you know Tony?" Hard as she tried, she couldn't keep the hostile edge from her voice.

"He's been around for weeks. I know everybody here."

She let him go upstairs. He greeted Tony—shook hands and touched fists with him in what looked like an elaborate gang greeting. Still chunky, Ben had stretched upward over the spring; he stood taller than Tony and almost as tall as she. His thick straight brown hair, now about two inches long, clung to his skull in contrast to Tony's, a lighter shade spiked up in front. He walked around her apartment, examined her computer and her books, and poked around her athletic equipment. He stopped at the huge map in her study.

"Is that the map your dad made?" he asked Tony.

Sandy flushed. Nick had obviously introduced the two boys, though she doubted he'd mentioned his dealings with Ben.

"Yeah." Tony explained the significance of the pushpins and showed the photocopy of the log that Sandy kept.

Ben flipped through the pages. "Except for your dad, I don't know anyone who has cancer."

They drifted back to the computer to check out some music sites. In spite of the heat, they wanted to go for a bike ride, so Tony borrowed Ben's old 18-speed and she borrowed Eddie's bike. During the ride, Tony told Ben about all the mountain bike trails he had done since taking up the sport at the end of sixth grade.

Spending time with a boy his own age seemed to make Tony happier than Sandy had seen him in a while. She wondered what he saw in Ben, because to her they had nothing in common. Was there something about Ben she didn't know? Or something about Tony? Or was it a friendship of necessity: with his school buddies at camp or out of town and him stuck at home alone caring for his father, did Tony simply hook up with the first kid who came along?

After they returned, Ben went home to take a shower. Sandy asked Tony what he thought of Ben.

"I like him. You know that bike he has?"

"Yes."

"It costs twelve hundred dollars. I looked at a bike like that, but Mom said we couldn't afford it."

* * *

She didn't see Tony on Wednesday. It concerned her because he only came if his father didn't need him. Nick hadn't yet purchased his next month's supply from Ben, and Ben wanted to know about his favorite customer. Sandy shrugged and said she had no idea. But she realized Nick had lied to her that afternoon at his house. He had told her what she wanted to hear and then done what he'd planned to do anyway without thinking of the burden it placed on Tony.

Nick located her the next day only by chance. She'd

planned to drive to Albany for the long Fourth of July weekend to spend as much time as possible at her parents' air-conditioned house. But she'd applied for several jobs in Cold Springs and had an interview on Thursday for an office clerk position at an SAT tutoring service. The manager had offered her the job on the spot. Twenty hours a week—two evenings and the weekends—at minimum wage. She'd miss the softball games for the rest of the season, but she needed the work. Her pay from watching Tony failed to cover the rent, and she hadn't figured into her budget the fact that Shady Ridge didn't pay teachers over the summer. She agreed to start after the holiday.

Sandy returned home to pack, and that was when the phone rang. Nick asked if she could drive Tony and a bag of soil samples to the college to give to Rich. His voice sounded distant, as if he were calling from far away.

She parked at the end of the driveway. Two mountain bikes leaned against the closed garage door, helmets dangling from the handlebars. On her way to the front door, she saw a shovel, trowel, and two pairs of battered work gloves lying in the dirt. The lawn, all patches of yellow and brown, reflected the neglect of a family distracted by more serious matters. Even the weeds appeared burned out.

She assumed Nick had called her to drive them because Rosie had taken the car or it had broken down. She rang the bell. Tony answered the door. He carried his red backpack from school, which was stuffed full and even dirtier than she remembered it from closing day. A Bob Marley tune played in the background.

"Car trouble?" she asked Tony.

"No. Dad passed out from the heat while we were digging up Mr. Brownfield's yard. He said he needed to rest."

"Excuse me." Sandy grabbed Tony's shoulders and pushed him aside. She shouted Nick's name but heard no answer. Just Marley wailing away.

She followed the music to the family room. Nick lay on

the sofa, sucking on a frozen juice pop, his skin ashen despite his tan. As an experienced jock, she knew a serious case of heat exhaustion when she saw it.

She turned down the stereo and felt his forehead. It was cool and damp. At least he didn't have heatstroke. Yet. She went into the bathroom. Avoiding the pile of filthy clothes on the floor, she scrounged three hand towels that she soaked with cold water. She wrung out the water and brought them to him.

"Take off your shirt," she said.

He didn't argue. All his body hair had fallen out, leaving his chest, stomach, underarms, and back a waxy yellow. His ribs protruded like large pieces of a broken cage. It seemed so long ago that she had snuggled against this body, explored every inch of it. But it was a different body then, firm and strong and whole. She wrapped one of the towels around his neck and chest and used the others to sponge down his head, face, back, and lower legs. As she worked, she gazed into his dull, sunken eyes, tried to find in them some spark of the Nick she'd known. Tony watched from the kitchen, his face twisted with concern. She asked him to bring his father another frozen pop.

She ripped the paper and handed the orange pop to Nick. He sucked it, his cheeks drawn inward. "Feel better now?" He nodded. He seemed a bit quiet for her comfort level, and she decided to check further. She moved one of his legs. He grimaced. "Cramps?"

"Yeah." His breathing quickened.

"I hope you don't plan to go walking around."

He shook his head.

"Do you have stomach cramps?" He made a so-so gesture with his free hand. "Do you think you can keep liquids down?"

"Sure."

She glanced up at Tony. "Get him water and one of those sport drinks."

"My water bottle's on my bicycle. And while you're there, put the bikes back on the porch, please," Nick said to Tony, his voice hardly more than a croak.

"You rode your bike over there in this heat?"

"It's six blocks," Nick retorted. "I know some people in the Heights drive across the street to get their mail, but I'm not one of them."

"And I assume it wasn't Tony's bright idea to go digging up a yard in the middle of the day in the middle of a heat wave."

Nick tried to sit. "No one would be out in the middle of the day to catch us."

Someone should put you in protective custody, she said to herself as she rinsed out the towels and began to sponge him down once more. "I'll take the samples, but I think you should call Holly to drive you to the hospital."

"I'll be fine. She's worried about her job. I don't want to bother her."

Sandy wondered about Holly's loyalty and why Holly had never once spoken to her in the time she'd worked as Tony's nanny. Did the fact that, in Nick and Tony's words, *she's against what we're doing* mean she'd gone back to Mr. Martineau and was seeing him at the office? "She should be worried about you."

"She would if I told her. She's the only reason I'm not in the hospital."

"What?"

"The doctor wanted to keep me there. She said she'd take care of me, but I doubt this is what she had in mind."

"So she left you with Tony who doesn't know any better."

"That was my idea." He flashed her a crooked smile. "He's with us and she isn't."

Sandy watched Tony refilling Nick's water bottle from the jug in the refrigerator and thought of how frightened the boy must have felt sneaking onto someone's property and then watching his father collapse from the heat. *Is this worth it*? she asked herself. Aloud, she asked Nick, "Are these soil samples really showing something?"

He licked his lips, orange from the juice pops, and handed her a wooden stick. "Oh, yeah. I got a bunch of matches. This house. The McDonoughs. The Ellsworths." He ticked off more names. "This is the third week Tony has helped me hit houses in the cluster. We sent out four sets of samples last week, and we have the Brownfields today."

Nick took the water bottle and blue sport-drink container from Tony and thanked him. He opened the top of the sport drink with his teeth and squirted the liquid into his mouth. She noticed red, swollen patches on his gums near his teeth. "Don't you think you and Tony should be doing something fun during your Thursdays together?"

"No. That's your job. I'm teaching him to become a man. Someone who cares about people and has something to contribute to society. What my parents—and your grandparents—would have called a *mensch*." He handed her the sport drink and squeezed the water bottle with both hands to create a pressurized stream that he gulped down. He lifted his left arm and squinted at his watch. "Listen, you two had better go. Rich may be willing to wait, but the post office won't."

She felt his forehead again. It was still cool. He'd begun to talk, and he wasn't hostile, both good news.

"Go on. I'll be all right," he urged. As she stood to go, he grabbed her arm. "Thanks, Sandy," he whispered. "You did good."

* * *

After the long weekend, Sandy joined Nick and Tony in the yard-digging business. She'd never realized what hot, hard work it was, for they had to dig deep beneath the topsoil to uncover whatever fill had been used to level the ground and build the houses. While Nick had obtained permission from a couple of the homeowners, they had to sneak onto two properties left vacant by families who had moved. They did much of their work in the heat of the day, when residents would not be around, and Nick insisted they wear masks and gloves.

While she and Tony dug and collected samples, Nick sat under a nearby tree or bush, gave directions, and wrote out labels for the containers. As both the heat wave and his treatments continued, she could tell he was getting weaker. The first week he stood lookout in case the cops or Marc Martineau drove by. The next two weeks he rested quietly in the shade while they worked and on returning home washed up, ate a snack, and went upstairs to lie down. She didn't know whether it was the cancer or the chemo that left him like this. She was afraid to ask him and just as afraid of losing him before all their work was done.

Tony now came to her only on Mondays. Ben waited for him. The two liked to go bike riding, but several times when they returned Sandy detected the odor of pot on their hair and clothing. Cheap pot too, pot that smelled like they'd stepped in dog crap. And once after Tony left, she opened an unfamiliar file on her computer and photos of naked women filled her screen.

The next time Tony came, she sat him down in her living room and told him she did not appreciate his smoking marijuana and downloading porn on her watch. She warned him, "Your dad's going to kill you if he finds out."

Tony gave her a contemptuous snort. "No, he won't. Except for class he barely gets out of bed."

She stood over Tony and stared him down. "You know what I'm going to do? I'm going to make you stay here by yourself. No Ben and no fun today. I want you to think about how your dad would feel if he knew what you've been doing."

She backed out of the room, congratulated herself for taking control, exactly what she would need to do if she found another teaching job. She grabbed a half-empty bottle of club soda from her refrigerator—one of a case Nick had left behind when he used to visit her—and poured a glass.

She heard Tony call her. She sat on the sofa next to him and put her arm around his thin shoulders. "What is it?"

He hesitated for what seemed like an eternity, though it couldn't have been more than a minute. "It's Dad. I've been taking care of him all summer, and I thought I was doing a good job, but he isn't getting any better." He wiped his nose with the back of his hand. "My whole life sucks, and I suck too."

She sighed. "Tony, your father is very ill. I know you feel responsible for him." Tony nodded. "But no matter what you do, no matter how attentive and caring you are, he's going to get weaker."

Tony interrupted. "I heard Mom tell a friend on the phone he was depressed. So I did screw everything up."

She didn't expect that from Tony. But even if he did get caught sneaking into his father's marijuana he couldn't blame himself for everything, she told him. All the while, she couldn't help but wonder. And worry. She had seen Nick angry, irritable, self-absorbed, but never depressed. She knew it ran in his family, though; he said once that both his father and his brother had been hospitalized for depression and that his father had later committed suicide. He'd asked her at the time if Judaism still considered suicide the unforgivable sin.

She decided to prod Nick a little. After he picked Tony up, pulling up in front of the house and honking as he had done all summer long, she signed on and began to compose an e-mail message, basically, *hi, how are you, haven't heard from you in a while*. And, *I miss you*.

She waited that night for a reply. Nothing. Nothing for the next couple of days either. They'd finished all their yards the week before, and then the heat wave broke with a spectacular nighttime thunderstorm that knocked out power to all of the suburbs east of the Yellow River.

When she got back from work the next night, a message

was waiting. Two sentences told her everything she wanted to know: *Don't take my silence as acquiescence. I'm fighting this thing every inch of the way.*

Twenty-five: Redemption Song

Except for the fact that her belly was flat rather than swollen, they looked like a slightly older expectant couple who had stumbled into the wrong room on their way to a birth preparation class. Nicholas and Holly stood about the same height, both slender and small-boned, which made them appear younger than their forty-four years despite the streaks of gray in their hair and creases at the corners of their eyes. They walked the gray-tiled hospital corridor hand in hand and joked nervously because it seemed the only sane response to a situation like this.

Nicholas remembered when he had accompanied Holly to those classes back in New York City. He remembered his triumphant smugness mixed with an overwhelming sense of responsibility for the pain he was about to cause her—had, in fact, already caused her because she suffered from morning sickness both times—and for the life of the new person he could then only imagine. He remembered the queasiness he felt on entering the classroom, in part sympathy with her, in part fear that he would not prove strong enough in spite of the absolute confidence he showed to the outside world. What he did not remember was the actual content of the class—deep-breathing exercises and other relaxation techniques—because when it came down to the final hours, the pain would be her problem and he figured he would just hold her hand or rub her back or listen to her curse him for having knocked her up in the first place. So he let his mind wander to the classes he would soon teach and the stories he would tell of people half a world away who dreamed and struggled and usually lost.

But this time it was his turn and he would have to pay attention. And despite the guilt Holly admitted, Nicholas considered her in no way responsible for his pain because there was no way she could have known; she had been deceived just like him and everybody else in the neighborhood. His doctor had suggested the class, and he'd signed up because that other class had worked so well for Holly. He couldn't understand it, though, visualizing a peaceful place on a beach somewhere when his idea of fun was hurtling down a twisting mountain bike trail and his idea of relaxation was chucking rocks through car windows in a junkyard or jogging along the bank of a poisoned river.

Still, he couldn't stay stoned for the rest of his life even if he hadn't caught Tony in his stash. He had to keep his mind clear for his teaching and for assembling all the evidence he'd collected on the chemical company and the toxic landfill. Besides, he'd begun to develop a tolerance, not unlike the tolerance the cancer would one day develop to the poison he fed it twice a week. The way he saw it, weed was like the lifeline on that game show everyone watched; if he laid off it now, he would have it when he made it to the million dollar question.

* * *

In Holly's place as caregiver, the kid did the best he could. The first time was the day of his thirteenth birthday, his Bar Mitzvah, but for Tony there was no prayer, no Torah reading, and certainly no party afterward. He'd gotten the idea of dragging his bottom-bunk mattress, formerly a storage area for loose CDs, to the screened-in back porch. He then hauled out his sleeping bag, a lamp, and a radio, and set up the equivalent of summer camp—believing, no doubt, that, like at camp, the two of them would have deep, heartfelt talks until the wee hours of the morning. And there Nicholas lay Tuesday and Friday nights, those surreal wasted nights that followed his treatments when nothing else in his crazed busy life mattered except getting through the next twenty-four hours. If there were any heartfelt talks to be had in those hours, he didn't remember them.

Submerged in a thick, swirling nausea, his head throbbing, the toxic chemicals burning in his veins, he vaguely perceived the ballgame on the radio as he drifted in and out of consciousness. He was of the last generation to lie outside on hot summer nights, to listen to the radio and dream of diamond glory before cable channels, satellite dishes, and regional sports networks brought everyone indoors and chained them to the television set. The fresh air helped a bit to settle his stomach, and located as he was on a bluff about halfway between New York and Boston he could usually catch the Red Sox, the Yankees, or the Mets when he needed them. On clear nights Tony would fiddle with the dial until he located a station as far away as Ohio or even Chicago. And then there were those superstations going strong at three in the morning with all the liberal-haters, anti-tax reactionaries, Christian patriots, white supremacists, and neo-Nazis whose ravings would have made Nicholas sick if he weren't already there.

"Damn it, Tony, can we find something else?" he groaned after hearing an especially odious anti-Semitic diatribe between dry heaves. By now he understood the neurobiology, but he wished he could convince his brain that the poison was flowing through his bloodstream rather than sitting in his stomach—his long-ago emptied stomach, its lining now stripped to raw muscle.

"I'll call them up and tell them to get fucked," Tony answered.

Nicholas pressed a wet towel to the parched skin of his face and head. "Don't bother. In this life, you have to choose your battles." The effort of pushing the words through his throat set off another spasm of useless retching. His thoughts came in gasps punctured by pain. *Choose your battles. Give everything you have to them. Toxic waste. Saving Tony. How much more could you have done without this damned sickness?* The strands of saliva he spat into the plastic bucket tasted metallic, like blood. He knew he should have been lying flat with his eyes closed, not moving or talking or thinking, but the kid had so much to learn.

Tony shut off the radio and stared at him with his hands over his ears and his lips quivering. As the nausea dissipated, Nicholas heard him stammer, "You're not going to tear out your insides from puking, are you?"

"Not a chance," Nicholas whispered. "Internal organs are pretty well attached. Like a roller coaster. Once you realize that, it takes the edge off." He gulped the cool night air, contemplated the profound soreness around the middle of his body and what if anything could make it more bearable. "Rub my back, will you, kiddo?" He eased himself face down on the mattress.

Tony's fingers grazed his skin through his t-shirt. "You're, like, on fire."

"I have a fever. It's the chemicals. They burn from the inside." Nicholas sighed. "Look, I know you're scared to touch me. But you're not going to catch anything, and you're not going to hurt me. You need to force yourself past your fear." He reached up and grasped Tony's wrist. His palm rubbed against his son's rough hemp bracelet. "Put your hand on my back until you're not scared anymore."

The physical contact made him calm and sleepy, and soon he dozed off. When he awoke, he heard Tony stir. The boy mumbled an apology and began to knead the space between his shoulder blades.

"How long was I out?" His throat ached, and a rolling queasy sensation signaled another wave of sickness on its way.

"Hour and a half. Feel better?"

Nicholas lifted his head and scanned the horizon for a hint of light. He saw nothing but darkness, a sliver of moon, and a few stars. "I won't feel better for a while," he answered after a moment. "But when I do, I'm going to kick some ass."

Tony laughed. Filled with pride at how the boy had stayed with him despite his fear, Nicholas rose to his knees, grabbed Tony around the head, and hugged him. Acid seared his throat and mouth, his stomach's protest at the sudden movement. He swallowed the bitter fluid and sent Tony into the house for a cup of ice.

The voice that scolded him inside his head sounded like Holly's. She would have told him to listen to his body. He listened, all right. But not liking what he heard, he got himself into a full-blown abusive relationship with it: Swear at it. Push it. Get kicked in the gut.

It all came with wanting to live.

Tony returned with the ice chips and his acoustic guitar. "Do you want me to read to you or do you want me to play?"

"Your decision. You're the one up all night looking after me." Nicholas filled his inflamed mouth with the crushed ice and lay back against the side of the house, letting the cool water trickle down his throat, not caring if it came right back up again. While Tony practiced the complex fingering of a song he was learning, Nicholas focused his mind on Dante's *Inferno*, a book he hadn't read since college. He began to speculate as to which circle of hell he'd been consigned and the multitude of things he had done in his life to end up there.

* * *

Though an Ivy League graduate, *summa cum laude*, Nicholas was clearly failing the relaxation class. The instructor spent at least half her group time working with him, urging him to let go of the tension that gripped his body.

He shrugged and glanced at Holly. "I don't know. I'm basically a tense guy."

He felt stupid and embarrassed and wanted to quit, but Holly had gotten into it. She enjoyed talking to the other spouses, and he knew how important it was for her to find support. His crusade had isolated her in the neighborhood, one of the things she'd told him when she returned from Minnesota, when they'd agreed to keep their marriage intact in spite of her betrayal.

He wondered if they had a resource room for people like him, the totally learning-disabled when it came to deep breathing and visualization. Or since his mind still wandered to his twentieth-century European history class and his new workshop on how to teach to keep students awake, maybe someone should diagnose him with adult attention-deficit-hyperactivity disorder and throw some Ritalin into the chemical stew he was mainlining on a regular basis.

Holly arranged a conference with the instructor and a social worker from the hospital. They asked him how he managed to continue teaching so effectively and what techniques and skills he could transfer.

He shook his head. "I can't really take apart my teaching like that. I mean, I could teach you how to teach." Seeing the shock and upset on the instructor's face, he tried again. "I don't mean you personally. It's just this summer workshop I'm running. Anyway, I'm sure what you're doing works for some of the others." He thought of apologizing for his frankness, not that he'd ever apologized to Sandy or to anyone else who had problems teaching, but he'd never been the worst student in the class either.

The social worker suggested an anger-management workshop. Holly thought it was a good idea. She didn't say it in those words, but he got the point: *How many cancer patients have a framed order of protection against them sitting on their nightstand?* Because Holly had begged him not to hang it on the wall, his stood upright against the table lamp amid orange pill bottles, cups of juice and water, a box of tissues, and a package of salted crackers.

He refused the workshop. He needed the anger; it kept him alive. He imagined himself in an interrogation room deep inside the abandoned Hometown Chemical Company factory. Sometimes the torturer was a company executive wearing a suit and tie and a black ski mask that concealed his identity. Sometimes it was Marc. The company exec kicked the back of his head, punched him in the stomach, beat his legs, hips, ribs, and spine with a crowbar. Marc always kneed him in the balls. Struggling against the pain, he told himself he'd pass out before he'd surrender and when he awakened he would beat the cancer and wreak revenge on his torturers.

But as the heat wave hung around like a houseguest who'd stayed too long, Nicholas felt himself wearing down more quickly than he'd expected. *Fatigue is a different type of torture, harder to fight against. You'd confess to anything to be able to sleep.* And he came to understand how he could be a cross-country champion in high school but never win at the college level: he'd never paced himself.

After his bout with heat exhaustion, he cut back his workouts and shortened his bike rides to the evening hours and his own neighborhood. He abandoned Tony's summer camp on the back porch for the air-conditioned master bedroom and Holly's back rubs when she arrived home from work. She never feared to touch him even at the worst moments. Patiently she stretched his cramped leg muscles and massaged the aches from deep inside his bones. She probed his shaking, feverish body for the places to hold, to stroke, that would calm the uncontrollable rebellion of an assaulted system gone haywire. She kept the records that allowed him to remain with her.

She always took out the journal as soon as she got home. Wednesdays were the hardest. He needed to show the doctors he could recover from the treatments.

A typical conversation: "Did you eat lunch today?"

"Yes. A glass of apple juice, a bowl of tomato soup, four crackers."

"Did it stay down?"

"No."

"How long did you keep it?"

"Couple hours. The meds wore off."

"Maybe you should try to find some pot. I don't know why you stopped."

"It's okay. I had a mug of tea and feel fine now."

He watched her list the composition of his lunch, and in the space after "emesis" she penned a large zero.

She encouraged him to redirect his rage, visualize the poison killing the cancer cells as they'd taught in the class. *Don't think about the chemical company, focus on getting better, Nicky baby*, she'd say to him. Even if the graphic and violent imagery of total warfare that he conjured from his knowledge of twentieth-century European history did nothing to soothe his agony—and perhaps because of his twisted imagination made it even more intense—he felt as though he had gotten something right every time he ripped up his insides in the name of victory. He called her his "special education tutor," the one who did his homework for him and sat beside him during the tests.

He knew he put a lot of pressure on her, for without her patron, her job at the advertising agency was no longer secure. She now crawled into work most mornings looking like a zombie, and although he appeared no less zombified, he could at least count on the adrenaline fix he got from his well-trained and expectant audience. He told her she should quit and take back her old job, but she said they needed the money. He didn't question her, for she paid the bills. Instead, he went to his college president, the Boston Brahmin ex-civil-rights activist who had always taken a special interest in the fellow political exile from his home state, and arranged to teach a workshop in the fall for new teachers in the area. One class, for as long as he could manage it, but he would receive his salary and benefits for the entire semester as though he'd taught a full schedule.

He told her what he'd negotiated. She seemed relieved, and he was happy to be able to take care of her after all she'd done for him. But she didn't quit the job. He suspected she was hiding something about their financial situation. He didn't want to ask, not only because he didn't want another reason to worry but also because he, too, had so much to hide from her.

He never told Holly and as much as possible tried to keep it out of his own consciousness, but after his bone-marrow transplant in California he'd come down with an infection that had left him with a damaged heart valve. When the doctors there warned him about it, he treated it like a computer error message: ignore it, try again, and if everything worked, proceed as though nothing had happened. And except for the occasional dizzy spell that he attributed to nerves, low blood sugar, or dehydration, or the chest pains he dismissed as an upset stomach, he never thought about it until the doctor reviewing his case for a second bone-marrow transplant exclaimed, "You did *what* with a heart in that condition?" But the heart valve that never stopped him from playing ball, mountain biking, rock climbing, or engaging in high-energy theatrics in the classroom ten to twelve times a week, got him turned down for a second transplant and every experimental therapy for which he applied, except the hair study for which he'd been on his best behavior.

Even if Holly's touch made the physical pain more bearable, she couldn't take away his fear that he would not finish assembling the information on the chemical company before he died. There was still so much to do. Results had to come in from the lab; he had to organize everything so some nearly clueless journalist or lawyer could understand it; he had to decide who should file the class-action suit, when, and how; and he did not yet have a smoking gun. In the debilitating July heat, he slept sixteen hours a day, rousing himself only to teach, eat, endure his treatments, and direct Tony and Sandy as they dug up the final yards on his list. As he drifted from consciousness, he would tell himself he wasn't dying but pacing himself, resting up for one final assault.

Although the chemotherapy hadn't induced a remission, it had brought the disease under control, setting up in his bloodstream an uneasy standoff between healthy and defective white cells. The doctors gave him a three-week break at the beginning of August to build himself up before trying a powerful new therapy.

His primary oncologist and one of the others didn't want to do it. Earlier rounds of chemo, they said, had strained and further weakened his heart, which was why he'd had so much trouble with the heat. "Your heart might not take this one," they warned.

"I'm dead in a month if I don't do it," he snapped.

His doctor explained that he could die instantly and that he would have to spend at least three nights, maybe more, in the hospital after every weekly infusion, on an IV and a heart monitor. "To be honest, with your heart, I don't give you more than a fifty percent chance of surviving the treatment."

"But it works," Nicholas told him.

"The remission rate is about twenty percent. And it should extend your life even without a remission—if you make it through the full course."

Nicholas ran the percentages through his mind, as well as the work he still had to do. "I'll take my chances."

They arranged to start the therapy on a Sunday afternoon, the third week in August. He met with his college president to schedule his class around it, beginning after Labor Day.

But on Monday, the final week in July, Nicholas had an unexpected visitor to his office, a delicately built light-skinned young Black woman who wore glasses and her short hair natural in a light-blue hairband that matched her sleeveless t-shirt and jeans.

She was Tasha Lockwood, from his class the previous fall. Her sister Diane had taken his class several years earlier. Their other sister, Monique, played ball.

His former students would often come back to ask for recommendations or advice on four-year colleges. Nicholas already knew that Tasha was headed to the state university in the fall to pursue a pre-med program because she'd asked him for advice and a recommendation, both enthusiastically granted. He'd also found her tutoring assignments to earn extra money. He guessed she'd come to thank him and get some final tips before leaving town.

She carried an envelope, which intrigued him. And she seemed nervous, which concerned him. She sat on his sofa. He pulled up his desk chair and sat across from her. They chatted about summer school, now in its second to last week. She looked as though she was about to cry, and he guessed that something had come up and she wouldn't be able to attend college. He started to ask her, but she spoke first. "Dr. Baran, promise you won't tell anyone I'm doing this. Not even my sisters."

"Promise." She handed him the open envelope. He took out the piece of paper inside, expecting an official letter, but on the page was a handwritten list.

Tasha took a deep breath. "I was a file clerk at Hometown Chemical Company last summer. My boss made me put metal clips in the files, and when the files didn't fit into the cabinets afterward, he made me take them out. I got to know those files real well."

He examined the list: "1980, dredging of Yellow River;" "1980-1990, landfill;" "1985- , rental of storage site." There were several other notations that involved dumping into the river and federal inspections of the wells in Yellow Springs Heights. Next to each notation were archive numbers that corresponded to cabinets where the relevant files were stored.

Tasha continued. "My oldest sister told me what you were doing. She heard from one of her friends who's helping you. I met her a couple of times, that teacher named Sandy who plays on their team."

"My son was in her class last year. She became involved

because some of the kids in the school were getting sick." He looked into Tasha's wide brown eyes. "You and Sandy have good hearts. I really appreciate that."

Tasha glanced down at her folded hands. "I heard what happened to you." She raised her head again, and her eyes met his. "I hope you get better soon. And I hope this helps you."

"Absolutely."

"Are you going to give it to the newspaper?"

"No. I need you to keep a secret too." When she assured him she would, he smiled. "I'm going in myself. I'd rather have the files in my hands, and then I'll decide what I want to do with them."

She drew back, stunned. He guessed she couldn't believe that her esteemed professor would do anything criminal. But then again, what were all the heroes whose stories he told in class but criminals in the eyes of their governments?

"Don't worry," he said to her. "If I get caught, I won't tell them where I got the information. They can pull out my fingernails, beat me, whatever. I've been through worse." She nodded as if she knew already. His eyes pierced hers. "We talk about how history is full of people who put their lives on the line to fight injustice. Right now I'm done with talking."

Her eyes were bright. "Good luck, Dr. Baran. I'll pray for you."

Before she left, she told him she would try to find another former student, an ex-boyfriend of Diane's who used to work as a plumber at the company and could tell him how to break in without getting caught. And again, she promised to pray for him.

* * *

Two days later, the heat wave broke. Two days after that, Nicholas went in for his last treatment. He had three weeks to get stronger and to make a plan. Three weeks for Tasha to get him the rest of the information.

The second week in August he borrowed Rich's jeep and took Tony, Ben, and Sandy up to Hamilton Hills for an afternoon of mountain biking. Ben showed off his expensive double-suspension bicycle, purchased, no doubt, with his drug money. But he didn't know how to ride a mountain trail. He sat on the cell tower's concrete platform while Sandy rode his bike. Nicholas took a seat next to him and stared up at the thirty-foot-high tower. Its thin metal beams glinted in the sunlight against an intense blue sky. In the heat that pressed in on him, Nicholas thought he felt the pulsing of radio waves, hundreds of invisible conversations, radioactive particles, electron beams—all with the power to rearrange and mutate.

"Aren't you riding, Mr. Baran?" Ben held a rolled-up magazine and swatted his bare lower legs with it from time to time.

Nicholas wiped his sweaty forehead with the sleeve of his t-shirt, "If I do something crazy and wipe out, the bleeding might not stop."

"That's too bad. Tony told me how much you like to ride." Ben unrolled the magazine, *High Times*. The article he was reading had to do with hybrids that grew best in cold climates.

"Did you have a chance to look at the Malcolm X autobiography?" Nicholas asked. Anticipating the worst from his next round of chemo, he'd purchased two ounces from Ben the week before and given him the money inside the thick paperback.

Ben's ears reddened. "I, uh, exchanged it at the newsstand." He held out the magazine. "For this."

Had it been Tony, Nicholas would have felt disappointment. And as a principal beneficiary he couldn't blame Ben for wanting to extend his growing season. Ben cared well for the clusters of plants scattered deep inside the vacant lot and harvested a good crop, chemical-free and so smooth the smoke didn't burn his irritated throat as he sucked it down.

He unfolded the newsletter he had brought to read while waiting for the others. It had arrived in the mail just before he left. Titled "River Journal," it appeared to be from one of the environmental groups he supported. But when he examined it closely, he saw the logo of Hometown Chemical's parent company headquartered in New York. "Would you look at this?" he said to Ben.

Ben glanced up from *High Times*. "Huh?"

"Do you know what propaganda is?"

Ben shook his head. Nicholas paged through the glossy newsletter filled with color photos of nature scenes and stories about how it was safe to eat the fish from the Yellow River and how eagles had come to nest in the surrounding areas. But in all his years living there, he'd never seen an eagle. "And as far as the fish are concerned, it's safe to eat them—because there aren't any left," he told Ben.

Ben laughed. His laugh seemed forced. Nicholas thought there was so much he could teach Ben if Ben could for one moment step away from his visions of riches in the drug trade. Nicholas tried to remember if he'd had those dreams when he was thirteen and lived in the trailer park, but the only dreams he could recall had to do with getting his mother back.

He read one more article before he returned the newsletter to his back pocket. It was a smaller piece that described the recently shut-down well. According to the article, the well had been closed because it was too old and expensive to run and a newer, more efficient well had been constructed on the eastern edge of Yellow Springs Heights.

More propaganda. He knew Global Millennium was worried, and he had to move quickly—before Labor Day at the latest. He hoped that the files had not been moved from the backwater Cold Springs office to New York City after the acquisition.

When he dropped Ben and Sandy off that evening, she

dashed upstairs and brought him an envelope. "Monique gave this to me, but when I opened it, the note said it was for you."

Inside were two tickets to a preview showing of an action movie at the North Springs Gigaplex on Saturday night. Attached to the note that read, "Please give this to Dr. Baran. Do not open," was a smaller envelope. He opened it and read, "I'm working the concession stand Saturday night. My friend's going to be there. Let's meet."

* * *

Tasha was at the concession stand when Nicholas showed up with Tony. She asked him to come by in an hour, after the stand closed for the night. So the boy wouldn't worry, Nicholas said he had to see someone with information about the soil samples and would meet him in the lobby at the end of the movie.

In the small office behind the stand, Nicholas saw her and DeShawn Fallon. DeShawn lived in Clear Springs, where he now worked as an independent plumber. He showed Nicholas pictures of his wife and baby daughter.

DeShawn took some folded papers from his pocket. Maps of the building. Diagrams of the heating and air conditioning system. A cleaning schedule that he'd gotten from a friend who worked for the company's janitorial service.

At home that night, Nicholas went out to the back porch and examined the papers under the light of the desk lamp that Tony had left behind. It was well past midnight, and everyone else had gone to sleep, but he felt wide-awake, full of energy, as if the cancer hadn't returned and he would live forever. Outside, crickets chirped, insects buzzed, and the cool wind rustled through the trees. He sniffed the fresh breeze and let it fill his body.

A year ago he had taken the first samples from the river and the riverbank and had come upon the body of a small child partially consumed by acid. So much had happened since then, and now he held in his trembling hands the final piece of the puzzle, the directions to the documents that would implicate the Hometown Chemical Company's officers. Soon the whole world would know exactly what they had done.

If the documents were still there.

He lay back on Tony's mattress and began to plan the break-in in his mind. He needed to choose a day. On Sunday afternoon he would start the new chemo regimen, and he wanted to wait a week so he would know what to expect. That put him at the last week of August, right before Labor Day, an ideal time because people went on vacation then.

He didn't want to go in alone if he didn't have to. Two people could help each other break into the building, search through the documents, carry them out, and photocopy them at his department office afterward. And while he felt strong now, he didn't know what condition he'd be in then.

He considered the possibilities. Only three existed—one of the kids or Sandy. He had dragged the kids through too much already. Sandy had volunteered.

He called her on Sunday morning while he packed his suitcase for a three-night hospital stay. They talked a little about the softball season. Then he told her about the information a pair of unnamed supporters had given him.

"Cool!" she shouted over the phone. He pulled the phone away a moment too late, and his ear was ringing.

"Okay." He lowered his voice, even though no one else was home. "Would you be willing to go in with me?"

"When?"

"The week after this one. I'll let you know. It'll be at night." It occurred to him that she worked two nights a week. He'd have to fit that into his plans.

"My office is closed for vacation next week."

"Do you want to think about it?"

"No." For a moment there was silence on the line, and

then Sandy spoke again. "We've come too far not to get them."

* * *

That was the thing about dying. People left you alone a lot because they thought you needed to rest, or they were afraid to be around you, or they didn't know what to say. Or like Holly they had to deal with everything else in their life. But when his body hurt too much for him to rest, Nicholas lay alone in bed thinking.

He had never considered himself an introspective person; he would much rather be out doing something or talking to someone or finding things he didn't like in the world and trying to change them. But there was a limit to what he could do while shivering in a flimsy hospital gown in the middle of the night, under heavy sedation but aching and nauseated, catheterized and tethered to an IV and monitor without Holly to climb into the narrow bed beside him as she had the night before.

When Nicholas was younger, he would boast to his friends that Holly didn't know half the crazy things he had done in his life. Over the past year or so, it seemed that the ratio of things she knew to things she didn't know had dropped to about one in ten.

He wouldn't tell her of his relationship with Sandy, how in his pain and his compulsion to perpetrate as well as suffer he had let things get out of hand, and then it had felt so good he didn't want to stop. He had made Sandy a promise that he intended to keep.

But except for the affair, and as soon as he pulled off the break-in at the chemical company, he pledged to himself that he would tell Holly everything. Without flinching, she'd followed him into this circle of hell to which he had been condemned in order to ease his suffering; for that, she deserved his honesty and his trust.

Twenty-six: Steal Home

Sandy had answered so quickly that it was only after she hung up she realized what she'd agreed to do: break into a building along with a crazy dying man who had nothing to lose.

She saw herself back at his house on a cold February night, him drinking straight scotch out of a water glass. Had she left that night, he would have finished the bottle and gone to walk the path by the river. After he had told her about his father, she knew she'd made the right decision.

This time she feared he'd take Tony if she backed out. Bar Mitzvah or not, Tony was a child. He deserved the protection of the adults around him, whether those adults were the officers of a company that had contaminated the only home he'd known, or his history teacher and his own father. But her resolve didn't chase away nightmares of the police closing in. Every time she drove through downtown Cold Springs, she went out of her way to avoid the fifteen-story building that housed the chemical company. She didn't want her visions attached to a specific place, one where she would be committing multiple felonies in less than a week.

Nick called again the following Sunday morning. She asked him how the chemo had gone. She hoped he'd changed his mind, decided he wasn't physically up to burglary and would give the information to a public-interest lawyer instead.

No such luck. "Well, I know what to expect, and I've made my plan. Are you on a portable phone?"

"No."

"Good." He paused for a moment. "We're going in Tuesday night."

"Aren't you supposed to be in the hospital that night?"

"Yeah." He laughed. "A perfect time to bust out with

nobody finding me. Doc's on vacation until Labor Day, so it's amateur week at Burnham Med. They pull my catheter on Tuesday aft—"

"Catheter?"

"Yeah, otherwise the chemicals fry my bladder. But it's a little hard to crawl through a building with a tube in your dick and a bag on your leg." He blew out his breath, making a single pop over the phone line. "I'll talk the attending physician into letting me out since they're always looking to cut costs. Then, I'll tell Holly not to visit that night, that they're running some tests. Tony will back me up."

At the other end of the phone line, Nick couldn't see her shaking her head in disbelief. "You're psycho."

"Tell me something I don't know," Nick fired back. "Listen, Holly will come to see me during her lunch hour on Tuesday, twelve thirty to one thirty. Bring Tony by at two thirty. He'll have a bag of stuff that I need. Afterward, drop him off at home, and get me by five. I'm going to tell them you're the nanny coming to pick me up."

"And then?"

"We'll go to your place and run through the final plan. I'll see you Tuesday at two thirty?" The way he made it sound like a question seemed to give her a way out. But she'd made her commitment.

"Okay." It occurred to her that he was speaking unusually frankly on these Sunday morning calls, so she asked where Holly and the kids were.

"Sunday Mass. She's gotten religious in the past few weeks. And technically, Rosie and Tony are Catholic." He hesitated, then added, "Some advice from one who's been there. Don't marry outside the faith."

He was wrong, Sandy told him. Things had changed since he'd walked out of the synagogue at age thirteen and had never gone back. Reform congregations accepted as Jewish the children of Jewish fathers, so Tony and Rosie could be Jewish if they wanted. But it did make things more complicated, which was why she'd dated only one non-Jewish boy in her life, way back in high school.

She offered to take Tony to Friday night services. Nick dismissed her with a grunt. Did he really believe religion to be the opiate of the masses? Or its nineties equivalent—for chumps? And when she thought about it, what did Judaism mean to her? Was it anything more than a social life, something to put on a résumé for college, and a set of rituals and abstract rules to live by? What kind of faith did she have if she couldn't even defend it to one of her own?

She considered her unanswered prayers. And the fact that she hadn't given up trying. "You don't get it, do you?" she said.

Nick sighed. "Get what?"

"They're all praying for you." When he didn't respond, she continued. "Holly and Tony and Rosie. Monique and Tasha."

"So you know about Tasha?"

"I suspect she gave you the information on the files. I know she's going to church every Sunday and praying for you." Sandy took a deep breath, tried in vain to control the tremor in her voice. "*I'm* praying for you." She held the mouthpiece away from her face.

"You're crying," he said softly.

"No, I'm not. But maybe if you knew all these people were making this effort for you, you'd at least appreciate it."

"Sandy, listen to me." Nick cleared his throat. "I don't remember much of what my rabbi told me when I was preparing for my Bar Mitzvah, but I remember one thing. 'Nicky,' he said, 'I know you're an athlete. I know many athletes pray to win. But that's not what you do. You work hard to win, but you pray that if you lose, you lose with courage and dignity.'"

Sandy shook her head. "That's beautiful. I never thought of it that way."

His voice hardened. "I don't intend to lose."

And I don't intend to give up. Maybe she wouldn't lead him back to his faith, but she wouldn't let him turn her away from hers.

* * *

As soon as she saw him in the hospital on Tuesday, Sandy knew Nick was flying. Laughing at his own jokes that weren't even funny. Being a goofy teenager, Tony didn't seem to notice, but it made her uncomfortable. She handed Nick the last batch of printouts that she and Tony had picked up from Rich. Nick glanced at the pages and tossed them to the foot of the bed, where they slid to the floor. Now even more worried, she stuffed them back into her purse. In less than eight hours, she and he would be pulling off a burglary—not an ideal time to get stoned and stupid.

Nick sent Tony downstairs to the cafeteria to bring him some ice cream. As soon as Tony left, Nick motioned for her to pull her chair closer.

Through his thin hospital gown left open in front, Sandy saw an IV tube taped to his chest and wires connected to monitor pads. A dark red liquid flowed into him from an almost-flattened bag hanging from a pole. A black bandanna on his head accentuated his pallor. Squeezing her chair between the bed and the pole, Sandy sniffed to detect the odor of marijuana, but a medicinal smell overpowered everything. She realized this was her first time in someone's hospital room, and so far she hadn't panicked. All she'd done to get there was follow Tony, who knew the way.

Nick grabbed her upper arm. "I talked to the chief resident this morning. We made a deal that if I ate all my lunch and kept it down, he'd sign me out."

She glanced at the door Tony had left open a crack. "Looks like you're doing more than that."

"It's called a serious case of the munchies. You wouldn't believe how much I've smoked."

"How did you get away with it?"

"I have my ways." He grinned, and she noticed his bloodshot eyes.

"Let me guess. Another one of your former students…"

He nodded emphatically before she could finish. "Now if some of them could get themselves elected to the state legislature and legalize it for medical purposes, I'd be really happy."

"So are you going to be okay for tonight?" she asked, the concern in her voice unmistakable even to one so incredibly stoned.

He assured her that the effects of the marijuana would wear off by then, but they hadn't when she picked him up at five. He wore the break-in clothes Tony had delivered in the red shoulder bag earlier that afternoon—a fresh bandanna, a black t-shirt, blue jeans, and black canvas high-top sneakers with thick rubber soles. To grip the metal ducts that they'd be crawling through, he'd explained earlier. In addition to the shoulder bag, he'd brought Tony's old school backpack to carry the documents. He giggled when she cut the hospital bracelet from his wrist, and he insisted on cooking dinner. He put together a couple of omelets from the odds and ends in her refrigerator and did a decent job, she had to admit. Better than boiling spaghetti, which was her idea, though she felt too nervous to eat. He finished the food on her plate as well as his and went into her bedroom to lie down.

"Wake me at nine," he said before he shut the door.

Left alone for three hours, she washed the dishes, watched a little TV, checked her e-mail, stared out the window at the setting sun, and imagined the police surrounding her and carting her off to jail. *Enjoy the sunset. The next one you see might be from behind the high walls of a prison yard.* The heat had returned the day before, and except for her bedroom, which had a fan, the apartment was still and sultry even after sundown. It seemed like an eternity until nine o'clock arrived.

When Nick rejoined her in the kitchen, his relaxed,

drugged expression was gone. She studied the whites of his eyes, shiny and the color of skim milk, and his pale eyelids without lashes to protect them. He filled a couple of water bottles, then took her club soda from the refrigerator and drank it straight from the bottle. She didn't think it was the healthiest thing to do for someone with a decimated immune system, but she kept quiet.

"Hot night." He followed his words with a loud belch.

"I know."

He took another long swig. "We'll need to carry extra water."

Sandy nodded. Nick went through a written checklist of the things they needed and repacked everything in the shoulder bag. He dropped fresh batteries into a pair of high-beam flashlights, then grabbed a handful of paper clips from her desk and stuffed them into his back pocket. Finally, he took two joints from the inside of his sock and hid them inside the three-hole punch in the top left-hand drawer of her desk. "I better leave these behind," he said. "Just in case something goes wrong, I don't want drug possession added to our rap sheet."

He opened a folded stack of papers and described the plan. The night custodians entered the building at nine and started cleaning from the basement up. She and Nick would follow at ten once that floor was finished, enter through the loading dock, and take a flight of stairs located next to the service elevator. Near the bottom of the stairs was a large custodians' storage closet. There they would climb through the air conditioning vent and crawl through the ducts until they reached the back room where the archived files were kept.

He explained that the incriminating files were located in a storage room behind the library, accessible only through the library. The library had a security system, but the storage room did not. There had once been a security camera, but it had broken and been removed the summer before. Thus, they could bypass the building's entire security and surveillance system by crawling through the ducts and slipping out inside the storage room. Once they had the files, they would put everything back as they had found it, climb back through the vent, crawl through the ducts, and leave the way they had come in. The goal was to leave no trace of their presence so that no one would know the files had been taken. Then they would go to Nick's office, photocopy the files, and come back to her place to sort them until morning, at which point she would drop Nick off at home.

"I'm a little vague on the scenario once we get to my office with the files," Nick said. "At some point, I'm going to crash."

Sandy's heartbeat stuttered. "So what will happen then?"

"I don't know. I'll handle it. But you might have to do more of the work, and it might take longer."

Would he handle it like he had handled his encounter with heat exhaustion? His cavalier attitude toward the dangers they faced left her with the urge to back out altogether, no matter how angry he'd be if she refused to go in with him. At that late hour, he couldn't take Tony, so the boy would be safe too. "Wait a second." She clutched his arm. "We need to talk about this."

He jerked his arm away. "No, we don't." He tapped the folded papers on her kitchen table. "Look at me."

She met his piercing stare. *I'm not going to let him intimidate me. Or lie to me, as he can do so easily.*

"I'll be honest with you, kiddo. I'm taking a bit of a chance here," he began. He told her that he was still toxic from the chemo and would be feeling its effects until well into the next day. He insisted that it was his problem, not hers, and that he had planned the break-in itself so carefully she had nothing to worry about as long as she followed his directions and didn't get scared. She recalled the time they'd climbed the bluff, the way he'd wanted to see how they worked together. Could he have known they'd end up in a situation like this?

She asked if he worried about what might happen to him afterward, and she held his gaze as he answered, as if she could keep him from lying to her.

"First of all, my pain is not your problem. And if it's not fun to watch, it's even less fun to go through, so I'd like to put it out of my mind and concentrate on what we have to do to get the files." He shoved the papers into his back pocket. "I'm sorry I even brought it up." He tossed the strap of his bag over his shoulder. "*Now* are we ready?"

She nodded.

"Let's go." They stood. He rested his fists on her shoulders, then embraced her. They went out into the steamy night.

In the car her heart raced. She asked him how he was holding up so far.

"Flying on adrenaline." He described why he preferred the adrenaline high to the drug high, how it left his mind so clear that everything seemed to come together at just the right moment, like when he was teaching. It was how he could envision the lesson and bring it to life right out of his head from only a bare outline. He took a deep breath. "So don't worry. I'll get us in and out. You'll see."

He asked her to park under the highway overpass that marked the boundary between deserted downtown and the bustling clubs and restaurants of the Market Square neighborhood, many of which Sandy had patronized in her grad student days. On one side of the highway she saw bright lights and jammed sidewalks. Above the highway's din, a cacophony of music spilled from the clubs' open doors. On the other side, two long boarded-up blocks and the construction site for the new Cold Springs Arena separated her and Nick from the Hometown Chemical Company office building, a well-lit compass in the sky. The few dark window squares made her think of missing teeth in a gold-capped mouth, and she guessed that environmental criminals didn't believe in saving electricity.

Sandy closed the car's windows. Nick handed her a pair of latex gloves. "Unless you want to leave fingerprints all over the place, you'll need these. Courtesy of Burnham Med." He snapped on his own, one after the other. She wiped her palms on her jeans and unrolled the gloves. They were too tight, and the band on the edge cut into her wrists. She wiggled her fingers but felt nothing. "You'll get used to them after a while," he said. "I've practically lived with these things on for the past year."

By the time they stepped outside, Nick was so wired he couldn't stop talking. Something about suburbanites afraid to drive into Cold Springs. Sandy tuned him out. She thought about all the safe things she could have done with her life. She could have gone back to Albany after she lost her scholarship, or she could have followed her boyfriend to Chicago. She could have said nothing when she learned of child after child diagnosed with cancer. None of the other teachers—teachers who still had their jobs—seemed nearly as appalled as she was. She could have even backed out of the break-in at the last moment. But as they passed the fenced-in construction site, her nerves ceased their struggle, and she felt calm, her mind clear as Nick had said. This was going to be her adventure. Despite everything that had happened at Burnham and Shady Ridge, she would not slink home with her tail between her legs. In the next few hours, one huge, spectacular act would keep Nick alive, erase all her failures, change the world.

Nick pointed to the large sign that announced the construction project and its several-times-delayed completion date. "Jail bait for Mayor Dellacagna," he remarked.

Sandy nodded. The mayor—who threw out the first game ball but never sent anyone to pick up the garbage in her neighborhood—might go to jail, but they wouldn't. She and Nick—they were invincible.

They crossed the street to the block that the chemical

company building occupied. Sandy glanced at the empty street—no cars, no people, only the dim light of buzzing streetlamps and the illuminated fifteen-story hulk that dwarfed everything around it. Soon, she thought, the building itself would be empty, abandoned, and dark, everything inside packed up and moved away.

Nick put his finger to his lips to shush her, although he had been the only one talking the entire way there. They pressed their bodies against the glass-walled building and surveyed the deserted loading dock. They dashed to the steps, scaled them, and hid behind a stack of boxes while they waited for the security guard to step away from his post in the glassed-in office just inside the building.

They squeezed into the sliver of space between the boxes and the wall. Nick pressed his sweaty body against Sandy's, and she felt his hot breath against her neck and face. Both his sweat and his breath had an odd, acrid smell, like burning plastic. Never having studied much chemistry, she wondered what would happen when adrenaline combined with whatever they gave him for his chemo. Would it do strange things in his bloodstream, like mixing baking soda with vinegar or bleach with ammonia?

He had his hand on her shoulder, and she wrapped her arm around his waist, pulled him even closer, so close she could feel his heart thud against her bare upper arm. Her body tingled. After all this time she found herself just as attracted to him, not the least because of his wild compulsion to push himself to the edge like this.

The bored-looking security guard stood and went into a back room connected to the office.

"Bathroom break. Let's move." Nick detached himself from her grip and motioned for her to follow.

Keeping below the line of the office window, they scooted into the building, spun to the right, and ducked into the stairwell. Nick inched the door closed behind them. They tiptoed down the stairs and into the basement. The door to the custodial closet was slightly ajar, and they slipped inside without disturbing it. Nick passed Sandy one of the flashlights. He switched his on, and she did the same.

He removed a surgical mask from the outer pocket of his bag, stretched the rubber strap around his bandanna-covered head, and fitted the curved plastic filter over his nose and mouth. Sandy held out her hand for him to pass her a mask. "You don't need one. You have an immune system," he muttered. "Now hold the shelf steady." She gripped the metal shelf that held toilet paper, paper towels, soap, and cleaning supplies as he climbed to the top like a wiry spider monkey. Holding his flashlight between his knees, he removed the spring clips from the vent cover and laid it on the top shelf. She envisioned bacteria and mold shaken loose and raining onto her. Her left eye stung.

He crawled inside the vent, maneuvered onto his stomach, and leaned out to steady the shelf and take her hand as she climbed up. She shivered in the cold air that filled the inside of the basement duct.

Nick took the folded-up papers from his back pocket and focused the beam of his flashlight on the map. She followed him as close to the rubber soles of his sneakers as she could without getting kicked. They crawled on their bellies through the basement ducts. At several points he shined his flashlight through the grates of some of the vents and kept on going. After several twists and turns, he stopped.

"This is it," he whispered, his voice muffled by the mask. "I'm going to check first to make sure they didn't replace the surveillance camera."

Nick unsnapped the vent cover and poked his head into the room. "There's a hole, but the camera's not there." He lowered himself onto a desk, careful not to knock anything over, and helped her down.

Nick lifted the mask, shook it out, and stuffed it in the bag. "The belly of the beast." He pointed to a tall metal cabinet. "Some interesting documents live here. That is, if they didn't move them all to New York."

Sandy tried to open the top drawer. "It's locked," she said.

"No problem." He pulled one of the paper clips from his back pocket and picked the lock while she shined the flashlight on his target. "We'll start with the river dredging." He flipped through the labels on the file folders. A grin spread across his face. "It's our lucky day. They're sitting right here."

The floor plan Nick carried had marked the dredging as beginning in 1980, but he soon discovered a previous dredging ordered by the federal government in the early 1970s, following the passage of the Clean Water Act. He popped open another cabinet and rooted through a new set of files. When he found a useful folder, he handed it to Sandy, who stuffed it into the backpack. While examining the documents, he mumbled a commentary on the key people of Hometown Chemical Company, Global Millennium Bio-Chem, the EPA, local officials, and other figures, people whose roles he'd researched over the past year and a half. It amazed Sandy how Nick had used the Internet and gone through old newspapers at the college library to research what seemed like the entire corporate history of the Hometown Chemical Company from its founding in the 1920s through its acquisition the previous year.

When they got to the section with documents on the landfill, Nick grew quiet. Sandy could see his gloved hands shaking as he held the individual letters and memos, mostly correspondence, he said, between the CEO of Hometown Chemical Company and the vice-president in charge of both river dredging and waste disposal and between that same vice-president and the developer of Yellow Springs Heights.

"What's that?" she asked him.

"Bingo." His eyes seemed to burn a hole in the paper illuminated by the flashlight. "We don't just have a smoking gun here; we have a fucking arsenal." He stuffed the files into his own bag and picked through some more folders. He shoved some papers in front of her face, orders to reroute the fill among several states to escape the detection of state environmental inspectors.

"Read this," he murmured. "Makes me sick to my stomach."

Sandy thought he didn't look sick at all. Instead, he looked energized, even elated.

By twelve thirty in the morning, they had gone through all the files, including ones on the rental of the abandoned factory site at the edge of the Yellow River to other companies seeking the disposal of their toxic wastes. Just as she started to shove in the last of the files, he stopped her. In his hand he held his camera.

"Take my picture," he said.

Sandy stared at him, her mouth wide open. "What?"

"I said take my picture. With the files."

Fine, she thought. Did he also have a spray can to paint, "Nick B. was here," on the walls? But he assured her he'd keep the photo hidden, just for the two of them to see. She pointed the flashlights at him and snapped a picture of him holding manila folders in both hands, his expression a mixture of defiance and triumph.

He put on a fresh mask and climbed onto the desk, again avoiding the family photographs and coffee mug of the person who worked there. Tasha's replacement, Sandy assumed. Or maybe that idiot boss of hers, whom Nick at one point had criticized for his lack of attention to the security of his archive storage room. They set their bags on the chair, and Nick boosted Sandy into the vent hole near the ceiling. He handed her the two bags and jumped into the hole. She pulled him up the rest of the way, thinking that he didn't seem much heavier than the bags she'd just lifted. He replaced the vent cover while she held the light on it. They retraced their path. Nick dragged his bag by the strap. Sandy pushed the backpack in front of her. Caught on a metal edge, Tony's Rage patch finally ripped off. Not wanting to leave anything behind, she shoved it into her jeans pocket. The mask muffled and distorted Nick's harsh breathing, which echoed in the long, cramped space. Sandy trembled from the penetrating cold and wished she'd worn something more substantial than a sleeveless top.

It seemed like forever before she spotted the open vent of the custodial closet. Nick leaned out to stabilize the shelf, and she climbed down, using his body as a bridge. He passed the bags down and lowered himself onto the top shelf to snap the vent cover into place.

Just as he touched solid ground, she heard footsteps. She seized his arm in panic. He lifted her backpack and guided her behind a box of toilet paper rolls. He crouched into a corner surrounded by brooms and mops. They switched off their flashlights and waited for the footsteps to pass.

Instead, the footsteps stopped. The door opened into the closet, and one of the brooms clattered onto the floor. Sandy held her breath and wondered if Nick had figured this into his plan. She tried to locate him in the light that poured in from the hallway, but dressed in black and blue, he remained camouflaged.

The uniformed custodian stepped inside. Sandy scrunched into a ball behind the boxes, took in the smell of plastic and soap. Murmuring something about having to clean the closet one day, the custodian rolled in a mop and bucket and pushed it straight into Nick. But Nick made no sound, and the custodian walked away, leaving the door wide open.

Sandy waited for the footsteps to fade away. She heard an elevator open and close. She slipped from her hiding place and stepped toward Nick, who was digging out from under the brooms and mops that had toppled on him.

"Are you okay?" she asked.

"Unbeaten and unbroken. But that was close." He

switched on his flashlight and picked his way over the piles of wooden handles. His mask hung from his neck.

Sandy's mouth felt like chalk. Nick had already finished one of his two water bottles, and the single one she'd brought was empty. "Can I have some of your water?" she said. He held the bottle several inches from her face and squirted a stream into her open mouth.

They took the stairs back to the first floor, climbing slowly because of their loads. Sandy's heart still pounded from the close call, and she felt pressure in both knees with each step. She wondered how Nick was holding up, weakened as he was by his illness and his treatments. He appeared fine, as strong as ever, and happier than she'd seen him in a long while. Again, they scooted along the wall toward the security office.

This time she couldn't be sure that the guard would take a break when they needed him to. Nick whispered to her that he would go first, watch for the guard to turn away, then signal for her to join him. Staying low, he scrambled to the other end of the hallway as if he were stealing a base and ducked behind the boxes. He made a sleeping gesture and pointed to the security office. Smiling so much her face hurt, she scooted down the hallway and crouched next to him on the loading dock.

All was hot, humid, and quiet in downtown Cold Springs at one in the morning, but it was only when they crossed the street undetected that they could carry themselves and their bags openly. Nick held up both his hands, and Sandy slapped them. She leaned against the plywood fence at the construction site. The terrifying images of cops and prisons that had tormented her for more than a week vanished. The buildings and the street spun around her, and she had to resist the urge to drop to her seat and let her dizzy relief wash over her.

She glanced over at Nick. He was leaning against the

fence and breathing in tight gasps. His clothes, like hers, were damp with sweat and covered with dust from the ducts. His face appeared yellow in the dim glow of the streetlamp, and she could make out dark unshaven patches on his jaw and chin where hair had grown back from the last round of treatments and not yet fallen out again. They stood for a long time side by side next to the deserted street, and then he murmured, "We have to keep going," so softly that she had to read his lips to understand him.

Her instinct told her he was going downhill fast, his adrenaline high wearing off. At the corner he lifted off his shoulder bag and lowered it to the ground. She picked it up and held it with both hands in front of her so that the two loads balanced each other. Even without the bag, he could barely stand upright. He grabbed his half-full water bottle from the side pouch.

"Go ahead, put your arm around me," she said.

"No, I need to throw up." He squeezed her shoulder. "Take the bags to the car." He curled his arm around the post of a flickering streetlamp, raised his gloved fist to his mouth, and swallowed. "If I'm not there in fifteen minutes, come get me."

He slipped through a gap in the fence and onto the construction site. In the weak light she could make out nothing but a huge hole in the ground and a pile of dirt more than ten feet high. The sound of anguished retching rose in the still air, but loaded down with the documents, Sandy could not see or help Nick. She crossed the street. The sound faded, then stopped altogether.

She staggered the rest of the way to the parking lot beneath the overpass. Only a few cars besides hers remained from the dozens that had been parked there earlier that night. The lights on the other side of the freeway, in Market Square, still shone, but the music had quieted. Above her, cars and trucks thundered past on the expressway, and she felt the pavement shudder beneath her feet when a large truck roared by. The noise and vibration made her even more lightheaded. With both hands, she tossed Nick's bag into the back seat of her car and flung the backpack on top of it. She realized she still had on her latex gloves. She stripped them off and threw them into the back seat, where they slapped against the bags and fell to the floor.

She glanced at her watch. Five minutes had passed since she'd left Nick. She watched the thinning Market Square crowds in the distance. Freshman orientation at Burnham had already started, and she imagined many of the young people to be eighteen-year-olds with fake IDs, away from home for the first time. She remembered her first carefree days of college—all the parties, all the fun, none of the problems and responsibilities. She thought one of these days she would look back on this moment and say, finally, definitively, she was no longer a kid.

She checked her watch again. Now fifteen minutes had gone by. *Please God let him be all right.*

She got into her car and turned the ignition key. Good, the car started. She made a right out of the parking lot, first heading away from the construction site because of the one-way streets. She took her second left and another left.

Only two blocks to the corner. Her heart thudded. She reached into the back seat to pull the bags to the floor, out of sight, and the car swerved. Then she saw parked at the end of the first block on her right the black-and-white car with the roof lights. She gripped the steering wheel. Red and blue lights flashed as soon as she passed. She pulled over and cut the engine, only half a block from where she was to meet Nick.

Was it her inspection sticker? No, that was current. Did they think she'd been drinking? The police car's headlights reflected in her rear view mirror. Both officers stepped out. One approached her.

She lowered her window and took a deep breath. The beam from his flashlight skimmed her face and the bags in the back. She squinted at him as her eyes adjusted to the light.

He folded his arms across her car roof and leaned toward her. She heard him breathe inward, his nostrils flared. His dark brown face was wide and shiny with perspiration. The name on his badge read "Williams."

"Is there a problem, sir?" she stammered.

"No, ma'am. My partner and I thought we heard someone sick in this area. A drunk kid who wandered over from the bars and might be in trouble." He glanced toward the overpass. "You haven't seen him, have you?"

Her first impulse was to shake her head and tell him she didn't know. But somewhere on the other side of the fence was Nick, and she, not the police, had to get him out. "I think I did see him," she answered. Memories of some of the scenes she'd witnessed as a student rushed to her consciousness. "A tall blond guy, about eighteen, couple of friends were trying to carry him?"

The police officer laughed. "That's about right."

"Last I saw, they made it to the parking lot under the highway. You might check over there."

"Thanks." He stepped backward. "You going to the U. with those bags?"

"I'm a little lost, aren't I?"

The officer circled past the front of her car. "I thought you New Yorkers knew your way around." He pointed in the direction of Burnham. "Take a right at the next corner, and after you pass the tall building, go right again. Keep going past the green, and you can't miss it."

The police car drove off. Sandy restarted her car and pulled to the corner. Nick squeezed through the fence and stumbled toward her. She pushed the passenger door open.

He gripped the door but didn't get in. His gloves were covered in dirt, and dirt streaked his face, clothes, and the water bottle he clutched in his other hand. "Heard you talk to the cop," he rasped, breathing hard. "Good."

"Feel better?"

"For now. You got some tissues?" She handed him the box she kept behind her seat for Tony and his allergies. Nick yanked out a handful, squirted water on them, and wiped his mouth and nose. He grabbed another wad, wet it, and cleaned the rest of his face and his neck, though when he climbed into the car he brought with him a powerful rotten stench.

Sandy shrank back and tried not to gag. "Do you want me to take you home?" she asked.

"No. We're going to finish this thing tonight." She edged the car forward. Nick cleared his throat. "Just like the cop said, take a right at the Hometown building."

"Don't I go straight to get to your office?" She approached the corner, traffic lights flashing yellow and red at this late hour.

"Yeah, but go around the corner. I want to see the building."

She turned and turned again. Nick told her to slow down. She approached the headquarters' grand front entrance: two-story-high plate glass, shiny new gilded letters for Global Millennium Bio-Chem, revolving doors, and a dark slab walkway with tiny specks that sparkled under the streetlamps. He lowered his window and leaned out. She then noticed the thick piece of metal in his jeans pocket, perhaps a bolt he had picked up from the construction site. He reached back with his gloved right hand, grabbed the metal chunk, and held it high as if to hurl it at the plate glass entrance.

Don't do it, Nick. She could have accelerated, flung his fragile body against the wide-open window, but her foot was frozen and she could only repeat the words in her head. "Fuck you, Hometown!" he cried hoarsely. He pumped once, but instead of throwing the metal at his target he let it drop with a hollow thud on the floor of her car. He slumped back onto the seat and closed his eyes.

Twenty-seven: Safehouse

Nicholas ached to hear the impact of metal against glass, see thirty-foot-high windows shatter, slide to the ground, and spray a thousand tiny shards across the unforgiving pavement.

Through his glove the metal bolt felt warm and heavy and powerful, and it pulled into him the energy he needed to fling it, the shortstop's bullet to home plate to end the game.

But he did not want the game to end like this.

He shouldn't have walked onto the construction site in the first place. Even a stalled project disrupted the earth, stirred up bacteria and fungi that could overwhelm his devastated immune system. The bolt was rusted and covered in cobwebs. He slipped it into his back pocket anyway, and it became the talisman of his hard, red-hot rage. After he dropped it onto the floor of the car, he became cold and weak, and the darkness enveloped him.

He heard the voice of his high-school track coach. *If you don't think you can take another step, take the next step*. It was what his life had come to—not the finish but the next step.

At his department office he turned on the copier, punched the buttons to collate three copies, and showed Sandy how to use the sheet feeder before he went into his adjacent office to lie down. She brought him his water bottles, squirted the cool liquid into his dry mouth, and patted his forehead with a damp paper towel. "Don't you have copies to make?" he snapped.

Without an immune system all he had left was the fever. And as he lay there, fever swirled through him, and he took in the acrid stench of scorched flesh. He saw his house, the fireplace in his living room, an ordinary fire like the one his family used to start on the coldest days of winter. He sensed himself spinning, shrinking, drawing closer to the burning timber, chained to a tree that had been cut long ago. At first he couldn't feel the flames, but he saw the fire glow red and orange and yellow as it consumed its fuel and collapsed the structure of kindling and logs. Immobilized in this miniature of a fiery hell he sensed the surface where he stood weakening and becoming hotter, the tree against his back infiltrated through its hollow core, the metal chain around him growing brittle from the intense heat. The framework above caved in, shot sparks like machine-gun spray. Sweat drenched him. The burning radiated through his body from his back and the soles of his feet, but he stood his ground until everything broke apart and he jerked awake.

The fire was inside him, in his mouth and throat. It churned like thick smoldering oil in his stomach and intestines. He reached out blindly and felt the plastic water bottle that Sandy had left on his trunk when he sent her to make the copies. Without opening his eyes, he sucked water into his mouth to douse the flame. He swallowed and in the next instant realized what happened when one threw water on burning oil.

He staggered to the door that connected his office to the department office. Leaning against the doorframe, he clutched his stomach. "You got any of that weed?"

Sandy hit a button and turned to face him. "You told me not to bring it, in case we got caught."

"Shit." He grimaced and backed into his office.

"Is there anything I can do?"

His guts twisted. He had but minutes to get to the toilet. Even if he kept some of the water down, it poured out the other end. The clock above the copy machine read ten to four. In just two more hours his least-favorite department member would be coming in to work. "Just finish up so we get out before sunrise. I have a colleague who wakes up with the roosters." He slammed the door.

He realized the fever wasn't his sole line of defense; his

body had become agonizingly thorough in trying to expel whatever contaminated it. When he next fought his way to consciousness, he found himself curled up and trembling on the rug by his sofa, propped against the file cabinet. A spike pierced his upper body, entering between his shoulder blades and exiting through his breastbone. The pain was constant, unchanged by his breathing or when he shifted position. He wondered how it had gotten there, if his heart had finally failed. Someone was calling his name, and he forced one eye open. The dim overhead bulb cast long shadows across the objects in the room. The metal cabinet felt cool on his cheek. Sandy crouched next to him and touched his back. He shuddered. "Nick, I'm done. We have to go."

"Good," he mouthed. He realized that at some point he must have changed from his jeans and black t-shirt to a pair of loose cargo shorts and a plain white shirt. A clear plastic bag on his trunk was stuffed with his break-in clothes and another white shirt, all soaked with brown fluid. His stomach lurched; he had kept nothing down.

Sandy stroked his head, still covered by the bandanna. It amazed him that she hadn't pulled away from him, for he could smell the sour, fruity stench of an animal decomposing from the inside out. "The bad news is, you have to walk out of here. And you have to help me carry a box," she said.

She handed him his water bottle. He squirted in a mouthful, but his throat had closed as if to shield the wound below. Water dribbled down his chin and onto his shirt. She asked what was wrong.

He ran his fingers along his breastbone. There was no swelling, no bruise, and his touch didn't alter the pain. Waves of nausea curled inside him. "I think I ripped something in here while dredging up lunch, dinner, and everything else." He squeezed his eyes shut and clenched his teeth. "Now how about not asking me any more questions?"

"You bullshitted me, telling me you'd be all right." The amount of anger in her voice surprised him.

"Yeah, yeah, and you know what?" He stopped and bit his lower lip. A series of convulsions seized his empty stomach; air and the taste of bile rushed through his torn esophagus and parched throat. Sandy cringed at the sound. He wiped his mouth on his shirtsleeve. "I flunked the class in pain management."

"Congratulations. So what do you think we should do now?"

"You go home and leave me here with the stuff. I'll be all right eventually." He let his head drop onto his upraised knees.

"I'm not leaving you here alone."

His head still lowered, he mumbled. "Then you tell me what we do."

She rubbed his hunched-over back. "Okay, you got me out of the chemical company building, so I'm going to get you out of here. Close your eyes, listen, and try to follow along with me."

He kept his eyes open, focused on the familiar objects of his office. The books and papers on his shelf. The Red Sox mugs on his desk. The poster of Marat bleeding, a knife in his back. Sandy's fingers stopped on the spot between his shoulder blades. The pain seemed to diminish and draw toward her. "Hold it there," he whispered.

She massaged his left shoulder with her other hand. His muscles softened. His eyes closed on his domain. Her words made no sense, but the syllables in her melodious voice lulled him. As if in a trance, he rose to his feet and picked up an end of the box. On the way to her car she heaved the plastic bag with his clothes into a dumpster. He held the box against the car while she opened the hatchback, and they slid the box into the space behind the seat. She slammed the hatchback shut, and then he heard something else. A muffled click like something breaking painlessly inside him.

Suddenly dizzy, he dropped into the passenger seat. The impact pushed his breath upward, and he felt something warm and sticky on his lips. He touched his lower lip. Sandy drove out of the parking lot and stopped at a traffic light. He held his index finger toward the light and saw the dark patch on his fingertip. He pressed two fingers from his other hand to the damp spot on his lip and held them there. He hiccuped and the warm liquid seeped between his fingers. He pulled them away.

"Shit," he murmured. He stared blankly at his fingers.

Sandy slowed the car. "What is it?"

"The place I tore. It's bleeding." He coughed, yanked the bandanna from his head, and spat into it. A small, round, wet spot glistened. His hands shook. His chest tightened in panic, and his breath grew strangled. The piercing pain returned.

Words ran through his head: *What is happening to me?* The pain and the blood were unfamiliar, unexpected. An infection would take a couple of days to kill him; internal bleeding could finish him off within hours. He'd thought he had more time left. He still had to sort through the files. He'd received a transfusion of platelets in the hospital before he checked out; he hoped they hadn't yet been destroyed.

It occurred to him that he should never have carried the box out of his office, and certainly not held it by himself while she opened the trunk. She had made him forget his weakness. "I guess we should have taken the originals and left the copies at the office," he finally said. "I sure won't be working on them now."

Sandy pulled into a vacant parking space in front of her house. "Will it stop bleeding?" He sensed the fear in her voice.

"Yeah, sure."

"I can take you to Mercy Hospital. It's three blocks from here."

He threw the blood-soaked bandanna to the floor. "No fucking way I go there. I'm not answering questions or dealing with cops."

"How would they know what we did?"

"I show up at this hour with you instead of my wife, looking like crap and spitting blood, someone will ask questions."

Sandy cut the engine. Nicholas thought the reference to a wife would have sealed the deal. But after staring at him for a moment, Sandy pressed on. "You have cancer. Just tell them that."

He stripped off his t-shirt and held it to his mouth. His irregular gasps scattered tiny dark droplets on the white cloth. "If you recall, I signed out against doctor's orders, lied to everyone in town, and can't account for the past thirteen hours. What I need is a safehouse to hide in and try to get through this thing." He started to get out of the car. "Now let's move this stuff upstairs."

By leaning his entire body against the car door, he could push it open, but everything began spinning when he tried to stand. Sandy lifted him and half-carried him up the stairs, for his feet and legs had gone numb. She propped him up against two pillows on her disheveled bed. He heard her tiptoe downstairs and back up several times. His hiccups started and stopped. The blood trickling into his stomach made him queasy, and he asked her to bring him a joint.

She handed one to him already lit, and she washed and refilled his water bottles in the kitchen next to her bedroom. He closed his eyes, about to drift off to sleep with the joint between his lips. He felt her shaking him.

"Nick, are you all right?" He opened his eyes. His head throbbed. She held the joint in one hand and his bottle in the other. "You've got to drink something."

She placed her hands around his on the bottle and squeezed. The fan hummed in the window and blew cool air on his bare upper body. He shivered a little, though his skin was dry and the night air steamy. She kept on talking to him, telling him about the files she had copied and shaking him every time his eyelids started to droop. From time to time she shoved the bottle in his face and forced more water into him.

"I need to sleep," he heard himself mumble.

"Are you going to be okay?"

He spat and wiped his mouth on the shirt. He didn't see any fresh blood. "Yeah. Let me sleep."

"I don't know." She took the shirt from his hands. He reached for it and almost fell over. She held him steady. "You don't look too good."

"I'm not going to die. I'm just really tired." His head sagged forward. She shook him again.

"How do I know you're not lying?"

"You're not going to keep me alive by shaking me." He looked up at her. In the faint light of the approaching sunrise her face was pale. He thought for a moment he would like to stay up to watch the sunrise, as he'd watched it so many times from Cold Springs Harbor at the end of an early morning bike ride. He didn't know if he would ever ride again. He couldn't even guarantee that he would wake up if she let him sleep. But he had to convince her. He closed his fingers around her arm. "Listen, Sandy. We've got to trust each other one more time." His dry throat tickled. He pointed a trembling finger at the bottle. She directed a stream of water into his mouth. His weakness and the steady dull pain in his chest made swallowing difficult and talking even more so. "Just stay here and watch me. Keep my airway clear and sponge me down because it's hot and I haven't held in enough water."

She nodded. He slid down on the bed and rolled onto his stomach. His belt buckle dug into his sore abdominal muscles, and he groaned and drew his knees toward his chest. She eased him to his left side, removed his belt, and gently set him back. Then she turned his head and placed his t-shirt under his mouth. The cotton cloth was soft and slightly damp beneath his cheek. She covered him with the top sheet. "Is that comfortable?" she asked.

"Yeah," he exhaled. The dull ache faded from his body. His breathing grew regular and relaxed. He couldn't die that night, he told himself in the moments before he slipped from consciousness. The chemical company files had to be organized. He had to deliver them to wherever they would have the best chance to get the mess cleaned up and the officers imprisoned. He hadn't said good-bye to Holly and Rosie and Tony. He had a class to teach in a week and a half and a family to support. He needed to arrange for Sandy to take his class and get credit so she could find a teaching position in the public schools.

Besides, he had promised Sandy he'd stay alive if she promised to take care of him while he slept. He figured she could chant a decent Kaddish but she wouldn't know what the hell to do with him if he died on her.

Twenty-eight: A Day of Life

A woman knows when someone she loves is in danger. Holly believed this, but too often her instinct had turned out wrong, a false alarm, and she'd worried for nothing. And both times the news of Nicky's illness came as a complete shock.

Yet on that Wednesday in late August she jolted awake as the day's first light filtered through the curtains. She patted the mattress with her left hand, expected to find Nicky asleep beside her even though he'd been in the hospital since Sunday and wasn't due home until evening. Perhaps it had only been a dream, the idea that he would sneak out and slip into the house to surprise her. It would be like him, she thought, to conspire with Rosie to do that.

She folded back the sheet and the thin thermal blanket. Still savoring her fantasy, she eased the bedroom door open and crept down the hall to Rosie's room. The beige carpet beneath the door glowed like a column of fireflies poised in their moment of glory. Her daughter, just past her seventeenth birthday, kept the overhead light dimmed because she didn't like to sleep alone in the dark. Holly turned the knob slowly so not to make a sound.

Rosie lay curled on her side, covers pulled to her chin, dark hair spread over her pillow. Holly returned to her own bed, her dream evaporated and a hollow space in her chest. She tried to fall asleep again; she rolled from one side of the queen-size mattress to the other in search of the perfect position that would let her drift far away from the closed-in room. Silence kept her awake—the absence of Nicky's regular breathing or his mumbled syllables when he slept on a full stomach. She missed his warmth, his cinnamon scent, the softness of his hair, the feel of his spine beneath his t-shirt. He always seemed so helpless and vulnerable when he slept that she thought she could make him promise her anything.

At six thirty she turned off the alarm clock. She would not back get to sleep again. She had to go to work. After a shower she called Nicky.

With each unanswered ring, her heart quickened. At home he usually awoke before seven, and days began early at the hospital with the changing of nursing shifts and the clatter of breakfast trays.

"Fourth-floor nursing station."

Holly's throat closed. Nobody had called her during the night, but she envisioned an empty bed, a crisis, Nicky taken away.

"I'm trying to reach my husband. He's a patient on your ward." She spelled out his last name.

She heard a rustle of paper. The nurse exchanged words with someone else, maybe another staff member. "He checked out yesterday evening, ma'am."

I'm his wife. I would know when he checked out. "Are you sure? He said he had some tests..."

"He signed himself out." The nurse sighed. "I didn't think it was a good idea. But your son was there, and I remember him telling me there was a family get-together that your husband wanted to be home for."

Holly thanked the nurse and hung up. The heat swallowed her again. Her palms were slick where she'd held the receiver. Her mind returned to the day before, when she'd visited Nicky and he'd told her about the tests. And Tony had said something at dinner. *Hope Dad's tests go well.*

She put on a bathrobe over her bra and panties. She didn't tiptoe to Tony's room. The door smacked against the rubber stop when she threw it open, and Tony rustled in his loft bed. It was a new bed, just two weeks old, purchased to replace the bunk bed with the ruined bottom mattress.

"Tony, get up. I have to talk to you."

"Five minutes, Mom," he mumbled.

"Now." She had to restrain herself from screaming. "Where's your father?"

"I can't tell you." He pulled the sheets over his head and burrowed deeper. "I mean, I don't know."

She reached up and tried to yank the sheets off him, to look him in the face. He rolled away from her toward the wall.

"He's in danger, Tony."

"I'm sure he's fine. He knows what he's doing."

"Do you know how sick your father is?" When Tony didn't respond, she said, "You had something to do with this."

A head, covered with tousled brown hair, broke through. "Yeah, sort of."

She grabbed the railing and shook the loft bed. "Why did he leave?"

Tony pushed the sheets back. His face was dark in the shadows. "He had to get something."

"Get what? And where?"

"Files from the chemical company."

That damned company, when will he ever let it go? She loosened her grip on the bed. "Your father could die if you don't tell me where he is. Is that what you want?"

"Let me try to find him."

She brought Tony the portable phone. He punched in a number.

"Hey, Sandy." His voice wavered. "How did it go?"

Holly grimaced at the name of the babysitter, the incompetent former teacher she knew as Miss Katz. A huge mistake hiring her.

"Cool!" Tony shouted. His voice dropped an octave and grew shaky. "Is Dad there?" He drew the phone back from his face. "Mom, Dad's at Sandy's."

"Give me the phone." Holly held out her hand.

Tony turned away and mumbled into the mouthpiece. "My mom wants to talk to you."

Holly snatched the phone from him. "What the hell is my husband doing at your apartment?"

Sandy answered quickly. "Nick and I got the files. We

have letters proving that company officials knowingly sold contaminated landfill to the developer of your neighborhood and conspired to evade state environmental inspectors."

"You sound just like Nick. Let me talk to him."

"He's sleeping." Sandy hesitated. "Should I wake him?"

Holly's chest tightened. "Is he a mess?"

"He's pretty wasted, if that's what you mean."

Interpret "wasted," in the lingo of a young twenty-something. For them it meant drunk or doped up, sick, filthy, and disheveled. Probably passed out. But Nicky could have been near death, and Sandy had no concept of the seriousness of his condition or what to do about it. "Give me directions to your apartment."

Tony leaned over the railing of the bed. "Can I come too, Mom?"

"No." She tossed the phone up to him. "Call work and tell them I'm not coming in."

Holly didn't have time for contact lenses or makeup. After dressing, she collected a fresh set of clothes for Nicky and the half-dozen bottles that contained his medications.

She shuddered when she drove into Sandy's neighborhood—the place where her fragile Nicky had ended up; the place where, without even looking or asking questions, she'd allowed Tony to spend his summer. Boxy apartment buildings with peeling siding and collapsing porches lined the wide avenue. Cars and castoff furniture lay scattered on the weed-covered patches that passed for lawns. She almost struck a boy on a bicycle who veered in front of her, and to each side she saw the children, swarms of children, who played amid the junk cars, refrigerators, sofas, and mattresses. Overflowing garbage cans stood at the curb; flies buzzed around them. The buildings on Wallman Street, where Sandy lived, were in better condition, most of them wood-frame houses with sagging roofs and small gardens in front. But again she saw the garbage and the broken sidewalks and the dented, rusted cars parked at the curb. On the next block was a burned-out pile of rubble that bordered an endless overgrown vacant lot. A small boy with olive skin and black hair sat on the porch steps of Sandy's house. She brushed past him and banged on the door. The former teacher answered.

"Where is he?"

Sandy pressed herself against the wall and pointed upstairs. "Back bedroom."

Holly's breath caught at the sight there. Nicky lay sprawled face down, naked to the waist on the bottom sheet of a double bed, the top sheet crumpled at his bare feet. His loose, unbelted shorts had worked their way to an inch below the waistband of his boxers. He clutched the bloodstained white t-shirt under his head as a baby would clutch a ragged blanket. His hair was matted and his skin translucent. Bits of dried blood caked his parched, cracked lips. She crouched on her knees next to him and inhaled his rancid odor. "Oh, Nicky, what have you done to yourself this time?" Her voice broke. She stroked his head and face. His lips twitched in response to her touch.

"I'm sorry, Holly. If I had thought he'd end up like this, I would have stopped him."

Holly turned her head in the direction of the voice. Sandy stood in the doorway.

"You stupid girl."

Sandy's mouth was a black hole. Holly held a swatch of the bloodied t-shirt.

"How did this get here?" When Sandy didn't answer, she raised her voice. "I have to know. His blood doesn't clot properly, and he could bleed to death."

"It wasn't much and it stopped right away."

"Where did it come from?" Her fingers gripped one of the rust-colored splotches.

"Somewhere inside him. He was sick to his stomach, and then he spat some up."

A stab in her chest made her wince. "I'm calling an ambulance."

Sandy leaned against the wall. "I wanted to take him to the emergency room, but he wouldn't go on account of all the felonies we sort of committed."

"Felonies…you…*sort of*…committed?"

"We didn't exactly get the stuff from the public library. We broke into the company headquarters and stole more than a thousand pages of documents."

Holly's lower lip trembled. She adjusted her glasses and examined the shirt. There were a half dozen stains of various sizes, from less than an inch to about three inches in diameter. The police might be looking for Nicky already. She cared nothing about the girl, but she couldn't have Nicky taken into custody. He'd had nosebleeds before, and nothing happened. Losing the small amount of blood on the shirt he would probably survive. He would not survive jail.

Sandy approached the bed. Holly extended an arm. "Stay away from him. You've caused enough trouble."

"Fine. You sponge him down." Sandy pointed at the unfinished wood nightstand next to the bed. She had left a washcloth draped over the rim of a ceramic bowl half filled with water. Holly dipped her finger in. The water was warm, and she noticed for the first time the window fan, which blew sultry air from outdoors onto them.

She lifted Nicky's right hand and saw blood on the lines of his palm and beneath his fingernails. "Don't you know enough to keep his hands and face clean?" She shoved the bowl in Sandy's direction. "Get some soap and fresh water."

She pressed her lips to the skin of his back, the quickest way to test for fever. His skin had a leathery texture that signaled dehydration but was only slightly warm—a low-grade fever if any. *He's fighting.* She held her hand to his face to check his respiration. His clear, regular breath cooled her hand. She thought she heard muffled sounds and put her ear to his mouth.

"Did he say something?" Sandy held the bowl, a fresh washcloth, and a bar of soap.

Holly sat up straight. Sandy's words drowned out whatever he'd said. "Let me ask you," she blurted out, "when you went into that building with Nick, did it ever occur to you that what you were doing was wrong?"

"Why are you saying it was wrong?"

She'd expected Sandy to evade the question the way Sandy had done when she'd asked about the bullying in the class. Sandy's challenge surprised her, and for a moment she didn't know how to react. She flung the washcloth onto the bed without wringing it out, and droplets of water splattered Nicky's ribs and armpit. "Stealing is wrong. Endangering his life is wrong."

"I didn't endanger him. He asked me to come to watch his back." Sandy's voice was calm, strong, and sure. Unrepentant.

"Do you do every crazy thing someone asks you to?"

Sandy shrugged. "If I believe in it."

Holly rubbed the washcloth on the bar of soap, dipped it into the bowl, and scrubbed Nicky's fingers, one by one. She avoided Sandy's eyes as she worked. Her vision was blurred, and she could hardly see the target of her efforts. "You are so naïve," she muttered under her breath. "You have no idea of the world."

"What would you have done if he'd asked you?"

Holly glanced up at Sandy, who stood in the middle of the doorway with her hands on her hips and a faint smile on her face. Holly recognized the tactic: *Strike where they're vulnerable*. Nicky hadn't asked her; instead, he'd asked Sandy. He'd drawn the kids into his obsession, enlisted Tony and perhaps even Rosie. She couldn't let Sandy see the hurt.

She took a breath and fixed her gaze on Sandy. "I would have talked some sense into him. He's not rational when he's in chemo." She reached for Nicky's other hand to wash it. "You wouldn't have known that."

"Rational or not, he planned that break-in perfectly. We used gloves, and we put everything back the way it was so they'll never know we were there."

Holly shook her head. "You think you have all the answers. And what are you going to do now?"

"Sort the documents and give them to the press."

"Nick's not sorting anything. Look at him." She pointed at her husband. "This is what you did to him."

Sandy spun around and left the room.

"Come here. I'm not done with you," Holly called. When Sandy didn't return, she raised her voice. "You're fired."

"I don't care." The voice came from somewhere else in the apartment.

Holly trembled with rage. She wondered how anyone could allow someone like Sandy around children.

Beneath her hand Nicky stirred. She stopped sponging and put her ear to him.

"Water," he whispered.

Holly glanced around the room for a bottle or cup. Seeing nothing except a vase of pink and white carnations on the dresser, she called again for Sandy. There was no answer. She slipped through the door but kept an eye on Nicky, who blinked several times and kicked the covers at his feet as if trying to run away from a bad dream.

Holly backed into the middle of the kitchen, with its chipped brown linoleum floor. The apartment seemed deserted, no one in the living room or bathroom. Another door next to the bedroom was shut but so warped that a sliver of the room was visible, enough for her to see Sandy sleeping on the floor. Holly recalled a news story she had once read. A teenager had killed several members of an opposing gang in a drive-by shooting, and after his arrest the boy had fallen asleep in the back of the squad car. *So lacking in remorse they fall asleep.*

She searched through Sandy's kitchen cabinets for a clean glass or cup. In a pantry nearly empty of food, she

353

picked up and examined a package of dried Ramen noodle soup with a price sticker of twenty cents and, curious, opened the refrigerator, which was also empty save for a jug of apple juice, a carton of skim milk, and a half-full bottle of club soda. The girl had no job, no money, no food in the house. And she wasn't going to help her cause by breaking into buildings.

Holly found a mug and, to be safe, washed it again. She brought the water to Nicky along with two pills, one for nausea and an antibiotic. After feeding him the meds, she swabbed the flecks of blood from his lips and wiped the rest of his face.

The antiemetic knocked him out once more. She squeezed onto the bed next to him and drew herself closer to feel his regular breathing. He mumbled something, and the syllables transformed into long, wrenching moans.

She rubbed his back. "I know it hurts," she whispered, though she didn't know what hurt him or if it was just another nightmare. *If I could give you my life, my health, and take your pain in return…*

He quieted without regaining consciousness. She wouldn't tell him he'd moaned in his sleep; he wanted to be so tough.

It was at least an hour before he stirred again. This time he raised his head and tried to roll onto his back but fell face down on the mattress. His arms were weak, clumsy, almost useless. "Do you want me to roll you over?" she asked.

"No, sit me up." His speech was clear, though a little breathless. She found two pillows on the floor next to the window and propped him up. The color in his face drained to gray.

"How are you feeling, Nicky baby?"

He belched. The pungent odor of stale blood hung in the air. He motioned for the water and drank it in tentative sips while she held the mug with a shaking hand. He stared at her, his eyes dulled. "I'm not home, am I?"

"No, you're at Sandy Katz's apartment. She brought you here after you broke…"

Nicky grinned. "Yeah, the safehouse. I got the files, right?"

"Yes." Holly wanted to slap him. Barely alive, he only cared about the files. "You want to lie down again?"

"No. Bathroom."

He pointed to his throat. Sandy's toilet was probably filthy, full of germs. Holly reached for the bowl on the nightstand and dumped its contents out the window. She crouched next to Nicky, helped him to his hands and knees on the bed, and gripped him around the waist. "Okay, relax. Bring it up gently." She raised the bowl to his chin. It wavered with the tremor in her hand.

Nicky squeezed his eyes shut and sucked in his breath with a high-pitched moan. Against her hand Holly felt violent twisting contractions, the only strength left in his body. A thick black clotted fluid spilled from his mouth. Its sour stench enveloped her. The jagged circle near the foot of the mattress resembled used coffee grounds. He gasped and spat. The knot inside him heaved again, and with a grunt he expelled a tar-like clot the size of a tablespoon.

His body went limp. She realized that she was no longer clutching the ceramic bowl but her husband, tightly with both hands; the bowl lay broken in two knife-edged pieces at her feet. She leaned Nicky back against the pillows and held the mug and washcloth while he rinsed his mouth.

"You need to go to the hospital."

"No, I don't." He swallowed the rest of the water. "Not if there's no fresh blood."

There wasn't any. She noticed fragments of the gelatin caps of the pills she'd given him and prayed he had absorbed enough of the antibiotic to fight whatever he had exposed himself to the night before. "It's not your decision, Nicky. I'm phoning your doctor."

"He's on vacation." Nicky made himself cough, brought

his hand to his mouth, and examined it. Again, no blood. "I think he's in Switzerland."

And you're in this hellhole, destroying yourself over an obsession. Holly imagined herself with Nicky on a faraway mountain. Somewhere clean. Somewhere safe. Tears filled her eyes. "I can't do this anymore. It's insanity. I'm calling an ambulance."

She started to get up. His fingers closed over her forearm. He glared at her. "Listen. It's my life, and I'm not letting anyone take it over. Not the hospital. Not the doctors. Not the cops. I got those files, and I'm going through them in the privacy of my own home." His outburst left him gasping. He took a few measured breaths. "Just give me some time to pull myself together."

It's my life… She wove her fingers between his. His hand was cold despite the heat. *How many times have I made up information, lied outright, or chosen not to bring your fevered body to the hospital, just to keep you with me?* "Okay," she finally said.

"Anyway, if I were going to die, I would have done it hours ago." He squeezed her hand. "Before you came."

Nicky dozed off, and when he awoke he asked her to clean him up and move him to another room. Holly lifted him from the bed and carried him to the bathroom. On the way she wished that she had Sandy to help her, that she hadn't fought with Sandy and chased her away. Sandy was strong and not afraid to touch him.

Holly could feel her arms weakening when she dragged Nicky to the sofa in the living room after his bath; the noise she made awakened Sandy. Sandy came out of the spare room with a dazed expression and her clothes rumpled.

Holly shrank away from her. Freshly washed, Nicky smelled sweet, like the apple juice he'd just been drinking. Sandy had an unwashed odor that suggested Nicky's sickness and the rotting garbage of her neighborhood.

"How's he doing?" Sandy asked.

Her voice was too loud, and it startled Holly. Holly tucked her arm around Nicky's head and snapped, "Shhh. Can't you see he's asleep?"

"Oh." Sandy backed away. "I guess I'll take a shower."

The next thing Holly heard was a long, high-pitched scream followed by a string of expletives. Nicky raised his head.

"What the…?" he mumbled.

Holly tapped his shoulder and listened. A bed stripped. Heavy footsteps. The thud of pottery dropped to the bottom of a plastic wastebasket. More curses in a breaking voice.

Nicky drew in his breath. "Hey, I'm sorry I trashed your room," he called out. He waited until Sandy appeared at the doorway, her eyes wide and her mouth gaping. "Look at it this way, Sandy. You haven't run a real safehouse until some wounded warrior hiding out there makes a really disgusting mess."

Though this wasn't the lesson Holly intended to teach, she began to laugh. The words "eat dogshit" came to her. Her beautiful Nicky had returned to life with all the joy and defiance, courage and hope, that had drawn her to him so long ago when, without thinking, she had pledged to accompany him through the sit-in and forever no matter what happened. She curled up behind him on the sofa and pulled him to her. She reached for his hand, and he closed his fingers around hers. She placed her other hand on his chest.

Beneath her fingertips, his heart beat in a strong, steady rhythm. His skin was warm, not hot. Soon she would bring him home. She would spoon-feed him baby food flavored with cinnamon until his system recovered, and she would hold his cup while he sucked water and juice through a straw. He would tell Rosie and Tony what he did last night, and they would listen in awe because they were still too young to know how complicated life could get.

Nicky exhaled a satisfied sigh. He twisted toward Holly and glanced at Sandy. "Sandy, would you please show Holly the map? She needs to see it." He motioned with his head toward the back of the apartment. "And bring me the bags while you're there."

Reluctantly, Holly detached herself from him and followed Sandy in silence. Sandy opened the door to her tiny spare room.

From the grimy open window, the midday light filtered in across Sandy's desk and a rolled-up sleeping bag that sat atop a foam pad. Squeezed between the edge of the pad and a desk chair were two bulging red bags and a closed-up box of copier paper.

"This is what we got last night," Sandy said. "I'll keep a copy, and you two take the originals and the other copies. I can carry them downstairs for you if you'd like." The former teacher spoke with confidence—so different from the way she'd sounded that day at the school when Holly had first met her. No breeze passed through the window, and the room had a musty odor of dirt and perspiration and garbage in the heat. Bookshelves made of boards and cinderblocks occupied the far wall, and when Holly turned around to face the door, she saw the map for the first time.

It covered an entire wall. On it were the names of familiar streets in unfamiliar handwriting. Every street in Yellow Springs Heights was there. Some were only black lines with their names beside them. Next to other lines, pushpins penetrated the paper and the wallboard behind it. The bottom edge and the entire right half of the map had a few blue pins scattered throughout. But in the top left corner, extending down through a quarter of the giant map, blue, red, green, yellow, and black-dotted pins crowded inside a jagged oval outlined with a red marker. Sandy said that the black dots meant children.

Holly found her street and house number. There sat a red pin, next to a penciled number one. A block and a half above it were two green pins that occupied the same spot, numbers two and three. Barbara and Roger McDonough. The mother of one of Rosie's friends had breast cancer. Holly located the house, for she had driven Rosie there many times. She saw the blue pin and the number fourteen. Someone else she knew had died of multiple myeloma several years earlier. That woman lived three blocks away from Rosie's friend.

And there was a yellow pin and the number seventy-eight.

Her neighborhood was riddled with cancer.

She recognized Nicky's handwriting and some numbers in Tony's hand. But Sandy must have labeled the streets and written in many of the numbers. And the map hung on her wall.

Why did Sandy have to do all this? I should have been there for him.

She picked up the bags, one in each hand. Her arms burned with exhaustion from taking care of Nicky. She let the bags drop at her feet. Sandy picked both up at once, and Holly realized why he had asked her to go in with him. If he'd thought he could have done it alone, he would have. But he was too weak and sick, even though he had a way to get the documents.

Sandy was a stranger whom they had brought into their lives. But she had risked her entire future so that Nicky could gain justice for the victims of a crime.

Holly knelt in front of the wall at the bottom of the map and touched the thin paper. Underneath her skirt the carpet's bristles dug into her bare knees. She repeated the words running through her head. "Forgive me, Father, for I have sinned."

A long silence followed, as if she were waiting for an answer that would never come. Then Sandy spoke. "I pray in front of the map all the time."

"What do you pray for?"

"The people here." Sandy pointed to the wall. "I want to honor those who died and pray that the ones who are sick will get well." She sighed. "But I couldn't do either."

"Why not?"

"To chant the Kaddish, the prayer for the dead, you need ten Jewish adults. It's a community prayer that recognizes we don't die alone. Or unnoticed."

Holly repeated Sandy's words in her mind. "I take it you don't know ten Jewish adults."

"Not around here."

"And what about the others? The ones who are sick?"

"I chant the Mishebeirach. A prayer for those in need of healing." Sandy took a deep breath and sang in a voice powerful and melodious, "*Mi shebeirach avoteinu. M'kor habracha l'imoteinu...*"

Holly rose to her feet. Her blood pounded in her ears in rhythm to words that flowed in song in an unfamiliar language. For a moment she thought she should ask Sandy to teach it to her, as if singing a Jewish prayer for someone who was Jewish would have the power to keep him alive. "Did you pray for my husband?"

Sandy nodded. "I mainly prayed for this kid, the little brother of a student. But he died." She stepped back from the wall. "I went in with Nick because prayers aren't enough; you've got to do something. But getting the files won't bring Stephen back or make Nick better either. I'm sorry."

Holly cleared her throat. "We're lucky if it doesn't kill him." She gazed at the map, at black lines on white paper, black dots on colored pushpins. Sick and dying children, their stories buried like the poisoned dirt unnoticed until Nicky dug them up, dug everything up. "But if bringing out the truth saves another child's life…" Her voice trailed off, and she feared that if she couldn't make herself believe her words she would allow Nicky to suffer and die in vain. She reached toward the bags in Sandy's arms. "I'll take these and the copies he asked for, and I'll work with him now. We won't be needing you anymore." It sounded so harsh, for all Sandy had done. Holly swallowed hard, tried again. "If you keep us in your prayers, that will be enough."

Epilogue: Heroes and Martyrs

Holly believed she fired me that day. She had no idea that to convert my substitute's license to a provisional teacher's license under the Cold Springs City School District's emergency certification program I had enrolled in a three-credit course in teaching methods at Springs Regional Community College. The instructor was Nicholas D. Baran.

He taught all but the last week of the course, and I hid my presence from Holly throughout it, even when she brought him to class in a wheelchair the day in mid-December that he told us good-bye. He and I had already assembled the files, worked on them every Friday afternoon after his class. The week before his final class he handed me the set of photographs that began with Luis Espada's disintegrated body and ended with him standing in the company's basement archive room illuminated by flashlight with the files in his hands. He said he could have set the camera to take a delayed photo, so there was no way anyone could confirm the presence of a second person. He also gave me the eleven-by-seventeen-inch scan of the cluster map, the original still on my wall, and the name of a New York Times *reporter he'd contacted. He told me to present myself as the executor of his estate to conceal my own involvement.*

He'd persuaded the reporter to come from the city to interview him, and later that week the article appeared with the title "A Fight to the End for the Truth." It detailed Nick's life, his four-year battle against leukemia, and his lonely investigation of the contamination of Yellow Springs Heights. He mentioned neither the break-in nor me; he wanted to protect me and to keep the stolen—or, in his words, "liberated"— documents a secret from the company. Before reading the words, I stared at the black-and-white photograph of Nick. Wearing an oversized hooded sweatshirt and covered with a blanket, he sat on the window seat of the screened-in porch. With his dark eyes and pallid face, it seemed as if he had passed already into the world of ghosts.

I was in Albany visiting my parents for the holidays when he died. I missed the obituary in the paper. I don't know the immediate cause of death—he'd said it would most likely be an infection, massive internal bleeding, heart failure, or his other organs shutting down one by one—the final offensive of a disease that gave little chance to even the most determined of warriors. I don't know if he was conscious to the end or if he died at home or in the hospital. One day I may go to the Vital Records Office at Cold Springs City Hall, where I first noticed the bruises on his arms, and see if his ex-student is still there and will let me look up the death certificate even though I'm not a family member and his family is now scattered and far away. I don't know if Nick's records will even be at Cold Springs City Hall. But I do know that, however he died, he was brave.

I had to be brave, too. On an icy February morning I drove to New York City and delivered a copy of the documents to the reporter. But it was not my copy.

The week before my meeting, Rosie and Tony came to my apartment. Tony went downstairs to visit Ben, and Rosie slipped into my study to see the map. She handed me the red shoulder bag she carried. Nick's bag.

"Mom sold the original documents back to the company along with the house for a lot of money," she said. She too traced the streets, and her finger paused at the pins that stood for people she knew. "They asked us to leave town, but I'll stay at a friend's until graduation. They made Mom sign an agreement that she wouldn't join a class-action suit."

It didn't surprise me that Holly had betrayed Nick, sold out to the company. "Does your mom know there are other copies out there?"

Rosie pointed to the bag. "This is her copy. She and Dad worked on it together. He said you had the reporter's name and since she couldn't do anything else, she wanted you to have this." I checked the table of contents against my own copy. The two were identical. He had replicated his work, spread it like cancer cells to ensure its survival and the success of his final assault on Hometown Chemical Company. And Holly had apparently directed her treachery not against him but against the corporation that took him from her. I couldn't ask her; I would never know what changed her mind. "Anyway, if those guys try to shred the originals, they're double fucked, because Dad gave each of us our own copies and Tony has the map on his computer."

I'd never met Rosie before, but I felt as though I knew her well; so much she had inherited from Nick.

She continued. "I didn't sign anything, and when I turn eighteen in August I can join any suit I want. Not that we need the money now, but..." She turned her back to me. I put my arm across her shoulders and let her bury her face in my sweater.

She could have been Amy Reed crying for Stephen, Tim Brownfield silently mourning his little boy, Nick witnessing his own fate in that of the McDonoughs. The pins were a chain of losses that stretched from victim to victim to the people who loved them, and I imagined their clasped hands encircling the poisoned neighborhood, their faces pleading, do something.

Do something.

I delivered the documents. The story broke. The trials began. After the criminal trials will come the lawsuits. This isn't enough.

I started to do the little things in my own life to cut waste and garbage because we have to start somewhere. Most days I walk the mile and a half to Cold Springs Southside High School where I teach. When I buy groceries, I choose brands with less packaging and ride my bicycle to the store. My trashcan no longer overflows. My clothes, bicycle, computer, stereo, and TV are secondhand. I never replaced the soiled mattress but simply disinfected it and flipped it over. It's amazing what bleach can do. The sheets I still use, too; the stains remind me of what a person can survive. I can't believe he's gone forever, so many times he'd brought himself back from the dead.

I finally joined the synagogue Neve Tefillah, and I'm helping Marissa with the youth group because kids need to know why a community is important and to belong to one. Sometimes I see Rich and Tasha and some of the other people whose lives Nick changed. Mostly, though, I see Ben. He's several inches taller than I am, with muscles where fat used to be. He's taken up wrestling and weight-lifting and plays center and linebacker for the Southside football team. He takes honors classes, so I won't get him. By the time I get enough seniority to teach honors, he'll have graduated. It's okay. My other classes are fine these days, and it would feel awkward to teach a kid I once bought dope from, whatever the circumstances. Last year the city gave up trying to build the highway and turned the vacant lot into a park. They carted away the remains of the tenement and mowed the weeds. In a single afternoon Ben's business disappeared. Eddie tried to talk him into working with a supplier, but Ben couldn't bear to give up half the profits or sell anything he hadn't grown personally. I've heard rumors around school he deals in steroids, but I don't ask. He's told me he has to do well and go to college because he's the one who'll take care of Paulie after his parents are gone.

"Whatever happened to Paulie?" I asked Ben one day while we walked home from school together.

"He was about two, and I don't remember much, 'cause I was only six. But he got sick, and we couldn't afford to bring him to the doctor. Pop was out of work as usual."

Ben doesn't get along with his dad, but most of the time they stay away from each other, especially now that Ben is bigger than Joe.

"That's too bad."

"Yeah, but he's alive. And he doesn't know anything's wrong with him. He gets to go through life not knowing all the bad things in the world. That ought to make him happy."

Ben is not happy. He worries about his mother and his brothers and whether he will make it in this world. He slams a lot of doors and likes football and wrestling because he can knock the stuffing out of people and he doesn't mind getting it knocked out of him in return. He says it's cathartic.

We talk about Nick all the time. I drive Ben up to Yellow Springs Heights sometimes and point out the places on the map. It amazes him how a neighborhood with big houses and rich people can contain so much suffering and death. We follow the court case in the local paper. We imagine what the place will look like in ten years, when the appeals finally run out. I imagine bulldozers and backhoes lined up on the bluff where Nick and I once stood arm in arm and watched the sun set over the half-frozen river. From his earth science class and his horticultural experience, Ben imagines the red and brown earth gashed, tree roots exposed, lawns and bushes plowed under. He says red earth indicates soil with a high clay content, which tends to hold in contaminants and make them more toxic. We drive by the Barans' house, now empty, and the McDonoughs' house, also abandoned with its weathered For Sale sign in the front yard. One day there will be block after block of houses vacant and boarded up, some in the process of demolition, their outer walls torn down and their interior rooms visible.

At times I think about Nick's crusade and wonder if he intended to kill himself with it as surely as his father killed himself with pills and booze. When Nick asked if suicide represented the unforgivable sin, I reminded him of Masada, of the martyrs who died for their Jewish faith atop that barren mountain fortress, and even though he did not accept the beliefs of Judaism, Nick possessed faith and pursued martyrdom. He followed the path of those who went before him—Jean-Paul Marat, Rosa Luxemburg, Antonio Gramsci,

Che Guevara, Salvador Allende, Stephen Biko—those whose wills proved stronger than their bodies and whose faith rested on the premise that imperfect people could create a perfect world.

One day after class, while we were working on the documents, he told me of a recurring dream. It came to him for the first time after we broke into Hometown and escaped to my apartment—sometime in the hours after dawn when, dehydrated, bleeding internally, his body chemistry totally screwed up, his heart stopped. And in the dream he saw where he would be going, and he said it wasn't so bad but he remained in no hurry to get there.

* * *

He saw himself on a dusty baseball field, on a hot, dry, late-summer day in southern Connecticut. The New England fourteen-and-under tournament championship game, bottom of the ninth, two out, two on, his team down by two. Squinting in the fading sunlight of early evening, he surveyed the field from the on-deck circle and listened to the announcer call his name.

The announcer described him—Nicky Baran, the Junkyard Dog—as a dangerous, unpredictable hitter and reminded everyone that he led the league that season in batting average and stolen bases. In eighth-grade English he had learned the word "impunity." He thought the announcer should have used that word in referring to the stolen bases.

He stepped up to the plate as the announcer speculated as to whether the pitcher, a Rhode Islander with a wicked fastball, would walk him intentionally and try his luck with the next batter with the bases loaded. But the next batter was a choker, Nicholas knew, so he would have to find a way to end the game right then and there.

The first pitch came in way wide. So the guy *was* going to walk him.

"Ya scared of me?" Nicholas shouted. "Why dontcha pitch to me, limpdick?"

The umpire called for time. He warned that he would not tolerate profanity and one more such outburst would get Nicholas thrown out of the game. Nicholas imagined his coach, the one who had given him a ride all the way to Connecticut, shaking his head and muttering that the kid was once again out of control.

The second pitch was wide as well. Nicholas swung at it anyway. And missed.

"Are you nuts?" he heard someone call out.

I can hit this. Just watch me.

The third pitch came in a few inches closer. Reachable. Nicholas didn't hesitate but stepped toward it. Wood connected with leather with a fierce crack that sent the ball sailing skyward and deep toward the right field fence. His mouth dropped wide open and his heart seemed to pause as he watched the ball disappear beyond the fence.

He sidestepped slowly along the base path and tried to locate the spot where the ball had dropped. His awed stare changed into a wide smile. "Man, I didn't think I could hit it that far," he mumbled just before he took off running.

Crossing home plate, Nicholas scanned the field. All was strangely silent, deserted. The players and spectators had gone; not even the coach and his son remained. Then he noticed her at the top of the bleachers. She was wearing a white dress. The sun had begun to set, but around her was bright light, as if someone had turned on the field's lights for a night game.

He scrunched up his face in an expression of surprise and disbelief. "Mom?"

"Nicky!" She held out her arms.

"I haven't seen you in years. What are you doing here?" he shouted up to her.

"It was the big game. I had to come and watch you."

Nicholas laid his bat, glove, and helmet on the ground

and approached her. He hooked his thumbs on his belt loops and focused his gaze on her pale face and dark eyes.

His mother smiled. "So have you been good, Nicky?"

He responded with a relaxed grin that showed a mouthful of crooked teeth. She knew him far too well for him to lie to her. "Hell, no." He climbed the first step up the bleachers. "But I *did* good."

LYN MILLER-LACHMANN is Editor-in-Chief of *MultiCultural Review* and the author of numerous books and articles on cultural diversity in literature and education. She received the 1993 Denali Press Award from the American Library Association, given to the outstanding reference book on cultural diversity in the United States, for her bibliography *Our Family, Our Friends, Our World: An Annotated Guide to Significant Multicultural Books for Children and Teenagers*. She is also the author of *Global Voices, Global Visions*, a guide to multicultural books for general adult readers, and the editor of *Once Upon a Cuento*, an anthology of short fiction by Latino authors published by Curbstone Press in 2003.

Active in human rights, social justice, environmental and peace groups since the mid-1970s and a seventh grade teacher in a Reform Jewish religious school, Miller-Lachmann sees her writing as a means of expressing her political commitment and her Jewish faith. *Dirt Cheap*, her first novel for adults, grew out of her experience of living and raising children in a suburb where consumer values had replaced concern for each other and the common good. She writes: "The toxic landfill is both a real consequence of our loss of communities that can act in opposition to corporate predators, and a metaphor for the toxic effects on individuals, families, and communities of placing the acquisition of things above caring for people."

Miller-Lachmann grew up in Houston, Texas. She graduated from Princeton University and has master's degrees in American Studies from Yale University and in Library and Information Studies from the University of Wisconsin-Madison. Before becoming editor of *MultiCultural Review*, she taught high school in New York City, worked as a reference librarian at Siena College, and founded an independent press to publish books for teens on controversial social and political issues. Shortly before the publication of *Dirt Cheap*, she moved, with her husband and two children, from a distant suburb into the city of Albany, New York.

CURBSTONE PRESS, INC.

is a non-profit publishing house dedicated to literature that reflects a commitment to social change, with an emphasis on contemporary writing from Latino, Latin American and Vietnamese cultures. Curbstone presents writers who give voice to the unheard in a language that goes beyond denunciation to celebrate, honor and teach. Curbstone builds bridges between its writers and the public – from inner-city to rural areas, colleges to community centers, children to adults. Curbstone seeks out the highest aesthetic expression of the dedication to human rights and intercultural understanding: poetry, testimonies, novels, stories, and children's books.

This mission requires more than just producing books. It requires ensuring that as many people as possible learn about these books and read them. To achieve this, a large portion of Curbstone's schedule is dedicated to arranging tours and programs for its authors, working with public school and university teachers to enrich curricula, reaching out to underserved audiences by donating books and conducting readings and community programs, and promoting discussion in the media. It is only through these combined efforts that literature can truly make a difference.

Curbstone Press, like all non-profit presses, depends on the support of individuals, foundations, and government agencies to bring you, the reader, works of literary merit and social significance which might not find a place in profit-driven publishing channels, and to bring the authors and their books into communities across the country. Our sincere thanks to the many individuals, foundations, and government agencies who have recently supported this endeavor: Community Foundation of Northeast Connecticut, Connecticut Commission on Culture & Tourism, Connecticut Humanities Council, Greater Hartford Arts Council, Hartford Courant Foundation, Lannan Foundation, National Endowment for the Arts, and the United Way of the Capital Area.

Please help to support Curbstone's efforts to present the diverse voices and views that make our culture richer. Tax-deductible donations can be made by check or credit card to:
Curbstone Press, 321 Jackson Street, Willimantic, CT 06226
phone: (860) 423-5110   fax: (860) 423-9242
www.curbstone.org